HUANZHULOUZHU
'The Master of
Pearl-Rimmed Tower'

Blades
From the
Willows

translated by
ROBERT CHARD

with illustrations by
MARK HAYWOOD

wellsweep

ACKNOWLEDGEMENTS

Cover design and illustrations by MARK HAYWOOD.
Cover typography by KEN REED.
Calligraphy for the title page by JOSEPH S P LO.

Translation copyright © Robert Chard

First published in 1991 by
WELLSWEEP PRESS
719 Fulham Road
London SW6 5UL

0 948454 05 9 trade edition (laminated cover)
0 948454 55 5 readers' edition (laid paper cover)

Our attempts to contact surviving relatives of Li Shanji in Taiwan have proved unsuccessful and we apologize for proceeding with the publication of this translation without their prior consent. We would be delighted to hear from them or anyone who can put us touch with them.

BRITISH LIBRARY CATALOGUING-IN-PUBLICATION DATA
A catalogue record for this book is available from the British Library.

The publisher gratefully acknowledges the financial assistance of the ARTS COUNCIL OF GREAT BRITAIN.

Designed and typeset by WELLSWEEP.
Printed and bound by BIDDLES LTD, Guildford.

Contents

Translator's Preface

THE PUBLICATION OF *BLADES FROM THE WILLOWS* REQUIRES A WORD or two of explanation; as far as I am aware, it is the first time that a novel of this type has been translated into English.

Blades from the Willows belongs to a class of Chinese popular literature known by the term *wuxia xiaoshuo*, which may be translated as 'novels of martial chivalry', or simply 'martial arts novels'. The wide appeal of the genre is evident in the extraordinary proliferation of novels, comic books, films, and television serials throughout the Chinese-speaking world, but it has seldom been taken seriously as a form of literature. Chinese intellectuals condemn it as being worthless or even harmful (though many of them read it in private); scholars of modern Chinese literature in the West have largely ignored it. Nonetheless, for those who consider themselves scholars of China to turn a blind eye to such a widespread cultural phenomenon because it is not good 'literature' seems rather narrowminded. Chinese popular literature of the past holds great fascination for the historian and literary critic; why should we neglect the best-sellers of the twentieth century—a continuation of the same native literary tradition—particularly when some of the better specimens might be of interest to a wider audience in the West? The current volume is an effort to fill this gap.

The martial arts genre is by no means a purely modern phenomenon. The exploits of chivalrous fighters have captured the popular imagination for more than two thousand years, and are celebrated in ancient historical works and poetry. More recently, elements characteristic of modern martial arts novels are conspicuous in vernacular fiction of the Ming dynasty (1368–1644). Novels such as the *Water Margin (Shui hu zhuan)* portray a subculture, or counterculture, whose members are usually at odds with authority, bound by an ethos of honour, chivalry, and fighting prowess. These heroes perform astonishing feats of strength and skill, or even magic; in other novels, such as *Journey to the West (Xi you ji)* and *Investiture of the Gods (Feng shen yan yi),* the supernatural dominates. By the nineteenth century, the martial arts novel had emerged as a distinctive genre in its own right; works like *Tales of Heroic Men and Women (Er nü yingxiong zhuan)* and *The Three Martial Fighters and Five Acts of Justice (San xia wu yi)* were the prototypes for the great flood of pulp fiction in the twentieth century. Most martial arts novels of recent decades are still set in traditional China, and use a latter-day version of the vernacular language found in popular literature of the

7

Qing dynasty. They are in fact a living continuation of the native Chinese tradition of vernacular fiction, in contrast to the 'plain speech' *(baihua)*, Western-influenced literature of twentieth-century intellectuals.

One of the rare scholars of the martial arts novel, Wang Hailing, divides the modern specimens of the art into several categories in order of descending respectability. At the top of the range are works which glamorize historical accuracy and realism; further down are those which emphasize martial training, exotic weapons, and superhuman skills. At the bottom of the scale are works of outright fantasy which portray immortal warriors, flying swords, and feats of sorcery, and ordinary martial arts play only a minor role. Wang is almost apoplectic in his denunciation of this category, which he accuses of having a pernicious effect on society, particularly the young. He identifies Huanzhulouzhu as the greatest master of this form.

Huanzhulouzhu, 'The Master of Pearl-Rimmed Tower', was the pen name of Li Shanji (1902–1961, birth date sometimes given as 1903), who later changed his name to Li Shoumin. During the 1930s and 1940s he enjoyed a wide following as one of the most prolific and original writers of martial arts novels, famous for the creation of an elaborate fantasy world of mysterious mountains and secret caves, inhabited by immortal warriors, sinister barbarians, evil sorcerers, and magical beasts.

Huanzhulouzhu was born in the southwestern province of Sichuan, and spent his childhood in different parts of China as his father, a government official, was transferred from one post to another. As a young man in his twenties, he served as a government functionary and later as military adjutant in Peking. His writing career began in the 1930s when he agreed to write a serial martial arts novel for a newspaper in the nearby city of Tianjin. Thus 'The Master of Pearl-Rimmed Tower' was born, and he began work on what was to be his best-known work, the enormous *Swordsmen of the Sichuan Mountains (Shu shan jianxia zhuan)*.

His writing was interrupted by the Japanese invasion of 1937. Burdened by a large family, he was forced to remain in occupied territory, and was imprisoned for refusing to work for a Japanese-sponsored journal. In 1945, at the end of the war, he went alone to Shanghai, where his main publisher, the Zhengqi Press, persuaded him to give up his official post and devote himself entirely to writing. Three years later he moved his family from Peking to Suzhou (Soochow), where he had lived as a child.

After the Communists came to power in 1949, martial arts novels were banned, and Li went to work as a writer for the Peking Opera Company. He did his best to adapt to the times; he changed his name to Li Hong ('Red' Li), and in 1956 published a self-criticism in the newspaper acknowledging the undesirable effects of his earlier work on society. He wrote two historical novels during this time, one based on the biography of a chivalrous swordsman in the first century B.C. text *Records of the Historian (Shi ji)*, and the second, never published, about the Tang poet Du Fu. He suffered a stroke in 1959, and died of cancer in 1961.

Huanzhulouzhu was an extraordinarily prolific writer. At the height of his career in the late 1940s he worked twelve hours a day, writing serial novels for several newspapers and publishers at once, juggling different casts of characters and complicated plots seemingly without effort. He did not produce 'respectable' literature, but was by no means lacking in literary talent. Wang Hailin, though highly critical of the content of Huanzhulouzhu's novels, acknowledges him as a gifted writer and storyteller, and praises his rich and original imagination. Certainly the enormous popularity of his work earned him a comfortable living; throngs of book-pedlars and readers would gather outside the publisher's office when a new volume of his latest novel was released, and a print run of ten thousand copies would sell out in three or four days. The appeal of his work remains undiminished to this day. The *Swordsmen of the Sichuan Mountains* and other novels have been republished many times in Hong Kong and Taiwan, and with the recent lifting of the ban on martial arts novels in the People's Republic, they have been reprinted there as well; book-sellers have difficulty keeping them in stock.

Blades from the Willows is not one of Huanzhulouzhu's best-known works, but it is an attractive choice for the translator on two counts. First, it is of manageable length, and comes to a definite and satisfying conclusion. Huanzhulouzhu's most famous novel, *Swordsmen of the Sichuan Mountains,* is immensely long, originally published in fifty volumes with a continuation of ten volumes (as opposed to six volumes in the case of *Blades*), and was never finished. Second, *Blades* precedes *Swordsmen* in the vast chronology of interlinked novels in Huanzhulouzhu's works as a whole, and is thus one of his few shorter works which assumes no prior knowledge of *Swordsmen.*

Blades from the Willows, whose Chinese title *Liu hu xia yin* may be rendered more literally as 'The Swordsmen's Haven at Willow Lake', tells the story of three mortal men, descendants of refugees hiding in the mountains of the southwestern province of Yunnan since the Mongol conquest of China in 1287, who stumble by accident into Huanzhulouzhu's strange fantasy world, and encounter immortal masters of the 'Flying Sword' arts. These masters and their disciples have the power of flight, and roam at will to the far corners of the world, furthering their own spiritual training and waging war against evil. They are Huanzhulouzhu's version of the 'transcendents' *(xian)* of Daoist religion, celebrated in over two thousand years of Chinese literature, from ancient philosophical texts such as the *Zhuangzi* (or *Chuang-tzu*), to Daoist scriptures, traditional tales, and medieval poetry. Most of these transcendents were once mortal men who achieved a form of physical immortality through certain practices such as meditation, breath control, the accumulation of spiritual merit through good deeds, and the smelting and ingestion of alchemical elixirs. In the world of Huanzhulouzhu,

9

these Immortals are locked in ongoing combat with their evil counterparts, sorcerers and corrupted monks and priests who prey on the virtuous, capturing the energies of living men or beasts and gathering the emanations of dead corpses to increase their own powers. The prototypes of these villains can be found in traditional Chinese tales, for example in the evil Daoist priests of the novel *Journey to the West*, but in Huanzhulouzhu's world they are lurid and horrible as never before.

Despite their mysterious powers, Huanzhulouzhu's Immortals and sorcerers, particularly their acolytes, are surprisingly human—they complain, scold, gossip, and argue. They also keep pets: animals who have absorbed cosmic essences over centuries and transformed into strange magical beasts. These creatures are captured in the wild mountains and tamed, to be put to work as faithful guardians, fighters, and beasts of transport. Again the inspiration for such creatures comes from weird tales and demonological lore in China's past; even in very early times animals who lived to a great age were thought to possess great powers, capable of taking on the semblance of gods, monsters, or human beings.

Prominent among the villains of *Blades from the Willows* are a barbarian clan belonging to the Miao race, a non-Chinese people indigenous to parts of the southwest. In Chinese tradition the Miao are thought to possess a deep knowledge of poisons and witchcraft, and are noted for a lack of restraint in relations between the sexes. Huanzhulouzhu exploits both of these beliefs to the fullest; in a strange sort of way *Blades* is also a love story, as the Chinese protagonists unwittingly attract the amorous attentions of two beautiful but dangerous Miao sorceresses.

The language of *Blades from the Willows* poses few problems for the translator, though it is at times more archaic and sophisticated than that found in contemporary martial arts novels. The main difficulty is in the style. Writers like Huanzhulouzhu were paid by the word, and their novels were issued in serial form. It was in the interest of the writer and publisher to keep the story going as long as the reading public's attention could be held, with the result that narrative and dialogue frequently seem unnecessarily wordy and repetitive. Other defects in *Blades* have been noted by critics, in particular large imbalances in the narrative as a whole. In the middle of the novel a huge digression occupies nearly a third of the whole, which in the English version will be published as the second volume. This tells the story of a character important in the final segment of the novel, but could stand on its own as a separate work.

In earlier drafts I translated the text in full, but, with the encouragement and assistance of the publisher, have subjected the final draft to extensive editing with an eye to readability, and removed much unnecessarily repetitive material. Sometimes this process entailed some reorganizing of the remaining text to preserve narrative cohesion. The chapters of the novel, which are very long, are labelled as 'Parts', and broken up into shorter chapters where natural breaks occur in the story.

Otherwise, the tale as presented is Huanzhulouzhu's own: somewhat streamlined perhaps, but complete.

The original used for this translation is the first Zhengqi Press version published in Shanghai in 1946. This edition differs from later versions in that it occasionally contains material in parentheses which identifies characters or events appearing in other of Huanzhulouzhu's novels; I do not know if this is from the hand of Huanzhulouzhu himself or his publisher. In the current translation such material is retained in the form of footnotes; translator's footnotes are enclosed in square brackets.

SOURCES & FURTHER READING

James J. Y. Liu. *The Chinese Knight Errant*. London: Routledge and Kegan Paul, 1967.

Wang Hailing. *Zhongguo wuxia xiaoshuo shilue* ('An Outline History of the Chinese Martial Arts Novel'). Taiyuan: Beiyue Wenyi Chubanshe, 1988.

Xu Guozhen. *Huanzhulouzhu lun* ('On Huanzhulouzhu'). Shanghai: Zhengqi Shuju, 1947.

Ye Hongsheng et al. *Liu Hu xia yin* ('Blades from the Willows', with preface and annotation). Taibei: Lianjing Chubanshe, 1984.

ALPHABETICAL LIST OF CHARACTERS

Names are given in Chinese style, surname first, using the standard Chinese system of Roman spelling. A few of the letter combinations are unfamiliar. As you read, pronounce 'Zh' as 'J', 'X' as 'Sh', and 'Q' as 'Ch'.

Bai Guiyi	A Daoist Immortal, one of the Two Short Men; also called the Chaser of Clouds.
Chen Graceful-Equity	A Daoist adept on the Mountain of Verdant Spots; wife of Zhu Blue-Lotus.
Cunning-Maid	Woman of the Miao people, and a powerful sorceress; sister of Moon-Maid.
Ding Shao	A Daoist adept and warrior living on the Mountain of Verdant Spots.
Drunken Daoist	A Daoist Immortal, sometimes in residence on the Mountain of the Goddess.
Fifth Brother	Used by the Drunken Daoist and others to refer to Zhu Blue-Lotus.
Grandmother Gold	(Luo Violet-Mist) A Daoist Immortal.
Hawuni	A corrupted non-Chinese Buddhist monk, a powerful sorcerer.
Hong Jade-Sheen	Powerful adept, disciple of the Old One in Green.
Jian Ice-Purity	A Daoist Immortal.
Li Gentle-Wisdom	(Third Sister) A daughter of the Old One in Green.
Li Hong	(Sixth Brother) Beloved son of the Old One in Green.
Li the Just	(Seventh Sister) A daughter of the Old One in Green.
Lin Lustrous-Gem	Daoist adept on the Mountain of Verdant Spots; wife of Ding Shao.
Lu Xiao	Disciple of Tao Si.
Luo Violet-Mist	(Grandmother Gold) A Daoist Immortal.
Moon-Maid	Woman of the Miao people, and a powerful sorceress; sister of Cunning-Maid.
Nineteenth Sister Xiao	Fellow disciple of Grandmother Gold.
Old Man Miao	(Old Man Dragon) Chief of a clan of Miao people, the Dragon clan, grandfather of Moon-Maid and Cunning-Maid.
Old One in Green	(Wanderer in Green) A Daoist Immortal living on the Mountain of Verdant Spots.
Ruan the Pellucid	Powerful adept, disciple of the Old One in Green.
Secure-in-Tranquillity	Daoist acolyte on the Mountain of the Goddess.
Shen the Lute	A Daoist priest on the Mountain of the Goddess.
Sixth Brother	(Li Hong) Beloved son of the Old One in Green.
Soaring Cloud	Adopted daughter of Zhu Blue-Lotus and Chen Graceful-Equity; adept in Flying Sword techniques.
Tao Si	A Daoist Immortal living in the South-End Mountains, close associate of Zhu Blue-Lotus.
Third Sister	(Li Gentle-Wisdom) A daughter of the Old One in Green.
Vortex-of-Tranquillity	Young disciple of Grandmother Gold.
Wanderer in Green	(Old One in Green) A Daoist Immortal living on the Mountain of Verdant Spots.
Wang Jin	A main character of the novel; sworn brother and constant companion of Zhao Lin.
Wang Pure-Wind	Abbot of the Daoist Abbey of the Pure Void.
Wei Lai	Adept living on the Mountain of Verdant Spots, betrothed to Soaring Cloud.
Zhang the Fourth	Boatman hired by Zhao Lin and Wang Jin at Lake Dongting.
Zhao Lin	Main character of the novel.
Zhao Xiu	A Song Dynasty general; one of the two founding leaders of Willow Lake, and Zhao Lin's ancestor.
Zhu Blue-Lotus	A Daoist adept from the Mountain of Verdant Spots.
Zhu Mai	A Daoist Immortal, one of the Two Short Men.
Zhu Man-Tiger	A main character of the novel; sworn brother of Zhao Lin and Wang Jin.
Zhu Qian	A Song Dynasty official; one of the two founding leaders of Willow Lake, and Zhu Man-Tiger's ancestor.
Zhu Shi	Village Master at Willow Lake, uncle of Zhu Man-Tiger.

I

A paradise akin to the Peach-Blossom Spring,
of incomparable natural beauty,
affords a secret haven;
men fly over the Gorge of Square Bamboo;
a remarkable child is extricated from
Southern fogs, miasmas, and rain.

CHAPTER 1

Willow Haven

A LARGE LAKE FEEDS THE LOWER REACHES OF THE COILING RIVER IN southern Yunnan Province. One end is enfolded in the plunging gorges of the Grief-at-Toil Mountains, forming fjords fed by mountain streams, and the other drains into the Coiling River far away. In between spreads a wide sheet of water, where endless waves lap over crystal depths. Because of the live current flowing from one end to the other, the lake bed is deep, and the water level steady. No matter how dry the season, the waters never diminish, and no matter how great the spring and summer torrents, they never flood, or show any but the faintest hint of swelling and agitation.

The climate of the region is mild. Amid a perpetual spring, flowers bloom over wide forests and green meadows throughout the year. Blossoming plums, peaches, willows, and cinnamon thrive everywhere about the lake, and among them grow a profusion of rare herbs and wildflowers. During the spring and autumn, when the floral display is at its height, the resplendent blaze shimmers like tapestried clouds, and the fragrances flow out on the mild breezes, perfuming wind and rain for miles around.

The land around the lake offers abundant resources. The soil is rich and fertile, perpetually moistened by an ample natural watershed. The lake itself yields a profusion of edible plants, such as lotus root, water caltrop, and arrowgrass, as well as innumerable species of fish, all uncommonly fat and sleek.

Suffice it to say that this mountain paradise is as perfect a natural setting as could be desired. And yet even in recent years it has had few human inhabitants. In earlier times, back during the Yuan dynasty of the Mongols, it was far out on the barbarian frontier in the southernmost reaches of Yunnan Province, completely cut off from civilization.

To reach it one still has to cross a vast wilderness of mountains and rivers, and track through dense jungles and forests, prowled by ferocious predators and infested with venomous reptiles and insects. Precipitous crags and deep chasms bar access to any but the most skilled of climbers. The lake water flows out into the Coiling River, but it emerges through a subterranean channel in the mountains, not only impassable to boats, but completely hidden from view.

As if this were not enough, the way is guarded by two additional natural barriers. One of these is a huge mountain gorge a hundred miles from the lake. The depth and precipitousness of the gorge, which already make it virtually impassable, are secondary to a far more deadly peril, a lethal emanation known as the Golden Miasma. Whenever this deadly fog appears—something which is liable to happen without warning at any time of the day or night—it can be seen from a great distance: a great conglomeration of bands and jets of auroral cloud, roiling and surging with shifting hues, filled with a multitude of yellow orbs of various sizes looking rather like gold coins, from which its name is derived.

If a mountain traveller is so unfortunate as to encounter the Golden Miasma, he immediately becomes aware of an unbearably foul stench, reminiscent of the vomit disgorged by someone who has consumed too much meat and wine, and soon drops lifeless to the ground. If he encounters the miasmal vapours in their full potency, his flesh dissolves almost instantly to a yellow slime, leaving only bones and hair intact. No man or beast can escape the slightest exposure. Even a bird careless enough to fly too low will lose consciousness, and drop to its death into the cloud.

The far side of the lake is guarded by a vast tropical forest untouched by human hand. The trees of this ancient wood grow exceptionally tall and strong, and with the passage of eons have proliferated to the point where at ground level the dense tangle of thick trunks leaves barely a thread of soil between them. The trees fight and crowd each other in a grim struggle for space over tens and sometimes even hundreds of miles of unbroken tangle. Here and there one might occasionally encounter a bit of clearing, but before long it gives way once more to the dense growth of gigantic trees. Up out of this impenetrable growth shoots a profusion of wildly spreading branches, driving frantically upwards toward the least crack of sunlight, forming a tight canopy of vegetation overhead. When every bit of space above is occupied, the vigorous life-force of the trees expends itself in yet more upward thrusts, adding level after level of new growth to the roof, crowding and pressing into a dense pack hopelessly tangled and interwoven above and below. These upper layers have grown so thick that they block the light of the sun completely. Far below on the forest floor, in pitch darkness, are massive heaps of rotting vegetation, riddled with serpents and vipers, overgrown with evil brambles and poisonous growths.

The branches far above the forest floor are heavily populated by all manner of ants, gnats, mosquitoes, and flies, buzzing in great swarms. Once dead their bodies fall to the ground below, in a constant rain. Most of these insects are endowed with rare venoms. Their bite or sting, while not necessarily immediately fatal, can at the very least cause several days of swelling, or transmit the contagion of deadly fevers. The atmosphere is steamy and foul, replete with evil miasmas and unhealthy emanations.

Filled as it is with poisonous life, small wonder that ordinary folk have always shunned the forest. Even a man of extraordinary abilities, well versed in protective techniques, armed with sharpened weapons and a good store of potent medicines, nine times out of ten would become trapped within the forest and perish. The dense mat of trees, spreading over tens and hundreds of miles, is completely without roads or trails. Beneath the trees, where not the slightest glimmer of light penetrates, it is dark as night. One wrong turn, and a traveller would lose his bearings and become hopelessly lost, unable to press on, equally unable to retrace his steps.

The lake, the fertile plain around it, its woods and meadows, and the surrounding crags and peaks lie directly between the forest and the miasma. From earliest antiquity no man had ever braved these two natural barriers to set foot in the valley. Only exotic birds and rare animals had ever lived there, having somehow made their way through the mountains in search of food and refuge. But all of this changed early in the Yuan dynasty.

At this time two great clans of officials and generals dwelt in the southern province of Hunan. Loyal vassals of the fallen dynasty of Song, they were unwilling to submit to the alien Mongol rulers. Reports of terrible pillage and depredation came to them from beyond the mountains to the north, and they eventually resolved to flee the ruthless claws and fires of the advancing barbarians. The clan heads chose a few of the most loyal and courageous from among their retainers and bondservants, and led their families and relatives into the mountains.

These former Song vassals were Zhao Xiu, a blood relative of the Song imperial line, and one Zhu Qian. Their respective clans had long been closely bound to one other through ties of marriage and friendship. As it happened, Zhu was in the civil service, and Zhao in the military; both served in the western marches of Hunan. Their tastes and ambitions ran close, and they had been intimate friends since boyhood. As the great upheavals began and the realm of Song was lost, both houses faced extermination or exile. Their trials and adversities firmed their friendship still further, and they swore a brotherhood of flesh and blood, an oath unbreakable in life or in death.

Zhao Xiu was of a clan long famed for its great martial prowess, and Xiu himself was no exception to the rule. His entire household—family, dependents, retainers, and bondservants—were all highly trained fighters, strong as tigers, endowed with lightning speed and superhuman agility.

Zhu Qian had been a scholar serving in the civil administration, but since boyhood, he had been fond of roaming through the mountain wilderness, and as a result had acquired an unusual degree of strength, speed, and alertness. He was fond of plots and strategies, and rich in practical knowledge and experience. He and his close friend Zhao Xiu were together day and night, and through a gradual process of osmosis, and a general desire to maintain his strength and fitness, Zhu too began to show an interest in the martial arts.

Earlier, when the Mongols had first mounted their invasion, Xiu had repeatedly urged Qian to devote more time to martial training. "We are entering a time of great lawlessness and disorder," he said. "The barbarian caitiffs grow mightier each day. It is difficult to say what evils might ensue. What if you should meet with a sudden change of fortunes? You might be forced to trek through the wilderness, subjecting your own person to all manner of obstacles and perils.

"Why not take up the study of the martial arts in earnest? With such training you could protect yourself, and increase your resistance to cold, hunger, and fatigue. Your entire household, from your nieces and nephews, sons and daughters, all the way down to your servants, retainers, and bondmaids have studied fighting arts from me and my son—worthless teachers though we may be!—but I am afraid that you and your lady, cultured and refined as you are, are too soft to have any martial ability. This could become a dangerous liability not far into the future. What if something unexpected happened to drive you from your official post? You might have to flee from tyranny, taking your family to seek refuge in the mountains, and await an opportunity to restore your former position. The mountains are home to tigers, wolves, snakes, and insects. Dangers lurk everywhere. You are not the usual scholarly weakling with barely the strength in your arms to tie up a chicken, but you're still going to find yourself in great difficulty if you plan to make long treks through the wilds and endure its perils!"

Zhu Qian had indeed noticed that the children of both clans, and even the servants, were applying themselves diligently to the fighting arts. He himself had long been uneasy, and felt that he should do the same. Stirred to action now by his friend's advice, he began to apply himself wholeheartedly to martial training. Having reached middle age, he had no hope of ever becoming a great adept, but thanks to his still-remaining strength and quick mind, he surprised everyone by the speed with which he managed to build up his strength and endurance.

As luck would have it, after Zhu Qian had been in training for two years, and was able to make some practical use of his newly acquired skills, the beleaguered Song government finally collapsed in the face of the overwhelming Mongol advance. The Zhao and Zhu families were able to hang on for two more years in Hunan Province, but in the end the alien race succeeded in establishing a regime of their own, the Yuan dynasty, and the old Song loyalists found themselves without a sovereign. As if this agony of grief were not enough, the invincible Mongol armies of the new dynasty had already penetrated to western Hunan.

The Zhao and Zhu clans took stock of their situation. There was no doubt that the Mongols were for the time being irresistible. But they were after all a foreign race, of a temperament uncommonly harsh and violent, and in the long run it seemed unlikely that they could do more than impose a temporary regime of cruel oppression. At the moment their power was too great to be opposed. That was no reason to turn traitor to the fallen Chinese regime, to be sure, but rather than stand fast, needlessly sacrificing the lives of their families, they elected to flee together into hiding.

Their first plan was to seek refuge in the remote mountains between the provinces of Hunan and Guizhou. When this base was secure, they

17

intended to make secret preparations, gathering confederates, concoct-
ing plans and strategies, and await the opportunity to participate in the
restoration of Chinese rule.

But the Yuan armies pursued a relentless policy of suppression and
extermination, ever wary of the spark of loyalty toward the old dynasty
which lived on among the people. Still worse, a class of Chinese traitors
appeared, hungry for wealth, luxury, and noble titles. These people
worked as agents for the enemy, leading Mongol search-and-destroy
missions to hidden patriot camps.

The situation deteriorated to the point where the Zhao and Zhu
clans, a party of one hundred and ten people, were forced to flee from
one place to another, wandering endlessly through the mountains. At
no time were they given a chance to settle in peace. During years of
headlong flight they suffered indescribable torment, disruption, and
privation, never free from peril.

Finally there came a time when, after a long and difficult passage
through mist-filled mountains, foul miasmas and torrential rain, they
somehow found their way into the Grief-at-Toil Mountains far south on
the Yunnan frontier. To do so they had gone through the dense
primeval forest, one of the two great natural barriers which barred access to the region. They had traversed even more perilous terrain to
reach the forest at all, during which they only just escaped the dark City
of the Dead. When they encountered the forest, they sent mounted
scouts to spy it out, and learned that the way was less arduous than some
of the wilderness they had already covered. Ordinary people might only
have left their bones mouldering within the forest's depths, but after
years of trekking through mountain wastes, surmounting countless perils and obstacles, the exiles had accumulated a store of skill and experience. They knew how to prepare for passage through dangerous terrain, and how to extricate themselves from difficult situations. Every
member of the party was driven by a common purpose; each was
stronger and more courageous than the next. They were well supplied
with food and water, medicines, and weapons.

Still, they stumbled about day and night in the darkness of the forest
for two months and more. They took their rest in shifts while others explored, fighting off poisonous snakes, savage beasts, mosquitoes, flies,
and other noxious insects. During the last two days of this ordeal, their
supplies of food and water nearly exhausted, and having lost all sense of
direction, they knew they were again on the verge of death. But when all
seemed lost, they saw a faint glimmer of light ahead. Quite by accident,
stumbling about at random, they had reached the end of the forest, and
now found themselves at the hidden lake.

OF THE ENTIRE PARTY, ONLY A FEW RETAINERS AND BONDSERVANTS
had been lost, felled by the plague and malaria, or killed by snakes and
wild beasts. Of the Zhao and Zhu families themselves, two had suffered
serious injury, one losing his left arm, but both had recovered. These

erstwhile farmers, accustomed to a gentler existence, had at last won through, saved by strength of numbers and the shrewdness of their leaders.

They ran out from the forest edge into this mountain paradise, and saw at once that it was an ideal site for a safe settlement. Their spirits soared. They pitched their tents on the lakeshore and sent scouts in each direction to make sure all was safe. Then, when they and their followers were comfortably established, they explored more thoroughly the land between the bounds of the two unique natural barriers which walled off their haven. They discovered there were fish to be had in the lake, and wild game on land, and that the fertile soil would, within a year's time, yield abundant crops. For clothing they could gather silkworms and use the pelts of wild animals. But there were still a good many things they lacked, of which salt was the most urgent, since their supply was nearly gone. Lacking the power of flight, they found the two great barriers a formidable obstacle. But a wise man is one who is satisfied with what he has. Here they could hunt, fish, cultivate, and produce everything they needed to survive. The scenery was magnificent. During nine years of constant perils and suffering they had thought only to preserve their lives. Now that this goal had been achieved, and they had found a good place to settle, they could accept a few deficiencies amid otherwise perfect surroundings.

During the years they had fled ever further into the mountain wilderness, their children had matured swiftly into adulthood. These children had benefited from the blood and family heritage of the two great ancient clans, and each of them was intelligent, courageous, thoroughly trained in the martial arts, and full of pluck and youthful vigour. All young people like to play, and sport about, and the emerald waters of the lake proved irresistible. At every opportunity they jumped into the water to swim, and when there were enough of them together they held races and contests of skill. Before long they all became accomplished swimmers.

A permanent lakeside village was soon established, and the group settled into a daily working routine. A small fleet of boats was built, and in the summer of the second year some of the junior members of the Zhao and Zhu clans, well provisioned with meat and wine, set off to explore the rest of the lake. It was a year of great drought, and the mountain torrents had not yet begun. The water was slightly lower than usual, and they discovered a subterranean outlet which penetrated the cliffs at the far end of the lake. They explored several branches of the watery cave within, and found that one of them led out to the Coiling River.

They hurried back to report this news to their parents. Zhao Xiu and Zhu Qian came out to see for themselves, and realized that the cave, opening up in the water at the base of precipitous crags, afforded a narrow and tortuous route to the outside. In some spots the ceiling was only two feet from the water, so that they were forced to lie down flat in their boats and push their way along with their hands. The exit, opening within a hollow in the cliffs along the lower reaches of the Coiling River, was well concealed behind a jumble of fallen rocks and an ancient growth of vines. The river beyond flowed deep and strong. Discovery by passing boatmen seemed virtually impossible.

Two agile and keen-witted youths were sent to clamber up the vines and survey the surrounding area. They reported that there were several settlements of Miao tribesmen ten or fifteen miles distant, with whom they could trade for necessities.

The villagers were overjoyed at this news. From that point on, they could make their settlement permanent, and devote themselves whole-heartedly to developing the valley.

For several years the two clan leaders entertained ambitions of working toward the restoration of the former dynasty, but after a decade of dwelling peacefully in the valley, their hopes began to fade. They knew the enemy was still too strong, and in any case, hidden as they were in a remote and isolated part of the barbarian-controlled wasteland, it was impossible even to communicate with the outside world, much less attract a following for an attempt to wrest the throne from the Mongols. Even though the members of both clans, men, women, young, and old, were highly trained in the martial arts, there were only a hundred or so of them. It would be much easier for them to remain secluded in this remote haven. They could devote their energies to developing the paradise around them, and formulate long-term plans for raising and nurturing children and grandchildren. The more they thought the more they realized that their grand ambitions would have no chance of success in their generation. Since the valley was ideal as a permanent home, they gradually gave up the idea of participating in world events, and began thinking only of paving the way for future generations.

Several general meetings were convoked to discuss the problem, during which they decided to modify their code of rules. The original goals were set aside, and they took the step of prohibiting anyone from leaving the valley without good cause.

Zhu Qian and Zhao Xiu each assumed their own fields of responsi-bility in educating the young of their new community. Zhu taught civil and literary knowledge, and Zhao fighting arts and military strategy. By necessity the non-military education was confined to a general study of the ancient Canons, along with readings in books of history, poetry, and essays, whose primary purpose was to inculcate a sense of traditional morals and family values.

The military side of their training was quite another matter. The com-munity was situated deep within the mountains, where snakes and fero-cious beasts ravaged at will. Even though years of settlement had made the lake a safer place than it had been during the first year or two, predators could still be encountered anywhere. Still more important was their constant vigil against revealing their presence to the outside world. If they were ever discovered, barbarians and Miao bandits would inevitably pour into the valley to indulge in looting and pillage. Thus serious care was taken to enforce rigorous and all-inclusive training in the fighting arts. Men and women of all ages were required to practice each day. Whenever there was a break in the agricultural schedule, everyone was ordered to participate in matches and bouts. These would allow each person's skill to be tested and ranked, and ensure that none could slacken in the severity of their training.

The administration of the village was at first conducted on an informal basis. The members of the group had shared much hardship and suffering in their years of exile together, and had grown intimate. Apart from Zhao Xiu and Zhu Qian, who acted as the chief and sub-chief of the village, and a few of the male juniors of both clans who were assigned periods of duty fulfilling certain administrative functions, the remainder of the community worked together in a spirit of harmonious cooperation, free from hierarchical constraints.

This worked well at first, for the territory was wide and the population sparse, leaving each individual free to choose fields for cultivation entirely at will. But the community grew rapidly. The subordinate status of the bonded servants, retainers, and household staffs had been relaxed, and they chose wives for themselves from among the bondmaids to establish households of their own. The children of the Zhao and Zhu clans intermarried with those of the other families who had followed them into exile. Thanks to the mild climate and the rich soil, all lived in comfort and happiness, and enjoyed good health and vigour. Not surprisingly, the conditions were conducive to high fertility. People and domestic animals alike reproduced at a great rate. Within twenty years of their arrival, the population had doubled.

Zhao Xiu and Zhu Qian, already nearing seventy years of age, possessed wisdom and foresight. They knew that the valley's great size and rich, fertile resources could support a large population, and that their system of education was able to impart to their youngsters a strong sense of the common good. Nonetheless they realized that if the population continued to grow at such a rate, it would not be long before dissension and disagreement would begin to set in. The two elders were lifelong friends, having shared good times and bad, and there was nothing they would not do for each other, nothing one would not forgive the other. But they knew that their own experience was unique. Their descendants, born to peace and prosperity, accustomed to sleeping on thick mats and wearing well-soled shoes—what would they know of suffering and hardship?

Even with the best of educations and a willingness to abide by the rules, people are inherently unequal in strength and intelligence. With the passage of time the comfortable environment would make their descendants complacent; without restraints they might slip into decadence and dissipation. Or perhaps parental favouritism would spur petty sibling rivalries into bitter jealousy and hatred. They might grow envious of the opulence of city life, and in their desire to escape stir up dissension, and bring disaster on all. Unchecked, problems of this sort would grow worse with time.

The two old men saw all of this clearly. Careful, long-range plans were required to maintain permanent tranquillity among future generations in their mountain paradise. They pondered and discussed the matter long between themselves, and on New Year's Day of the succeeding year, they proclaimed a new code of laws and regulations in the community temple.

According to the new code, a Village Master would from that time forward be chosen by general consensus to head the community for a term of five years. During his tenure, he would exercise almost absolute power. In case the village was ever without a leader, there was also to be a Council of Elders, which was to offer advice and assistance to the Master in the administration of the village, and which was given the power to oversee and control the conduct of the Master.

A system of punishments for crimes by ordinary citizens was drawn up. It was designed for maximum simplicity. Corporal punishment was to be applied at the discretion of the Master, who would summon the parents or other senior relatives of the guilty individual as well as the injured party, and apply the sentence in their presence. The idea was to make the guilty feel shame and punish himself with his own conscience, since the punishment itself would not be particularly severe. The equivalent of prison sentences could also be meted out for periods of up to half a year or more.

In the case of more serious crimes requiring banishment and hard labour beyond one year, the verdict determined by public consensus would have to be unanimously approved by the Council of Elders before the sentence could be applied. It was stipulated that the convicted man would have to be obviously set in his evil ways, considered an outcast by all members of the community, and show no sign of shame or remorse.

Another even more drastic measure to be included in the punishment of the most incorrigible criminals was that of hamstring mutilation. If during the period of the sentence it became evident that the convict had no intention of mending his ways, then when the term of punishment was over, he would be barred from ever leaving the valley. This would be ensured by slitting at least one of his hamstrings. It was feared that a felon of this sort might climb out of the valley and deliberately lead in enemies from outside. From then on the hobbled criminal would be given only light work requiring his hands but not his feet. He could still enjoy the benefits of the community, but would be a social outcast.

The death penalty was provided for as well, but was only to be applied with extreme caution.

All in all, the village laws were both just and severe. They allowed no special consideration for relatives or personal friends in any way, and prohibited anyone from manipulating them so as to take advantage of others or work selfishly for individual profit. Much more could be said about them, but here it suffices to say that they were both precise and all-encompassing, complete in letter and spirit.

Old Zhao and Zhu were the natural leaders of the community, loved and admired by all, and they had taken turns governing for many years. When they formulated the new code of rules for the administration of the village, both had reached old age, and wished to retire from their duties. Having made such careful provisions, they might have expected that their children and grandchildren would live long and peacefully, satisfied with the comfortable life afforded them by the abundant resources of the valley. But they knew that it is ever the way of the world that unity leads to disunity, order is followed by disorder; prosperity and decline always follow one another in close succession. They wanted to see their newly established institutions tested before their deaths, so that any flaws could be corrected, and it was clear that the system functioned smoothly.

After two Village Masters had been elected and served under their tutelage, old Zhao and Zhu felt that they could set their minds at rest. By this time they were nearing their dotage, and were able to contribute less and less owing to their diminished physical and mental powers. Now that the institutional foundations of the community had been laid, it was clear that the village was prospering as never before. Talented people were emerging in each new generation, each making major contributions. The potential for trouble always existed, but the two old men were inclined to let matters rest, since they had done all they could. They both passed away, one right after the other, before the second Village Master's term of office had ended.

The villagers were grief-stricken, and carried out the mourning and funeral rites with the utmost solemnity and respect. In the years afterward they scrupulously followed the regulations left by the two old leaders. Village Masters were chosen one after the other in the prescribed manner.

AFTER SEVERAL DECADES, THE COMMUNITY ACHIEVED A GOLDEN age of prosperity. The peerless natural beauty of the mountains and lake was enhanced over many years by the labour of hundreds and later thousands of people. Magnificent architecture—houses, towers, estrades, and pavilions—spread over the mountains and were reflected in the lake's clear waters. Between its shores—lined with blossoming trees like a mineral forest of gems—emerald waves lapped, set against a crystal-clear backdrop of unbroken mountains and shining clouds. Sky and water, separated by an unbroken ring of flowering trees with gently waving branches, each held the other in its embrace, dotted only by a few boats traversing the limpid void.

Within the transparent waters the fish stood out so clearly that an observer on shore could almost count them individually. Every now and then one would leap from the water, and fall back with a distinct plop. On the shore, where the waves lapped under the shade of the willows, young boys and old men dangled their hooks in the current. Every now and then a quick flick of the wrist would bring up a huge fish, twisting and flopping in a flash of silver scales beneath the pole.

No matter what the season, there were always flowers in bloom. Sometimes it was a brilliant snowfall of apricot, striving to outdo all other evidence of springtime, sending forth a cool fragrance to drift ten miles or more. At other times it was water lilies in the pools which lay at intervals over the ground, their floral splendour bursting out here and there over thousands of acres. In autumn, the rich beauty of the flowering plum, the languid fragrance of the peach trees, the sweetness of blossoming cinnamon, the perfume of the orchids, and the drifting vermilion of falling maple leaves wove a huge, lusciously scented tapestry that gave even longer and greater enjoyment than was afforded by the springtime display.

The fields, wildlands, and even the marshes and swamps around the lake had mostly been developed, and sustained the community in comfort and enjoyment, forming a veritable earthly paradise far from the world of men. The villagers should have been satisfied with what they had, but of course men always desire something new, and take what they have in hand for granted. The valley lacked salt, iron, and various other odd necessities, and with their own rich surpluses, it was only natural that they should begin to trade with the outside world. Every three years they sent a party out through the watery cavern, offering furs, leather, grain, herbal medicines, and gold dust in exchange for the goods they required.

The trip was at first arduous, because of the difficulty of traversing the cavern and the perilous terrain beyond. It was a thankless task. Out of each party of twenty, only two men, proficient in the Miao tongue and familiar with the route, were obliged to go along on every trip. The rest were chosen at random to go once only, and would be exempted from other labour duty in compensation. Great care was taken throughout the expedition. The secret entrance to the valley had to be guarded at all costs. The seasonal market fairs held by the Miao were crude and rustic in the extreme, but most of the traders who frequented them could be counted on to do business in a scrupulous and honest manner. The villagers from the valley and the Miao merchants, once they had dealt with each other for a while, mixed as readily as milk and water, and soon developed a fair degree of mutual trust.

But the market fairs were also frequented by less pleasant folk. Barbarians and Miao bandits, accustomed to prowling half naked through the wilds, came to mingle with the crowds. Such men were cruel and fierce. Worst of all were Chinese fugitive criminals and army deserters. These rogues were vicious and cunning, capable of any evil. When encountering such folk one had to be prepared to yield to them, and wait to seize the advantage later by clever strategy. Otherwise, if conflict broke out, these felons would either slaughter their victims forthwith, or else creep back at the first opportunity to murder them in secret. If anyone once surrendered to their bullying, they would be marked forever as weaklings, and the scoundrels would never weary of preying on them. The trading parties from the valley were always made up of men carefully picked for their resourcefulness and fighting ability, and could defend themselves with little trouble even against such cutthroats as these. And indeed, incidents occurred on every trip.

What with the difficult terrain to be traversed and the frequent conflicts with local bandits, it was small wonder that most saw this task as a dangerous undertaking. If not chosen by the Village Master, very few would volunteer. But the valley population soon grew to the point where one trip every three years was not sufficient. The Village Master argued before the Council of Elders and at general community meetings for more frequent forays, and the interval was changed first to two years, and later to one.

As the years went by they began to find the Miao traders unreliable. These simple folk were inept when it came to managing complex affairs, and were liable to forget things from one year to the next. Items ordered the previous year would often be unavailable in the agreed amounts, having either been appropriated by the traders for their own use, or swindled away by Miao bandits.

Finally the year came when neither of the two most urgently needed items, iron and salt, had been procured in sufficient amounts. The authorities were on the point of meeting to discuss the feasibility of a second trip to the Miao fairs that same year, when a sudden landslide blocked off a major portion of the underground route out of the valley. While checking the extent of the damage, a work party found another cave, filled with stalactites and stalagmites, leading off from a fissure in a branch of the original tunnel. They followed it, and found that it led to a spot high in the crags above the river outside.

The Village Master holding office at the time was a clever man of forceful personality, and under his influence even a sizable faction of the reigning Council of Elders was known to display an uncharacteristic boldness. They knew that one of the greatest problems facing the community was the difficulty of the narrow and dangerous water route that was their only link with the world outside. The landslide could not have been more fortuitous. They decided to reopen the subterranean route, and, while they were at it, make it larger and more easily passable than before, though not without constructing certain defensive devices to seal it should the need arise. There was little concern over the newly discovered cave above. Its outer opening was far up in the crags where no man could ever climbed, safe from discovery by outsiders.

The new setup would certainly be far safer and more convenient than the old, and the villagers, ever ready to avoid trouble and travail if at all possible, heartily endorsed the project. Stalwarts from the village were mustered, and after half a year of construction, the new way was open. As planned, it was easily defendable and strategically sound, as well as completely undetectable from the outside, but at the same time far more easily traversed.

The new passage was so much more convenient, in fact, that they realized that the risks of travelling as far as the nearest cities no longer seemed as great as they had before. It had been many decades since their elders had fled to this spot. All traces of their flight would long since have vanished. Why not send a few people to the small cities nearby to look around? They could bypass the Miao market fairs entirely, and procure what they needed directly from the cities.

After such a long time in the mountains, their only contact with the outside world through the primitive Miao, they were apprehensive of falling victim to the assaults of Mongol soldiers. Great care would have to be taken to preserve secrecy. But unbeknownst to them, the regime of the barbarians had already entered its decline. The alien rulers had grown arrogant, lazy, and dissipated. Their officials were cruel and corrupt to the point where the people's very survival became difficult. The situation was worst in the frontier prefectures, where the officials were relatively free from government supervision and did what they pleased. There was no evil to which these brigands would not stoop.

During their first few trips to the nearby cities, they were strictly warned by the Council of Elders never to become involved in any trouble, lest the valley's location be revealed and disaster strike the village. The first few times they witnessed cases of cruel injustice, they were able to suppress their outrage, and did nothing beyond slipping a little money to the injured party, urging him and his family not to do anything reckless. But as time went on, expeditions were sent out of the valley more frequently, and the scope of their activities grew wider. The more cities they visited, the more injustices they witnessed. Each party was as a rule led by a pair of older, more experienced men, but the rest were youthful, high-spirited stalwarts with a strong sense of chivalry. These latter soon reached the point where they could no longer restrain themselves, and began to take action. The corrupt officials and local strongmen, for all their minions, were no match for these heroic and deadly fighters, trained from childhood in the ancient secret fighting arts transmitted for centuries within the Zhao clan.

At first it was a matter of two or three youths slipping away to redress some wrong in secret, but as time went by, others joined in. Eventually even the older leaders could no longer contain their indignation and rage, and it was the entire party that went on the offensive. Once things had progressed to this point, it soon became the rule to use their full numbers and fighting prowess, guided by a careful application of strategy, to intervene in cases of oppression and injustice. After this had gone on for some time, though without in any way endangering the village, the Village Master and Council of Elders finally learned of it. At first they attempted to prohibit it, but in the end they were forced to acknowledge that compassion and chivalry were firmly rooted in human nature. Short of cutting off the procurement missions entirely, there was no way to prevent their own citizens from attempting to ameliorate the misfortunes of others. After several years, during which time no trouble reached the village, they decided to look the other way, and paid no further heed to the matter.

CHAPTER 2

The Wanderer in Green

THIS YEAR THE TASK OF LEADING THE PROCUREMENT MISSION OUT OF the hidden valley had fallen to Zhao Lin. Zhao, only twenty-seven years of age, would normally have been considered too young for a position of such responsibility, but his competence was nonetheless unquestioned. He had taken part in the expeditions since the age of sixteen, and now, after ten years of experience, his qualifications to lead were formidable. He knew his way around outside the valley as well as anyone, and had developed a fluent command of both the various regional Chinese dialects and the Miao tongue.

Zhao Lin was a direct descendent of Zhao Xiu, one of the revered founders of the hidden mountain community. As such he was heir to a position of considerable prestige and authority within the Zhao clan hierarchy. But he had shown brilliant promise in his own right. Since boyhood he had applied himself to his literary studies and martial training with exemplary diligence, impressing his teachers with his keen intelligence and remarkable physical coordination. He also possessed a loyal and kindly nature, and early in life had achieved a reputation for a strong sense of chivalry and justice.

Accompanying Zhao on this trip were two other young stalwarts, Wang Jin and Zhu Man-Tiger. Both were much admired among the younger generation of the village. They and Zhao Lin had been inseparable companions throughout their youth, and it was only natural that the two had determined to join Zhao on this expedition. With Zhao Lin in charge, they intended to take advantage of this opportunity to see the great cities of Kunming and Dali, and visit some of the famous lakes and rivers for which Yunnan Province was noted. Last of all, they wished to ascend the Mountain of Verdant Spots not far from Dali to pay a call on a man they had befriended during the expedition of the previous year.

Leading an expedition out of the mountains was a difficult and complicated business. The members of the party would usually dress as itinerant merchants, and pretend to be travelling separately. Whenever they encountered injustices perpetrated against the populace by the local authorities—a common enough occurrence in those chaotic times—one or two among the party travelling ahead of the others would come openly to the aid of the victim. The main party, following later, would pretend to be unconnected with the incident, but, if necessary, offer secret assistance. They might add to the general confusion by identifying their own fellows as villainous outlander bandits and claiming that they too had been harmed, then direct pursuing forces in the wrong direction. On the trip back to the valley they would again travel separately, with the men who had fought lagging far behind the others, deliberately making their presence known, thus diverting the attention of those who might otherwise have been able to track the main party back to the village. Sometimes the fighters would even wait until the next outbound party had passed through before starting back. Any suspicion that they were in any way associated with the others was avoided at all costs.

On this particular expedition Zhao Lin discharged his duties as leader in exemplary fashion. All the necessary supplies were procured, and the group managed to avoid becoming embroiled in any violent incidents. When it had become apparent that the difficult and dangerous part of the mission was completed, Zhao resolved to part from the group. He gave instructions for the goods to be transported back to the village in the usual manner: overland to the stockade the villagers had in recent years constructed near Raven-Rock Gorge midway up the Coiling River, then downstream by boat to the valley. Zhao himself, meanwhile, struck out for the city of Dali, accompanied by Wang and Zhu.

Dali was in a region of western Yunnan Province famed for its scenery. The air was clear as crystal, and the landscapes on every side exotic and beautiful. Not far from the city was the Mountain of Verdant Spots, one of the area's best known landmarks. This peak towered between two and three thousand meters above sea level, piercing far above the sea of clouds which surrounded it. Its top was cloaked year round with the accumulated snow of many seasons, little diminished through the summer despite the tropical clime. But even at the higher altitudes flowers and trees flourished, sheltered from the frost in deep glens watered by springs bursting forth from the rocks. From a distance the beauty of the mountain was breathtaking, presenting a pattern seemingly painted by the brush of an imaginative artist. The fertile glens dotted the mountain with an electric green interspersed with the varied hues of exotic dyes and pigments. From the earliest glimmerings of dawn to the last fading glow of dusk, the mountain displayed constantly shifting colours. It was the verdure of these glens that gave the mountain its name.

The Mountain of Verdant Spots was home to a mysterious man Zhao Lin and his colleagues had befriended the previous year under rather strange circumstances. They had been embroiled in one of their chivalrous escapades, effecting the rescue of a hapless peasant kidnapped by a brutal local strongman. This brigand kept a sizable troop of stalwart young fighters about him, but they had proved no match for Zhao Lin and his companions, who mounted a surprise attack and swiftly overwhelmed them. The kidnapped victim was rescued, but the strongman escaped. Zhao Lin was just making up his mind to track down the villain and finish the job when a man of unusual aspect appeared and spoke a quiet warning into his ear.

"This brigand has won the friendship of a dangerous and evil Buddhist monk, known as the Barbarian Monk in Red," the stranger said. "He is a formidable master of dark sorcery, and his powers are great. If you do not stay your hand now, and succeed in killing this villainous bandit, the Barbarian Monk will become aware of your existence, and exact a speedy and dreadful revenge upon you for the death of his friend."

Zhao was quickly persuaded; once entangled with a sorcerer of this magnitude, misfortune might follow them endlessly. They did not have the means to oppose the spells of one such as the Red Monk, and their party would risk extermination. Worse, the trail to their secret mountain haven might be discovered, and a baleful demonic power brought to their very doorstep. Never again would their fellow villagers dwell in peace. With the security of their entire community at stake, they had no choice but to let the matter rest.

This Barbarian Monk was a master of the Teachings of the All-Pervading Red, in particular the arcane and difficult art of the Image-Viewing Crystal Sphere. Had he used it, the party would have been struck down by a swift and terrible death. But, fortunately for them, the brigand had violated training precepts laid down for him by the Red Monk, led astray by lust and selfish greed. He had suffered an embarrassment in an encounter with the haven's mysterious band, and lost a captive of no great importance. As long as he had not been driven to the point where his life and family were in danger he dared not call upon his deadly master, whom he greatly feared. The strange band of fighters had struck against him with almost inhuman speed. He had no idea of where they were from or where they had gone. They left behind no trace of themselves, and dropped nothing that they had been carrying, which made the Red Monk's magic more difficult. Working the Image-Viewing Crystal Sphere required a dangerous expenditure of blood and vital humours, and unless it were a matter of great urgency, the Monk would never consent to apply his spells at full strength.

The brigand was himself a powerful river pirate. His real name had long been secret, but in earlier years he had been known as the Magistrate of Land and Water. He was now also called Qin Kuo, the Lion of Flames. His own fighting abilities were minimal, but a violent temper, willingness to commit evil deeds, and devious cunning had taken him far. Seeing that the mysterious attackers had not inflicted any serious losses on his own forces, the Lion of Flames comforted himself with the thought that it had been a minor incident, a passing encounter in which the other party had felt compelled to draw their blades to satisfy an obscure point of honour, and wished no further trouble. At that very moment they must be lying low somewhere, anxiously watching for signs of his own retaliation. Since there was no sign of further mischief, he would be satisfied to lick his wounds and let the matter rest. If they should ever run afoul of him again, he vowed grimly to himself, let them beware!

ZHAO LIN AND HIS COMPANIONS HAD ENCOUNTERED THIS STRANGER a number of times before. He was a middle-aged man of scholarly mien, with a clean and refined aspect, and his bearing and speech reflected a certain mild elegance. He invariably wore a green tunic, and styled himself the 'Wanderer in Green'. He never revealed his true name to them. Over a period of several years, Zhao Lin had encountered him on every trip out of the valley. At first he thought this pure coincidence, and paid little attention to the man. But as time went by Zhao grew curious. The stranger always wore the same green tunic, no matter what the season, and his person was always immaculate. His speech and attitude reflected excellent birth. The expeditions Zhao Lin joined went to a great many different cities, and the routes they travelled were never the same, and yet they always encountered him at some point along the way.

Zhao Lin gradually became aware that there was a genuine mystery behind the man. Owing to the ban on admitting outsiders to the secret valley, Zhao was accustomed to associating with people on the outside without revealing anything about himself. Here, however, was someone who was equally mysterious about his own origins. On the two occasions they had exchanged conversation, the man had treated them with great courtesy, but as strangers. After a few polite remarks had been exchanged on either side, he would offer an excuse and depart. Several times they had tried to befriend him, but on each occasion they met with a courteous rebuff as he slipped away once more.

Then, finally, the previous year, he appeared again as they attacked the strongman's estate. During the course of the fighting they became aware that there was a capable fighter aiding them in secret, making their task considerably easier. As they were puzzling over this, the Wanderer in Green revealed himself. It was only after this encounter that the stranger finally agreed to befriend them.

Before this time they had never before spoken with the Wanderer in Green beyond exchanging the simplest of pleasantries, and were astonished to learn that he seemed to know everything about them. He said that he had been told of them by a close friend, whom he would not name. His entire family, he told them, lived on the far side of the Mountain of Verdant Spots, sheltered in a high glen never before trodden by human foot. Finally he said that he always took refuge there from the heat of the summer from the sixth through eighth months, and that they too might join him at their convenience.

Zhao Lin's expedition departed the valley at the end of the third month, and by the time all the necessary supplies had been procured, it was the first week of the seventh month. He and his two companions had from the beginning planned to take advantage of the Wanderer in Green's invitation, and since he had not made his customary appearance during the course of their travels from one city to the next, the three were all the more eager to see him again. In the heat of the summer season, their packs were light and simple; when they reached Dali at midday, rather than lodging in an inn, they struck out directly for the Mountain of Verdant Spots.

The far side of the mountain was a wilderness where men never ventured. The way through it had been described to them in great detail by the Wanderer in Green, but Zhao Lin and his two companions had not paid sufficient heed when the Wanderer had warned them that his abode was well guarded by the natural features around it. The three were strong and courageous, and confident of their wilderness skills. Raised deep within the mountains, they had, since their teens, routinely braved barbarians, foul miasmas, and torrential rains, had traversed dangerous mountain wilderness and forded raging rivers. Difficult mountain terrain they had seen in full measure. They had listened to the Wanderer's instructions, but not taken them enough to heart, and the year's interval had not improved their memories. All they recalled was that the man lived in a secluded valley not far from the summit. Some of the mountain trails described in the Wanderer's directions they had forgotten completely, and even where they had not, it was still the first time they had seen the route.

The ascent was easy enough at first. Climbing the Crest of the Immortal's Aurora, the Emerald Snail Coil, and the Hundred-and-Five-Step Celestial Ladder was for them as easy as an immortal monkey going up a tree to pluck fruit. When these obstacles were past, and they had scaled three more cliffs, they reached the upper elevations of the mountain, and crossed over to its shadowed side. It was only when they got this far that the terrain became truly difficult.

They paused to take stock of the direction of their travel, and decided they were still on the right track. Confident of their agility and strength, they plunged boldly on, paying little heed to the increasingly arduous terrain. They scaled steep crags, clinging desperately to vines and creepers, teetered along the edges of frightening chasms, and threaded their way over lofty and precipitous ridges. They went along like this for nearly four miles—the going getting rougher all the while—and after many hours finally arrived at a spot where further forward progress was quite impossible. To the right towered a nearly vertical wall of rock that swept far up into the clouds; to the left a sheer chasm yawned, apparently without bottom, cutting over to meet the cliff to the right and blocking the way ahead. The ledge on which they now stood came to an abrupt end, and the cliff plunged directly into the chasm for a thousand feet or more in front of them.

The rock wall above them was thickly carpeted with bright green moss and lichens, glistening with dew. Below them the chasm dropped straight down, its bottom hidden in murky dimness. On the far side of the chasm rose a stately crag, not quite as tall as the cliff beside them, but equally imposing. The chasm cut between the two precipitous upthrustings, separating them by no more than two hundred feet. On both sides ancient pines clutched at the rock face, thrusting outward in a twisting dance amongst the contorted stones.

The sun was blocked by the cliff on their right, and everything around them was in shadow. An eerie echo made the gloom more sinister. A single word would be flung back immediately by the chasm, leaving behind it lesser reverberations that took nearly a minute to subside.

32

Endless piercing after-echoes reached their ears, a chorus of angry howls from a mob of mountain goblins in the concealing murk of the chasm bottom, venting their hatred of the human strangers above them.

And yet despite the fearful gloom below, the lapis vault of the sky above was still serene and bright, lit by the hidden afternoon sun and crowded with fleecy clouds. A clean and mild breeze imparted to their clothes a faint suggestion of dampness. The contrast of emerald cliff, verdant chasm, and the ancient pines amid the contorted rocks suddenly took on an aspect of beauty and purity. It was a scene of rare and unearthly splendour which transcended the world of men, drawing their souls into flight as they gazed upon it, completely entranced.

Zhu Man-Tiger was the first to speak.

"We seem to have come to exactly the right place," he said, his voice tinged with wonder. "Isn't this steep cliff in front of us the 'Green-Clad Thirteen Twists' the Wanderer described to us?"

"I recall something of what he said about the way," mused Wang Jin. "This wall of rock with the chasm beside it must be the 'Green-Clad Cliff' he mentioned. But he warned us that looking at it from the outside it would appear so dangerous that even an ape or monkey could not get across it, which explains why no one else ever came this way before. He said he cut the 'Stone-Stairs of the Thirteen Twists' in the cliff so that anyone knowing something of Light-Body techniques could negotiate it, but the cliff wall is covered from top to bottom in slippery wet moss and lichens. Not even a snake could slither across that, much less one of us using our hands and feet. Where do we go from here?"

"This cliff must go up a thousand feet," said Zhu Man-Tiger. "The dwarf pines are too far apart for us to climb from one to the other. We can't have found the Thirteen Twists yet. There is clearly no way through here, and yet he said that it would be easy. The old man must have been sincere about wanting us to visit, or he wouldn't have been so careful to give us such detailed directions. Why would he deliberately want to make us to do something we cannot?"

"He was sincere," said Wang. "But we were too confident and careless to listen to what he said. Just point us in the right direction, and we can find anything. We simply weren't paying attention when the old man was describing the Green-Clad Thirteen Twists. When we parted he told us that once past this point, it would only be a few simple turns, rises, and falls in the trail before we got to his home..."

Before he could say more, Zhao Lin, who had been carefully inspecting the terrain above and below, suddenly broke in.

"I almost wonder if the old man, judging from the type of person he seemed to be, and from the way he spoke and acted, were not deliberately setting a test for us. The obstacles we have already crossed were dangerous enough, and yet he spoke of them in a rather casual way. Perhaps the trouble is that he is so used to travelling this route that he does not find it difficult, and he overestimated our abilities. In any case, the Thirteen Twists is something he only recently constructed, so there must be a way. Perhaps it is secretly and cunningly concealed, difficult to find through a casual inspection. I say we should search more carefully, and if we really can't find it, then we'll just have to find another way through. It would be shameful to turn back now."

Zhu Man-Tiger listened with growing displeasure. He was a very proud and reckless young man, a direct descendent of Zhu Qian, and as such had grown accustomed to living in ease and comfort. Clambering over one obstacle after another for the better part of a day was an exhausting business, and Zhu's original enthusiasm had flagged considerably. He was not pleased at Zhao's words, and was formulating a protest, when Wang Jin spoke up once more.

"I see a slope down below," he said brightly, peering down into the chasm. "There are little pines and creepers growing all over it. You can't see it very well from here, but if we descend the cliff at this point, I think there are enough trees that we can stop ourselves if we lose our footing and start sliding. The direction along the chasm looks like the one I remember the Wanderer described. The Thirteen Twists must be on the cliff wall below us. It would indeed be a shameful thing for us to turn back now. You two wait here until I've tried the way down to see if it's safe."

Wang Jin was the descendent of one of the Zhu family's household servants. He was honest, prudent, and endowed with considerable humility. He and Zhao Lin were the closest of friends. Wang had always been loyal and true to Zhao, and as soon as he heard Zhao say that turning back would be a disgrace, he decided to risk great danger to himself and try out the path. Zhao realized what he was up to the instant he spoke, and leaped forward to stop him in alarm.

"Wait, brother!" he shouted. "It's too steep and slippery down there! You mustn't go!" As he spoke he reached out to grab him, but Wang was too quick for him.

Wang Jin's native athletic ability and his command of the martial arts were superb, and he never shrank from applying himself to a difficult task. He was astute and clever, and knew full well that Zhao Lin, who loved him better than he would a younger brother of his own blood, would never allow him to put his life in danger. Wang had spied out the way before he announced his plan, and was over the edge and sliding down the nearly vertical cliff face before Zhao could reach him.

From where they stood the cliff wall, bordered by the chasm and towering up over a thousand feet, seemed to permit only one way ahead. This was a natural rock road, seventy or eighty feet long, created by a series of boulders projecting directly out of the cliff face. Unfortunately, this began some way ahead; there was no way to climb to it, and it was in any case too precipitous and slippery, full of impassable gaps. But down where Wang Jin was headed, a distance below the protruding midsection of the cliff, there did seem to be a less steeply sloped outcropping running along the rock face.

Zhao carefully inspected this sloped shelf. It looked like it extended far enough to provide a way through ahead, and seemed to have pines, vines, and protruding rocks scattered over it, though it was difficult to see clearly. Although it was less steep than the rest of the cliff face, it tilted downward alarmingly, and was covered with slippery moss and lichens. One false step and a man clinging to it would plunge immediately into the bottomless chasm beside it, to be dashed to bits far below.

Zhao Lin had already spotted this route, but decided it would be too dangerous to risk. He never suspected that Wang Jin would go down on his own. Now that Wang had already slid down onto the cliff face, Zhao dared not speak for fear of distracting him. Anxiously he watched his friend's progress.

Gazing intently downwards, Zhao observed that Wang Jin was applying his climbing techniques with extraordinary deftness and speed. As soon as he was over the edge he began to apply the secret Zhao family Light-Body technique known as the 'Flying Snake Traverses the Wall'. The sloping shelf was a bit over thirty feet below where Zhao and Zhu Man-Tiger stood watching. Climbing down a cliff was not a particularly difficult feat for anyone with the skills these three men had acquired; the problem was the moss and lichens which blanketed the rock face, which were as slippery as if covered with oil. With the near vertical pitch of the cliff, there could be no margin for error. One slip, and the climber would slide right across the slope into the gulf below. He could not allow his hands or feet to pause even for an instant.

As extraordinarily treacherous as the way was, Wang Jin handled it with apparent ease. First he dropped lightly straight downward, clinging tightly to the cliff face. When he had gone ten feet or so, he made an abrupt reverse spin to one side, and seized hold of a small pine tree briefly in passing, slowing his downward momentum. He continued to use this technique: downwards, then left or right towards a pine tree. These small trees kept him from building up too much speed as he progressed; if his downward momentum got out of control he would slide too quickly and lose his purchase on the slippery face of the cliff. He never paused, and looked for all the world like a giant gecko walking about on the nearly vertical wall, appearing and disappearing among the pines trees. In little more than the blink of an eye, he had reached the incline below, and stopped himself against the base of a thick dwarf pine about half the height of a man.

He looked about him for a moment, sitting astride the pine tree at an angle, and then looked up.

"This incline seems to connect with level ground around the corner up ahead," he said. "My guess is that it is the same flat area that our host described, though I can't be completely sure. The moss here is thick and fairly firm, and there are young pines and creepers all about. With your skills, neither of you elder brothers should have any difficulty. All it will take is a bit of the Breath-Lifting technique. Your worthless younger brother will go on ahead to try it out."

Zhao Lin was proud and gratified at Wang Jin's display of skill and uncharacteristic initiative. The two of them had grown up together, but Wang's humility had always kept him from showing off his remarkable skills in any way. In this he differed from Zhu Man-Tiger. Zhu had always been confident, and could generally be depended on to be thoroughly pleased with himself. Zhao could not repress a glance in Zhu's direction as he answered.

"If we're going to go, let's go together! We three have always shared dangers and pleasures alike. I've tested the moss and lichens too, and with enough of a slope, I think we can support ourselves on them. The way looks long and steep, though. We'll have to go along the incline supporting our weight with our hands, which could become dangerous. Still, I am certain we can figure out a way to keep going. Let's descend together!"

First, he tossed their packs down to Wang Jin, and then told Zhu how to negotiate the cliff face.

Zhu Man-Tiger was by this time feeling considerably fatigued, but his competitive nature made him unwilling to show any sign of weakness. He could not have stayed behind alone, so there was nothing for it but to summon up his courage and follow after Zhao.

Zhao and Zhu moved down with palms pressed tightly against the cliff face, flipping sideways one way or the other to catch hold of the small trees and slow their downward momentum as Wang had done. When they reached the small sloped area below, they each chose a small pine tree to stop themselves. While they rested, they inspected the way ahead.

The steeply inclined outcropping stretched out before them, twisting, turning, and bending like a huge snake. It did provide a way through, but was not an easy road. It was long, and sloped treacherously toward the chasm. The moss and lichens were far too slippery to allow purchase for their feet, and were, in any case, too weak to support the full weight of a human body. They would indeed have to employ their Light-Body skills, using the Breath-Lifting technique. One slip of a hand or foot, one missed Lifted Breath, and they would be dashed to a pulp below.

They knew their chances of making it were not perfect. They found themselves facing the ordeal with uncharacteristic caution. They settled their packs on their backs, and secured weapons and climbing tools where they would be ready to hand. Then, with Wang Jin still in the lead, and Zhao Lin following closely behind Zhu Man-Tiger, they moved out across the face of the slope.

Zhu Man-tiger was a very unhappy man. He had grown accustomed to passing his days in comfort. In the years he had been accompanying his comrades out of the valley, the only real hardship he had endured was during fights with their adversaries. He had taken to wife a woman of uncommon beauty and voluptuousness, and doted on her far more than was good for him. He was no match for Zhao and Wang in toughness and skill, as those two had continued to pursue their martial training with single-minded dedication. Wang Jin, furthermore, was not long out of his teens, and had the added benefit of youthful vigour. Zhu was uncomfortably aware of his own degrading position in the middle of their formation, and began to feel a combination of embarrassment and indignation. He saw that Zhao Lin had unfastened his Flying-Rope Pliant Claw, one end attached securely to his waist, and the other gripped between two fingers of his left hand, so that the Claw hung over the back of his hand. Although Zhao was thoroughly occupied with his own slippery progress, his glance fell again and again on Zhu. It was obvious that he knew Zhu's skills were not completely up to the task, and, fearing that Zhu might slip, was secretly ready to come to his rescue.

This was a bitter pill for Zhu Man-Tiger. As children he and Zhao had trained together, and it had been Zhu whose native ability outshone that of his peers. But when he had achieved a truly remarkable command of a few techniques, he grew pleased with himself, and slackened off considerably in his training. Now he found himself being herded along like an animal, and the more he thought about it the more ashamed he became. He was still in a state of considerable distress when the three of them dropped onto a large rock projecting from the surface of the slope, and sat down to rest.

As they sat, they became aware of a peculiar white vapour, rising in great puffs from under the rock beneath them to coalesce in a cloud which loomed motionless a few yards above their heads. As they puzzled over this, they heard a strange cry, clear and piercing, from the top of the cliff far above. It echoed back and forth and seemed to shake the empty crags. The sound had not quite died away when a weird howl, savage and thunderously deep, came from somewhere along the way ahead. It seemed to be a fair distance away, and sounded as if it emerged from a deep glen. It was their impression that it was answering the first cry they had heard.

By this time the Hour of the Monkey was giving way to the Hour of the Rooster,* and down on the midsection of the cliff it was growing even darker than before. The first sound came too suddenly to leave much of an impression on them, but they knew full well that whatever creature had made the second—bird, beast, snake, or other reptile— was undoubtedly ferocious and malign, and they were anxious not to meet it. Unfortunately, the perilous path gave them no option but to ignore the sounds and continue forward.

Just as they reassured themselves the howl was repeated, this time from the top of the cliff above them. It came again and again, growing

---

* [In traditional China there were twelve hours in a day, each the equivalent of two hours in the West. The Hour of the Monkey (*shen*) was 3–5 PM; the Hour of the Rooster (*you*) was 5–7 PM.]

ever more frenzied. Their sense of security vanished. If they encountered the monster on the steep slope, they would be in serious trouble. They looked at each other helplessly, at a loss for a way out of their predicament.

Wang Jin was uncomfortably aware that he was the one who had put them in danger. The unpleasant expression on Zhu Man-Tiger's face, in which anger and accusation were combined, increased his sense of shame and regret. The way ahead might be dangerous, but at least it was still open. And as fierce as the unseen monster's howls and roars sounded, it looked thus far as if it were content to rage on the cliff above, and did not intend to come down after them. This surely signified that it was after all an ordinary mountain predator of flesh and blood, and not some spectral being. He estimated that his capabilities were up to what might lie ahead, for a while at least. Fighting his native caution, he decided it would be better to take the lead forward than stay where they were, waiting passively for death while their situation grew steadily worse.

When he had thought this out, he stood up.

"Danger lurks all around," he said. "Staying here doing nothing can only make things worse. Why don't I beat a path on ahead? If we can get off this cliff and back to solid ground, we will be less vulnerable."

"I'm a little better at hard fighting techniques," Zhao answered hurriedly. "And I have more specially-made knives and throwing darts. I'll go first, you back me up, and Second Brother Zhu will bring up the rear. As soon as I reach solid ground, if I can't kill the monster, I can at least draw it away, and we'll be out of trouble."

As they spoke the white vapour emerging from under the rock continued to rise, puff after puff, feeding the expanding curtain of cloud above their heads. The cloud grew ever whiter and more luminous. The unseen monster's ferocious howling went on and on. A violent wind sprang up, booming and shrieking in the crags and gorges around them. The din smote their ears, and the entire cliff seemed to shake. The tempest grew ever louder and more frightening, until at last they could no longer make themselves heard to one another, and were forced to communicate with signs and gestures.

Zhu Man-Tiger, though the weakest, was also the keenest of hearing. He sat beside a pine tree, letting the others argue over who would go first. He did not speak, and his attention was not distracted. When the chill wind began to shriek, and the evil beast redoubled its howling, he seemed to hear someone shouting far away behind them through the din. He listened carefully, but could make out nothing further.

Wang Jin, meanwhile, did not even wait for Zhao Lin to finish speaking. He had spied out the way, and now moved sideways across the steep slope in the same way as before, gripping vines and clinging to small hollows in the rock. All Zhao could do was hurry after him, ready to render assistance if necessary.

"Follow behind me, Second Brother, and back me up!" Zhao shouted back to Zhu as he leapt to his feet.

Wang Jin had not gone twenty feet across the cliff wall when a jet of the white vapour, four or five inches in diameter, shot out like an arrow straight toward him from under the rock. Realizing that Wang was in deadly peril, Zhao reacted instantly, and shouted at him to duck. He had no time to think what manner of thing the vapour might be. His left hand came up and cast the thirty-foot Seven Star Pliant Claw, dangling at the ready over his arm, to seize Wang and prevent him from falling. His right hand raised his repeating projectile catapult and began to fire. He was dimly aware of someone shouting behind him, but was too intent on Wang to look.

The Claw was a rare and marvellous implement. Zhao Lin had collected the ends of Seven-Star Hooks growing on the tails of a peculiar variety of poisonous snake found in the territory of the Miao tribesmen. He steeped them in the sap of potent medicinal herbs, and attached them to an intricate mechanism which flexed like a human hand, relaxing or stiffening the digits as the wielder desired. The long line to which it was fixed was fashioned from the back muscles of another snake, the rare Iron-Thread. It was little thicker than an ordinary hempen rope, but stronger than steel. Not even the sharpest knife or axe could sever it. At the same time it was so remarkably pliant and elastic as to seem to be alive. When it was cast, the seven digits, each a foot long with an array of rubbery barbs, would relax and spread out in perfect unison. When they reached their target, man or animal, the wielder would flick the handle upward at a precise angle, and the digits would stiffen and flex, seizing the victim in a tight grasp from which he was unable to escape, and yet left him uninjured. It was an intricate but at the same time a dependable and effective implement.

Zhu Man-Tiger grasped what was happening more clearly. He could see that the white vapour was not solid. He drew out his precious throwing knives, the weapons he used with the greatest proficiency. These knives were forged from the finest steel with a small admixture of gold, smelted and annealed a hundred times over, like willow leaves in thickness and shape. They came twelve to a set, and when thrown flashed out like a beautiful golden lotus, scattering in a deadly rain of glittering flowers, rising and falling as they flew spinning through the air. Zhu's control of them was superb and inhumanly quick, and once released the intended target could not escape injury. These flying knives were complicated to manufacture, but he was ready to hurl them all if by doing so he could aid his friends. His ill-humour of a moment before was forgotten in his anxiety for Wang Jin. The strange wind continued to shriek as before, and in his desperation over what was happening in front of him, he too failed to look behind.

A great deal happened very quickly in the seconds that followed. The white vapour jetted out from under the rock; Zhao Lin shot at it with his catapult. Zhao caught the briefest glimpse of something hurling down like a bolt of lightning from the top of the cliff, and had an impression of three emerald stars, the size of peas, shining with a chill green light, diving straight toward the white vapour. When they struck, the vapour began to writhe and twist as though hit by a massive charge of electricity. Wang Jin seemed to have been poisoned by it, however, and without a sound or backward glance, his grip loosened, and he tumbled sideways, then straight down into the bottomless chasm.

Wang should have been smashed to bloody bits far below, but he was saved at the last instant, thanks in part to Zhao Lin's Pliant Claw. Zhao cast it almost instantly, so by the time Wang Jin was overcome by the poison, the Claw seized him and held him fast.

Zhao, in his relief at having prevented Wang from falling, relaxed his concentration ever so slightly. He forgot that Wang was now dangling right over the spot from which the poison vapour sprang. Wang Jin had been dropping like a stone when he was caught by the Pliant Claw, and it took all of Zhao's great strength and coordination to keep him from striking the rocks and being bashed to death. There was no way he could have kept Wang away from the poison orifice.

As he relaxed slightly, mustering his strength to haul Wang to safety, Zhao's nostrils were bathed in a sweet and exotic fragrance. He staggered under a wave of faintness and dizziness. Before even a cry of alarm could escape his lips, everything went black before him. A shout came from up above: "Hold on, you two!" He was dimly aware of being snatched up and carried into the air in a rapid diagonal ascent. Before he could move or make a sound, he lost consciousness completely.

CHAPTER 3

The Cloud-Spewing Beasts

GRADUALLY, AFTER AN UNKNOWN INTERVAL OF TIME, ZHAO LIN regained consciousness. He grew dimly aware that he was on solid ground, lying somewhere warm and comfortable. There was a slight soreness in his left arm, but it did not seem serious. Slowly and laboriously his mind began to work, and he struggled to remember what had happened. His present surroundings were certainly no dream.

But where was he? The question had barely occurred to him when he remembered Wang Jin. Wang's life had been hanging from Zhao's hand, and he did not know if he were alive or dead. Galvanized by a sudden shock of alarm, he opened his eyes to look about him.

He seemed to be in a chamber of stone, fully furnished, lying on a stone bed, covered with a thick quilt. It was quite dark, and even with the excellent night vision he had developed over the years, he could only make out the vaguest outlines of his surroundings. The room was not large, and contained only the one bed. Zhu and Wang were not there. There was no one else with him either, and it occurred to him that the stranger who had saved him, seeing that he had not yet regained consciousness after breathing the poison vapour, must have left him sleeping to recover.

Zhao peered around the room, but it was too dark to see where a door might be, and there was no one around to ask. Strange recluses with unusual powers were often eccentric, bound to a rigorous schedule of training and self-cultivation. If there was no one about, whoever it was must have gone away to attend to something important. His benefactor obviously had no evil intentions, but Zhao was reluctant to do anything rash. He was paying a visit here for the first time, alone in a secluded cave on a wild and mysterious mountain, and there was nothing he could do to hasten the return of his host. He did not even know what time it was. If he had been lying there a long while, it might already be late at night, in which case it would be rude of him to raise a clamour. But at the same time he was desperate with worry for his friends, his sworn brothers, with whom he had shared all dangers. Now it seemed that he alone had escaped; there was no sign of the others.

He continued to inspect his surroundings as best he could, trying to locate the door, and perhaps ascertain the hour by getting a look at the sky. He might also be able to find someone he could ask about his friends.

Just as his mind was spinning with anxiety and worry, and he was making up his mind to get up and feel his way around the wall to take stock of his surroundings, he heard a clear cry echoing sharply from a great distance over the desolate mountain outside. It was similar to the cry they had first heard while on the cliff. Now, however, it was evident that it was not the voice of an animal, but of a human being.

Barely had the sound reached his ears, when three chill green lights about the size of peas flashed near him in the darkness. It struck him that this was something he had seen before. The lights, part of a dim shadow two feet long and two feet wide, sped toward the wall behind the bed. A stone door was suddenly revealed, opening briefly outward to admit the bright light of a lamp beyond. The cold green lights and their accompanying shadow shot out the door with lightning speed and disappeared.

Before it revealed its lights, the thing, whatever it was, had been crouched motionless in the corner behind the bed. Zhao had noticed nothing except for a vague form he had taken for a bamboo barrel. When it made its presence known, he caught only the most fleeting glimpse before it vanished. Except for the three cold emerald lights at its front, there had been nothing but a shadow, with no visible head or tail. But the three emerald stars were somehow familiar.

An instant later he was startled by a series of thunderous roars that seemed to shake the sky, followed immediately by the sudden howl of a violent wind. The unbearable din echoed deafeningly through the mountains in every direction. The roaring was exactly what they had heard on the cliff face. The wind too was the same as that which they had experienced before, powerful enough to tear the leaves from trees and raise booming echoes through the mountains like a giant ocean surf. Now, as then, he thought it one of the most terrifying sounds he had ever heard. Strangely, though, the source of the sound was rapidly receding.

It appeared that the formidable creature with the three green eyes was some sort of pet kept by his benefactor. Its strength must be very great, as it had soundlessly and almost instantaneously pushed the heavy stone door open with no apparent effort. Since there was lamplight outside the door, someone must be there. Why not venture out and find someone to ask about his friends? He rose and went out the door.

ZHAO FOUND HIMSELF IN A CAVERN. ITS OWNER HAD PRESERVED ITS natural configuration, but had enlarged it and carved additional chambers out of the living stone. This outer room was long and narrow, and rather less neatly laid out than the bedchamber within. It was brightly lit by two flames in a small bowl-sized lamp hung from the high ceiling. The cave walls were smooth and glistening, as if fashioned of white jade, dotted here and there with small deposits and outcroppings of minerals. Stalactites and stalagmites clustered near the walls. The whole chamber, lit by the rays of the lamp, glittered with an unearthly phantom gleam.

The furnishings were sparser than those of the inner bedchamber. The room was dominated by one large table, carved out of a solid block of white marble, beside which were placed two stone drums. On the table were arranged a few incense censors, teacups, and other similar implements. Against the inner wall was a crystal screen constructed over stalagmites growing from the cavern floor, shining and sparkling transparently in the lamplight. Behind the screen was the rear wall of the cave, covered with uneven mineral encrustations.

There was no trace of anyone in this outer chamber. Zhao began exploring through a small forest of stalactites in what appeared to be the front end of the cavern, hoping to find the exit. After threading back and forth through the maze for about twenty feet, he emerged from the mouth of the cave.

The moon hung directly in front of him, its rays slanting into the entrance. By its light he saw that the cavern was located in a secluded valley of considerable size, covering several hundred acres. Along the valley rim jagged peaks stabbed high into the night sky, and imposing cliffs swept the clouds. The cave opened from the bottom of a vertical wall of rock carpeted with a profusion of moss, lichens, dwarf pines, and creepers, intermingled here and there with various wildflowers. The wide valley floor was almost perfectly flat and clear. Fragrant herbs and grasses, rich and succulent, grew everywhere, forming a soft carpet little more than an inch thick.

On Zhao's left grew a stand of a hundred or more giant bamboos, perfectly straight, tinkling now and then like nephrite chimes in the breeze. Not far to the right was a solitary summit, beautiful and perfectly proportioned, its peak cloaked by a small cloud, a pillar supporting the sky above. From an opening not far from its summit a small waterfall spilled out, a silvery band three feet or so in width, which plunged finally into a deep pool far below. From this pool the water flowed through a number of outlets, feeding channels which radiated out in all directions. The fall might have been an extension of the Milky Way, a luminous sash of misty gossamer and frosty silk dangling from the sky, escorted by flying pearls and splashing fragments of jade. Down below transparent ripples moved through deep long channels, driven by the waterfall out over the terrain like silvery snakes writhing along the ground in the moonlight. Beside some of the channels Zhao saw that compact square rice paddies had been cleared. Small bamboo lodges and pavilions were scattered on the ridges and along the stream banks.

Above, a moon just past full hung in the fathomless cobalt void. Nothing else was visible in the sky, save for a handful of stars sparkling like a decoration around the moon, and a few clouds shrouding the peaks around the horizon. Silvery moonbeams bathed the entire scene around him: verdant cliffs and peaks, cut by waterfall and springs, and the flat valley floor, punctuated here and there by solitary trees, dwarf pines, contorted rock formations, flowers, and giant bamboos. Through the crystal atmosphere the scene was sharply lit, like a new painting about to spring to life. All was in complete silence, broken only by the murmur of the springs, the soughing of the pines, and the faint tinkling and musical whistling of the bamboos. The entire effect was of an eerie and secluded realm quite cut off from the common dust of the mortal world, a setting whose beauty was equal to but utterly unlike that of Zhao's own valley home.

Far away the howl of the monster with the emerald lights had faded out of hearing. Zhao had tarried only a moment or two in the cavern's outer chamber, and yet outside all was now completely tranquil. The wind he had heard only moments before, violent enough to fling sand and rocks about, had apparently accompanied the creature into the distance. The wide valley floor amid the towering crags surrounding it seemed like the bottom of an immense well. In the time it had taken the monster to utter a few howls, it had crossed to the side far opposite the cave entrance, scaled the cliffs, and sped into the distance beyond. If his host was able to control a monster of such supernatural abilities he could only be an Immortal. But then, if he had indeed achieved immortality, why would he waste time growing crops on the valley floor in such a diligent manner?

AS HE STOOD THERE, ABSORBED IN WORRY AND INDECISION, HE WAS startled by a young woman's voice addressing him from behind.

"Honoured guest, the poison has not yet worked its way out of your system. Why are you up walking around like this?"

It was a lovely voice, gentle yet clear. An instant earlier Zhao had been completely alone below the mountain cliff. There had been no one in either chamber of the cavern when he had found his way out, and it did not seem possible that someone would approach him across the deserted landscape outside without his being aware of it. In such tranquil surroundings his senses, trained for years to detect the stealthy approach of an enemy, should have been keen enough to detect a leaf hitting the ground, much less the footfalls of a human being. And yet this person, a young woman at that, judging from the sound of her voice, had come right up behind him without his knowing it.

He did not really think that the woman behind him was a malevolent mountain imp or other demonic being, but he was greatly startled. When she spoke he slipped instantly to one side to avoid any possible attack, and then whirled around to look.

Standing perfectly still in the moonlight was a young woman of perhaps sixteen or seventeen years of age. She was remarkably lovely, dressed in a snow-white silken garment which glowed in the moon's frosty brilliance. Her sylph-like form looked like the cold jade-white body of an Immortal. She seemed to be aware of Zhao's suspicious reaction, and was not much pleased. Her phoenix eyes narrowed slightly in vexation.

"Do you understand what I am saying? You are safely rescued, but the poison that struck you is no ordinary one. The medicines you people were carrying with you are only efficacious against the poisons from common miasmas, and would have been useless. You have been

44

brought back to life and are out of serious danger, but the poison remains in your system. The main danger at present is that you might catch a chill, or over-exert yourself. You will not be completely recovered until the poison has completely dissipated, by around noon tomorrow. It might seem pleasant and peaceful out here, but when our Snowy goes on a rampage he stirs up quite a wind wherever he goes. My mother and cousins are not home, and if Snowy happened to come back fresh from a savage mountain battle with you standing here gazing at the moon, you would surely be injured by the wind he raises!

"You must forgive me. I have always been impatient and a bit too quick to open my mouth. My mother ordered me to remain in the rear cavern and prepare a medicinal ointment for your companions. I never thought that you would be able to endure your pain to rise and go wandering around. But here you are, bold as you please, ignoring your discomfort. You and your two companions were rescued from certain death in the very nick of time. I am asking you to go back to bed for your own good. Why are you so suspicious of me?"

Young as the girl was, a mysterious gleam of unearthly potency shone in her clear eyes. Her speech was bold and completely unaffected. It was obvious that she was no ordinary woman. He listened quietly to her explanation, and concluded that she must be one of the junior inhabitants of the cave. As equal measures of alarm and joy danced through his mind, he hastened to perform a formal salute, and answered her.

"We three ignorant brothers came to this mountain in response to an invitation issued by a man calling himself the Wanderer in Green. We lost our way, and ended up running foul of a strange poisonous miasma on the face of a precipitous cliff. We are very much in your debt for rescuing us and bringing us to be here to be revived, and will remain eternally grateful..."

The girl suddenly smiled and interrupted him.

"When my brothers rescued you and brought you back, all three of you were in a deep coma and near death. If it hadn't been for my mother's knowledge of medicine and the potent drugs she keeps secretly prepared, you would never have survived. We had to treat each of you separately. Since there is only one bed in each room, and also because we were afraid you would strain yourselves by trying to talk to each other, we kept you apart. You are all out of danger now. One of the others is still unconscious, but the third has already awakened. My mother gave me instructions when she left not to let him speak, and to leave him a written note informing him that all three of you were safe, but that you must rest until tomorrow noon, when you could see each other again. We had no idea who you were, where you were from, or why you were here. Now I understand how you found your way up into the mountain. The Old One in Green often wanders abroad, but never before has anyone come here looking for him. You seem to be well-trained in martial arts, but are scarcely advanced enough to associate with someone like him. You are extremely youthful as well. Wherever did you meet up with him? How is it that he invited you to come here to visit him?"

Zhao Lin gave her a rough account of the circumstances under which they and the Wanderer in Green had sworn friendship the previous year.

"Well!" she laughed. "There is more to our three honoured guests than meets the eye! So you made the acquaintance of the Old One in Green as of last year. This explains much. No wonder you regained consciousness so much earlier than we expected! I thought that you had staggered out of your bed in great pain because of curiosity or anxiety over your friends. But I see that your complexion has returned to normal, which must mean that the poison has dissipated, and that you aren't in much discomfort at all. Your other companion, the one who woke up ahead of you, must also be nearly recovered."

Listening to what she said Zhao realized that she must be speaking of Wang Jin, and was overjoyed, though since the young woman was alone in the cave, he knew that he would be committing an impropriety if he asked her to take him inside to see Wang. He informed her that he felt no discomfort except for a trace of soreness in his arm. Then he asked her name, and whether or not she was acquainted with the Wanderer in Green.

She smiled. "The poison must indeed be completely dissipated. But since your arm is still sore, perhaps it would be safest if we went into the cave out of the chill to talk."

Zhao Lin, seeing that she showed no signs of awkwardness in speech and manner, began to feel somewhat more at ease with this mysterious young woman. She was completely free of the tiresome affectations common among girls her age in the world outside. Knowing that it would be discourteous to refuse, he politely assented to her request. The girl nodded her head and walked into the outer chamber of the cave, Zhao following behind.

"The room in which you slept is where my eldest disciple-cousin performs his practices and exercises," she said, smiling once again. "There is no lamp lit in there, so let's sit out here and talk."

Zhao Lin had hoped she would take him into the inner cavern to see Zhu and Wang, but was reluctant to make the request, and so had no choice but to sit down where he was. The young woman sat down opposite him on the other side of the table, and began to question him in greater detail on how he had come to be on the mountain.

As he sat facing her in conversation, Zhao Lin could not help being stirred to some extent by her not inconsiderable feminine charms. He had always been a man of the most upright morals, never much given to romantic thoughts, but confronted with her dazzling beauty and the distinct scent of orchids on her breath, he found himself softening toward her, and felt slight stirrings of desire.

After a while she asked the name of the mountain where Zhao and the others lived in hiding, where it was located, and how it might be

46

found. The strictest rule in Zhao's community was that against ever revealing the route to the valley to any outsider, and he hesitated briefly before answering. The girl sensed his reluctance, and her phoenix eyes betrayed a certain vexation.

"You are unwilling to tell me. Are you afraid that I will go off at once to look for it?" she asked with a cool smile.

Zhao saw a faint flush of annoyance on her jade-white cheeks. Afraid that he had displeased her, he smiled and made haste to answer.

"Miss, you are a sylph from beyond the confines of our world. If you were to deign to descend to our barren little mountain and visit us, it would bring us the honour of a lifetime. We would not presume to ask you to demean yourself in such a way. How could such as we be unwilling to receive your visit?

"Many years ago, when our ancestors led their clans and followers into the mountain refuge, fearing only that it was not remote enough to escape persecution, they worried that a formal name for our home might eventually be revealed during the course of a procurement mission on the outside, so they decided not to give it one. Many names suggested themselves, what with the distinctive lake, mountains, flowers, and trees there, and the many learned men among the original settlers would have been eager to think of an appropriate one. Now, as our population has grown and we have spread out over a greater and greater area, we sometimes use informal names among ourselves for the sake of convenience, but only at home, never when we go out into the world. We have little else than our spacious open lake, whose shores are mostly lined with weeping willows. This we are accustomed to calling 'Willow Lake'. Every time we go back to it while travelling on the outside, we only say that we are 'going home'. Our barren little village has never had a proper name, so when you did me the honour of inquiring about it, I was unable to answer. That is the reason I hesitated. Please don't be annoyed!"

The girl laughed. "I understand very well what is in your mind; say no more! I am sure I'll find my way there sooner or later. There is no need for you to reveal it and risk being punished by your leaders."

Zhao Lin took the opportunity to change the subject.

"But here I have been wasting time on myself, and haven't asked you your name, Miss, or how our kindly benefactor rescued us and brought us here; might I prevail upon you to reveal something of these matters?"

"There are some things I can't yet talk about as freely as you have about your own affairs," she replied. "Fortunately, you should be able to see the Old One in Green in half a day's time, and he will reveal all you want to know. As for how you came to be rescued, that I can tell you.

"Last month a strange mutant beast appeared on our mountain, Heaven knows from where. It has the ability to spew forth a smoky vapour which rises to form a cloud, which it can manipulate in midair exactly as it wishes. It can expand the cloud or contract it; it can send it forth and draw it back in. The vapour is unimaginably poisonous. I was out on the mountain gathering medicinal herbs, and quite by accident discovered it lurking on the opposite side of the Gorge of Square Bamboo, on the same rock where you were resting your feet yesterday. It was belching out its vapours, poisoning the living creatures all around it. In form it is something like an enormous lion, but covered with greenish fur and hairy bladders. There is a whole cluster of strange eyes on its forehead, which shoot forth a baleful gleam in all directions. Right in the middle of its belly it has an extra claw. When threatened, this monster responds by inflating its hairy bladders like great balloons, so that its entire body appears to expand almost instantly. It can then float through the air, rising and falling at will. All five of its taloned claws spread out, ready to strike in unison.

"When I saw this creature, it was spewing its vapour and spreading it into a thick canopy. Then it blew out several thin threads of the stuff and began waving these about in the air. There was a strange fragrance, and birds flying near would swoop downwards, tricked into seeking its source. As I watched, a flock of several dozen birds was poisoned and sucked into its mouth. Its strange lipless maw breathed in and out slightly, making chewing motions, and then gaped wide to blow out a huge cloud of feathers, which danced and fluttered through the air. It had made a meal of the whole flock! Truly a most dreadful and malevolent beast.

"I understand that this particular specimen is a mere male. The female is rather different in form, and much more dangerous. The species is a mutant one, called the Fire-Eyed Emerald Distentor, or sometimes the Cloud-Spewing Beast. It lives only in remote mountain areas. It apparently spews its clouds and fogs entirely for its own amusement, and after many years of practice develops considerable powers and wisdom. Once it reaches this stage it will not again use its vapours to take the life of any living thing without reason. I didn't know this when I saw it, and had no idea that its clouds were poisonous. It had inhaled the flock of birds just to frighten me away. But at the time I was thoroughly angry with it for being so wantonly malicious, and made up my mind to get rid of it.

"Thank goodness I approached it with caution! I was puzzled at how such a heavy and clumsy looking monster (it was over ten feet long!) could ever have climbed on and off that rock across the slippery, nearly vertical cliff face. Also, I didn't have any idea where its lair was, or whether there were others of its kind about. In any case I was confident it would be unable to escape once I decided to do away with it, so I was in no hurry to do the job. I decided to observe its movements for a while and find out where it had come from. While I paused to watch it, it had already made up its mind that I was an enemy, but at the same time was a little afraid of me. It did not attack, but put on a great display of fierceness, roaring savagely. Then when it saw that I stood by without doing anything, it decided that I intended no harm. At that moment the voice of a human child crying out impatiently came up from far below.

48

The monster stopped its aggressive posturing, and growled softly toward the chasm, then puffed up its bladders and flew downwards.

"I saw then how its strange mutant body could expand and contract at will, and how it could fly about with great quickness and mobility. It also became evident to me that its breaths were laden with a rare poison. If I had tried to kill it, I might have found myself in serious trouble. I thought it strange, too, that there would be a human child down in that unhealthy chasm. I did nothing to harm the creature, and peered down in the direction it had gone.

"It dropped far down toward the dark mists that lurk in the lower half of the chasm. The chasm bottom is an unwholesome place. There are innumerable venomous snakes, pythons, poisonous spiders and insects of every description, all trapped there by the vertical cliffs, which they cannot climb. They inhabit nests, lairs, or perches, each after the fashion of its kind, where they grow and breed, and fight and kill one another for territory. The low chasm bottom is damp and filthy to begin with, and the venomous discharges of the reptiles and insects combine with other foul emanations to form a fearfully toxic miasma which pervades the lower reaches of the gorge. The sun never penetrates to the bottom, and between walls several thousand feet in height the miasma can never escape. The chasm is inaccessible to man or beast, so it poses no real danger. Every few days during the spring and summer, when the bright noonday sun shines directly downward, the poisonous fog evaporates, rises, and condenses into rainbow clouds, which thicken and let fall a poisonous rain within the chasm. Fortunately these clouds never ascend more than a hundred feet or so below the protruding rock on the cliff, so the area affected by the rain is extremely small. The clouds are actually quite beautiful, roiling and twisting one after another in great shimmering puffs. Wherever the rain falls, no plant can grow, and the rocks and cliffs on both sides of the chasm are as slippery as wet jade. You saw only the moss and lichens far above, which are green and lush. Only two hundred feet below where we rescued you the cliff curves inward, and nothing grows at all. There is no possibility of clambering around on that slippery naked rock!

"Anyway, I tried to make out the monster's lair, which must have been the place where the poor child had cried. I could see a hollow cave, and there really was a human child in it, perhaps two or three years old. He was wearing very fine clothes, though they were a bit worn and tattered. The cave entrance was small, blocked off by a large rock. The child couldn't get out, and was crying anxiously inside. When the Emerald Distentor got down to the level of the cave, it floated over to the entrance. I couldn't see what it did, but the rock shifted inward, uncovering the entrance. The child came out to meet the beast. He struck it twice with his fists, then hugged its head, and they went together into the cave. It looked as though he were upset with the creature for being slow to return, and struck it twice to vent his pique, then started feeling fond of it again. Both actions showed affection and intimacy. The next thing I knew the rock had once more been moved to seal off the cave entrance.

"It was an ordinary human child, though perhaps stronger and more agile than one would expect. The more I thought the stranger it seemed. There was no accounting for what might have brought about such an unusual situation, and I couldn't help but be impressed by the child's unusual appearance and obvious intelligence. I made my way home without delay, and reported everything to my mother.

"At that time my oldest disciple-cousin had just returned to the mountain from a journey to visit a friend. On the way back he passed through Glaucous-Envelope Mountain. There he encountered a strange two-headed creature called a 'Linked Culmen,' which happens to be the Emerald Distentor's only natural enemy. The Linked Culmen is also a mutant vapour-spewing beast, only its appearance is even more repulsive. The Emerald Distentor is a vivid green all over, has seven eyes growing on its forehead, and blows out snowy white clouds. The Linked Culmen is covered with short grey hair as stiff as needles. Its body is stubby and short, almost rectangular in shape. It stands on short straight legs, lean and hard, which terminate in feet with six hook-like talons capable of ripping the most savage beast or deadliest snake to shreds. No armour or shell can withstand it. Its strength is virtually limitless. Most peculiar, though, is the two heads growing on the front part of its body. These it can extend and retract at will. Usually it keeps its heads and necks retracted inside two cavities between its shoulders, so that only its two weird faces are exposed. Each face has a lion-like nose and a gaping mouth stretching from one jowl to the other, filled with rows of sharp teeth. It has two triangular ears, one on the outer side of each head. Three dragon-like eyes, large and spherical, sprout from each forehead, and a third grows in the space between the two head cavities. Usually this middle eye is closed and invisible. When the beast meets an enemy, it takes a threatening posture, retracting both heads and emitting a penetrating green light from all three eyes at once. Once the glow of its eyes is fixed on its target, all but those who beat a hasty retreat will be caught by the luminous green vapour it spews, transmuted from the vital elixir breaths circulating in its belly. The victim, whether man, beast, or snake, will fall unconscious on the spot, and the monster will tear it to shreds with a few strokes of its claws. Unlike the vapour the Emerald Distentor emits when disturbed, the Linked Culmen's fog is not lethal, and as long as its victim has not been torn by its claws, it will in time regain consciousness and recover. But it is still an extraordinarily dangerous creature, particularly for the Emerald Distentor, which knows no other natural enemies. Fortunately this particular Linked Culmen was a young one, its powers not fully developed, and my cousin was able to capture it. It can expand and shrink its body at will, and extend and retract its heads. It can run and jump with incredible agility, moving faster than a flying bird. But its kind does not have the Emerald Distentor's ability to inflate itself and drift up and down through the air.

"When my cousin caught this beast on Glaucous-Envelope Mountain, it had somehow been seriously wounded, and was near death. But it was still capable of putting up a menacing display when threatened, and vigorously stoked up the breaths from its internal elixirs to defend itself. It was only by trying every trick he could think of that my cousin was finally able to subdue it. The beast has a fiery disposition, but once tamed it becomes loyal to its master, and will never betray him. My cousin managed to endear the beast to him by treating it kindly. Later when my mother and I spent night and day treating its wounds with rare and potent medicines, it became friendly, and is now loyal to us as well.

"But we still couldn't do anything about the child. The Linked Culmen had not yet recovered its strength, so we couldn't send it against the Distentor, natural enemy or not. My mother went to the Gorge of Square Bamboo to observe the situation, and concluded that the child and beast were together for some good reason. The Old One in Green had not yet returned from his wanderings, and there were several things we needed to ask him before we intervened. A rash move might cause irreparable harm or bring us up against unforeseen obstacles. My mother is not afraid of trouble, but she is accustomed to living in peace, and had no desire to cause an unpleasant incident. It was evident that the Distentor had been tamed by someone, and had become sensitive and intelligent, unlikely to harm any living thing without good reason. In any case it had taken refuge in a secret and dangerous spot safe from any outside enemies, so my mother decided to leave it and the child alone for the time being. She forbade my disciple-cousins to tease or disturb the beast in any way, fearing that it might realize that we wished to subdue it, and flee with the child to a distant spot beyond our ability to follow.

"We decided to wait. The Linked Culmen was still not at full strength, so we healed it and trained it, all the while watching for the return of the Old One in Green. Two months went by, but the Old One sent us no word of his return. It may be that he was already back, but did not intend to see us, perhaps occupied with other affairs of his own, and was unwilling to involve himself in this matter. If the Old One invited you here, then he must have anticipated being home at this time. Had we known that you had been invited here as his honoured guests, the others probably would not have been in such a hurry to go off and tend to the child."

Zhao Lin asked what his absent hosts were now doing, and added, "It has been a long time, over a year in fact, since the old gentleman made his invitation to us. How could he have known we would come on this particular day?"

The girl laughed. "I am only guessing that the Old One anticipated your arrival today. As for what is happening tonight, I can tell you more. After the Emerald Distentor had seen me it wasn't much disturbed, but when my mother went to look, it grew more wary. It began making preparations to flee to a place of greater safety with the child. We sus-

51

pect it had not already moved the child only because it was having difficulty locating a new hiding place. Every night it shut the boy in the cave while it roamed far and wide in search of a suitable refuge. At first we weren't aware of what it was doing, but then my disciple-cousins discovered it, and informed my mother. We guessed that it would depart sooner or later. Meanwhile, my oldest cousin had left the mountain and learned something about the child. I'll tell you more about that later.

"We resolved to subdue the Emerald Distentor with all of our combined strength on a day of our choosing, come what may. The monster was aware that we were up to no good. It redoubled its efforts to find a new place of refuge, sallying forth to search during the daytime as well as at night while my cousins watched from their hiding place on the cliff.

"Today they reached their observation post later than usual, just as you three had lost your way. By an unhappy coincidence, you determined to traverse the cliff face with your Light-Body techniques above the monster's lair. If you had kept going everything might have turned out all right, but you paused to rest right on top of the protruding rock. My younger cousin had taken the Linked Culmen to that very spot a few days ago to frighten the monster and give it a warning. Originally, motivated by concern for the child, he had hoped to convey to the creature that it would be best for all concerned if it would surrender the child and come with him to our house, where all would be safe. He tried to make it understand that if it was unwilling to trust us, then at all costs it should not leave its present lair. Unfortunately, not only did it fail to apprehend this message, but, because of the presence of its enemy the Linked Culmen, its suspicions were confirmed. It became angrier and more afraid as time went on, and when you appeared on the scene, its wrath and frustration had reached the bursting point. Under the circumstances, it is not surprising that it assumed that anyone on the rock was an enemy.

"When we discovered your presence, my mother and oldest cousin were away. Only my youngest cousin and I were up on the cliff top. An immediate rescue would have been difficult, because we would have been the monster's poison breath, which, in its agitation, it would be sure to use. We made haste to signal the alarm to the others back home. By the time my mother and cousins had hurried to the scene, bringing the Linked Culmen, you were in mortal danger. A slip of the foot would have plunged you into the deadly chasm beyond any hope of rescue. You came within a hair's breadth of disaster, but happily they arrived in time to save you. My mother instructed the Linked Culmen not to attack the Distentor, but to roar threateningly, stoke up the vital elixir breaths in its abdomen, and discharge the energy through its three mutant eyes. Meanwhile, she and my oldest cousin descended towards you at best speed. They reached you just as you were struck by the poison, on the verge of falling unconscious into the gorge. They managed to rescue all three of you, and brought you here.

52

"We left my youngest cousin up on the top of the cliff to keep watch. Later in the evening he returned to report that the Emerald Distentor seemed to be making preparations to flee. At dusk it had ascended cautiously to reconnoitre. Seeing that there was no one on the cliff, it shot back down in a great hurry, and re-emerged with a bamboo box in its mouth, which it carried off into the southeast at great speed. After about an hour it returned to its lair, this time fetching up a leather bag containing a brightly glowing object which must have belonged to its former master. My mother's worst fears were realized: the monster was fleeing rather than risk confrontation and the loss of the child or treasures. My cousin showed himself and shouted at it to stop. The creature reacted with astonishing speed. It roared when it saw him, then turned and fled, loosing a jet of its deadly breath. My cousin, though prepared for this, only just escaped. Fortunately for him the Emerald Distentor was wary and cautious; after the one spurt it withdrew its poison and beat a hasty retreat. My cousin knew that it would probably not reappear until it could modify its plans. He hurried back to bring us the news.

"When my mother heard this report, she knew that a dangerous confrontation was inevitable unless we were prepared to allow the creature to carry the boy away. She had once been acquainted with the child's parents, and did not wish to allow the glowing treasure, an otherworldly periapt of great potency, to fall into the hands of an enemy who might use it to work great harm. She resolved to confront the misguided monster. In great haste she led my cousins to the cave where the child was confined. But the rock blocked the entrance, and nothing they tried would remove it. They dared not use drastic measures for fear of injuring the child. Had they succeeded at that point the child would now be here safe and sound, and the whole affair over and done with. They did not take the Linked Culmen with them because it was needed here to circulate its vital elixir breaths and counteract the poison in your bodies. It should have been kept here until dawn. You were the most severely poisoned, so the Linked Culmen was remaining by your side. It must have seen that the poison had dissipated and that you were reviving, so it closed its eyes and retracted its heads, and sat still and silent. In the unlighted room, you wouldn't have seen it when you awoke. Just now it answered my mother's summons from the Gorge of Square Bamboo, which must mean that they have lured the Emerald Distentor out into the open and trapped it, but have failed to persuade it to open the cave and surrender the child. They do not wish to injure the creature, and need the Linked Culmen to help them subdue it. The Linked Culmen isn't strong enough to defeat it, but it is the only species the Distentor fears. I'm sure the advantage is already on our side, and that they will return soon."

Zhao Lin listened to this account with great wonder. His hosts were the very sort of mysterious and unearthly adepts he had always longed to discover. The Wanderer in Green he had come to seek turned out to be an exalted figure of great mystery, held in awe even by his present hosts. The Wanderer must have cut off most contact with the world long ago, and retired to this mountain to live in seclusion. Zhao rejoiced at the good fortune that had led this man to deign to befriend them and invite them to visit. He wanted to ask more about him, but heard a sharp howl far off in the distance, and hesitated.

The girl saw him pause, and spoke first. "Just now you asked my name. People who have withdrawn from the world do not usually reveal this to others, but you seem a kind and honest man, and are in any case a friend of the Old One in Green, so you are not really an outsider. Now that the troubles at the Gorge of Square Bamboo are over, the child rescued and the Emerald Distentor all but subdued, a great load has been taken off my mind. When my mother returns she will reveal all to you anyway, so I might as well tell you our names. My father is Zhu Blue-Lotus, and my mother is Chen Graceful-Equity. My name is Soaring Cloud.

"My father discovered this mountain fifteen years ago when he came here to meet a friend. The friend never appeared, but on his return he passed near the Gorge of Square Bamboo. Being well-versed in the art of geomancy, he perceived at once that the configuration of the mountain terrain was highly unusual, harbouring terrestrial energies of great potency. Out of interest he traced the energy meridians beneath the ground and found this valley. He noticed that there were many potent medicinal herbs growing here, and that the peculiar peak on one side was covered with mineral springs gushing from stalactite-covered areas in the rock. He resolved at once to move his family here. During the first two years or so we cleared away some of the stalactites and channelled the water of the springs into a waterfall feeding a network of watercourses, so there was no longer any need to depend solely on rainfall to water the fields. Gradually he began to invite some of his former students and disciples to come with their households and join us here. As of now we have only seven or eight families scattered about, and are insignificant by comparison with the wide territory, big population, and beautiful scenery of your Willow Lake. But it is secure and peaceful, and doesn't seem particularly lonely. My cousins often leave the mountain to wander about the world, but I must usually remain here to take care of various minor affairs, and am not allowed to go abroad without good reason. Perhaps I could go visit your Willow Lake sometime, do you suppose?"

Zhao Lin's response was automatic: "Yes indeed!" The girl, seeing that his thoughts were elsewhere, did not press him further.

Zhao asked about the Old One in Green, where he lived, and what his real name was. The girl smiled again.

"Tomorrow we will take you there, and you will see for yourself. No need for haste!"

As she spoke, a thunderous roar battered the cavern, and a wild gust of wind blew sand and rocks into the air outside. It was the same sound he had heard after regaining consciousness. Startled, the girl looked up.

"If they were successful, why is our Snowy still raising such a fuss? I'd better have a look."

There was a breath of wind, and the lamp flames shuddered slightly. A third person stood in front of them, a handsome youth in a white tunic with a long sword hanging at his waist. The girl stood.

"Well?" she demanded. "Is it all over? Why have you all been gone so long? It's nearly dawn..."

The youth interrupted her impatient questioning.

"The creature was more stubborn and dangerous than we anticipated," he said. "None of us is conversant with the speech of beasts, so we could not coax it to submit. We didn't want to hurt it, so after we managed to corner it, we summoned the Linked Culmen to help. It still wouldn't surrender. It stood there calling softly in a most pathetic manner, not fighting, but refusing to give up. Then it suddenly erupted with all of its strength, catching us completely unprepared. It lashed at us with all of the force of the vital elixir breaths it has refined over the years, spewing poison so strong it burned like pure vitriol. Even the Linked Culmen was hurt, only just escaping severe injury, and was still howling madly just now when we were coming back. If we hadn't worked out how to get the two creatures calmed down, they would still be waiting for their first opportunity to fight to the death.

"In the end it was Oldest Brother who figured out what the Distentor was trying to convey to us. It wanted the child to accompany it at all times, and wished that an unearthly gem of power left behind by its master, along with the potent protective talisman whose magic it was using to seal up the cave, be strapped to the child's body, never to be removed or handed over to another for safekeeping. We naturally agreed to these conditions. The child is quick, intelligent, and brave. He was beginning to stifle in the cave, which had been sealed for quite a while. When we had more or less mollified the Emerald Distentor, we called to the child through the rock and explained what the situation was, and he agreed to come out. The Emerald Distentor roared in great agitation up on the cliff, warning the child not to unblock the entrance, but the child paid no heed. He removed the magic talisman, and the entrance was unsealed. Our mistress then went down, removed the rock and went in. She came back up with the child, the leather bag, and the talisman.

"The child had readily agreed to come along with us, but when he saw that the Emerald Distentor had been trapped, he threw a frightful tantrum, clawing and scratching with all of his might, trying to activate the magic of his father's bright jewel to do us injury. Our mistress restrained him, and spoke calm words to him, making him understand that he was to behave himself, and that our valley would be safe for him and great fun besides. Finally he settled down and became obedient, and ordered the Emerald Distentor to submit to us as well. Our mistress, to win the trust of the monster, returned the magic jewel to it, putting it into the pouch inside its mouth. The creature was finally convinced that our intentions were good, and seemed delighted. It knelt down before her and wept huge tears while she praised it for its loyalty to its dead master, and for keeping his poor orphaned son from harm. She gave it some cinnabar pills to eat, and it went off to fetch the bamboo box, which we have now brought back and stowed in Oldest Brother's cave.

"The Linked Culmen was still stubbornly belligerent. Ever since it first saw the Emerald Distentor it has been spoiling for a fight, itching to unleash the elixir breaths built up in its belly and vanquish its enemy. It had already been prevented from doing so twice. Now it was injured and in some pain as well. The Linked Culmen is really quite an admirable little beast, and when it puts on a threatening posture I think it is much more impressive than the Emerald Distentor. Anyway, I didn't want the two of them to be lifelong enemies, so I told it that since it had been such a big help in rescuing everybody and dealing with the monster, if it would agree to be friends with the Emerald Distentor from now on and promise not to fight with it, I would feed it some of the potent cinnabar pills Elder Sister got last year. I thought you surely wouldn't mind, since you love the little beast so much, and are always praising it..."

"What!" the girl said angrily. "I had to beg and beg the Old One for that cinnabar! Except for the two pills I gave you I didn't give any to the others, not even Oldest Cousin! Now you start handing them out on my behalf, and to an animal! And try to tell me that it is because you made a promise to it! The Old One smelted this cinnabar himself at great trouble, mixing in three hundred rare medicinal herbs over a period of years. It's much more potent than the stuff we make! It can quicken the formation of an immortal embryo within the body, begin transforming one's bones, and even revive someone nearly dead! I know he makes large quantities, but you know how strange the old man is when people ask him for things. With the two I gave my mother out of filial duty, the two I took myself, and the two I gave you, I only have six left. Have you forgotten everything the Old One has told you over the years? How could you throw them around so carelessly? All the two beasts did was blow their breaths around at each other, and perhaps deplete some of their internal elixirs. They can't have been much damaged. A few days and they would have recovered anyway. What do you mean by this lavish generosity with my belongings?"

The youth interrupted her with a smile.

"All right, all right, Elder Sister! You're quite right. But you know me. I never break faith, not even with animals. I have promised, and the beast has thanked me. It would be a disgrace if I went back on my word."

"I know how your crafty little mind works," she said, glaring. "You knew perfectly well that if we talked it over in advance I would never have agreed, so you promised first, knowing that I always stand behind you and would never let you embarrass yourself. Admit it!"

"I'm always honest with you, Sister," he said. "You're perfectly right. But can't you say yes just this once?"

"This whole thing was a deliberate trick," she said, still unmollified. "You're rotten through and through, and yet speak of honesty!"

"It's only because you are always so kind to me, Sister," explained the lad, now visibly perturbed. "But it's not fair to say I am cheating you on purpose!"

He glanced at Zhao Lin, paused, then spoke again.

"Don't you want to go meet the little boy? I'll take you out to see him."

The girl laughed. "I know what you are thinking. If we have something to say we'll say it right here. We have a guest. You should have humbly implored him to give you teaching, but instead you come in here like a house afire and start an argument. What sort of manners is that?"

The youth once more glanced at Zhao, and seemed about to say something.

"You'd best not take him lightly," she warned. "He is here on personal invitation from the Old One in Green, which should give you an idea of his accomplishments, and what is in store for him in the future."

The youth quickly interrupted to explain. "I already know about Elder Brother Zhao, but because I was in such a hurry to get the pills from you, and you wouldn't let me get a word in anyway, I never really had a chance to greet him properly, that's all."

"How did you know who he was, and how to address him properly?" asked the girl, rather puzzled. "I only found out from him myself a moment ago."

"The Old One in Green sent Seventh Elder Sister over to tell us. He had long since calculated that they would come today. He returned from his travels quite some time ago. When we tried to visit him last month it was evidently not yet opportune for a number of reasons, so Seventh Sister was ordered to send us away with his regrets."

"Well!" she said. "At first I wondered if these guests were presuming on the Old One's kindness, because they are so much younger than he is. But his actions are always difficult to fathom, so I thought, who knows? Maybe he really did befriend them despite his exalted status. I was refraining from addressing him as Elder Brother until I had found out for sure, but now the Old One himself has confirmed it. Elder Brother Zhao is a man of great honesty and a strong sense of justice, very similar to my disciple-cousins. The natural surroundings of his home at Willow Lake are quite remarkable, and I would like to visit there myself some time in the future."

"If you go, Big Sister, I will have to go too," the youth said eagerly.

"Of all my cousins, you are the most disgusting," she said. "Elder brother Zhao and his people have dwelt apart from the world for many years, and won't be especially willing to have outsiders show up on their doorstep!"

Zhao observed that the girl genuinely intended to visit Willow Lake, and began to ponder how this might be accomplished. Befriending accomplished adepts of mysterious power could be of great benefit to him and his people. He made haste to answer.

"Honoured airborne sylphine warriors, we never could have hoped that divine and noble personages such as yourselves would ever deign to visit even if we were to invite you! Of course we would be willing to let you come! When we return to our valley we will notify the people of our village of your coming, and I myself will return here to escort you there. Would that be to your liking?"

"We have grown accustomed to neglecting good manners," the girl said gravely. "I have forgotten to introduce my younger cousin to you. This is my father's disciple Wei Lai. He is only one year younger than myself, but as you can see is childlike and immature, and will undoubtedly give Elder Brother Zhao much cause for amusement."

As she spoke Wei Lai walked up and respectfully saluted Zhao.

"You must forgive us," he said. "We have never been much bound by rules of good conduct and manners, and are accustomed to speaking in a rude and familiar fashion. I hope Elder Brother Zhao will accept our humble apologies."

Zhao modestly protested against the youth's addressing him as "Elder Brother," but to no avail. The girl broke in.

"I have examined Elder Brother Zhao's complexion, and though the poison has dissipated, he is not yet at full strength. I suggest that he rest quietly for a while. Tomorrow at noon he may rejoin Zhu Man-Tiger and Wang Jin, and I will take you all to meet my mother and the Old One in Green. Is this acceptable?"

Zhao Lin assented with a polite smile. Wei Lai addressed him again.

"This honoured Elder Sister of mine, Soaring Cloud, has always been quick and impulsive in word and deed. She has a warrior's heart and a strong sense of justice. She will subject herself to great danger for a friend, and will confront anyone, no matter how dangerous they may be. She has never yet found herself in serious trouble, but she has made no small number of enemies. Therefore our mistress has in recent years forbidden the two of us to leave the mountain without good reason. If you see the Old One in Green tomorrow, Elder Brother, perhaps you could put in a word or two for us, suggesting that it is your own intention to invite us to Willow Lake. If the Old One so much as nods his head once, our mistress will be obliged to agree."

"You say *I* like to make enemies and stir up trouble," laughed Soaring Cloud. "Why then does my mother also forbid *you* to leave the mountain? You are brash enough to conceal your own glaring defects, and bring the matter up as if it were all my fault! Here you are meeting Elder Brother Zhao for the first time, and you demand an invitation from him! What a joke!"

Zhao Lin hastened to intervene. "It is my own humble intention to have you visit our valley, so if I see the Old One I will make this request of him without fail. But I will have to return first to our valley, and come back at a later date to escort you two honoured guests, if that is not objectionable."

"That is of no consequence," said Soaring Cloud. "But now, Elder Brother Zhao, you must get some rest. It is nearly dawn. No matter what you might hear inside or outside the cave, do not be alarmed. We will be able to handle anything that might come up, so please do not trouble yourself to come out and look. There is wholesome spring water of great potency in your chamber. If you are thirsty you may drink some of it, since it will do you good. Unfortunately, you must not take solid food until midday tomorrow, so I cannot offer you anything to eat now. Youngest Cousin and I have a little business to attend to outside, so we must leave you."

Zhao assured her that he was not hungry in any case. The two of them left the cave, Soaring Cloud in the lead and Wei Lai following behind.

Zhao, who still felt some discomfort in the area of his spleen, followed the girl's advice and went directly back to his bed. After lying for a while he began to feel a burning thirst, accompanied by a feverish heat in his chest. Soaring Cloud's mention that the potent spring water was beneficial came to mind, and he felt a strong desire to drink some of it. Unfortunately the room was in darkness, and the layout unfamiliar. He was reluctant to poke through his host's possessions, but surely the water would be in a bottle or basin of some sort, which should be easy enough to find.

He sat up and peered through the darkness. His eyes were good, though somewhat dimmed from the ill effects of the poison, and some lamplight came through the door. He could make out a few implements on the table, but nothing that looked like a water vessel. His thirst was rapidly becoming unbearable. He got up and began to hunt about. At first he was sure that there would have to be some easily recognizable container for the water, and searched on the table and desk, then the rest of the room, but in vain. There was no one in the outer chamber he could ask. In his acute discomfort he began to consider whether he should disobey the girl's wishes and venture out to drink from the springs below the waterfall.

Just then he caught sight of something white, roughly the width of two fingers, down near the floor in the corner to his left. He bent down to look, and discovered a small crystal beaker about four inches tall and one inch in diameter, tucked into a small groove in the rock wall. He felt tiny depressions in the side of the vessel which seemed to be engraved writing. He removed it, took it over to the light and read 'Milk of the Immortals from Numinous Rocks'. The water inside was clear and lustrous, glowing in the faint lamplight with an unearthly silver sheen. He recalled what Soaring Cloud had said about the potent mineral water

59

from the stalactite-laden springs. The sparkling fluid inside the crystal beaker must be from these springs.

He took off the stopper and sniffed. It had no particular odour, but as soon as it touched his nostrils he became aware of a delicious penetrating coolness which cleared his head almost immediately. He tried a small sip, and felt the shock of a chill colder than ice against his teeth, almost more than he could bear. Before he could spit it out, however, he had already swallowed it.

It was quite evident that this fluid, which he now noticed glowed faintly with a silvery light of its own, was not ordinary water. Soaring Cloud had spoken of potent spring water from energy-laden springs that was beneficial to drink, but this was clearly something more than that. Anything kept in such a tiny and well-crafted beaker must be extremely precious. What had he done? He had no idea of the proper dose or method of ingesting the fluid, or even whether it was toxic. He held out the beaker to look again, and discovered to his horror that a full third of its contents was gone. He quickly replaced the stopper, and stepped over to return the beaker to its niche, mortified with sudden guilt, wondering desperately how he would explain to his hosts the next day. In his haste, he failed to pay sufficient attention to where he was going, and banged his knee painfully on something hard just below the niche in the wall which held the crystal beaker. The object rocked sideways with a muffled gurgle of water. He bent down to look, and discerned a container shaped like a stone drum. The water still sloshed faintly around inside it.

He replaced the beaker, intending to investigate the water inside the vessel. But then he paused. His thirst and discomfort had vanished. He felt very tired. There were a great many strange things here, and he had already made one serious mistake. Since he was no longer thirsty, he had best stop disturbing his hosts' personal effects. He left the water vessel alone and lay on the bed, and soon slipped into a deep sleep.

CHAPTER 4

The Miao Sorceresses

ZHAO AWOKE TO THE SOUND OF A LOW VOICE SPEAKING IN THE chamber. He kept his eyes closed and listened.

"This guest of ours is a great one for courtesy, isn't he?" it said in sarcastic tones. "We befriend him with the best of intentions, and he ransacks the room when our backs are turned. Even some of the Jade Elixir Stone-Milk is gone. If he drank it, it's too late now, and we'll just have to say he was destined to get it. How unfortunate that he had to do something like this!"

Zhao Lin recognized Wei Lai's voice. The Stone Milk he had swallowed was indeed an elixir of great potency, just as he had feared. Acutely embarrassed, he continued to feign sleep, and listened to what else Wei might say. He heard Soaring Cloud's voice beside him.

"Look here. The water urn is completely full. He never touched it. He must have been feeling thirsty and uncomfortable from the after-effects of the poison, and stumbled on the Stone Milk by accident while searching for the water. My own carelessness and negligence is to blame. I should have told him that the spring water was in the urn. It's all your fault for promising Snowy the cinnabar pills. The Old One told me last year that every two less pills means the loss of one full level of protection. I couldn't help but be worried, and you kept insisting. I was eager to see the boy, too. With all that on my mind, I assumed that someone as alert as he would find it without being told, and never bothered to come in and check. Now look at what has happened! From the look of things—him sleeping here like a baby—he must have swallowed some of it and no mistake. This stuff is not as potent as the true Milk of the Immortals made from thousand-year-old hollow Bice the Old One described to us, but it is still a great treasure for anyone who practices the arts of immortality. It brightens the eyes, firms the complexion, lightens the body, strengthens the vital energies and breaths, and extends life. Just a drop or two is miraculously potent, and with as much as he's taken, it's bound to work changes in his body.

"It looks to me as if he felt its marvellous effect the minute he tasted it, and hastily put it back. This shows impressive honesty. If it had been some ordinary person—like that lout Zhu who came with him—he would have feigned ignorance and drained it all down. He must have been greatly ashamed of his mistake, and put the beaker right back without any further thought for his own benefit. After he awakes he will be horribly embarrassed. I suggest we pretend we didn't notice.

"Anyway, Mother said yesterday that they were virtuous men, and she was prepared to administer a few drops of the Stone Milk if the other medicines did not suffice. Not this much, of course. Thank good-

61

ness he did not swallow it all! What could we have done to make up for it when Father returned? He knows nothing about the cultivation of immortality, and has no knowledge of how to circulate the elixir in his body for maximum effect. Imagine the frustration of knowing that a rare treasure had been completely wasted!"

"True enough," Wei Lai admitted. "But if Mother finds out she won't be pleased, and Eldest Cousin is bound to be even more unhappy. Mother has done much for Elder Brother Zhao, but she might not have done less if she had known something like this would happen. If she discovers it now, we will lose our only chance to visit Willow Lake. Why not accept the responsibility for what happened? Let's not say anything about it now, and wait until Mother has introduced him to everyone and initiated him into the teachings of our art. Then I will step forward and confess to doing it. Do you think that might work?"

Soaring Cloud seemed rather angry. "Yes, yes, I suppose it would. But you would be well advised to remember to call my mother 'Mistress.' You're always saying 'Mother' this and 'Mother' that. It's a good thing that there is no one else in the room to hear. Elder Brother Zhao might not make anything of it, but what if Seventh Sister were to hear you? She would laugh and tease most unmercifully. If you make the same mistake once more I will never speak to you again!"

"Don't be angry, Big Sister!" The youth seemed quite perturbed. "It just slipped out. I don't say it on purpose!"

"Don't try to tell me it wasn't on purpose!" she snapped. "Of course it was on purpose! If it weren't, you would be squawking 'Mother, Mother' in public all the time, wouldn't you? That would be even more disgusting."

"I won't! I won't!" Wei Lai replied anxiously. "I'll be more careful!"

"Well, I suppose it isn't really important," said Soaring Cloud, somewhat mollified. "The bonds between us are deeper than they are between any of the others. Mother and Father have said that if two people become intimate with each other there is nothing to be ashamed of as long as their own consciences are clear. If we are planning on practising the arts of immortality together, we will always have each other if we are successful in extending our youth. We need not fear what anyone says, but their yammering is annoying.

"Now that Elder Brother Zhao has ingested the elixir he mustn't be exposed to the sun's rays until noon. He's not awake yet in any case. Let's wait until the lout Zhu is completely recovered, and then call them out of bed to see each other."

The two of them left the room, talking and laughing softly all the while.

Zhao lay quietly on the bed, his head reeling. So the Stone Milk was an elixir of the sort highly prized by Daoist immortality seekers! This explained the relief of his thirst and the peaceful clarity of his mind. He was overcome by a strange emotion, a mingling of shame and delight.

After eavesdropping on the conversation of the two, it was apparent to him that they were lovers. This explained much about their behaviour with each other the night before. It was fortunate that he had been cautious and circumspect when he had first met the girl. Thank goodness it had not been Zhu Man-Tiger instead of himself! Sitting alone in a dimly lighted room face to face with a woman of such perfect beauty, a woman free of shyness and other affectations usually found in girls her age, a man would have to be a saint not to be stirred to some foolishness. Zhu would surely have entertained fanciful thoughts, and committed a serious violation of decorum.

In his anxiety he could barely restrain himself from rushing out to find Zhu and castigate him roundly for his folly. But Zhao himself had done something which did not bear speaking of. Soaring Cloud and Wei Lai were planning to cover up for him, but he could not allow this. He had always felt that a true man conducts his affairs in an aboveboard manner, and takes full responsibility for his actions. It would never do to allow another to take the blame for something he had done. He resolved to make a full confession to his hosts when they met, no matter how unpleasant the consequences. All he could do now was exercise caution in all he did and said. What was done was done; it was beyond his power to make recompense.

Unfortunately, though, try as he might, he could not fall asleep. The elixir had not only cured him of the after-effects of the poison, but had left him alert and clear-headed, fairly bursting with far more than his usual strength and vigour. He continued to worry about Zhu and Wang, and could not wait to see them. His mind spun furiously one way and then another, which kept him far from the realm of dreams. He forced himself to close his eyes and rest as best he could.

After a little more than an hour, he heard a strange clamour outside the cave. First there was an incredible cacophony of birds and animals, among which he made out many calls and howls he had never heard before. At first the sound came from a great distance, but then grew steadily nearer, and finally seemed to descend from the sky to ground level. Angry cries of wild beasts continued, among which he recognized only the voices of tigers and apes; the rest were unknown to him. The ground shook, and a wind swept like an ocean tide through the trees. Other cries answered from a distance. The savage and ferocious sound made Zhao's blood run cold. The clamour continued unabated until the Linked Culmen uttered a thunderous bellow that seemed to shake the sky. Two musical notes sounded, like strings plucked on a silver zither. The clamour subsided, except for a few scattered cries; these soon gave way to complete silence.

Not long afterward Zhao heard young women laughing and talking outside the cave. Though he could not hear them clearly, he could tell that none of them was Soaring Cloud. As he lay there wondering, he heard a young woman's voice shout in anger, and then an agonized yell, which he recognized as the voice of his friend Zhu Man-Tiger!

He leaped out of bed, not waiting to listen for what might follow. He jumped into his shoes and rushed out of the cave, anxious for Zhu's safety.

Not far from the cave mouth stood two women. They were draped in garments of a brilliant green which left their jade-white arms and legs bare, and were bedecked with sparkling gems. Both were in the full flower of youth, and glowed with sensuous vitality. They gestured in the direction of a tall pine, scolding angrily, but at the same time making an effort to suppress laughter. In the tree were two large beasts. They looked something like apes, but were taller than men, and covered in brilliant white fur. Both were hanging head downward, gripping branches with their feet. Their taloned hands held the unfortunate Zhu Man-Tiger, one at his hands, the other at his feet. Red eyes gleamed malevolently as the two beasts looked down toward the women, paused for further instructions. Zhu Man-Tiger made no sound, but was evidently in great pain, his teeth clenched and his face white as paper. The beasts were obviously far too much for him. He hung quietly without making any struggle, enduring the pain as best he could.

Zhao's blood boiled with rage at the sight of his friend's plight. The creatures were formidable, with hooklike talons and obvious savagery, but any hesitation he might have felt was far outweighed by the bonds of friendship. He felt for his knives and other weapons, but all had been removed the previous night. In his fury he had no leisure to make any other plans, and with a great shout of rage rushed to attack with only his bare hands.

A sudden gust of wind struck his face from one side.

"Stop! Brother Zhao! Don't do anything rash!" someone shouted. A blur of shadow moved swiftly along the ground; the two lovers Wei Lai and Soaring Cloud dropped to the ground in front of him to cut off his path.

Up in the tree another beast lurked, a gigantic yellow ape. Up to now it had not moved, but now it dropped out of the tree and charged at Zhao. Soaring Cloud turned to block its way and shouted, "Stop! They're our guests! What do you think you're doing?"

The yellow ape uttered a weird shriek, and retreated to its perch in the tree.

One of the bare-armed young women gestured at the white apes in the pine and called sharply. "Our hosts have explained. What are you waiting for? Release him!"

The two creatures obediently hoisted Zhu over to Zhao, who hastily took him out of their clutches. Seeing that Zhu was unable to hang on, and fearing that he was seriously embarrassed, Zhao shouted his thanks to Soaring Cloud and Wei Lai, and helped Zhu back into the cave.

Zhu Man-Tiger lay on the bed panting, his eyes closed, saying nothing. Great red welts, all badly swollen, marked where the apes had seized him. Fortunately he had not received any other injuries to speak of. Zhao groped in his own pockets, and found that his medicinal plasters were still there. He began applying them to Zhu's wounds. He knew how proud a man Zhu was, so while his wounds were still troubling him he thought it best not to ask him what had happened. He spoke a few words of encouragement to Man-Tiger and went out.

He had not been in the cave for any length of time, but Soaring Cloud, the two strange women, and the three ape-like creatures were gone. Only Wei Lai was still there, fetching water from the pool below the waterfall. Zhao scanned the whole area around him and was surprised to find the others nowhere in sight. It seemed unlikely that they could have left the mountain-ringed valley so quickly. He noticed that the sun was still not high, and recalled Soaring Cloud's warning not to expose himself to the sunlight before noon. He wondered if he and Man-Tiger had done themselves any harm by disobeying this instruction. Wei Lai had by this time filled a jug from the waterfall, and was heading back toward the cave. When he saw Zhao, he stopped and smiled politely.

"Has your honourable friend suffered any injury, Elder Brother Zhao? Is he bleeding at all?"

"Thanks to your help, Elder Brother Wei, my worthless friend is not badly hurt," replied Zhao. "He only has some swelling where he was seized. There is no bleeding. I have never seen creatures like this before. Are they a kind of ape?"

"It is a good thing that he is not bleeding," replied the youth. "Otherwise it would be rather troublesome. Your honourable friend behaved with great audacity, and it pains me to say that in character and disposition he falls short of you and Elder Brother Wang. He started trouble with no apparent purpose, and aroused those two demon queens. Elder Sister Cloud has soothed their tempers somewhat and led them away, but I am not sure that the affair is finished. Your Zhu has been behaving inappropriately since early this morning. As soon as he regained consciousness he insulted Sister Cloud with some ill-chosen remarks. But we did not anticipate that he would slip out and create serious trouble just a little while later. I'm quite frankly amazed that people capable of such preposterous behaviour exist in the world."

Zhao, anxious and thoroughly ashamed, realized that Zhu must have committed a great impropriety. It was Zhao's duty to find out what had happened so that he could deal with it properly. He addressed Wei Lai.

"The three of us, in our unpardonable ignorance, have behaved in a most reprehensible manner since you so magnanimously rescued us and brought us into this Mountain of the Immortals to heal us of our wounds. I myself am no exception. Last night Elder Sister Soaring Cloud gave me clear instructions, telling me that there was wholesome spring water to drink. I lacked the sense to search for it properly and mistakenly swallowed something labelled as Stone Milk. I didn't realize that it was something precious until it was too late. I am unable to make amends, save to offer my most humble apologies to its owner for my unforgivable carelessness. As if that were not enough, now my sworn brother in his ignorance has committed some act of great folly. My shame and embarrassment know no bounds. How can we make amends?"

Wei Lai laughed. "Your honesty does you credit, Elder Brother! I wish I could say the same for your honourable friend. I know nothing of your history before coming here, judging from the two incidents that have taken place since this morning, it seems unlikely that you will be permitted to visit the Old One in Green. Sister Cloud has ordered me to fetch water to mix up some medicine for his injuries, but if as you say there is no bleeding it will not be necessary. I'm not particularly eager to associate with someone like him anyway. Let's remain outside, and I will tell you what happened."

Zhao Lin, thoroughly embarrassed, assented.

"By coincidence," Wei began, "there was another party of guests scheduled to arrive this morning. They are some of the brothers and sisters of the Dragon clan from the Fortress of the Immortal Gibbon on the highest peak of Jade Dragon Mountain. They were coming to pay their respects to our Mistress and to request some of our potent spring water to ferment liquors and mix medicines.

"The history of this Dragon clan is of interest. They are of Miao extraction. Seventy years ago their master, a Miao man of extraordinary courage and honour, discovered a beautiful spot with a gentle climate on the peak of Jade Dragon Mountain, and there constructed an impregnable fortress. Since then he has spent a lifetime in seclusion and comfort. It is a place where no outsider ever goes, and clan members do not leave their stronghold except at urgent need. When they do go forth they travel in twos and threes, dressed as ordinary civilized Miao tribespeople. The old man's children and grandchildren are strong and skilful fighters. They raise many strange and unusual beasts. When abroad they are charged by the old man never to seek trouble with others, but they are dangerous and peculiar, given to unpredictable changes of mood. Their women are incomparably beautiful, and perilous. Woe to any man who is beguiled by their sweet and saint-like appearance! He will find that he has caught hold of the very Demoness of Pestilence instead!

"These women have a fondness for strong and ambitious men. If such a one catches their eye and they take a fancy to him, they are likely to take him right then and there as a husband, and kidnap him to their mountain fastness.

"Once Sister Cloud, admiring their beauty, suggested that they try infusions of herbal drugs made with our potent spring water to moisten the skin and firm the flesh. Delighted, they immediately asked for some. Sister Cloud and I met with them and gave them water and some of the herbs we had collected. They in turn permitted us to gather some of their herbs. Sister Cloud reported to her mother, and our Mistress decided to give them the formulas and let them mix the drugs themselves. In this way we enjoyed good relations with them.

"Then, two years ago, our Master, my father, was conversing with the Old One in Green, and they began reading the future with their mystical vision. They warned that if our association with them became too intimate, evil would come of it, particularly for Sister Cloud. Not long afterwards there was indeed an incident, and since that time we have grown somewhat estranged from them. Sister Cloud and I go to their mountain less frequently, and they come here to mix their medicines just once each year. The last few times they have visited there has been tension on both sides. The most unpleasant thing about the whole business is the large numbers of them that always come. Their old master doesn't often permit them to come out of their mountain, and this trip for spring water is a rare opportunity for them. They invariably put together a large party of men and women, and bring a whole menagerie of flying and crawling beasts, which make a dreadful racket and track all over the valley.

"We had received word that they were coming, and worried that you guests would be disturbed and alarmed. We feared what might happen if you encountered them. Sister Cloud and I went into the rear of the cave to explain the situation to Zhu and Wang. Elder Brother Wang is an honest and prudent man, and listened carefully to my explanation and warning. He's been lying quietly in his bed ever since, waiting patiently to see you. But that fellow Zhu was another matter. When he saw Sister Cloud he seemed to get all sorts of strange notions. The minute he opened his mouth he made the most foolish suggestions. Sister Cloud had no desire to deal any further with him, and went off to speak to you.

"Meanwhile the brothers and sisters of the Dragon clan, a dozen or so strong, had already arrived.

"The two women you saw are sisters, named Moon-Maid and Cunning-Maid. Moon-Maid is twenty-four, and Cunning-Maid is nineteen. They are very close, and stick together like a man and his shadow. The Miao generally marry young, but these two have reached adulthood without being betrothed. An elder sister of theirs married a Chinese man, a failed candidate for the civil service examinations. Moon-Maid and Cunning-Maid live with their mother next door to this sister, and since childhood have absorbed something of Chinese ways from their brother-in-law. They claim that they will not marry unless they find Chinese men of good education and martial prowess. It is the custom of their clan to adopt all sons-in-law into their family. Once married, it is expected that the husband will remain for the rest of his life with his wife in their fortress, as if he had sold himself to her. He will never want for food or clothing, and will live a life of luxury and ease, but his movements are no longer free. Any man of character or ambition would never consent to such an arrangement.

"Moon-Maid and her sister have high opinions of themselves, and are contemptuous of the average Chinese rabble. The old master of the fortress prohibits them from travelling abroad at will, fearing that their beauty will cause trouble and result in their injuring and killing outsiders in self defense. Their chances of meeting a satisfactory mate are considerably lessened, and they have to this day been unable to find suitable matches.

"Your friend Zhu heard the roars and howls of the animals, and came running out of the cave to see what the stir was about. It is unfortunate that the sisters brought their three apes along on this trip. The last time the apes were here, they discovered that the two ancient pines here outside the cave bear a great quantity of nuts. As soon as they arrived this morning they slipped away from their mistresses and hurried here to gather pine nuts. The two women came after them, fearing that their lust for the nuts might lead them to fight and damage our beautiful old trees, or that they might enter the cave and start pawing through the things they found inside. No one but the sisters can control them, so they hurried over with the intention of disciplining them before they could cause trouble. But when the sisters got here, they discovered that the creatures were feasting quietly on the pine nuts without fuss, and they decided to let them continue. The girls stood by the cave entrance for a while, waiting until the apes had eaten their fill.

"Then, quite unexpectedly, the fellow Zhu came out and found them. They are pretty, much like the Miao girls of the mountains, except that they have the additional attraction of being able to speak the Chinese language. He walked up and began to flirt with them most outrageously in the Miao tongue. He apparently thought they lived with us, because he asked them why the girl he had seen this morning had been dressed in Chinese clothing. The girls in turn thought he was one of us, and, though offended, were unwilling to do him any harm. But after a while it became apparent that he was an outsider. He didn't even know Sister Cloud's name. His speech was bold and familiar, and he used a filthy and coarse variation of the Miao tongue. Would you believe it? He told them how wonderful his family was, how he owned great pastures and farmland covered with herds of horses and cattle, and large quantities of jewels and other treasures. He bragged about his strength and fighting skills. He invited them to return with him to be his concubines, to lead a life of comfort and luxury. The more he said the angrier they became. If it had happened anywhere else, they would have exploded into violence and slain him right then and there. Out of respect for their hosts, though, they held themselves in check, rebuking him in the Chinese tongue: 'You ignorant bandit! Have you lost your mind?' As they scolded him, the white apes, who take great pleasure in teasing and bullying human beings, were listening. They understand human speech quite well, and could see that their mistresses were unhappy. They are always eager to please the girls, and made ready to pounce on him. The ridiculous Zhu, however, befuddled by his lust, never even noticed these beasts in the tree. When the girls started cursing him, the apes leaped down, grabbed him, and dangled him from the branches.

"Those beasts are incredibly strong, and their claws are covered with venom. If the two girls hadn't given the order to stop, Zhu would have been seriously injured. Had they wished, they could have torn him in half. That fellow certainly was asking for trouble with all of his lewd suggestions. The sisters have strange tempers. For the time being they have let him go for Sister Cloud's sake, but you can be sure that you will find them waiting to cause you trouble when you depart."

Another voice interrupted.

"Where did you ever get the idea they let him go for *my* sake?"

Zhao looked around, and saw Soaring Cloud. Somehow she had come up soundlessly behind him once again.

"What do you mean?" Wei Lai broke in. "They didn't do it for your sake? Don't tell me they are planning more trouble for him on our territory! Why did they let him go with so little fuss?"

Soaring Cloud laughed. "What a simpleton you are! No shop ever opened up that was not prepared to do business; every bit of merchandise has its buyer. There will always be someone to purchase even the worst piece of rubbish. What makes you think that the sisters bear Zhu any ill will? From what I saw, they were unhappy at first when Zhu spoke to them in such rude fashion. But they were impressed at how Zhu made efforts to resist those monsters, very nearly slipping away, and how he hung there bearing the searing pain without a single groan. You know they have long been unhappy for want of satisfactory mates. They could see that this fellow was far from ugly, a young Chinese man with fighting ability and courage to match. That started them both thinking right then and there, and if I hadn't showed up they probably would have let him go anyway. Actually, if Zhu had addressed them courteously in the Chinese language, instead of blustering in that coarse, ill-mannered version of Miao, they might have listened to his proposition, and he would not have suffered at all.

"I have taken the sisters over to the cave at Five-Cloud Cliff to get settled. Originally we planned to pay a leisurely visit to Eldest Cousin and his wife, but the sisters insisted that I hurry over and speak to you, and convey your reply as soon as possible. They've asked me to act as a go-between, you see. To think that they would take a fancy to someone like Zhu!"

"That explains it," said Wei Lai. "I've never seen them so ready to forgive an insult. So they had secretly taken a fancy to him all the time! Well, that simplifies things, doesn't it? Elder Brother Zhao need have no more concern for the welfare of his friend."

"It simplifies things, does it?" said Soaring Cloud. "It makes more problems than ever. You don't know the half of it yet!"

"If they like each other, and both sides are willing, what problems could there be?" Wei Lai asked.

"Nothing in this world is ever that simple," said Soaring Cloud. "Where did you ever get that idea? First of all, the inhabitants of Willow Lake are Song dynasty loyalists, refugees from the Mongols. Ever since they went into hiding, they have had no contact with outsiders, much less intermarriage. Also, Miao women like these two are emotional, and their customs are strange. Once a man has made a proposal to one of them, she will be convinced that he loves her. Or, if he already has a wife, particularly a young and pretty one, she might also think that he is insincere and unfaithful. Either way, it means trouble. My guess is that a lecherous fellow like Zhu must have a wife and concubines at home already. We have a serious problem on our hands, and you talk as if everything were settled."

"Didn't you hear what Zhu said to them?" asked Wei. "He wanted to take them home as concubines!"

"What?" said Soaring Cloud, startled. "I didn't know. He must have said that before I arrived. Well! If that is true, Moon-Maid knows perfectly well that he is married. If she still wants him in spite of that, she must have taken a real liking to him. The problem may be easier to solve if we don't have to follow their formal marriage customs, but it's still going to be difficult to untangle. It's all your fault! You were right nearby when Zhu came out, and had plenty of time to stop him. If I had arrived there a fraction of a second later, even the Old One in Green wouldn't have been able to put things right again!"

Wei Lai began to look anxious. "You know I've had a brush or two with those she-devils before, and I wasn't particularly eager to confront them again. Besides, how could I have anticipated that the Zhu fellow would do something so stupid? I say give him what he asked for. It wouldn't be bad to get such a beauty, now would it?"

Soaring Cloud pursed her lips and hissed at him in exasperation, then turned her back on him, and spoke to Zhao Lin.

"Tell me about this Zhu Man-Tiger! Does he have a wife and children?"

"You must understand that Brother Zhu is really not a bad sort," Zhao said, increasingly worried at the seriousness of Zhu's predicament. "But he is an only son, and was badly spoiled as a child. He has grown up with an unfortunate lack of restraint and a tendency toward arrogance. As for the matter of concubines, the rules of our community are strict: only if a couple has reached middle age without children can the matter even be considered.

"My brother Zhu is the only one of us who is married. I have heard it said that if a man of the Miao race changes wives, he need only present a quantity of silk or livestock to the aggrieved woman, and the matter is considered honourably settled. I understand that they call this 'shame-hushing money'. Man-Tiger has an aged mother and a beloved wife at home, and it would never do for him to be adopted in marriage into a Miao clan on a far-away mountain.

"Would it be untoward of me to implore you, Elder Sister Cloud and Elder Brother Wei, to reply to the sisters on his behalf? Perhaps tell them that he rose from his bed while still ill, and that he only behaved as he did because his faculties were impaired by delirium. Fortunately he confined himself to lewd propositions, and did not actually lay a hand on them. Now he realizes that he behaved most disgracefully, and wishes to make amends by offering them some gold, jewellery, and silk to 'hush the shame' of what happened. If you could persuade the sisters to abandon their notions, we would be deeply in your debt."

"From what you say it appears that neither you nor Elder Brother Wang is married. Is that correct?"

Zhao Lin nodded.

She laughed. "You certainly seem eager to take the part of your friend. But what about you? Didn't you realize that they have taken a fancy to you as well?"

Zhao was startled. "How can this be? When I heard the clamour outside and saw my friend in danger, I lost my temper. I did notice that there were two women under the tree, but I never even got a clear look at them, much less a chance to engage them in conversation!"

"All right, all right!" Soaring Cloud broke in. "Don't be anxious, Elder Brother Zhao. Miao women are generally passionate and emotional, and tend to be naive and straightforward about certain things. They are confident of their charms, and most of them are in fact very comely. The few ugly ones among them are too ashamed of their appearance to seek love from any man. They feel that love between a man and a woman is a natural thing; not like us Chinese people, who have cloaked the whole business in constraints and ceremony. When Miao women have taken a fancy to someone, no matter how unattainable he may be, they will have him if they have to fight to the death to get him. If the man persists in refusing her, and she fails to charm him, she resorts to a most peculiar expedient. She lies in wait for him in a secluded spot, and when he walks by she embraces him, and attempts to arouse him to the point where he has his way with her. She weeps and cries, implores and begs, trying to get the man to love her. If he doesn't respond she will not desist, and persists to the point where he curses her, shoves her, and finally beats her. No matter how violent he becomes in his efforts to fight her off, she will not put up the least resistance. Sometimes the girl is so stubborn that she risks her own life, allowing herself to be horribly beaten, refusing to release him until she really is beaten to death. Killing her might seem the easy way out; after all she did waylay him, so under tribal law the man is guilty of no crime. But if she is killed, and the man is a Miao, all the young Miao women will take note of his cruelty. No one will be willing to marry him, and even during the great licentious festivals of spring and autumn, the Moon Dance and other observances, no girl will pair with him, which a Miao man would find intolerable. Therefore, as long as a woman is not afraid to risk marring her beauty as her face is bashed and bruised, she will persist in holding on to him, and there is considerable hope that he will relent in the end. Soft-hearted men of course cannot bear to beat them at all, and generally surrender forthwith.

"If the man they have fallen in love with is Chinese, they resort to similar methods, but with a difference. If the man refuses, and it is evident that there is no hope for her, the Miao woman will kill herself before his eyes. If, as sometimes happens, her tribe knows that her advances have been entirely one-sided and the man has done nothing to harm her, then they let the matter rest. If not, then all Miao women in the region swear vengeance upon him, and will murder him in the most horrible way.

"The more noble Miao women, those of higher status who have a greater regard for themselves, like the sisters of the Dragon clan, do not take the initiative quite so directly. If, as is the case with Zhu, the man is the one who makes advances, only to change his mind and refuse them, that is an insult of major proportions, and they will not let the matter rest. The custom of 'shame-hushing money' is indeed found among the Black Miao, the House-Beauty Miao, the Cultivator Miao, the Lampshade Miao, and a few other tribes, but not in the Dragon clan. Furthermore, the Dragon clan has been gathering wealth for generations. Their treasure hoards are enormous. Even they have forgotten how many rare and strange objects are in their possession. I am afraid items like silk will make little impression on them, particularly when something as important as marriage is involved.

"As for how you managed to get mixed up with the two sisters without ever having so much as spoken to them, it's really rather amusing. Cunning-Maid, the younger one, is stronger-willed and more dangerous than her sister. She is much loved by their entire clan and particularly by their old leader. It is she who raised and trained the white apes. Even if Moon-Maid had tried to take the initiative and ordered the apes to drop Zhu, Cunning-Maid might have refused. You appeared before either of them had come to a decision. Cunning-Maid got a close look at you, and determined that you had ten times the character, strength, courage, and sense of honour that Zhu did. She was overwhelmed with admiration and love.

"She has announced to me her determination to wed you and no other. If it had not been for the two year's schooling that she received from her Chinese brother-in-law, she probably would have followed you straight into the cave and proposed to you in person. But she feared that you would look down on her, and asked me to act as go-between in the proper Chinese fashion. Fortunately, she does not know that you are unmarried. You never expressed any intentions toward her, either. We can fabricate some sort of a reply and probably get you out of trouble. But if she ever finds out that you are unmarried and have refused her, no good will come of it."

Zhao did his best to repress the frustration he felt, and forced himself to smile.

"When men and women marry, it is because they both desire it. By what right can she force her wishes on me? I do not refuse her out of contempt or disrespect. It is simply that I have other plans and ambitions, and do not plan to take a wife at all. I do not lie, and will not offer the falsehood that I am married to avoid this predicament. Elder Sister Cloud, please convey to them that it is my humble intention not to take a wife in this lifetime, and that in any case the rules of my people strictly forbid my being adopted into the family of an outsider. As for Brother Zhu, say that if indeed the lady favours his unworthy person with her true affection, and she is willing to accompany him to Willow Lake as a lesser concubine as was originally proposed, so be it."

"You certainly make it sound easy, Elder Brother Zhao," sighed Soaring Cloud. "I knew this job of go-between was going to be troublesome. The only thing I cautioned her in advance was that you might already be married, and that as beautiful and passionate as she may be, you might not necessarily be willing to leave your wife for her. I did not anticipate that you, the oldest among you three, would be unmarried! I will do everything I can for you, but your friend Zhu is another matter. No one here is willing to involve themselves in his affairs. He got himself into this mess, and can solve his problems himself."

"Once more I am greatly in your debt, Elder Sister," said Zhao. "But we three ignorant brothers are sworn to share all things in life and in death. If one of us were to return home without the worthless Zhu, however could we face his wife and aged mother? If you could find some way to extricate him from the coils of these frightful Miao women it would be a great blessing to us. If this is not possible, Wang Jin and I will be obliged to fight to the death by his side."

Soaring Cloud smiled slightly, but said nothing.

"Your sense of honour and justice is truly admirable, Elder Brother Zhao," said Wei Lai. "But are your friends as willing to share all things in life and in death with you?"

"Elder Brother Zhao is clearly determined," said Soaring Cloud to Wei Lai. "There is little point in arguing about it now. There is no need to convey a reply to the sisters this very day. It's almost noon now, and our three guests have not eaten since yesterday. We'll let them see each other now, and then take them to see Mother. Maybe she can help. It is certainly better than wasting our time here in idle talk."

"Is my third brother Wang completely recovered?" Zhao asked eagerly. He had missed Wang Jin most of all.

"He is well," said Wei Lai. "I must say that Elder Brother Wang is a fine man, much like yourself. There is no comparing him to Zhu. He asked anxiously after your safety, and was cooperative about resting properly. He knew he was almost completely recovered, but didn't start running around the way Zhu did, though it is true he was in one of the deepest rooms of the cave, where sounds from outside are not easily heard.

"You've already seen Zhu. Why not wait here while I invite Elder Brother Wang to come out and join us? The lower levels of the rear cave are deep, and it is a bother for all of us to go up and down. We can talk for a while, then fetch Zhu and go to see our Mistress."

Zhao Lin realized that there was a large rear section to the cave he had not yet seen, deep within which was another chamber. There was a great deal about his hosts that was difficult to fathom. This much was evident: the master of this valley, his wife, daughter, and disciples were clearly people of great power and mystery, immortal warriors, or at least adepts well advanced in the arcane practices by which men transformed themselves into Immortals. Local Miao tribesmen, no matter how belligerent, would scarcely trouble such a class of beings. And yet Soaring Cloud spoke of this band of Miao in a way that suggested a cautious attitude. He had long heard legends of men and women of frightful demonic powers among the Miao barbarians, sorcerers in command of grim spectral forces, particularly those involving the lethal arts known from ancient times to the men of China as *Gu*. That the two sisters had the power to control fierce birds and evil beasts could only mean that they knew something of this secret lore. Recalling the terrible strength of the apes, he knew that he had been fortunate indeed not to meet them in combat. Had he not at once helped Zhu into the cave to tend to his wounds, and stayed behind to vent his anger on the two sorceresses, he might have already fallen prey to their witchcraft. Soaring Cloud spoke to reassure him.

"Do not worry!" she said. "I know that you are a man of honour. These two sisters have dreadful powers, and my mother is unwilling to provoke them. This situation is going to be awkward to solve. My young cousin Wei Lai might have been of some help, but unfortunately he has decided once and for all that Zhu is a mean, shameless fellow with no notion of his proper station, and has sworn not to help him in any way. Wei Lai is strange in this regard. I might force him to agree on the surface, but in his heart he would remain defiant. Actually, I have another plan, if Elder Brother Zhao permits. Remember that you three are here together by invitation. If you were somehow unable to return home together, we as your hosts would suffer acute embarrassment. I know it looks bad, but remember that there is another you have not yet met. Who knows? He might break his usual rule and intervene on your behalf."

Zhao Lin remembered how respectfully their hosts spoke of the Old One in Green. His powers must be far greater than theirs. They had come in response to his invitation. He had acted to help them the previous year; surely he would not stand by with his hands in his sleeves if they were in serious danger.

74

The Shame of Zhu Man-Tiger

ZHU MAN-TIGER RECOVERED MORE SLOWLY THAN THE OTHERS, EVEN
though he had received a lighter dose of the poison exhalations. He was
weaker than Zhao or Wang, having lost something of the vitality of his
younger days.

When he regained consciousness and looked about him, he found
himself in a cave, lying on a stone bed between thick embroidered
quilts. All about him were objects he had never before seen. The chamber was large, well lit by two lamps of coloured glass hanging from the
ceiling. The furnishings were beautifully made and highly refined. His
memory of what had happened to him was curiously indistinct, like a
dream. In great wonderment he sat up, preparing to descend from the
bed and find someone. He paused when he heard the sound of someone laughing and talking outside, and a strikingly beautiful girl came out
from behind a crystal-encrusted screen built over stalactites and stalagmites. When she saw that he was awake, she smiled at him.

"Are you better now?" she asked.

It was at this moment that Zhu Man-Tiger's evil luck began. As it happened, he was lying in Soaring Cloud's own bedchamber. The furnishings were not those of a typical woman's boudoir in the outside world,
but they betrayed a certain feminine elegance. When he and his companions had been rescued, Soaring Cloud's mother saw that Zhu had
been exposed to less of the poison than the others, and did not require
the presence of the Linked Culmen. Without giving the matter any particular thought, she put him in Soaring Cloud's room. Now Soaring
Cloud and Wei Lai had come down together to check on the status of
their guests, and warn them that they must not come out until midday,
lest they encounter some of the Miao. To save time, Wei Lai went in to
speak to Wang Jin, and Soaring Cloud went into her own bedchamber
to see Zhu.

Soaring Cloud had always had a free and familiar manner in dealing
with others. She had been impressed the night before by Zhao Lin's
upright character and loyalty toward his friends, and assumed that Zhu
Man-Tiger was the same. As she walked in she smiled pleasantly at him,
which set the vain young man's fanciful mind spinning with lascivious
thoughts. Zhu had many strange events the day before, and it had begun
to seem to him as though he was moving in a waking dream. When he
saw a girl of jade-like beauty, like an immortal sylph maiden, smiling at
him and speaking to him in gentle tones, his emotions betrayed him.
He completely misunderstood her friendly manner. He thought that,

like the famous squires Ruan and Liu centuries before him,* he had stumbled upon the grotto of a maiden Immortal who desired him as her husband. His head swam as though drunk, and he stared stupidly at her, unable to speak.

Soaring Cloud, a bold and simple girl, thought that he was simply surprised and disoriented. She never realized that he was lusting for her. Again she spoke, wishing to reassure him.

"You and your friends were felled by a rare and dangerous poison yesterday. All three of you were rescued and brought to this place. Are you all right? Do you feel any pain or discomfort anywhere? Why don't you speak up, instead of staring at me like that?"

Zhu Man-Tiger, still dizzy with the thrill of seeing her, heard only the last two sentences she spoke, which only strengthened his mistaken impression. The sylph-maiden was gazing directly into his eyes with no hint of embarrassment, and she was speaking gentle words of concern for his comfort. He did not trouble to question how he had come to be where he was, or how a beautiful young girl would be living alone in such elegance within a remote mountain cave. When she spoke his heart leaped, and without the slightest restraint he opened his mouth and addressed her in a most lewd and preposterous fashion. Fortunately he did not touch her, but what he said was discourteous in the extreme.

Though usually quick-tempered, Soaring Cloud restrained herself. She assumed a stiff and wooden expression, and waited until he had finished, intending to let him make a fool of himself before she rebuked him. Unfortunately, Wei Lai walked in while Zhu was still speaking.

In fury he strode toward the bed. Soaring Cloud shouted at him to stop, knowing that his temper was even worse than her own.

"What is the point of bothering with a man like this?" she said. "Come, let's go." She grabbed his arm and forced him out of the room. When she had pushed him past the crystal screen she stuck her head back into the room for one brief moment.

"If you know what is good for you, you will stay right here. If you hear a commotion outside, do not run out to look. After midday someone will come and conduct you to see your companions. If you do anything else foolish, you will have only yourself to blame for what happens."

Wei Lai, still in a rage, was little pleased when Soaring Cloud issued this final warning.

"Who cares what happens to this shameless scoundrel?" he shouted angrily, and hurried her away.

---

* [According to a legend of medieval times, two young men named Ruan Zhao and Liu Chen lost their way in the Tiantai Mountains, and were saved from starvation by two immortal maidens. The mortal youths spent some months in romantic dalliance with these maidens, then returned to their homes. But time flows differently in the immortal realm; they discovered that centuries had passed in the mortal world, and their friends and families had long since turned to dust. Eventually they went back to their immortal lovers.]

76

Soaring Cloud tried to soothe his rage, and asked him about Wang Jin's recovery.

"Wang Jin is in excellent condition," the youth reported, his temper gradually cooling. "He appears to be an honest and good-hearted fellow. He is even more cautious and restrained in manner than Zhao Lin."

Even now Zhu Man-Tiger did not grasp the true nature of his circumstances. When Soaring Cloud had turned back to speak to him again, he began to entertain still wilder notions. He had heard Soaring Cloud and Wei Lai address each other as 'Brother' and 'Sister', and concluded from this that they were actual siblings. The girl had listened to his declarations of love without protest or anger, which could only mean that she was attracted to him. It was unfortunate that her brother had burst in at the wrong moment. He had been distressed by what he found, which was of course typical of brothers everywhere. The girl, too, would of course have to maintain decorum and pretend to spurn him at first. She could scarcely be expected to declare her feelings for him so soon in front of other members of her family! But she had turned back as she left, which could only mean that she loved him passionately. He had not even had the chance to ask her name, or how he had come to be here. By the look of things she would come back and see him again at the earliest opportunity. What a lovely fairy tale it would make if he had encountered a lonely sylph-maiden to wed as Liu and Ruan had of old! Perhaps she would even be willing to accompany him home to the mortal world as his concubine!

He lay there dreaming, making plans on how his fantasies might be fulfilled, and waited for the girl to reappear. But though he watched eagerly, she did not come. After a time he heard a clamour of birds and animals, accompanied by a violent wind blowing sand and rocks through the air. The sound was evil and savage in the extreme. He began to wonder if the cave was situated near the lairs of mountain beasts. It was clear that the animals were numerous, and he began to fear that the girl would be threatened or injured by them. Since awakening he had felt stronger and more vigorous than usual, and, inspired with his excitement over the girl, was eager to test his powers and impress her with his fighting skills. He saw that all his precious knives and other weapons were on a marble stand to his right. He went over to inspect them, and noticed a set of cosmetic bottles and boxes there as well. Their manufacture was exquisite, and he detected a subtle fragrance in the air. They were obviously things for a woman's use, which spurred his lecherous thoughts to new heights.

As he armed himself, the thunderous racket outside quieted. Fearing that he was missing his opportunity, he hastened out.

The chamber was deep within the secret rear section of the cave. There was a heavy door which separated the secret rear chambers from the area in front, and the operation of this door was known only to the cave's inhabitants. But Zhu's misfortune was now inescapable; Soaring Cloud and Wei Lai had been absorbed in their chattering and arguing, and failed to close this important door properly. Man-Tiger was nothing if not resourceful, and soon found his way around the screen in the direction of the animal cries he had heard a moment earlier. He was able to find a shortcut directly to the complex passages in the front of the cave, bypassing the two outer chambers completely. As he emerged, he saw Moon-Maid and Cunning-Maid standing idly below the solitary peak to his right, admiring the waterfall.

The two women were remarkably beautiful, and their dress was ornate and sumptuous in the extreme. Their arms and legs were bare, exposing perfect jade-white skin, which contrasted nicely with the green sparkle of their jewellery. He felt they were lovelier than any women he had seen in the outside world. Their exotic beauty was quite equal to that of the girl he had met a little while earlier, though certainly different in style.

Man-Tiger had spent much of his life frequenting the market fairs of the Miao, and knew something of their tribal customs. He was fully aware that most Miao women would prefer to marry Chinese men if given the opportunity, and were thus easy marks for conquest. In most cases, he had found, teasing and flirting were accepted as a compliment. Very few reacted with anger. He marvelled at how all the women he had seen on this mountain ranked among the greatest beauties of the Empire. It seemed that both Chinese and Miao dwelt here, each costumed after their own fashion. There was a mystery here, one that should have urged him to caution. But his judgement was clouded by lust. He gazed hungrily at the two women, so dazzled that he never saw the terrible mutant apes lurking in the tree above. The more he stared the more infatuated he became. He walked boldly up and accosted them, using some of the common phrases he had learned from the Lampshade Miao.

Cunning-Maid lost her temper at once. But Moon-Maid, who had seen him emerge from the cave inhabited by their hosts, assumed that he was a friend of Soaring Cloud and her family. Out of respect for their hosts, she restrained Cunning-Maid from committing violence.

If anything, Zhu Man-Tiger felt that their anger made the two women all the more seductive. Retreat was the last thing on his mind. It was then that he made the mistake of asking them the name of the girl who lived in the cave. At the same instant he reached out to stroke Moon-Maid's exquisite jade-white arm.

The sisters realized at once that he did not know Soaring Cloud at all. Their reluctance to punish him was forgotten. As he reached out to touch Moon-Maid, they reacted with fury, and warned him off sharply. Zhu was abruptly snatched off his feet by the two white apes, and found himself dangling helplessly by his hands and feet from the tree. Only then did he realize that he had made a serious mistake.

Zhao Lin rushed out of the cave to help him, and Soaring Cloud and Wei Lai dropped out of the sky to rescue Zhao. Zhu finally began to have an inkling of what was actually happening. Bemused by ancient fairy tales, he had indulged in vain and romantic fantasies. His life had been saved, but he had repaid his hosts in ludicrous fashion. Without even having so much as asking the girl's name he had come to the conclusion that he had entered an immortal paradise, and accosted her in an unseemly manner. He had ended up making an utter fool of himself, humiliated in plain sight of all. He had disgraced his sworn brother Zhao as well. The more he thought the more embarrassed he became, and fervently wished for a place to hide.

Zhao Lin put him on a bed and inspected his injuries without a word. A moment later he hurried out. The pain of his injuries lessened somewhat, thanks to the medicinal plasters, but the swelling did not go down. After Zhao had been gone for quite some time, Man-Tiger heard someone speaking outside the room.

"I do not presume to count anyone like your excellent friend among my companions. Perhaps you could go in yourself, Elder Brother Wang, and inform him of Moon-Maid's proposal. When you have finished, fetch him out to meet the rest of us outside the cave. Then we shall proceed to the pavilion over the water on the Lesser Isle of Ying* and enjoy some wine and a meal. After that we shall visit my Mistress, and see how your luck goes."

Another voice replied briefly, too softly for Zhu to hear. The first voice laughed contemptuously, and said nothing further. Footsteps faded away toward the cave entrance. The first voice he recognized as belonging to the youth he had already met. The second was that of his sworn brother Wang Jin.

Zhu recalled the circumstances under which he had sworn friendship with Zhao and Wang. Of the three of them only Wang Jin had been of inferior birth, descended from household bondservants of the Zhao clan. In the beginning Zhu had felt that Wang was not worthy of associating with the other two on such an intimate basis. But Zhao Lin, whom he respected as an older brother, was extremely fond of Wang, and had long since sworn friendship with him. The rules of the village left behind by its founders forbade any discrimination on the basis of a family's original status in the outside world, but old customs died hard. Zhu had accepted Wang with reluctance. As time went on, however, he was impressed by Wang's respectful modesty. Wang always yielded to others and never showed off his abilities, though they were in fact considerable. After many years of close association, Zhu seldom remembered Wang's lowly ancestry, and eventually came to accept him as an equal member of their fraternity. But now they had ventured out into the world, the three of them together, and it was the highborn Zhu who had disgraced himself. If it had been Zhao who had come alone to fetch him, it would have been somewhat easier to bear. But he had always

---

* [The Isle of Ying is one of the floating island paradises of the Immortals in the Eastern Ocean.]

prided himself on being a second elder brother to Wang Jin, and felt it degrading to face him now.

As he lay there in shame and embarrassment, Wang Jin entered and greeted him politely.

"Are you fully recovered, Elder Brother?"

Zhu, proud and vain, was sensitive about losing face in any way. He was so mortified over his humiliation that he did not realize that Wang was referring to the effects of the poison.

"Your ignorant and ignoble elder brother did indeed act in somewhat reprehensible fashion," he admitted hastily. "But those two Miao girls are clearly no good at all. They deliberately set those horrible beasts on me to maim or kill me. When we return home, I'm going to find out where their tribe lives. I'm going to repay them for this, or I'm not a man!"

Wang Jin knew full well that the blame for the incident lay squarely with Zhu. The Miao women had perhaps reacted with excessive violence, but it was going to be hard for Zhu to explain why he had greeted his hostess, to whom he owed his life, with lewd propositions. But Zhu was never one to admit his faults, and Wang did not argue with him.

"I wasn't referring to that, Brother," Wang explained with a smile. "But don't forget that we three have sworn an oath of life and death. We won't let you down now."

It was obvious to Wang that Man-Tiger was thoroughly repentant, and would cause no more trouble. He suggested that they go out to meet their hosts.

"We have not been allowed to eat until after midday because of the effects of the poison," he explained. "Eldest Brother Zhao and our host are waiting for us outside. We are to go to a place called the Lesser Isle of Ying for wine and a meal, after which we will see Madame Chen, the mistress of this place. We'd best go right now; I understand there is a matter Eldest Brother and our hosts wish to discuss with you."

Zhu Man-Tiger had no stomach for meeting the inhabitants of the cave. Had he not been in their home he might have fled rather than facing them. He felt rather like an ugly new bride about to be presented to her parents-in-law for the first time. But he was hungry, and had no choice but to get up and accompany Wang out, his head hanging and spirits low. There was nothing Wang could say to cheer him up.

When they emerged from the cave, Wei Lai was nowhere to be seen. Only Zhao Lin and Soaring Cloud were there, standing in earnest conversation. When they saw Wang and Zhu, they walked over to meet them. Zhao seized his companions' hands and anxiously asked how they were feeling, and even Soaring Cloud smiled and spoke to Zhu in friendly fashion as if nothing had happened. This was entirely due to Zhao's efforts. He had pleaded long and earnestly with her on Man-Tiger's behalf. After a time Soaring Cloud was embarrassed by Zhao's entreaties, and agreed not to bear a grudge against Zhu.

When Zhao Lin had formally introduced Man-Tiger to her, Zhu began to feel a little better, though he was still greatly ashamed. Zhao then asked whether they could meet Wei Lai.

"My youngest cousin has a stubborn temper," she explained. "It's just as well that he has gone. You didn't see him slip away because we were talking and your back was turned. He is going to scout the way for us. The way to the Lesser Isle of Ying begins at a deep cleft in the cliff opposite us on the far side of the valley. The cleft is the beginning of a long gorge which leads for several miles across the side of the mountain. It is too far to walk, and we would be rather remiss as hosts if we asked you to run. Also, we have to consider the animals brought by the Dragon clan. Every one of them is savage and cunning to a rare degree, and they vie to please their mistresses with acts of violence. The creatures must by now have learned of what happened. Even if their mistresses never ordered it, there is no guarantee that some of them might not take it into their heads to lie in ambush along the way, waiting for a chance to attack. After some discussion, my youngest cousin and I decided it would be best to proceed as if unaware of any trouble. We have summoned Snowy and the Distentor, whom we have named Emerald, to bear us there. When they arrive we will have your excellent friend Master Zhu mount on Emerald and lead the way, and Brothers Wang and Zhao ride together on Snowy. I will follow along in the rear on foot. These two magic creatures strike terror into the hearts of all ordinary animals. Only the divine beasts of the Immortals, who have grown and cultivated themselves for a thousand years or more, to the point where they have achieved miraculous powers, have no fear of such as these. Any Miao beasts lying in wait for us will withdraw. This will preserve our dignity and avoid unnecessary trouble."

As she spoke, two tiny round shapes appeared in the sunshine at the other end of the valley. They approached at incredible speed, one flying right after the other. The first seemed even at that distance to be extremely large, shining a brilliant halcyon green in the sunlight. Their shapes were indistinct; it seemed as if a tiny greenish cloud with a white light flashing about it were speeding toward them across the sky. Soaring Cloud began to laugh.

"What a ridiculous creature! Conveying us will only take it a few minutes of its time, but it is still too worried about the safety of its little master to leave him behind. Look! There is the child sitting on its back!"

So rapid was the progress of the two beasts that in the time it took the girl to make this observation, the green and white shapes had already glided in for a landing in front of them. Zhao Lin was prepared for the sight of the numinous animals from Soaring Cloud's detailed descriptions, and he had already had a glimpse of the Linked Culmen. Wang and Zhu had never seen either beast. They knew only that one of them had nearly killed them with its poison, and that the other had saved them.

II

Talk of magic milk in the Nephrite Cave;
the Golden swords fly in tandem,
and meet the chivalrous warriors;
through freezing clouds,
they are enchanted by distant green;
a tune on pipes of iron disperses the barbarian maids.

CHAPTER 6

Flight to the Isle of Ying

THE EMERALD DISTENTOR WAS A MONSTER OF FRIGHTENING AND impressive aspect. It stretched nearly twenty feet from nose to tail, with a
massive head as big and round as a dinner table. From its forehead
sprouted seven weird eyes, each the size of wine cups. These protruding orbs opened and shut independently, and beams of golden light
flickered at random dozens of feet in every direction. Nostrils gaped as
large as spittoons. Its wide blood-red mouth, which stretched from one
massive jowl to the other, was open a crack. A billow of dense white
vapour jetted forth every now and then to a distance of four or five feet,
only to be abruptly sucked back in. A terrible strength and agility, now
almost completely held in check, was evident in every movement. The
creature's body was a bright emerald green, covered with long shaggy
tufts of green fur. Its coat gave an appearance of a soft uneven woolli-
ness, as though the whole animal were draped in a huge felt rug. It stood
on short stout legs, claws safely concealed inside velvety green tufts of
fur on the toes. A three foot tail, splayed like a fan, jutted erect from its
rump. Soft green wool grew particularly thick and dense on its broad
back.

Seated firmly behind its head was a young boy, perhaps two or three
years old. He was fairly bursting with health and vigour. His lips were
bright red and teeth snow white, skin white and firm. He had long and
pronounced eyebrows which slanted back to his temples, framing eyes
which sparkled with energy and mischief. His hands were as quick and
agile as the claws of a bird. He looked particularly handsome and fierce,
and his dress was unusually fine. A golden clasp bound his long hair. He
wore a pair of short yellow trousers, and a cloak of shining green feathers covered his shoulders. His arms and legs were bare. At his breast
hung an ancient talisman of white jade. At first glance he appeared no
different from an ordinary child the same age, but on closer inspection
Zhao and the others were struck by his obvious intelligence and his
amazing strength and health. His arms and legs were firm and well-
muscled, like refined metal or white jade. His voice was strangely clear
and penetrating, deafening when he raised it. His movements were extremely quick and agile, like those of a bird.

When he was still more than twenty feet away, he uttered a long
whoop, and leaped off the beast's back. He flew through the air into
Soaring Cloud's arms, and hugged her with exuberant affection. The
Emerald Distentor stopped and stood motionless, its huge blood-red
mouth split open in what looked like a smile. The entire constellation of
golden eyes was now open and fixed on the child.

The Linked Culmen had landed close behind it. It was nowhere near as impressive as the Distentor. It was weird and ugly in appearance, with a flat rectangular body and four short legs straight as sticks poking into the ground. Twin heads grew side by side between its shoulders, retracted almost fully into their cavities. Its three mutant eyes were all half closed, mostly concealing a potent emerald gleam that was at the moment less bright than the golden shine of the Distentor's eyes. It was little more than two feet high, and looked almost like a small rectangular table with two animal heads carved at one end. It was a small beast to begin with, and standing quietly next to the enormous Distentor it seemed unimpressive, insignificant and frightfully ugly.

Wang Jin was already aware that most of the people and animals in this valley were mysterious and unusual, so he was not disappointed by the appearance of the little beast. Zhu Man-Tiger on the other hand marvelled at the ugliness of the creature. Its movements seemed quick and agile, but it was awfully small and short; how on earth would it be able to carry two people? As he wondered about this, the creature's three eyes snapped open and fixed on him, startling him with the frightening potency of the light that they contained.

Only Zhao Lin fully understood the awesome powers of the Linked Culmen. He could see that Zhu Man-Tiger was not much impressed by it. Zhao knew that the creature had preternatural powers of perception, and was afraid that it had taken offense at Zhu's lukewarm attitude. He turned hastily to his companions.

"This is the remarkable numinous animal known as the Linked Culmen," he announced in a respectful tone. "When our search for the Old One in Green went awry and we lost our way upon the face of the cliff, this other numinous beast, the Emerald Distentor, misread our purpose, believing that we had come to attack it. Out of commendable loyalty to its young master, it called upon the elixir breaths in its belly to fell us. We were very fortunate that our hosts brought along this most excellent beast, the Linked Culmen, who used its own elixir breaths to save us and restore us to health. I have already offered my thanks to Elder Sister Cloud, but because I did not know where this numinous beast was to be found, I was unable to express to it my respectful gratitude for saving our lives."

By the time Zhao had finished this speech, the Linked Culmen had lidded its eyes, and the deadly green light was concealed once more. Zhao led Wang and Zhu before it, and the three of them saluted it respectfully to offer their thanks. It did not seem eager to accept their gratitude. It uttered a faint low rumble, and then leaped nimbly away. Soaring Cloud went over to soothe it. Zhao Lin continued to praise it.

"Both of these remarkable numinous beasts have been cultivating their inner energies and humours for many years in the mountains of the Immortals, and have as a result become highly intelligent and very powerful. The loyalty and awesome power of the divine Distentor we have already witnessed; it needs no further description. This excellent

Linked Culmen is also a master of transformations. It can shrink and enlarge itself at will. With one great roar it can expand its body to much greater size, and the light of its eyes flashes like lightning. When it flies it can cover a thousand miles in a few moments, raising a terrible wind in its wake. So strong is this wind that sand and rocks are flung through the air. I have never before seen a creature of such supernatural strength, or one capable of uttering such a mighty roar. I suspect that it noticed that we were here talking to Sister Cloud, and is taking care to act in a polite and unobtrusive manner for fear of frightening us."

The beasts seemed to understand that they were being praised, and were visibly pleased. Both turned to look at Zhao as he spoke, and rumbled deeply in their throats when he finished. Zhao caught sight of Soaring Cloud nodding unobtrusively to him in approval, and he knew that his words were having their desired effect. He went on to say more about how they had been rescued. Zhu and Wang were amazed to learn that the thunderous roaring they had heard while on the cliff had been uttered by this tiny beast. Soaring Cloud said nothing and made no move to proceed until Zhao had finished the story, allowing him to flatter the beasts as much as possible.

As they prepared to leave, the little boy clung tightly to Soaring Cloud and insisted she accompany him on the Distentor. If she would not, he demanded to be carried in her arms as she went along on foot. The Distentor made it clear that it would accept only the former arrangement, and that it did not care to have a stranger riding alone on its back. Soaring Cloud thought a moment, and then decided on the only reasonable alternative. Zhu`Man-Tiger would ride on the shoulders of the beast, and she, holding the child, would ride on its rump.

As they clambered up on the creature's back, two strange bird cries, sharp and wild, reached their ears from high up in the sky.

Zhu Man-Tiger now knew that Soaring Cloud was no ordinary girl, and how dangerous it had been to provoke her. Much to his dismay he now found himself riding with her on the same beast. His lecherous fantasies were completely quelled, and he was conducting himself with great caution and reserve. If anything, he had become overly sensitive. He paid little heed to the strange bird cries in the sky.

Zhu was puzzled as to how a creature as tiny as the Linked Culmen could fly through the air with two men on its back. Zhao had said that it was a master of transformations, capable of changing its size at will. Zhu wondered how it accomplished this. As he sat there, lost in thought, he heard a series of animal howls far off in the distance. They were answered by a tremendous earth-shaking roar behind which deafened him, and a violent gust of wind drove sand into his face. The sound echoed back and forth off the cliffs and crags as it gradually faded.

Almost immediately afterwards, the green velvet bladders on the Distentor abruptly inflated, and the creature surged into the air. It rushed forward and upward at great speed, and in barely an instant had reached an altitude of two hundred feet. The sudden takeoff caught Zhu by surprise; his ears rang and vision whirled. If he had not had a firm grounding in the martial arts, he might have fallen off. The beast soon reached its chosen altitude and levelled off; its back became steady as a boat. They glided smoothly along as if riding on a cloud, moving swiftly toward the cliffs at the far end of the valley.

Zhu, still overwhelmed by shame, felt as timid as a bird which has been shot with a catapult. He seized fistfuls of the soft green fur on the creature's neck and held on for dear life, fearful of an abrupt change of course. Then he tried to pay attention to what was going on around him.

Once airborne, the preternatural beast flew at incredible speed. The wind roared in his ears. Rocks, trees, and water flashed by in a confusing blur, too fast for him to make out anything clearly. If a beast like this were able to move through the air at such a great rate, he wondered, how much faster the flight of the mysterious swordsman-Immortals of whom he had heard so much? These exalted beings were said to fly through the void like shooting stars, travelling a thousand miles at one brief stretch. Their flight must be unimaginably faster than this.

Now that the Distentor was flying so rapidly, he began to wonder if the Linked Culmen would be left behind with two men on its back. He wanted to turn and look, but checked himself, fearing that Soaring Cloud, sitting behind with the child in her arms, might misunderstand his motives.

He was startled when Soaring Cloud shouted directions at the beasts.

"Brocade-Spring Gorge is directly ahead!... The Lesser Isle of Ying is not far beyond the entrance. Snowy, don't try to show off! Follow carefully behind Emerald and make no trouble! Brothers Zhao and Wang, sit tight! If anything happens I will take care of it."

This time Zhu Man-Tiger could not restrain himself from taking a look behind him. He was greatly startled to see that the Linked Culmen had expanded to roughly the same length as the Distentor. It actually seemed bigger and broader because of its flat rectangular shape. Its two mutant heads were extended out side by side to their fullest extent. Brilliant emerald beams lanced like lightning from its three weird eyes. Greenish flames and vapour spurted forth at intervals from its mouth, shooting out a few feet and then immediately withdrawn once more. Every hair of the white fur over its entire body stood on end, gleaming brightly in the sun. In its present state it was even more frightening than the Distentor. He had never seen creatures like this before, and now had seen two in a single day. The greatest wonder of all was that they were so tame, responsive to their mistress' every command.

Once again Soaring Cloud spoke, this time to the Distentor.

"Here is Brocade-Spring Gorge! Take care, Emerald!"

They wrenched to the right; the sunlight was abruptly cut off as they entered a deep and narrow gorge. Zhu, twisted around to stare at the Linked Culmen, never saw the opening.

Before they had entered the gorge the two beasts had been flying swiftly along at an altitude of four or five hundred feet, Emerald in the lead, and Snowy following behind. Once in the gorge they abruptly slowed to half their original speed. Zhu was able to see his surroundings more clearly. Vertical cliffs towered two thousand feet on either side to enclose a thin strip of sky far above. Looking up from such a depth the sky was a deep blue, broken every now and then when a white cloud sped across the gap. The bottom was relatively smooth and clear, perhaps thirty feet in width. The rock walls were carpeted with dark green moss and lichens, vines, and small trees. The gorge turned and twisted like a writhing snake, doubling back and angling in unexpected directions. The landscape within it was dark and mysteriously beautiful, the atmosphere curiously rich, like no place Zhu had ever seen. It was more shadowy than he might have liked, but otherwise extremely attractive.

As the walls of the gorge bent and twisted before them, now advancing, now receding, it often seemed to him that there was no way through the crags and precipitous slopes ahead. A solid wall of rock would leap toward them, threatening to crush him under a great weight, but then the enormous head of the powerful Distentor would turn suddenly to one side, and a whole new section of the gorge would be revealed as though by magic, and they would continue forward. On either side waterfalls broke the green of the cliffs, long white dragons stretching downward, cloaked in misty gossamer and coruscating beads of crystal. Ancient pines danced and cavorted, like young, green flying serpents striving to soar into the sky. Queer crags and pinnacles stabbed up into the clouds, revolving slowly to present ever-changing shapes as the beasts raced past. Everywhere the exotic beauty of the landscape seized Zhu's attention, trying to lure him into its many splendours. The mountain springs splashed, and the wind roared through the pines and raised eerie howls and whistles from strange formations and orifices in the rock. Beautiful fowl and rare birds sang, their music clear and crisp to the ear. Zhu's senses were overwhelmed, incapable of registering it all.

After flying on like this for quite some time, the Distentor took a quick turn to the left. The light brightened suddenly, and the thin crack of sky between the stone walls leapt apart to a width of several hundred feet. The twisting cliffs to either side now shot past them like twin dragons flying abreast, their heads curving in toward each other to merge into a single body far ahead. There they melded and swept up into a pair of high peaks, set closely side by side, rising out of a common base. From the point where they had entered to the two peaks ahead, the spacious valley measured nearly two miles in length, and as much as half a mile in width at its centre. The cliffs and crags were covered with flowering trees of an unfamiliar variety, each about thirty feet high, branches laden with bowl-sized blossoms of a deep rich pink in full bloom. From a distance they resembled flowering plums, but with a subtle sweet scent reminiscent of cinnamon blossoms, penetrating the nose with wave after wave of exotic fragrance. They looked like miles of clouds glowing in a splendid sunset, layer upon layer of shimmering auroral mists, covering the cliffs and crags almost completely; only traces of emerald moss and lichens showed through occasional breaks. Set against the blue-green mountains in the background, the pink trees created a peerless landscape of rare beauty.

Zhu recalled that their destination had been called the 'Water Pavilion on the Lesser Isle of Ying', a name which suggested some sort of a terrace overlooking a body of water. He had seen several waterfalls along the way, but no sign of anything so large as a lake. The two peaks ahead marked the end of the valley, but there was no sign of water or buildings. He began to wonder if the place in which they were to be entertained lay in another area beyond the peaks. If so, was the Distentor really capable of clearing crags and peaks of such great height? In the time it took his thoughts to run this course, they covered more than a mile along the length of the valley. Soon they would reach the end. The peaks melded smoothly into lofty ridges on either side, forming a single unbroken wall of rock only a hundred feet or so below their summits. The space between the peaks extended downward only a few dozen feet further before being completely blocked. The upper part of this huge escarpment leaned precariously, extending beyond the base below, looming threateningly above the onrushing party. As they sped forward it seemed to Zhu that it was about to fall and crush them. It was far grander and more precipitous than any feature they had yet seen along the way. On its upper reaches a multitude of rocks and outcroppings protruded in strange contorted shapes, among which numerous caves and other cavities opened, difficult to see because they were so well hidden by the flowering trees.

The three men felt their airborne mounts accelerate beneath them, putting on a terrific burst of speed as they neared the escarpment. They were now travelling even faster than they had been in the first stage of their trip. It began to seem as though they were going to ram directly into the cliff wall ahead.

Zhao Lin, travelling behind on the Linked Culmen, was surprised to see Soaring Cloud put down the child and stand easily upright upon the rump of the green Distentor. She seemed to be preparing to do something, though he could not imagine what. As he wondered, he caught sight of a large stone gateway just below the peaks ahead. Above it were carved the characters 'Lesser Isle of Ying' in a quaint seal script of great antiquity. The entrance had been hidden from their view by several massive flowering trees many spans in diameter, each covered with a profusion of blossoms. Coming at it through the air at an altitude of several hundred feet, it had not become visible until they were almost upon it.

As they swept toward the cliff, Zhao Lin was startled by a sudden booming roar in front of them, like the crash of a huge brass gong. The Distentor lifted its head, and a massive cloud of white vapour jetted upwards. Soaring Cloud shouted out angrily.

"How dare you disobey your mistresses? I must teach you manners! Emerald! Pay no attention to them!"

She extended her arms, and two threads of bright green radiance shot upwards toward the vegetation above the gateway. Then she left the back of the speeding animal, flying smoothly upward toward the spot from which the sound had come. The Linked Culmen dipped abruptly downward, dodging two brightly coloured shapes which streaked down from the cliff and whipped past Zhao's head. Zhao could not make out what they were. The beast beneath them uttered a deafening roar, and lifted its heads to see where Soaring Cloud had gone. An instant later they shot through the gate like a bolt from a crossbow. As they plunged briefly through a dark tunnel, a clamour of birds and animals roaring and squawking broke out above the gate behind him. The sound receded into the distance, the creatures having apparently scattered in all directions, and all was quiet once more. They hurtled underground through the rock for two hundred feet or so, and then burst out into the sunshine over the rippling waters of a broad lake. A single island rose from the centre of its sapphire waters. They came down too rapidly to get a good look at it. They had a brief impression of green peaks and deep blue water, of ridges and crags linked together in complex turns and twists, a separate world with unique and exquisite scenery.

CHAPTER 7

Lad-of-Heaven

THE TWO BEASTS FLEW ALONG SIDE BY SIDE, SKIMMING LOW OVER the waves toward the island. When they reached their destination they decelerated abruptly, and dropped lightly down to the shore. Zhao and his companions, their heads spinning, dismounted and turned to see a grand two-storied hall. Wei Lai and another youth emerged to meet them, and saluted their guests politely. Wei Lai began to lead them into the building, but the other youth, after greeting them with a smile, turned suddenly to scold the Distentor, who was following them toward the building.

"Halt!" he barked. "We go to feast our guests. Your little master is welcome to join us, but you and Snowy must wait outside. If you still feel you cannot trust us with the child, I am afraid he will have to ride back to the cave with you. There of course he can eat only ordinary foods, and won't be able to play with the rest of us..."

The child reacted with alarm. He leaped over to the Distentor and hugged its huge head.

"No need for you to go in today," he shouted urgently to the beast. "Listen to Third Brother! Let me play with them for a while, can't I? Please?"

The Distentor's reluctance was plain, and the child responded with a violent tantrum. He seized the beast's shaggy tufts of fur and began to yank wildly, shouting all the while.

"I don't want to play by myself! Don't tell me what to do!"

The Distentor allowed the child to tear at its fur without reaction. Golden beams from its seven weird eyes flickered and flashed, scanning the spacious building inside and out. Then it uttered two rumbles of tender acquiescence. The boy, who understood the language of beasts, had been given permission. He began to regret yanking at its fur. He hugged its head and massaged the spots he had attacked, and shouted happily to it.

"I'm sorry, Big Green Brother! I shouldn't pull your hair. When we go back I'll love you some more!"

The creature leaned its head gently against the boy in tender affection. The others, watching the drama unfold, smiled with amusement.

Something hissed through the air above them, and Wei Lai called out.

"Back already, Sister Cloud? There can't have been much trouble!"

Zhao saw a flash of green as Soaring Cloud dropped to the ground. The child abandoned the Distentor and bounded over to her.

"Sister! Sister!" he shouted, seizing her hand. "Where is your giant monkey and your ape? Why didn't you let me go see them? My Big

Green Brother said I could stay here and play with you, and have nice things to eat!"

Wei Lai and the other youth interrupted to ask her what had transpired.

"Setting an ambush like that!" Wei Lai said angrily. "How dare they intimidate us? Were the two Miao sisters directly involved?"

Soaring Cloud laughed. "Look at you! Nearly grown adults, jabbering and fussing like our new Baby Brother here! You have left our guests standing outside the door. Why not invite them in to sit? We may talk at our leisure inside."

"That was my intention," said Wei Lai. "But we were distracted by our Baby Brother and Emerald, and simply had to stop and watch."

He invited Zhao and his companions inside. Zhao noticed that Wei and the other treated Wang Jin and himself with great courtesy and respect, but were cool and indifferent toward Zhu Man-Tiger. Zhao could not help feeling grieved at this.

"The Water Pavilion has two levels from which one can enjoy the scenery," Wei Lai explained. "The lake is of course nowhere near as large as your own Willow Lake, but it offers pleasant prospects of bamboo groves and flowering trees over the water. A table has been prepared upstairs, from where the entire vista can be seen more clearly. Permit me the discourtesy of leading the way."

They followed him into the interior of the building. On the lower level a grand and beautiful hall stretched a hundred feet to either side, filled with exquisitely crafted furnishings. They went around a screen set in the middle of one wall, and mounted a flight of stairs. The upper level, a fair amount higher than the ground floor below, was built entirely of fragrant Nanmu hardwood. The wood had been left in its natural state, unencumbered by varnish or carving. The furnishings were at once simple and elegant. The hall was carefully designed so as to give the impression of floating high in the air over the water. There were no solid walls, and huge windows afforded an unobstructed view on all sides. Mild breezes blew through from time to time, bearing a hint of floral perfume. Zhao and his companions had not yet seated themselves, but already they felt refreshed. The cares of their travels fell away, leaving them feeling clear-headed and revitalized.

Places had been set for them on a mat in the left rear corner, directly above the sapphire waves. Outside, the mountains beyond the lake faded away in layer upon layer of blue, drawing the viewer's gaze far into the distance. The three visitors exclaimed again and again at the magnificence of the outlook.

After all seven of them were comfortably seated, Zhao Lin and his companions formally thanked their hosts for their rescue and hospitality. Introductions were made, and they learned the second youth was named Ding Shao. A woman dressed in green came up to serve them. They began with wine and four platters of appetizers. Even before he began to ply his chopsticks Zhao Lin could see that the food was of excellent quality, prepared with meticulous care. The platters and bowls were antiques of great beauty and value. Except for the first four platters, crafted from an identical porcelain like black jade, no vessel was like any other. Each piece had the look of ware from Geru and other famed kilns of the long-vanished Song dynasty craftsmen.

"Your tableware is superb!" Zhao exclaimed. "You treat us with excessive kindness. We have no means to repay your excellent hospitality."

In response, Soaring Cloud raised her cup to toast the company.

"I must tell you the story of our porcelain ware," she said. "In prior years, before my father practised the Dao, he often said that it is better to have fine porcelain than fine food. The worldly and vulgar man, eager to display his wealth, hires a craftsman to manufacture a complete set of tableware to his specifications, decorated with uniform designs of the most common sort, engraved with his name and sobriquet. Each strives to outdo his fellows in ostentation, hoping to enhance his social standing. But then the ware is used to serve an elaborate array of rich foods with a meaty, rancid odour. A starving man might derive satisfaction from it, perhaps, but is poorly suited for daily consumption. Not only does it look vulgar and unwholesome, but everything on the table nourishes the fire-humours within the body, to the detriment of one's health. A man with a weak stomach loses his appetite just looking at it.

The wealthy who spend tremendous sums in the preparation of such lavish spreads understand nothing of the artistry in the preparation and consumption of food and drink. It should delight the eye, please the palate, and fill the stomach pleasantly without causing discomfort and indigestion. Only those with some sense of elegance can hope to achieve this. Most ridiculous of all is that after feasting all year around, the worldly man comes to detest the sight of banquet food, and invariably dreads the next formal dinner. And yet when it is his turn to act as host he takes great pains to prepare the same fare for his friends, believing it the only honourable way to entertain guests. He carefully balances the Five Flavours, and takes great pains to preserve the soft rich fat. He taxes the limits of his ingenuity to find novel combinations, confident that his guests will never tire of his fare. A great joke, indeed!

"My father refused to hold formal banquets at all. Sometimes on a holiday or festival, at a time when there was excellent weather or fine views to be enjoyed, he might invite a handful of intimate friends to drink tea and wine, and pass the time in easy and refined conversation. Sometimes they would spend days and nights at a time in this wise, never growing weary of it. The foods he served were always clean and light, never more than they could comfortably eat. His dishes and vessels were all products of the great kilns of the ages of Tang and Song, exquisitely crafted in the refined designs of the ancients, and there was never more than one of a kind, each different from every other in shape and size. His companions were people of similar tastes, retired counsellors and ministers of state, or men of lofty principles dwelling in seclusion in the countryside or mountains. While eating and drinking, they would delight in appraising and appreciating one another's pieces. My father took great pride in his collection.

"Twenty years ago, he retired from office, abstained from grain foods,* and devoted himself to the pursuit of immortality. When he withdrew to this mountain, he stored all his fine implements away, and used them no longer. Last year at our New Year's dinner, I happened to recall this collection, and we decided to fetch them out and use them again.

"But enough of that! We take great pleasure in entertaining you as honoured guests, and must make amends for keeping you from eating for nearly a full day. We feared you would be famished by this time, and have quickly prepared a few things to satisfy you for the time being. We apologize for the hasty preparation of the food, and for the fact that the tableware is only what we have for daily use. We hope that in future days when you honour our barren mountain with your presence once again, you will permit us to entertain you in proper fashion."

It was clear to Zhao Lin that Soaring Cloud, who had the power of flight, was a warrior of considerable powers. If her father had ceased eating grain foods to cultivate longevity, it was quite possible that he had by now become an Immortal, or was well on his way to doing so. Despite all the strange things Zhao had seen, he was startled by this revelation, though it was not entirely unexpected. Before he had time to formulate a reply, Wei Lai, who had been straining to contain his impatience as Soaring Cloud spoke, interrupted.

"Why all this endless chatter, Elder Sister? Tell us what happened!"

"You're always so impatient," she retorted. "Can't you see that we are trying to eat? There is nothing we can do about it at this moment, so what is the point of disturbing our guests' meal? Wait until we're finished eating and have gone to see Mother. I don't wish to ruin everyone's spirits, and I don't feel like telling the story twice."

"There is something you don't know," said Wei Lai. "A few minutes ago Sixth Brother and Fifth Sister disobeyed the wishes of the Old One and came to spy out what the white apes were up to. They informed me that those two friends of ours, the ones who came last year, are coming again today. Fourth Brother is willing to aid us as well, as long as he can do so without being found out. If all of us act in concert, none can stand against us. The Dragon clan has grown unruly and violent over the last few years, and I for one have had enough of it. But our Mistress forbids us to confront them, so we sit on our hands, trying to swallow our anger. Why not take this opportunity to band together and teach them a lesson, and make them think twice before making trouble for us at every turn?"

---

* [Abstinence from all grain was often one of the precepts followed by Daoist immortality seekers. It was believed that grains nourished the Three Corpse Worms within the body.]

93

The other youth Ding Shao broke in.

"Younger Brother Lai is still in a dreadful temper over what happened several years back," he said in a conciliatory tone. "We should remember, though, that the older members of the Dragon clan still abide by the rules bequeathed by the Grand Masters Celestial Confluence and Luminous River.* As arrogant and unruly as the Dragon juniors are, their laws are strict, and they commit no great evil. Also, and forgive me if I speak plainly, remember that the trouble we are having now has come about because Elder Brother Zhu here, in a moment of weakness, allowed himself a slight indiscretion. The fault lies with us, not with the Miao. I know what you are thinking, Younger Brother. The brothers and sisters of the Dragon clan have been at odds with you and Elder Sister Cloud for quite some time now. Mistress won't let you act, and you have been unable to vent your anger. Today's events provide you with the excuse you have been waiting for."

"You're not far off the mark, Third Elder Brother!" laughed Soaring Cloud. "My father and the Old One concur that Brother Lai has great potential, but is prone to taking shortcuts and direct action, traits unsuitable in one who aspires to the arts of the Immortals. I doubt that he will ever be able to control his temper, and it's going to limit his progress."

"I'm a simple fellow," said Wei Lai with good humour. "I don't aspire to any great accomplishments. All I want..."

"'All I want,' indeed!" Soaring Could snapped, phoenix eyes narrowing in anger. "What do you want to do? Tell us! You're worthless! You lack all ambition, and yet have the gall to announce your plans to us!"

Wei Lai, seeing that she was really angry, hastened to explain. "I have my ambitions! I want to prolong my life in this secluded paradise beyond the world, spending my time in carefree wandering through the clouds and mists as a simple practitioner of the arts of longevity. What need to achieve transcendence as one of the Divine Immortals of Heaven? Here I can attain a life span as enduring as Heaven and Earth, and enjoy pure bliss forever, every now and then, descending through the winds and dust of the mortal world, righting wrongs, aiding the good, and helping the poor. If I achieve this I shall be happy and satisfied indeed."

Soaring Cloud ignored him, and turned to address Ding Shao.

"If we let the Miao women have their way with Elder Brother Zhu, the problem is at once resolved, and we will have earned their increased goodwill. Otherwise, the blame is on us, and our position difficult to explain. On the other hand, their proposal to Brother Zhao lacks merit, as he has never so much as looked them full in the face.

* The Elders known as Celestial Confluence and Luminous River were masters of the Blue City school. They were contemporaries of certain other personages of the late Song dynasty such as Zhu Mai the Short; the Perfected Master Jiang Shu, Queller of Demons; and the Perfected Master of the Long Eyebrows, the founding patriarch of the Omei Mountain sect in Sichuan. By the early Yuan period all of these luminaries had departed the world and joined the ranks of the Immortals.

"When I was bringing our guests here, the animals the Miao brought along with them had the audacity to lie in wait for us on the peak above the gateway. They were evidently planning to capture Brothers Zhao and Zhu and carry them off by force. Such a blatant attempt at coercion right on our very doorstep is intolerable, and strengthens our bargaining position with the sisters. At first I was under the impression that this shameless crowd of birds and beasts had acted against orders, but my suspicions were aroused as I chased them out, and surprised the old one-armed ape directing the operation from what he thought was a safe hiding place. At that very moment the Dragon sisters flew up on a simurgh, saying they had heard Emerald and Snowy roaring, and feared that trouble had broken out. They apologized handsomely for the attack, and claimed that it had been mounted without their knowledge. But I knew they were hiding something, and believe that they had been aware of it, and had done nothing to prevent it. Had the venture been successful, they would have permitted the two white apes to carry Brothers Zhao and Zhu back to their mountain on their huge old bald vulture.

"However, I must admit that the two sisters are not bad as people go. I have never thought of them as close friends, but we have always enjoyed good relations with them, and they are far less objectionable than the rest of the children of the Dragon clan. They apologized most abjectly, and begged me to continue acting as a go-between, and I could not refuse them, though it's certainly brought me much grief.

"Elder Brother Zhao has pure and high-minded ambitions, and it is clear he will go far. I find no trouble making excuses on his behalf. Elder Brother Zhu already has a wife, and his somewhat quixotic behaviour was no doubt due to his illness. It is my intention to do everything possible for both of you, though I had originally planned only to 'snatch the firewood out from under the axe', as they say, and attempt to persuade the sisters not to do anything rash.

"Brother Lai, it seems, has something quite different in mind. He wants to use this incident as an excuse for confrontation and revenge. The consequences of such a course would be disastrous. The Dragon clan would be hard pressed, and suffer much death and injury. Once open conflict began, they would be bound to avenge themselves no matter what the cost. The result could only be the final extermination of their entire clan.

"You may have the wholehearted support of some of the Li brothers and sisters, and those two devilish friends of yours, but I tell you right now that I for one want no part in it. Mother will be even less pleased. You know how kind and caring a woman she is. You are allowing yourself to be guided by personal animosity, which is risky in actions of this sort. What will you benefit from all this trouble?"

All this time Zhao and his companions ate ravenously. They were reassured by the informal manner of their hosts, and were in any case too hungry to be much interested in ceremony. The food and drink were excellent. As the conversation turned toward more serious topics, they listened with greater concern.

When Soaring Cloud had finished, Wei Lai sat silently, deep in thought.

"Your thinking is inept," Soaring Cloud continued. "Do you have any idea what Sixth Brother is up to? He is as young as you are, and like you has yet to outgrow his childishness. He has his eye on those two black monkeys of theirs. He's been itching for revenge ever since our unfortunate incident with the arrogant children of Old Man Miao. He and Fourth Brother have been known to say that malicious Miao like these ought to be removed. The only thing holding them back all this time has been the risk of their parents' displeasure. Now, to their great rejoicing, this incident has occurred. Their two friends just happen to be coming for a visit, too. All of them are young and fond of trouble, exactly like you. It is a perfect time to strike. You haven't given a thought to what unpleasant consequences might ensue. Even if it all goes smoothly, think of how many people could be hurt or killed!"

"All right! All right!" Wei Lai protested. "I admit you have read most of what is in our minds. But you're wrong about the monkeys! Sixth Brother is one of my best friends. I know he's busy with his strict training, and can't spend as much time with us as he would like, but he still cares a great deal for all of us. Now he is willing to avenge our honour, and you say it is for the sake of robbing those Miao strumpets of their pets! You are unfair to him! You know how great his powers are, and how fond of him all of his brothers and sisters are. If he wants anything, he has only to ask. Why would he covet the Miao girls' beasts?"

He was interrupted by a glorious shout from outside.

"My brother speaks the truth! We are indeed good friends! I have a message for you. You need not go to the Green Longevity Pavilion to see your Mistress after all. She has gone to my house, and has commanded me to tell you to take enough time to allow our guests to eat well, stroll about and enjoy the scenery. At the Hour of the Monkey,* she wishes Big Sister to take them alone to my house to meet her and my father together."

Zhao Lin and his companions had taken note of the beauty of the view, and the wide expanse of rolling waves, but had not otherwise scrutinized the terrain outside, preoccupied with eating and the conversation going on around them. When they heard the clear voice calling, they directed their attention outside, and saw in the middle of the water fifty feet distant a column of stone thirty or forty feet in height. It was heavily draped with moss, marked here and there by clumps of red flowers. Its proportions were symmetrical and pleasing to the eye, somewhat wider at the top than at the base. On its flat top, ten feet in diameter, stood a boy who looked to be about twelve years of age. He

* [3–5 PM.]

was fair-skinned and plump. Even at that distance they could see that his eyes shone with a strange light. His forehead and features were refined and handsome. His voice rang out clear as a bell with no discernible effort on his part.

The pillar of stone floated like a cloud of rock in the sky, surrounded only by lapping waves. How had the boy managed to climb it? As Zhao and his companions stared in wonder, Soaring Cloud made haste to shout back to him.

"Why not come in, small Sixth Elder Brother? Are you angry with me?"

"Well, you did say I was greedy behind my back just now, and in front of outsiders at that!" the boy replied. "Do you think I would dare beg for a meal after you said such a thing?"

"I would be surprised indeed if you weren't interested in those little black monkeys," laughed Soaring Cloud. "You and Younger Brother Lai are a pair of crafty wolves, always up to something or other! You'd best be careful, or I'll inform your father!"

"This humble little grandson is not afraid," the boy shot back gaily. "If you want to tell him, go ahead!"

Wei Lai interrupted, calling out loudly: "Why does our Mistress want only Sister Cloud to go with the guests, and not me as well?"

"I only repeat what she said," the boy answered. "I have no idea why. When our two older cousins come, they will come here to look for you. I must go now!"

Zhao Lin, thinking that the boy must be the son of the Old One in Green, was about to call out a greeting, but a silvery cloud flickered strangely about the top of the stone, and the child disappeared without trace. Zhao and his companions looked around in astonishment, but could not see how he had departed. Soaring Cloud explained.

"The seven brothers and sisters of the Li family, of whom he is the sixth, all have great powers. Second Sister and Sixth Brother are especially zealous in their training, and adept in the arts of the sword. Strange stories are told of Sixth Brother. Evidently he has been the beloved son of the Old One in Green through successive incarnations, and the bond between them is particularly close. The first time he was born to the Old One and his wife he was their only child, and they loved him dearly. He had accrued much guilt in previous incarnations, and as a child suffered terribly from constant illness and frequent accidents. His parents stood by him through all trials, and out of gratitude he swore a great oath not to embark upon the path of immortality until they too had done so. Three times since then he has undergone a fatal karmic nexus and had to leave the world of the living, but each time his soul managed to find the same parents and be born to them once again. Over the centuries he has endured more for their sake than can ever be told. The rigours of his vow and the terrible illnesses and disasters of his karma are beyond the understanding of any normal human being. With each new incarnation his Daoist powers have increased. In his recent births

97

he has come into the world with his intelligence, knowledge, and magical arts intact and fully developed.

"But these very powers and the immutability of his vow have left him vulnerable to dark enemies, terrible demonic sorcerers and spectral entities, who have in each previous lifetime succeeded in bringing about the destruction of his body. It is because of his vow to his parents that he has undergone these fatal karmic nexuses again and again.

"In each lifetime he leaves his parents before the age of ten to seek out his kindly teachers, two Grand Masters who have willingly delayed their own progress many years for his sake. We have learned that he has found his old masters in the third month of this year. He has not yet departed because he cannot bear to separate from his parents. He obtained permission from his masters to remain with his family for the space of one additional year before rejoining them. When he does go to them he will reclaim the magical talismans and Treasures of Power he has carried for many lifetimes, and take up his cultivation of the Dao once more.

"In each life, from the time he is born to the time of his passing through the Translation of the Sword,* he never survives longer than one sixty-year cycle. Despite his youthful appearance, he has already passed forty years of this lifetime. He won't begin his Daoist cultivation until next year, which leaves him little time before he must undergo his next karmic nexus. He should have grown into an adult many years ago, but out of love for his parents he retains the form of a child throughout each lifetime, unwilling to grow up. His appearance remains identical from one reincarnation to the next, which causes many problems. His enemies, demons, devils, and other spectral entities, are able to recognize him on sight. They hate him bitterly, and do their utmost to destroy him or hinder his progress. He makes no attempt to conceal himself, and goes on about his business with no trace of fear. He relies on his confidence and dedication, driven by his centuries-old vow, and faces all obstacles and trouble with bland indifference.

"He may not look very impressive to you, since he has not yet recovered his periapts from his masters. All he has at the moment is one magic flying sword, and he cannot manifest his full strength as yet, but after he goes forth and rejoins his teachers next year, his powers will be frightening. And yet he keeps his childish manners throughout. He maintains an innocent and eager demeanour, and indulges in tantrums and mischievous pranks. All in our family love him dearly, and he is particularly fond of Brother Lai here. It is a shame that we cannot visit him more regularly."

"Our excellent guests will soon have the good fortune to meet him," said Wei Lai. "Sixth Elder Brother is kind and good-hearted, and will

---

* [This is one means by which Daoist adepts transcend to a state of immortality or extended life. They seem to die, and are laid out in a coffin, but their bodies soon disappear, leaving behind only a sword or a sprig of bamboo.]

98

sooner or later be of great help to you. The Old One himself has not ventured forth much of late because he wishes to spend as much time with his beloved son as possible before they must part. Also, the Old One has many enemies, evil sorcerers of great power. Were he to manifest his powers openly on your behalf, it would create a stir in many circles. Word would be passed around, and a great evil alliance formed to destroy him, and it would cost him much to resist them. If these demonic powers were attracted here before his son returned to his masters, Sixth Brother would be in mortal danger. My family too would be caused serious inconvenience, and might be hard put to defend ourselves."

Zhao Lin and his companions listened with awe and amazement. Zhao and Wang in particular began to feel a great longing to cultivate the arts of immortality themselves.

The young boy, meanwhile, free from the watchful eye of the Distentor, had been indulging a prodigious appetite. His surname, Zhao and the others learned, was Bu, and his given name Lad-of-Heaven. He was thin, for all his amazing strength, and yet ate enough for several adults. The instant he was seated he attacked his food with reckless determination, devouring everything within reach, heedless of what transpired around him. He paused to watch when Sixth Brother appeared outside, but resumed his eating when the other boy departed. Zhao Lin began to wonder who his parents were, and how it came about that the Distentor had taken refuge with him in the cave at Square-Bamboo Gorge. He opened his mouth to ask, but Soaring Cloud, who seemed to have read his intention, cut him off with a warning look.

"Our Sixth Brother is named Li Hong," she continued. "You will surely be allowed to see him, though it is hard to say whether you will have the opportunity to meet any of his brothers and sisters. I have heard it said that the Old One and his wife will undergo their own karmic nexus in another fifty or sixty years, and will at that time transcend as Immortals. You are indeed fortunate that the Old One has invited you here to see him. Even we younger ones, dwelling but a single ridge away, are rarely granted this privilege. Only my mother and two others of the older generation spend much time with him, having been his good friends for many years. An excellent opportunity like this must not be wasted. If there is anything that troubles you, or if there is anything you desire, do not fear to speak plainly. You have some time yet, because the invitation was for the Hour of the Monkey, but do not worry about other people's affairs for the time being." She glanced meaningfully at the child as she said this. "Think over carefully what you wish to say to the Old One. He will already know all about the incident involving the Miao sisters, and if he is willing to intervene, he will give you much secret aid. If not, there is no point in asking him about it at all. Unless he brings the subject up first, you should not mention it. Brothers Zhao and Wang in particular should not waste this opportunity on account of worry for Brother Zhu; he will be taken care of one way or another, do not fear."

Zhao Lin thanked her for this advice.

Everyone had by this time finished their meal, except for the insatiable Lad-of-Heaven, who continued to eat with great energy. Suddenly, though, he threw down his chopsticks and clutched Soaring Cloud's shoulder.

"Sixth Brother is really wonderful," he cried. "He knows the Flying Sword, just like my Mother and Father. But he flies even faster! One blink, and he was already over that ridge over there! And it flashes so much better too! I want him to teach me, so I can kill my parents' enemies. Take me there, Big Sister, please? Take me there quickly! I'll stop eating all of these nice things!"

He began to blink and roll his eyes in an effort to keep tears from rolling down his cheeks. His grief was obvious, though his expression was at the same time one of grim determination. The Distentor began to rumble deeply outside, and Lad-of-Heaven turned to shout at the faithful beast.

"I know this place! There are no bad people here! My enemies won't hear! If they don't let me go along now, everything will be ruined!"

The Distentor rumbled once or twice more, then ceased its protests. It was clear that it was able to communicate with the boy in its own animal language.

Soaring Cloud began to scold Lad-of-Heaven. "Didn't I warn you not to talk about this in front of other people? You must not be so wild and impulsive! If you want to say something, say it properly! There is no need to grab me so hard, either! It's a good thing it was me and not someone else. If you grab other people like this, you will hurt them. If you behave in this way again, I won't like you any more!"

Lad-of-Heaven loosed his grip at once. "Nice Sister, I'm sorry!" he said anxiously. "Every night I can't sleep, and I always dream of my mother and father. They want me to get revenge for them, and scold me for not obeying them more quickly. I don't know what to do! I can tell that even all of you brothers and sisters are not strong enough to defeat my enemies. Emerald teaches me to pray to the Buddha every day so that I will grow faster. But it doesn't work! Now I've seen Sixth Elder Brother. I know he can help me! He can teach me the Flying Sword, I know he can! I was so happy that I grabbed you harder than I meant to. Don't be angry, Big Sister! I promise not to be wild and impulsive!"

Zhao Lin was amazed at Lad-of-Heaven's strength. Soaring Cloud was clearly an adept in the arts of the Flying Sword transmitted among the Immortals, and yet even she had complained about his grip. His speech did not seem like that of a small child either, for all his lack of restraint. He bore his grief solidly in the manner of an adult. Soaring Cloud did not wish Zhao to ask about the child, but Zhao had divined that he was somehow involved in events of great import. He could not restrain himself from praising the child.

100

"This little brother is so young, but his character surpasses that of most men. His courage and intelligence are the most outstanding I have ever seen. Truly remarkable!"

The child glared at Zhao. "I don't like people telling me I am little!" he shouted angrily. "If you weren't Elder Brother Zhao, I would grab you right now!"

Soaring Cloud broke in immediately.

"Stop that nonsense!" she snapped. "Elder Brother Zhao is a good friend of ours! Sixth Brother's father, the Old One in Green, likes him very much! If you keep on like this, the Old One will know that you have offended Brother Zhao when we go to visit, and will be angry! Sixth Brother will never help you then!"

Soaring Cloud spoke thus out of fear that Lad-of-Heaven's temper would lead him to hurt Zhao, and her words had the desired effect. The child, greatly perturbed, flew straight at Zhao with one quick leap. Zhao, curious to know just how strong the boy really was, did not dodge, but prepared himself by directing inner *qi* energies into his arms to fend off the child's attack. Lad-of-Heaven dropped to the ground right beside him, but did not touch him.

"Brother Zhao! Brother Zhao!" he cried anxiously, his face a bright red. "You're a nice man, and baby Lad-of-Heaven was too stupid to see it. I didn't mean to offend you! Please don't tell Sixth Brother about this, all right? Please? Help me just this once? My parents in Heaven tell me that you are a very good man, just like all my other brothers and sisters here!"

Zhao Lin recognized Soaring Cloud's effort to control Lad-of-Heaven. The boy was simple and innocent, and obsessed with the idea of avenging the wrong done his parents. Zhao was moved by strong pity and love for the grief-stricken child, but was at a loss for words.

Lad-of-Heaven saw Zhao sitting there silently, and looked even more unhappy.

"I only said something bad to you. I didn't really grab you. Why are you still angry with me, Elder Brother Zhao?"

"I'm not angry," Zhao explained hurriedly. "I like you very much, and your plight causes me great distress. I fear that I am too insignificant to be of any help to you. I wouldn't be angry with you even if you did grab me. I am only hoping to begin my studies now, at a late point in my life, and have very little strength or influence. It will be difficult for me to ask the Old One to help you."

Lad-of-Heaven's anger and upset vanished, and he jumped up eagerly.

"How stupid I am! I knew everyone here was good, and that these two elder brothers and Elder Sister love me most of all. You are Elder Sister's friend, so I should have known that you would never be angry with me! You're a very nice brother. But I don't quite understand what you said. I only asked you not to tell Sixth Elder Brother that I was cruel to you. Just tell him that I will be very good and do everything he asks. If you do that, I'll like you even more. As long as no one tells him I am no good, then he will be my teacher, and I don't have to worry about him not wanting me. If you tell him that I am good, but he still doesn't want me, it won't be your fault!"

Zhao smiled and nodded, which delighted the child to no end. He whirled about and shot back to his own place with one quick leap. It was hard to believe that he was only three years old. His agility, intelligence, and alertness were astonishing. He was somewhat unruly, but that only seemed to add to his innocence. Everyone was now smiling at his antics.

"Look at you, jumping about like a monkey!" laughed Soaring Cloud. "If you keep on acting up like this, whoever will accept such a naughty child as a disciple?"

Lad-of-Heaven laughed. "Watch! Third Brother taught me this a little while ago. I still remember exactly how to do it. If you don't believe me, just watch, and I'll do it once more for Big Sister."

The child leaped up from his place, and assumed a serious expression. He took two steps forward with deliberate slowness, then stopped and stood still for a moment in an attitude of deep respect, then took a few more slow steps forward. Suddenly he dropped to the ground and prostrated himself. Then he began to speak in a solemn, tearful, and heart-rending voice.

"Your humble disciple Bu Lad-of-Heaven once lived with his parents in seclusion, practising the arts of the Dao," he intoned. "But my parents were slain without warning by two enemies who had long plotted their destruction. Their evil is higher than the mountains and deeper than the sea. I cannot bear that they and I should live under the same sky. But alas! I am young and weak, and have not the power to avenge my father. I beat my breast and weep tears of blood because I am not worthy to be his son. I have been accorded the honour of being admitted into your presence, O Old One, and I humbly beg the Old One and Sixth Elder Brother to grant me the favour of your vast kindness, unworthy though I am. Take pity on your humble but earnest disciple, orphaned and helpless, and permit Sixth Elder Brother to take me into your school, so that I may sooner avenge my father..."

"What!" cried Soaring Cloud. "You should ask the Old One to be your teacher, not Sixth Elder Brother!"

"But isn't Sixth Elder Brother stronger?" the child asked, barely able to contain his tears.

"Ridiculous!" said Soaring Cloud. "The Old One is his father, so of course he is the greater. Also, you must not forget that you are still very young. How can you talk of going right out and getting revenge?"

"But I am so anxious and desperate," the boy wailed.

"You must understand that the Flying Sword techniques of the Warrior-Immortals cannot be acquired overnight," replied Soaring Cloud. "Being anxious and desperate is of no help at all. Even the rare magic treasures left you by your parents cannot be wielded until you are old enough to master them. You must cultivate patience and a calm mind, and apply yourself to your training with earnest diligence. Do not fret over whether the Old One takes you as his own student, or entrusts you to the care of another for your training. No matter who your master may be, you can be sure that he will be very fond of you, and take great pains to transmit his lore to you. In the fullness of time not only will you be able to avenge your father and mother, but will have achieved great strength and powers in your own right, to use for your own purposes. You should keep this in mind; harness your bitter and earnest determination, and bring it to bear!"

Lad-of-Heaven was now so unhappy that his eyes were blinking and rolling more than ever in his efforts to squeeze back tears.

"But Sixth Brother smiled and nodded to me when he flew away!"

"You just can't forget Sixth Brother, can you?" Soaring Cloud said. "He has to leave the mountain next year to seek his own masters. How could he take you as his student now? You'll have a good teacher of your own, that I can promise you. Don't be stubborn, and above all don't be impatient! If you don't believe me, ask Emerald. Do you think Emerald will let you go into danger before you are ready? Just now Third Elder Brother was testing you, to see if you could remember and repeat a speech. You remembered every word, which you could not have done unless you were very clever. With such intelligence you can achieve anything you wish! You won't require your speech anyway, because the Old One will know all about the matter already. All you have to do is behave yourself, and everything will be all right. Third Brother also made you learn the speech because he wanted to make sure that all of our brothers and sisters would love you and commiserate with you, nothing more. Eight to ten years will pass before you know it. Your enemies won't die and escape you in such a short time. Don't be in such a hurry!"

The entire company was moved by the child's plight. They were amazed at the grave and serious demeanour he assumed when he gave his speech. He seemed a completely different person than he had been just a few moments before.

Wei Lai, who had spoken long with the child the previous night and understood more of his predicament than the others, hastened to reassure him.

"Don't be so sad, dear little Lad-of-Heaven," he said with a smile. "Sixth Elder Brother doesn't accept any students, but he is one of my very best friends. Next time I see him I will talk to him, and tell him all about you. I will ask him to give you every aid and assistance in the future when the time has come to avenge your parents. Would that please you?"

Lad-of-Heaven ran to hug Wei Lai.

"You're a wonderful brother!" he said happily. "Once my parents are avenged, I will be willing to die for you, too!"

He stood up and began posturing and shadow-boxing with his bird-claw hands, snatching furiously at the empty air.

"When I find my enemies, I'm going to squeeze them to death with my hands! Then I'll chew up their bones and flesh into tiny pieces and spit them out on the ground, and grind them into a mush with my feet! But even that won't get me my parents back, will it?"

The child's teeth gnashed with rage, and a savage gleam came into his eyes. Every hair on his head stood on end. But when he realized that his parents would not able to return, tears poured forth. Seeing his grief, everyone felt great pity for him. But at the same time they could not help but be somewhat alarmed at his savage temper and bizarre performance. There was no doubt that the boy was remarkably gifted, but at the same time he had within him a streak of violence. It was indeed fortunate for him that he had been in the care of the kindly beast, who through some intuition had borne him here where he would encounter the Old One in Green. Once he had encountered a good man as his master there would be little chance of his being seduced into evil. Had he fallen in with treacherous and evil men, however, his natural simplicity might swiftly have been corrupted, with unfortunate results.

Soaring Cloud, Wei Lai, and Ding Shao, who knew his story, were particularly concerned for his future. They anticipated that he might not return to them from this visit to the Old One, and that it might be a long time before they would see him again. They were taking this final opportunity to urge him to calm and patience. His violent temper would have to be curbed, so that he could cultivate a tranquil mind. Only then would he be capable of sustained progress. After he had completed his training he would of course be honour-bound to avenge his parents. But for now the most dangerous thing for him was his obsession with murdering his enemies.

"You are after all still only a three-year-old child," they warned him. "Your parents have been murdered by their enemies, so of course it is only natural that you are torn by grief night and day, and have sworn an oath to avenge them. But remember this: nowhere in this world is there anyone who does not have children and dear friends of his own. If you kill someone, another person will suffer what you are suffering now. This can trigger an endless cycle of retribution, abhorrent to anyone who aspires to immortality, and a great hindrance to spiritual progress. Murder incurs a burden of evil karma which grows heavier with each passing day. Heaven above will be angry, and man below will cry out in resentment against the murderer. Hosts of enemies will arise, and the murderer will eventually come to a cruel end. But if you follow in the footsteps of your parents you may ultimately achieve Release by the Sword, and transcend to the realm of the Immortals. Good fortune beyond measure will be yours. You must always be careful to compare your own heart with those of others, so that you can commiserate with them. Never lose sight of your own compassion."

Lad-of-Heaven listened attentively, and promised to follow their advice.

It was evident to Zhao Lin and Wang Jin from the tone of their hosts that they expected this child to make remarkable progress, and felt certain that his future would be a bright one. They too added words of encouragement, assuring him of his ultimate success. Children all take delight in praise, and Lad-of-Heaven was no exception. He began to feel increasingly fond of Zhao and Wang.

CHAPTER 8

The Cave of Pearls

ONCE AGAIN ZHU MAN-TIGER FELT THE ODD MAN OUT. HE REMAINED enormously ashamed of his indiscretions, and was uncomfortably aware that Wei Lai in particular disliked him intensely. Soaring Cloud had whispered to both Wei and Ding Shao for a moment, after which they at least began to address him as 'Elder Brother' as they did Zhao and Wang, but there was little cordiality in their manner. Zhu also feared the uncanny powers of the Miao women, and was apprehensive about his chances of escaping them. He had found the child's face and general appearance strange, and at table had been startled to see him devouring his food like a starved wolf. He could not restrain himself from looking at the boy every now and then. At first Lad-of-Heaven paid little heed, thoroughly absorbed in the satiation of his tremendous appetite, but soon he concluded that these covert glances were a sign of Zhu's contempt, and was secretly displeased. Afterwards his dislike of Zhu lessened somewhat, but he felt little fondness toward him. While the others were urging the boy to curb his impatience and remain calm, Zhu too chimed in once or twice, but Lad-of-Heaven ignored him. Somewhat disgruntled, Man-Tiger rose and walked over to gaze out over the scenery outside the pavilion.

Upon his arrival Zhu had been too absorbed in eating, drinking, and listening to the conversation to pay much attention to his surroundings, and had only a general impression of the magnificence of the scenery. Now, as he looked about in all directions, he discovered that the setting was pure and unearthly, little different from an actual paradise of the Immortals. The lake was confined on every side by cliffs and crags, rather unlike Willow Lake, which lay amid thousands of acres of gentle fields, meadows, and flowering trees. At first glance this lake seemed somewhat smaller, but as he gazed at it he was no longer sure. Its surface was wide enough that the waves on it built up considerable force by the time they finally crashed upon the rocks below him. The waters seemed cleaner and deeper than those of Willow Lake, and there was no doubt that they were less calm.

The surrounding crags looked like the walls of a vast roofless fortress, its top open to the sky, protecting a great liquid mirror. From the waters at the lake's exact centre the island on which he stood leaped aloft, an equal amount of water and cliffs on every side. The rocks of the isle itself were covered with moss and a profusion of peculiar flowers and exotic foliage. Here and there stood groves of graceful trees. Zhu went to each side of the building in turn to lean out and gaze into the distance. In every direction the brightly coloured glow of flowers lit his eyes, and light reflected from fragrant herbs and grasses, waving softly in long halcyon streams, bathed his face in green. Every now and then a mild breeze would sigh past him, bearing a rare perfume that brushed pleasantly past his nose. The clean exotic beauty of the landscape restored his spirits, and he felt himself transported away from the world of men into the realm of the Immortals. He stood transfixed, enraptured by the indescribable natural beauty around him.

As he stood enchanted, leaning on the rail at the edge of the building and gazing outward, he noticed the Emerald Distentor and the Linked Culmen flying swiftly through the air, skimming just over the waves. They circled the building, and alighted near the entrance. He heard Zhao Lin call to him: "Where are you, Second Brother?"

Zhu shouted in response, and hastened to rejoin the others. Wei Lai was scolding the Linked Culmen.

"And where do you think *you're* going? Even I have not been permitted to go along!"

"Why don't you let the silly creature go too?" laughed Ding Shao. "Emerald can expand himself to carry you all, but the stretch of tunnel by the exit has many sharp turns. How could he ever squeeze all five of you through at once? Remember that he remains faithful to the orders given to him by Lad-of-Heaven's mother before she died, and won't leave the boy even when there is no danger. If Lad-of-Heaven does not return with you, how will you convey our guests home? Why not let Snowy accompany you, and divide the passengers between the two beasts?"

"I am not exactly forbidding him to go," said Soaring Cloud. "It's just that Brother Lai insisted on feeding it some of the potent cinnabar the Old One gave me because he felt sorry for its wounds. I'm afraid the Old One will detect this and be displeased."

"Since when have we been able to keep anything from the Old One?" said Wei Lai. "Do you think that he doesn't already know? Mistress has probably told him."

"Maybe so," laughed Soaring Cloud. "But I would prefer that he not see it himself. I suspect that you weren't invited to go with us precisely because the Old One is displeased by your lack of zeal and ambition, and doesn't particularly wish to see you. Perhaps Third Elder Brother has been excluded because of his close association with you."

"That's not necessarily the case," Ding Shao objected. "The Old One has always been fond of our younger generation, particularly the three of us. When the mood takes him he has frequently invited the lot of us to his house, or had one or two over for many hours at a time. You know as well as I that the real reason we can't go there whenever we wish is because Mistress doesn't want us to interrupt our training. She's also afraid that we'll become too familiar with the Old One's children, and band together to leave the mountain and stir up trouble. Our Master hasn't yet returned from the South-End Mountains, and if we run into trouble of the sort we did last time, the Old One would have to come out himself and rescue us. Mistress has been close friends with the Old

One and his wife for years. The last thing she wants is to cause trouble for them. Today is certainly the first time the Old One himself has given any indication that he didn't want us to visit. I suspect Sixth Brother was up to his usual tricks, and was planning to sneak off and go adventuring with Younger Brother here. The Old One must have known what he was planning, and put a stop to it by keeping Brother Lai away. Remember also those two other friends of ours who are coming to visit the Old One today."

Wei Lai stood up, looking as though he had something important on his mind.

"It is already the Hour of the Monkey," he announced. "There are a few things I have to do, so I must leave first."

"Ha!" laughed Soaring Cloud. "I knew something was afoot!"

"Hey!" Ding Shao interrupted. He was looking down toward the entrance of the building. "Sister Cloud! Snowy's angry because you won't let him go, and he's getting ready to vent his frustration on Emerald! If you don't let him go along, we'll have a nasty fight on our hands!"

Soaring Cloud went over to the railing and looked out. Wei Lai slipped quietly away. The two beasts below had faced off against each other in threatening postures. Beams of golden and emerald light flashed between glaring mutant eyes. Fearing discovery and punishment by their masters, neither had uttered a sound, but their attitude was one of menace and ferocity.

The child Lad-of-Heaven charged straight toward the railing, shrieking at the top of his lungs. "You little two-headed white dog! How dare you bully my Big Green Brother! I'll squeeze you to death!"

Soaring Cloud caught him before he reached the edge, and scolded him with feigned anger.

"Look at you! You're just as crazy and impatient as ever! I do believe I really will not love you any more!"

"But Green Brother is afraid of him!" the child wailed, his eyes fixed on the Linked Culmen. "I won't squeeze the white one if you make him stop!"

"Snowy!" Soaring Cloud barked. "Stop it! I'll take you along, don't worry! The two of you must be friends from now on! If not, see what happens if I catch you fighting again! Just this morning we told you to be friends, and you both promised. It's been less than a day! Have you already forgotten?"

Both beasts veiled their eyes, and their fur, which had been standing on end, relaxed and fell flat. By the time Soaring Cloud had finished speaking, they were leaning against each other, crooning affectionately.

In a flash Lad-of-Heaven's fury gave way to joy.

"Look!" he whooped. "They were just pretending to fight! They tricked us, because they both wanted Big Sister to let Snowy go along! They made me get angry for nothing!"

"It just goes to show that you should never be impatient," scolded Soaring Cloud. "If you had done something foolish and hurt him, it would have been wrong of you. It would have been even worse if you had annoyed him and got yourself hurt as well. Remember not to be so hasty next time!"

"Don't be angry, Big Sister!" said Lad-of-Heaven. "I won't do it again!"

Soaring Cloud summoned the two animals up beside them. She herself, holding Lad-of-Heaven in her arms, climbed on the Distentor's neck, and directed Wang Jin to sit on its rump. Zhao and Zhu she instructed to mount the Linked Culmen. They saluted to Ding Shao in farewell, and Soaring Cloud directed the Linked Culmen to lead the way.

"Snowy, you have been through the watery tunnel before with the smaller Elder Cousin. When we reach the far end, I'll point out our new direction. We won't be flying over the ridge because I don't care to meet any more of those animals."

The Linked Culmen and the Distentor dropped off the edge of the building and swooped close to the water. Flying at a somewhat more leisurely pace than when they came, they made a turn to the right, and skimmed low over the waves toward the bottom of the cliff at the edge of the lake. There Zhao Lin saw a fissure in the rock, obscured by dangling vines and pine trees, next to a crag which jutted out sideways into the water. The fissure was twenty feet wide, and not very deep, narrower and harder to detect than the gateway through which they had entered the valley. Its sides were perfectly straight and clean, as though sliced out by the enchanted axe of the ancient giant Five-nail.

As they circled around the overlapping crag on one side of the fissure, the mouth of a cave within it came into view. The opening was thirty feet high, its lower portion submerged. Trees and vines covered it, hanging low into the water, partly concealing light which could be seen shining through from the interior. Zhao Lin, sitting the furthest to the front, found it odd that the daylight from the far side would penetrate the massive rock cliff.

The twin mouths of the Linked Culmen gaped wide, and the creature blew the vegetation hanging over the cave entrance to either side with a great gust of breath, allowing them to slip through the gap thus created. The passage within was the same size as the entrance, thirty feet high and twenty feet wide. It was far deeper than had been evident from the outside. It twisted and angled one way and another, and the beasts slowed to a leisurely glide. After several turns, they were well past the point where the daylight behind them could have penetrated, and yet the interior of the cavern was still suffused with light, revealing an underground realm of strange enchantment. The walls were streaked with moss in varying shades of green, and flowers, plants, baby pines, and other tiny contorted trees sprouted in great profusion from fissures in the rock. These vegetation-filled cracks twisted like green scaled serpents coiled to leap into the air. Innumerable stalactites formed a multitude of fantastic shapes; limestone ribbons and gem-encrusted curtains sparkled in a multihued canopy over their heads, drifting by in a never-ending succession of shifting patterns. The phantom illumination reflected green and gold from the walls and ceiling, spreading a shimmering sheen over the surface of the water, enhancing still further the mysterious beauty of the strange underground paradise. Try as they might, Zhao and his companions could not make out the source of the light. Seeing their puzzlement, Soaring Cloud spoke.

"What do you think of the view in this cave? Originally it was completely sealed off from the outside. Last spring there was an earthquake, and a part of the cliff wall fell away. Only then did we discover its existence. The brothers and sisters of the Li family went in to explore, and found it strangely beautiful, deep and secluded. The only thing they disliked was that it was pitch dark, blacker than the deepest night. The method they used to light it has a strange story behind it.

"MANY YEARS AGO, THE OLD ONE IN GREEN'S WANDERINGS LED HIM to the county of Putuo on the northern coast of Guangdong Province. He was accompanied by a friend, like himself a man of the Dao. As they stood idly on the beach, enjoying the pink clouds around the setting sun, there was a sudden disturbance out on the ocean. A violent squall blew up, and gigantic waves capsized hundreds of the fishing boats that had been tranquilly plying their nets. Strangely, in the distance both sky and sea were calm, with no sign of any storm. Fearing that this was no natural phenomenon, they hurried to render what aid they could. Beneath the waves they encountered a frightful monster of the sea. It was nearly two hundred feet in length, with hundreds of legs, like those of a centipede, growing down either side of its body. They made haste to kill it, and the disturbance subsided. The fishermen in the water were rescued, except for the few which had been devoured by the monster. The Old One and his companion, believing that the creature's corpse was full of blubber, had thoughts of dragging it up on the shore and extracting its oil, which the bereaved fishing families might put to good use. But they soon discovered that the creature was permeated with a horrible poison which no man could withstand. They decided to destroy the huge corpse, but feared that residual poisons would escape and contaminate the seawater, bringing death to the marine life of the region. They saw no alternative but to use their combined strength to drag the hideous mutant body to a large uninhabited island some distance out to sea. There they dismembered it with their Flying Swords and buried the pieces far underground, summoning up the True Fire to reduce what was left. Ordinary fire, they reasoned, might spring back to life from a spark after they had departed, and allow some of the deadly ash to escape.

"At that time the Old One's powers were not so great as they have since become. Little did he know that this unpremeditated deed would reap for him a great reward. Only later did he discover that this was one of the hideous mutant spawn of the Millenium Coldwind. The Coldwind was the most feared of all the monsters in the great Outer Ocean, dwelling in the strange luminous watery realm just outside the Circle of

Magnetic Glow at the Minor South Pole. Fortunately, the Coldwind is a mutation that has occurred only once in all the ages of the world. There is only that one, a female. She was born with a strong complement of the poisons and essences of uttermost Yin radiated by Heaven and Earth. Her malignant venoms were incomparably potent, the most concentrated poisons known.* The monster encountered by the Old One was spawned by her, and contrary to her habit she did not kill it after birth. It managed to escape from the Lesser South Pole, and eventually made its way to the coast of Guangdong. Barely a century after its birth it had already developed great powers and intelligence. Its entire body—skin, flesh, ligaments, and bones—was imbued with powerful magic forces. Hidden along its spine grew a vast quantity of luminous pearls of many different sizes and shapes. Although they were at that time unaware of how these might be used, the Old One and his friend retained these pearls.

"The mutant corpse was putrefying by the time they had dragged it to the island, but was still extremely dangerous. Natural prodigies of that sort are always permeated with foul fluids and slimes, replete with evil demonic energies. If they had used their Flying Swords to dismember it in the water, its reeking blood and body fluids would have flowed in all directions, posing a great menace. If they had used common fire to burn it, it would have emitted a lethal gas, scattering a hideous stench mingled with an exotic perfume. As this spread, it would attract demons, monsters, ogres, and other horrors to fight over the corpse. The mightiest human sorcerer in the world would have been hard pressed to fend off such a terrible onslaught. Had the odour penetrated as far as the Luminous Realm of the South Pole, it might have awakened the great old she-monster there, with grim consequences. Her offspring are all derived from embryonic impregnations by her own vital Cinnabar Energies, a process quite different from the reproduction of normal animals, and are imbued with elixirs of inestimable value. Thus she usually devours them not long after they are born for the potent energies they contain. If she too had left her lair in hopes of devouring the corpse, she would have touched off a cataclysm of unthinkable proportions.

"The Old One had no inkling of this, and merely feared that the fire would release acrid poisons into the winds and bring harm to living creatures within its influence. Fortunately, he and his companion took great care to establish a protected area tightly sealed by powerful spells, and dug a deep pit for the remains. A great tragedy was thus averted. They worked seven days and seven nights without rest before the task was complete. Not so much as a drop of the creature's bodily essences

* [This great female monster of the South Polar Luminous Realm is described in greater detail in the second *Swordsmen of the Sichuan Mountains* cycle, which tells how Golden Cicada and the rest of the Seven Short Men combined their strength to slay the dreaded Coldwind and open the great treasure house of the Luminous Realm.]

escaped. Only afterwards did they learn of the true nature of the monster from a more senior master of the Dao.

"When the job was done, they each came away with two bushels of luminous pearls. The Old One kept a fifth part of the largest for Daoist magic, and gave the rest to his children and disciples with orders to sell them, and donate the gold and silver thus obtained to the poor and needy. Even now some of this wealth remains to be distributed.

"He retained over a hundred of the largest pearls for his own use. These are objects of great potency, which repel venomous insects and snakes. Aside from the ten or so that he distributed among the rest of us, the others have all been set into the walls and ceiling of this cave. All of us joined in the task, which took quite some time, as we frequently had to experiment to find the best places to fix them. They shine from carefully concealed spots, situated so that their radiance is reflected to best advantage from the crystals and stalactites. You cannot see the pearls themselves unless you go up to the level of the ceiling and look very carefully."

HER VOICE FELL SILENT. THEIR MOUNTS GLIDED SLOWLY FORWARD, navigating the complex twists and sharp curves of the winding underground route. After some time the tunnel narrowed and slanted sharply upwards. The Linked Culmen shrank itself to a third the size it had been when they started, but still could barely avoid scraping the walls as it went by. They negotiated two sharp turns, and then flew out into the open air.

They had emerged over a small clear stream. The two beasts flew over the water and alighted on the opposite bank, then began to lope upstream at a leisurely pace.

The stream was wide and flat. Transparent waters, nowhere more than a few feet deep, flowed over a bed of pure white sand. Water plants waved in the current, and fish darted back and forth across the bottom. On the opposite bank, below the cliff from which they had emerged, was an unbroken line of peach and willow trees, which cast a luminous green shade on the ground below.

On the right bank, the one they were now following, was a level grove of a variety of trees, casting a soft shade over a lush carpet of artemisia and other fragrant herbs and grasses. Not a trace of dust or earth was visible. The scene was not as exotic as others on the mountain, but its clean and simple beauty was no less entrancing.

112

CHAPTER 9

The Immortal

THE TWO BEASTS, RESPONDING TO A SIGNAL FROM SOARING CLOUD, slowed their pace. The path led deep into a stand of giant bamboo. Ranks of stately emerald pillars extended along the bank of the stream. The bamboos were enormous, their trunks several inches wide, so tall they seemed to pierce the clouds. A gentle green glow of sunlight filtered through the leaves, lighting the faces of the company. Here and there on the surface of the stream were beautiful clusters of red and white lotuses, with stems a foot or more in length. The bamboos sighed and whistled in the breezes; the stream burbled and murmured. Zhao and his companions sat entranced by the pure and simple beauty of the setting, and the perfect harmony of natural music, waves of floral perfume, and halcyon canopy above. Beyond the grove massive cliffs and black mountain ridges formed an impressive backdrop, jutting fiercely into the sky.

They followed this path through the bamboo for nearly a mile. Lad-of-Heaven, riding in the rear on the Distentor, craned his neck and shouted, "Here comes Seventh Sister!"

"Make sure of who it is before you shout!" laughed Soaring Cloud. "That is Third Sister. She's not the one you met this morning."

As she spoke a girl dressed all in purple came into view on the bamboo-lined path ahead. She appeared to be about sixteen years of age, a little younger than Soaring Cloud. If anything, she was even more elegant and lovely. She carried a small garden hoe, from which hung a basket of flowers. As she approached them at a leisurely pace, Zhao and Zhu sensed at once that she was quite different from anyone they had yet encountered on the mountain.

Soaring Cloud called the two beasts to a halt, and walked forward to meet the girl, leading Lad-of-Heaven by the hand. She made introductions all around. The strange girl was Li Gentle-Wisdom, third child of the Old One.

"Collecting medicinal herbs, Third Elder Sister?" Soaring Cloud inquired.

"I am the victim of one of Sixth Brother's jokes," said Gentle-Wisdom. "He told me a magic dodder plant had matured on Flying Cloud Ridge, but it is obviously a ruse to get me out of the way."

"You haven't gone there yet. How do you know he wasn't telling the truth?"

"I don't have to go to know it isn't true. He loves weird plants and animals, and a magical dodder of the sort he described would be a rare and potent addition to his collection. If it were really as marvellous as he claimed, he would have gone up himself and spent night and day trying

113

capture it. Such a treasure would take precedence even if Cousins Hong and Ruan came to visit. No, it can only be because he is the only person besides myself capable of opening and closing the Dharma-spells guarding my house, the ones first set for me by the Grand Master Superior Moonbeam. My place is secluded, far from the Pavilion of Green Longevity where Father lives. Sixth Brother has probably made arrangements to use it as a meeting place where he can hatch secret plots. My guess is that he's going to meet that Devil-star of yours, Brother Lai. At first I was going to expose his little plot, but then I changed my mind. He is my little brother after all, so I ought to let him have his fun if it means so much to him. I even reduced the strength of the guardian spells around my place so that he will have an easier time getting in and out and replacing them when he leaves. I've never been as strict with him as Second Elder Sister is, which is why we have always been particularly close. He is a fine boy, really, despite his tricks. There are enough of us on hand to get him out of trouble, and Cousins Hong and Ruan are arriving today to visit. There are plenty of other plants to be found on Flying Cloud Ridge, including a huge clump of enchanted fungi with fat sclerotia, which Mother wants to make a fine liquor. I pretended to be taken in by his ruse, because I don't care to be involved if trouble comes of it. Second Sister would be displeased with me if she thought I acquiesced to this mischief. I spent the morning at my Brother's place before setting out for the Ridge. But why have you arrived so early?"

"Why do you say we are early?" said Soaring Cloud. "Sixth Elder Brother brought us the message that I was to come alone at the Hour of the Monkey with our honoured guests. I brought Lad-of-Heaven here because he is under my mother's care."

"Both you and Sixth Brother got it wrong," laughed Gentle-Wisdom. "He must have assumed that you would fly over the ridge, which would have taken longer, rather than using the shortcut through the cave, which these two remarkable beasts of yours can navigate with such ease.

"Our cousins Hong and Ruan should be arriving any moment now. Sixth Brother must have gone ahead to meet them and delay them for a while. My father is home and you can see him at once, but I think it best not to bring up your difficulties with the Miao sisters until Cousins Hong and Ruan are on hand. If you give them a brief account of the circumstances before you depart, they may be willing to intervene on your behalf, which would help your case considerably."

"If Sixth Brother has gone off to meet Brother Lai, then it is on account of this Miao business for sure," said Soaring Cloud. "But I don't see why they wanted to delay their rendezvous until after our two cousins visit the Old One."

"Sixth Brother frequently does the unexpected," said Gentle-Wisdom. "I know he is up to something, but not who he is going to meet. You must realize that Cousin Ruan never intervenes in any affair without first making a close investigation of the people involved, and he will want to meet our guests. If he receives a bad impression of someone, then he refuses to help, and no amount of persuasion will induce him to modify his opinion. If the enemy is unquestionably evil, he may bring misfortune upon the malefactor afterwards, but do nothing to help the victim in his hour of need. You must keep this in mind when you see him!

"I also heard Eldest Brother mention that the Dragon clan has grown immensely powerful in recent years. They have offered the many rare medicinal herbs growing on their mountain in exchange for various services from outsiders. In this way they have gradually accumulated a sizable force of deadly fighters, and are not to be taken lightly."

"You are as wise as your name suggests," Soaring Cloud sighed in admiration. "Prudent and meticulous in all things. When trouble strikes you have always formulated a complete strategy in advance; never do you lose the advantage in any conflict. I, on the other hand, am sloppy and careless, and always seem to fall short."

"And you are also prone to excess flattery!" laughed Gentle-Wisdom. "You may conduct our guests over at once, but remember, don't leave before cousins Hong and Ruan arrive. If possible, contrive it so that one of you, not one of you, brings up the subject of your difficulties. You may leave the beasts here. I will be getting along now; I must return as soon as possible. I too have business to discuss with Cousin Ruan."

She saluted politely to them in farewell, and continued downstream on her way through the bamboo forest.

As she spoke, Emerald uttered one clear cry and wagged his head in an almost human nod. Snowy chimed in as well. When Soaring Cloud ordered the beasts to wait where they were, Emerald did not object.

Not far ahead was an entrance to a deep valley, toward which the party now headed. Zhao Lin, observing the leisurely pace at which Gentle-Wisdom had left them, assumed that her destination was somewhere nearby. On questioning Soaring Cloud, however, he was astonished to learn that the ridge was not on the Mountain of Verdant Spots at all, but well over a hundred miles away.

"All the members of the Li family are masters of the sword arts of the Warrior-Immortals," she explained. "They have cultivated their powers over many lifetimes of dedicated training, and are now of great age. In their efforts to achieve the status of Celestial Immortals, they always pass on through Corpse Dissolution together. Their two associates Hong Jade-Sheen and Ruan the Pellucid, whom you will soon meet, have also been intimately associated with them over several lifetimes, particularly Ruan the Pellucid. He always incarnates into a family with the surname Ruan, keeps the same given name, and takes on the same aspect he had in the previous life. At present he is a youth seventeen years of age. He and Hong Jade-Sheen are of similar temperament, and are intimate companions. Both have cultivated great powers over lifetimes of training, and in each reincarnation their knowledge and faculties are fully developed right from birth. During childhood they are carefully protected from their enemies by their former masters and fellow disciples of previous incarnations.

"Since Ruan's physical form never changes, his many enemies, who hate him bitterly, have little trouble finding him. Out of fear that he might inadvertently lead his foes here and disturb the Old One's spiritual progress, he has no fixed abode, and with Hong cultivates the Dao while wandering in the world outside. To outsiders they mention only the master of their previous lifetime, never the name of the Old One. They come here every year or two to receive instructions from their master, and in doing so they shroud their coming and going in great secrecy. If they should happen to encounter him in the outside world, they pretend not to know him. The Old One and his family are nearing the end of their spiritual training, and have spent the last century in solitude on this mountain so that their practices will have the maximum effect. Any interruption at this critical juncture would be disastrous. Hence the entrance to the valley ahead is guarded by strong spells, which no outsider can penetrate.

"When you meet Hong and Ruan today, tell them of your problem if the opportunity presents itself. They will not neglect you if you are guests of the Old One. It would, however, be inappropriate to make any direct request of them. If they have any advice, they will communicate it to you.

"I am surprised that Emerald is willing to allow his young master to go on without him. This beast is intelligent and highly perceptive. I believe he recognized Gentle-Wisdom from previous incarnations, or perhaps had seen her when his former master was alive. He knows full well that this meeting with the Old One is crucial to the future of his young master."

Zhao Lin and his companions listened in wonder. They had by this time reached the entrance to the deep valley ahead. It was smaller than the other places they had seen that day, but far more strange and unearthly. It seemed to them that they had entered the realm of the Immortals. On either side shining green cliffs rose up into crags sweeping the clouds far above, enclosing a precinct of incomparable purity and seclusion. From the floor to the highest crags the valley was pure marble, its surface covered with green and white striations of varying shades, bending and coiling into a multitude of natural designs. Its surface was as smooth and shiny as jade, unsullied by dirt or dust, or any trace of moss and lichens. The only growing things were a few dwarf pines spurting in an airborne dance from the rock high on the cliffs above. The deep blue vault of the sky and dyed green stone encompassed an ancient realm of lofty and pristine splendour.

They followed the path along the valley around a few turns, until they came at last to a solitary peak standing like a gigantic tooth in the centre of the valley, a towering edifice of gemlike stone rising three hundred feet into the clouds. Like the valley in which it was encased, it was of pure marble, though even finer and more lustrous. Its surface was engraved with numerous secluded ravines and grottoes, the largest of which were fronted by shelves of level rock ten feet or so in width. A few of these grotto entrances had been artificially enlarged so that they opened wide and high, and on the shelves in front of them towers, pavilions, and estrades of solid marble had been constructed. Many of these had been carved directly out of the living stone of the peak in an ancient and vigorous style, each harmonizing perfectly with its setting. The crag had not a grain of dust or soil anywhere on it, and no vegetation grew that had not been planted.

As Zhao and his companions stared in wonder at this massive jade-like edifice, they became aware of the roar of a great torrent of water. They followed Soaring Cloud around the left side of the peak, and saw the source of the sound: a solid white band descending from a gully high in the green marble cliff opposite the peak, an immense dragon dancing, a bolt of lightning cloaked in shimmering mists and wreathed with crystal pearls in flight, thundering in violence as it plunged into a chasm hundreds of feet below. It was far larger than the one Zhao had seen in the moonlit valley the night before. The cliff was almost exactly twice the height of the marble peak, and the gully from which the water issued spanned a full hundred feet. Even at this distance they felt its icy coolness on their skin, a chill that set their hair on end.

Directly ahead the path came to an end. The only way forward was a steep stairway carved into the marble, leading up from the base of the peak beside them. It curved sharply upward, following the natural features of the rock, twisting and looping back and forth at frightening angles, finally reaching the summit three hundred feet above. They began the ascent. The steps were narrow, slippery, and steep, and a keen wind blew, but Zhao and his companions, relying on their Light-Body techniques, had little difficulty. Lad-of-Heaven, with his small stature and short legs, was forced to leap from step to step. This proved no handicap for him, however; his unusual strength and light build allowed him to hop upward with the easy agility of a small bird. Finally Soaring Cloud, fearing that he might slip into the deep pool at the bottom of the gorge beside them, snatched him and held him until Zhao and the others moved ahead of her, then carried him the rest of the way.

The three men, applying their Breath-Lifting techniques to good effect, made excellent progress as they wound their way around the various outcroppings and gullies in the smooth marble surface. After several sharp curves, they glanced back, and discovered that Soaring Cloud and Lad-of-Heaven were no longer behind them. They began to wonder what they would do when they arrived at their destination with no one accompanying them, but then heard a shout above their heads.

"The way to the Pavilion of Green Longevity is beside you! You've started on the wrong path, which leads to the summit!"

They looked up. Not far to one side were seven or eight steps carved tightly into the nearly vertical rock, steep and sharply slanted. At the top stood Soaring Cloud, laughing and talking with a girl sixteen or seventeen years of age, dressed in a shimmering white garment of cicada-wing gauze. Lad-of-Heaven was nowhere to be seen. The other girl was just as lovely as Gentle-Wisdom had been, and in fact looked so much like her, except for the colour of her clothes, that they might have thought it was Gentle-Wisdom herself already gone and returned.

Zhao and his companions changed their course. So steep were the marble steps at that point that they could see absolutely nothing of what lay above. When they had clambered up this last precarious stretch and looked about them, they cried out in surprise.

They stood on a shelf of pure white marble midway between the valley floor and the peak. It was not large, less than half an acre in size. Its surface was as smooth and polished as a mirror. So clear were their reflections in the fine and perfect stone that they could distinguish every hair on their heads. Behind the shelf towered the top half of the peak, and opposite it loomed the green marble cliff with the dragon waterfall plunging down into the ravine below. Although there was no trace of soil on the flat marble surface, to left and right stood over a hundred bright green bamboos, unlike any they had ever seen before. Their colour was the purest emerald, and they grew uncommonly tall and slender, stabbing straight up as though to pierce the mists above. Their halcyon branches whistled and tinkled gently in the wind, in musical harmony with trickling springs and pines soughing on the cliff.

Two huge and ancient pines grew from the marble face above the shelf. One erupted like a huge mutant python from a tangled mass of intertwined roots five or six spans in diameter. It coiled and squirmed with great energy, seemingly prepared to rise up and strike an enemy directly in front of it, its strength gathered and ready to be unleashed, but as yet held in check. The second tree leaped directly out of a fissure in the rock, then stretched upward across the rock face for twenty or thirty feet like a dragon lazily extending itself, only to double back and curl downward once again in an attitude of languid comfort. The needles on both trees were slender and long, growing thickly on a profusion of branches to form a dense canopy above.

Just below the cliff was a pavilion built of bamboo, tall and spacious, roof thatched with huge iridescent feathers shimmering green and gold in the sunlight. They were too long and broad to be the tail feathers of any peacock or pheasant, and were unlike the plumage of any bird Zhao could identify. Beside the pavilion was an enormous tree peony over twenty feet high, with massive trunk and enormous flowers the size of water basins, well over a foot in diameter. These blossomed in several soft hues, purple, silver, and crimson, amid the dark green leaves. Each was in full bloom, displaying an astounding profusion of multi-layered petals. The whole tree presented an auroral tapestry that seemed more a many-coloured illusion than reality, its shimmering hues filling the air with an enchanting fragrance. It was well past the season for peonies, and the three men wondered why this tree was still blooming with such glorious vitality.

Zhao Lin, peering into the pavilion, saw a man and woman seated within. Lad-of-Heaven knelt before them. The woman had the aspect of a married lady in her twenties. The man was none other than the Wanderer in Green they had befriended the year before. These two were in earnest conversation with the child. Zhao hastily beckoned to Zhu and Wang, and straightened his cap and clothes.

Soaring Cloud introduced the young girl, whom she identified as Seventh Elder Sister, named Li the Just, and presented Zhao and his companions to her. They exchanged polite greetings.

"My father is now eagerly waiting to meet our honoured guests," said Li the Just, motioning them toward the pavilion.

As she spoke, the Old One in Green stepped out to meet them. The three hurried forward, intending to kneel at his feet. The old man spoke, making an almost imperceptible motion with his hand.

"Our friendship was never burdened with such ceremony before," he said. "Why do you suddenly insist on these vulgar gestures?"

As his hand moved, Zhao and his companions were held by an unseen force which prevented them from bowing down, no matter how they tried. Soaring Cloud signalled to Zhao that a simple salute would suffice, and they complied. The Old One responded with a similar gesture, and waved them into the pavilion. He indicated the young married woman.

"I would like to present to you Madame Zhu, née Chen, at whose home you rested last night," he said. "There is no need for modesty; ordinary manners will suffice. Please be seated, and we shall talk."

Zhao and his companions, respecting the Old One's casual regard for ceremony, saluted the woman politely and seated themselves. Soaring Cloud also entered, bowed to the Old One, and whispered briefly to the young woman, who was her mother. Then she and Li the Just went out to enjoy the flowers.

Lad-of-Heaven was still kneeling abjectly on the floor.

"You gain nothing by kneeling in such a fashion," said the Old One with a smile. "I am not destined to be your teacher; there is no karmic affinity between us. Sixth Brother too must go forth into the world to seek his own master, and is in no position to take you as his student. The master I have promised to find for you is more powerful than I, and is furthermore better suited to your own character and temperament. His home is not far from the lair of your enemies, an added convenience. That makes a total of three advantages over me. Your impatience is quite useless."

"Didn't you say that this teacher is on the Isle of Earth and Wood, dear Master?" said Lad-of-Heaven in a tearful quaver. "That is so dreadfully far away."

"You need not address me as 'Master' if you are not my student," said the Old One. "As for your enemies, they came from beyond the sea. Fearful of discovery, he wove a mask with sorcery to create a false aspect when he struck. Your mother penetrated this disguise, but did

119

not tell your Numinous Distentor, fearing that it might abandon you in its impatience for revenge, and hurl itself straight into the tiger's mouth. Now that you are safe, you may tell the beast that their enemies are none other than the demonic sorcerers they encountered ten years ago while gathering medicinal herbs on the Isle of Black Sands. The Distentor will remember who they are."

Lad-of-Heaven bounded to his feet and rushed forward.

"Why, that's perfect!" he shouted. "So my enemies are there too! Please, call my teacher here right away, dear Master! Have him wield his Flying Sword for me to watch! If he is not as powerful as you, I don't want to be his student! I've never seen your powers, but I've seen Sixth Brother's Flying Sword. You are his father, so you must be even stronger. My father and mother were always so much stronger than I was."

He sobbed once, and then made a fearful effort to suppress it, struggling as if trying to swallow a cow whole. The Old One and the young woman smiled kindly at these antics, and the old man took the boy's hand.

"It gives me great pleasure to see you display your feelings so openly and spontaneously," he said gently. "It is indeed lamentable that there is no karmic affinity between us.

"You must remember that it is the rule for a student to go to his teacher, not the teacher to the student. It is not possible to have your master come here and await your convenience. If you do not have confidence in him as yet, then I advise you to be patient. Very soon two of my disciples are due to arrive, and I shall command them to conduct you to him. As for mastery of the Flying Sword, even these two fall far short of your teacher-to-be, my Companion in the Dao, Master Shang, Lord of the Isle of Earth and Wood. But my two disciples are stronger than the Sixth Brother you believe in so firmly. Compare them in this way, and you will have no difficulty. And please, you are not my student, so you must stop calling me 'Master.'"

"I'm only a child, so I don't know," said Lad-of-Heaven. "It was Big Sister who told me to call you that. What should I call you?"

The young woman smiled at him. "The Old One is a close friend of your teacher, so you may address him as 'Master-Uncle'."

"Nice Master-Uncle!" said the boy. "And what should I call the two who are coming to take me there?"

"They are my students," said the Old One. "One is surnamed Hong, and the other Ruan. You may address them as 'Elder Cousin'."

"Master-Uncle, you do have disciples then," the child said forlornly. "And you've taught them such great powers. But you say we have no karmic bond, and that you won't take me. If you just let me stay with you, I will speak only sweet words, and do everything I am told. When all my Brothers and Sisters see how good I am, they will come along and help me get revenge. How wonderful that would be!"

The child was deeply disappointed. The young woman drew him over to her, and comforted him with kind words.

Zhao Lin and his companions, mindful of the true powers and status of the Old One, waited in respectful silence while all this transpired. Then at last the Old One turned to them with a smile.

"The three of you have travelled a long distance to visit, and had the misfortune to arrive when we were preoccupied with other business. I was unable to send any of my children to meet you, so it is truly my fault that you ended up by mistake in Square-Bamboo Gorge. Though you have now been rescued and are resting in comfort and safety, I am sure that you have suffered more than enough danger and fright. You have endured much on my account, for which I must make amends.

"Masters Zhao and Wang, I know of your yearning for the Dao, and what it is that you have come here to seek from me. I regret that our karmic bond is one of friendship, not teacher and student. I have just now spoken with Madame Zhu. Her husband, my Companion-in-the-Dao Master Zhu, is now cultivating spiritual purity on the South-End Mountains in the North. He has accepted many disciples. He aspires to the free and easy roaming existence of the Immortals, but is as yet unwilling to take his place among the Immortals of the heavens. Practising the Dao under him will enable you to bypass many of the troubles and difficulties you would have had to undergo had you studied with me. In a moment I shall supply you with a letter of introduction. With this letter and my poor influence, you will be well received wherever you might wish to go. In addition, I shall give each of you three cinnabar pills. Even if you never retire to a mountain to study the Dao, these will greatly lengthen your span of life. With these tokens, it is my hope that your arduous journey here will not have been made in vain."

They hastened to express their heartfelt thanks.

Zhu Man-Tiger had not understood that both Zhao and Wang had been secretly yearning and praying for what the Old One was now offering them. He began to realize that he was face to face with a true Immortal, and that a rare and wonderful opportunity was passing him by. From the Old One's words it was plain that Zhao and Wang were to be introduced to an Immortal master, and that he alone was not. Unhappy and grieved, he thought of entreating the Old One, but he recalled that Soaring Cloud and Ding Shao had indicated that Zhao Lin was to act as spokesman for the three of them. Also, the Old One had already intimated that he would not be able to assent to any further request any of them might make, so the only result could be embarrassment for Zhu in front of all. Also, he was restrained by the old man's serene and abstracted air, which left him too awed and respectful to speak out. He hesitated, and the opportunity was lost; the Old One said something about writing a letter and disappeared into the bamboo grove outside.

Zhao Lin turned to the young woman sitting with them. She appeared to be only twenty-three or twenty-four years old. Her face was refined and beautiful, her bearing graceful and elegant. He knew that she was Soaring Cloud's mother, and the wife of his future master. They had greeted her with a formal bow a few minutes before, but had not had the opportunity to thank her for saving their lives. With Zhao taking the lead, the three of them bowed formally once again, and expressed their profound gratitude. Zhao and Wang both addressed her as 'Mistress'.

Graceful-Equity treated them with an air of great modesty. Although they had not yet been formally accepted as her husband's disciples, she responded by rising to her feet and making a half bow. Zhao Lin took the opportunity to confess to having mistakenly drunk some of the Stone Milk.

"I believe this was destined to happen," she said. "You and Esquire Wang Jin will be going to my husband on the South-End Mountains, and will from that time be as members of our family. There is no need to be so contrite! The Numinous Stone Milk is in any case nowhere near as valuable as the extracts of thousand-year-old bice or other rare minerals in potency."

Lad-of-Heaven pulled at her hand, and began jumping up and down. "What Numinous Stone Milk? Can I have a little too, Mother? It was so easy for *them* to find a teacher."

Graceful-Equity smiled at him. "They are in the same situation as you, are they not? They are being introduced to another teacher elsewhere for study. Even for this you are jealous! Anyway, the Numinous Milk at the Isle of Earth and Wood is very much better than mine."

"Brother Zhao and his friends can learn the Dao with you at your place," said Lad-of-Heaven. "But when will I get to see you? Where are those two elder cousins that are supposed to be coming? If I have to leave today, I won't be able to see you when you fight with the Miao ladies and catch the big monkeys."

As the child spoke, a thundering roar became audible, approaching them through the sky far above. Outside Soaring Cloud and Li the Just burst into laughter.

"Here they are now! Don't be so impatient!"

Zhao and his companions looked out of the pavilion. There, coming across the sky from the southeast, came two streaks of light, one golden, one red. They moved with the speed of thunderbolts, spanning the sky like a huge rainbow, and descended toward the ground in front of the pavilion.

III

Astride a crane, the brave squires are escorted off;
one takes pity on the pretty maiden in her mortal struggle;
penetrating the grove they go off with a friend;
passing through distant mountain passes,
they pay a call on a god of the Immortals.

CHAPTER 10

Flight Under Cover

LAD-OF-HEAVEN LEAPED UP AND DOWN AND SHRIEKED WITH delight: "Look how good they are!" Barely an instant later two men flashed into view outside, and strode into the pavilion.

Both were of youthful aspect. One was dressed in rustic garments of yellow linen. He seemed not much over twenty years old. He was not tall, and quite chubby. He had an old leather sack tied to his belt, but bore no weapon. He seemed unusually energetic, and had about him an air of scholarly refinement, but otherwise was not particularly impressive to look at.

His companion seemed only sixteen or seventeen years of age. He was tall, handsome and elegant, his skin white as jade. He had phoenix-like eyes, in which double pupils* gleamed like stars, concealing great hidden power. He wore a garment of green silk gauze. Strapped to his waist were a long sword and a long thin leather sack; on his left hand he wore two rings of iron. An undeniable heroic flair was reflected in his bearing.

As these two entered the pavilion they knelt down before Chen Graceful-Equity. By this time Soaring Cloud and Li the Just had also hurried in, and greetings were exchanged all around. Zhao and his friends had already guessed that the pair were Hong and Ruan, the two disciples of the Old One they had heard spoken of before.

Lad-of-Heaven rushed up to the pair, and seized their hands.

"Master won't accept me as his student," he shouted. "He said that when you two Elder Cousins arrived you would take me to the Isle of Earth and Wood to meet my new teacher. He said my new teacher is even more powerful than either of you two Elder Cousins. Is this true?"

Ruan the Pellucid, the tall and elegant one, burst into great laughter, pleased by the boy's innocence and intelligence.

"The two masters Shang on the Isle of Earth and Wood have been adepts at the Dao for many years," he said. "Their magic is indeed very great, though it is not quite the same type as we have been studying. For someone of your gifts and temperament, having either of them as your teacher would be a great blessing."

"Then take me there, Elder Cousin!" shouted Lad-of-Heaven, thoroughly delighted.

Both Hong and Ruan burst out laughing.

---

* [In Chinese traditional physiognomy, double pupils were a characteristic found in certain unusual men, such as the great general Xiang Yu, or sometimes in those destined for immortality.]

"Why the hurry?" said Ruan. "We've only just arrived. Surely you can't expect us to take you right now, before we've seen our Master or Mistress, or any of our older and younger cousins! Your enemies are dangerous! If you want to avenge your parents, you must undergo at least ten years' training. One or two days' delay now will make no difference!"

"I wanted Master Uncle, you two Elder Cousins, and Sixth Elder Brother to be my teachers," said Lad-of-Heaven, growing anxious once again.

"If you learn with us it will take even longer," said Ruan the Pellucid.

Lad-of-Heaven stood in dejected silence.

Li the Just laughed. "Perhaps your master will take pity on you and take revenge on your behalf. If so, it could be much sooner."

Lad-of-Heaven was delighted for a moment, but then his face fell once more. "I wouldn't want that," he said dejectedly. "Before my mother became an Immortal she commanded me to strike with my own hand."

"That I fear will be difficult," said Soaring Cloud.

"When Master Uncle finishes writing his letter and comes out, surely he will tell you Elder Cousins to take me off right away," said Lad-of-Heaven. "I will miss all of the excitement when the Flower Ladies come to take Zhu away, and Big Brothers Zhao and Wang refuse and fight with them. But I suppose it is more important to learn the Flying Sword and get revenge."

"What nonsense are you talking?" said Soaring Cloud angrily.

"Oh dear!" said Lad-of-Heaven hastily. "I made a mistake! I wasn't supposed to talk about it in front of the fellow Zhu!"

Man-Tiger knew that the child was innocently repeating what Soaring Cloud and the others had said, and once more was overcome by shame.

Zhao Lin, worried for Man-Tiger's sake, was moved to mention their predicament. But Soaring Cloud signalled to him, glancing over at Hong and Ruan and shaking her head slightly. The two young men must already know about the whole affair, and perhaps had agreed to offer assistance.

The Old One emerged from the bamboo grove. Hong and Ruan immediately went forward to bow to him, addressing him as 'Dear Master'.

"Your Mistress is in the cave with the rest of them smelting mineral elixirs, so she cannot come out to greet you," said the old man, with a happy smile. "She is eager to see you, so why not go directly in?" He turned to Graceful-Equity. "Madam Zhu, my wife invites you in as well."

Graceful-Equity rose and entered the bamboo grove, accompanied by Soaring Cloud, Li the Just, and Lad-of-Heaven.

The Old One produced the cinnabar pills he had promised, and divided them equally among Zhao and his companions. He handed the letter he had written to Zhao Lin, who tucked it safely away.

"My Dao-Brother Zhu is an affable man," said the Old One. "When the two of you go this time you will certainly receive Registers from him.* I regret that my rustic mountain dwelling here is ill-equipped to offer you hospitality. The cave is cold and bare, and we cannot provide enough beds. But over at Madam Zhu's home they have accommodation for many students and their dependents, and their cooking fires never go out. You are already staying there anyway, and have met both mother and daughter. I have some business to discuss with my wild and unworthy younger ones, and so cannot keep you company for the time being. My third little daughter, who has just returned, has given the two intelligent beasts clear instructions to bear you back to Madam Zhu's home. I will have someone see you out of the valley."

The three of them bowed in gratitude. As they did so, a shimmering silver cloud entered the pavilion and vanished, revealing the boy Li Hong they had seen back at the lake. He rushed up to the Old One, calling him 'Father'.

"You always start moving around when you've been sitting still too long, don't you, Little Hong?" said the Old One fondly. "You must be up to some mischief!"

"No, it has nothing to do with that," laughed Li Hong. "Where's Mother? Why won't she come out?"

"Your mother is in the rear cavern smelting mineral elixirs. Everyone else is in there too. You've come at a good moment. The stairway down the peak is a difficult climb. Why don't you take our guests to the valley entrance for me?"

The boy readily assented, and the Old One rose to his feet. The three of them knew that they could stay no longer, and bowed to him in farewell. The Old One saluted them politely and walked away. The three of them greeted Li Hong with some relief, addressing him as 'Sixth Elder Brother'. Li Hong seemed delighted at their courtesy.

"Let's go!" he said, smiling happily. He waved his hand, and they felt themselves suddenly snatched into the air. A silver cloud flickered and blazed around them, so bright that they saw spots before their eyes. An icy chill penetrated their skin and scalps. They heard the roar of a great wind gusting by, though they felt nothing. In a flash their feet touched earth. They recovered their balance and looked around, and found themselves in the bamboo grove outside the valley.

The Numinous Distentor and the Linked Culmen had not strayed from the place they had left them. Li Hong instructed Wang and Zhu to mount Snowy. Then he turned to Zhao Lin, smiling merrily.

* [The initiation rites into the secrets of Daoism included the transferral of 'Registers' from master to disciple, sacred texts of divine potency which detailed the techniques or practices being transmitted. The disciple acquired new registers at each stage in his or her training.]

"I've already ridden on Snowy," he said. "I hear that Emerald is very intelligent. Why don't I accompany you all the way over the ridge, so I can try him out?"

Emerald raised his head and uttered a low-pitched growl of protest. A frightful scowl contorted Li Hong's chubby red-lipped face, and he glared balefully at the creature.

"You mutant spawn!" he barked. "My Third Elder Sister has already explained everything to you! What do you mean by this stubbornness? I had hoped to spare you this embarrassment. Do you want something unpleasant to happen to you? Do you think I can't handle you?"

As the boy spoke, Emerald shook his head repeatedly.

"Ah, I see," said Li Hong, mollified. "You just want to find out about your young master, don't you? I'll whisper it all to you." His small mouth began moving, and the Distentor nodded and rumbled in response, its attitude one of affectionate submission. "Now you know why he can't come along, and who I am. Let's be on our way!"

Li Hong tugged at Zhao Lin, and they climbed on the Distentor's back, with the boy in front. Rather than following their previous route, the two beasts mounted straight into the sky. Zhao, worried about their difficulties with the Miao women, could not restrain himself from sliding forward to speak to him about it.

"You must know something of our predicament," Zhao said. "My brother Man-Tiger awoke after his illness with his wits addled, and got himself into trouble with those two Miao sisters. We have sworn brotherhood to the death, but I fear that our own strength is insufficient to resist them.

Li Hong hesitated for a moment, and then spoke. "Do not fear! When the time comes someone stronger than myself will be there to help you. Now I have seen your friend Zhu I know he is not really bad. He has a wife and child, and a mother as well, the poor fellow. I'll speak to Younger Brother Lai when we get there, and put in a good word for him.

"We could take you directly back to Willow Lake now, but I am afraid that the sisters might be able to track you down. You trade at Miao markets, and the Dragon clan, with all of their power and influence, could find your secret refuge with little trouble. The two sisters are masters of the deadly arts of the Flying Trident, and have control over all manner of animals and serpents. Sooner or later they would locate you wherever you might be, with serious consequences. Far better to arrange a meeting with them as a ploy to reduce tensions for the moment, and give us time to think of a plan for dealing with them. Old Man Dragon's children are growing ever more numerous and unruly, and several of them have even sought out evil sorcerers as masters. I have the feeling that their family fortunes are soon to run out."

The Miao sisters were even more dangerous than Zhao had feared, but Li Hong was obviously reluctant to say more, and Zhao dared make no further inquiries. As he fretted anxiously, the two beasts flew over the ridge into the valley they had left that morning. Rather than heading toward the cave they had stayed in before, the beasts turned to the left, and moved toward a wide ledge at the midpoint of the cliff rushing up to meet them. They had a brief impression of a sizable villa on this ledge, surrounded by spacious arbours and lofty pavilions, with two terraced rice paddies on a slope below.

Ding Shao was waiting to meet them. Li Hong bade them farewell and flew off. Ding Shao conducted them into the house, where his wife Lin Lustrous-Gem emerged to greet them.

Their host treated them with great civility, but deflected all questions about the Miao sisters. He said only that there would be no trouble, and that all would be made clear on the following evening. But after a while he began to speak to them with an air of great seriousness.

"It is on our account that you three excellent guests have come to this mountain, and through no fault of your own you have encountered difficulty. Both you and the Miao sisters have refused to moderate your positions. The sisters have not responded to Sister Cloud's efforts to placate them, the best we can do at this point is to fulfil our obligation as hosts and keep you here in safety for a few more days. Once the Dragon sisters have departed, we can see you on your way as far as the region of Meng Hua, though it will be awkward for us to accompany you to the Grief-at-Toil Mountains. You must understand that we who have left the ordinary world of men cannot interfere in the marriage customs of others. The Dragon sisters are not acting out of malice. I deeply regret that we have no choice but to leave you three honourable guests to solve the problem in your own way after we part company."

Zhao Lin sat stunned, at a loss for words. Only Soaring Cloud had seemed truly willing to help, but she was no longer with them. Lustrous-Gem stood up and walked over by a window to fetch something. As she returned, her back to the window, she moved her eyes, apparently indicating something in the window. Zhao, thus alerted, glanced casually in that direction, and saw several points of gold and green light moving and flickering outside a crack in the window. Something strange was spying on them, and he understood why Ding Shao had spoken the way he had.

Zhao raised his voice.

"We three all have wives and children of our own," he said. "My Second Brother Zhu awakened from his illness with mind confused, and jested with them in an improper manner without really knowing what he was doing. As for me, I have never spoken with the Dragon sisters, or even had a clear look at their faces. Marriage is a matter between willing parties, in which intimidation has no part. We had hoped that you would be able to render assistance in this difficulty, because we saw that the Miao sisters have power over exotic birds and beasts beyond our ability to resist. Unfortunately, though, Elder Sister Cloud and I have not seen eye to eye in our conversations since yesterday, and I fear she will not again honour us with her presence. Elder Brother Ding has now

128

made clear answer to the same effect. Since the Miao sisters are your close friends, it would be inappropriate of us three ignorant brothers to compel you to aid us. At dawn we shall bid you farewell, asking no more than that you grant us the kindness of escorting us far enough so that we do not lose our way. We three ignorant brothers are sworn to share all dangers unto the death. If necessary, I will meet knife or axe with my own body!"

Zhao kept his eye on his hosts to make certain that he did not say something wrong. Ding Shao sat with an icy smile on his face, but Zhao was relieved to see Lustrous-Gem, whose back was still to the window, smile and wink slightly in genuine warmth.

"You three excellent guests have only just recovered," said Lustrous-Gem. "You should rest and husband your strength. Our Mistress has asked that you not depart until we have made some medicines for you, which will be ready in three days' time. There is no need to be in such a hurry to leave!"

As she spoke she signalled again with her eyes, and the three of them accepted her invitation to stay with thanks, though were careful to maintain an expression of dissatisfaction on their faces.

After a short time they heard a gust of wind outside, and a faint whirring of wings. Ding Shao left his seat and slipped out, then returned wearing a smile of relief.

"Forgive us, Elder Brothers!" he said. "As you saw, we were unable to speak freely."

Lustrous-Gem, a woman tall and elegant with an intensity of gaze, was of strong and direct character.

"These barbarians are getting further and further out of line," she snorted to her husband. "This morning Sister Cloud said they were planning some devilry. After the Miao sisters left, they had the audacity to send the mutant spawn under their command to come and spy on us. I see no reason why such creatures should be allowed to live. It was only your timidity that prevented me from going out to finish them off as soon as they appeared!"

Ding Shao laughed. "You're quite right. Unlike the rest of you unpolished rustics, I believe in caution. All of you would rather act first and talk afterwards. What does it gain us to kill a pair of animals? The Miao sisters are constant and singleminded in their affections, and I for one feel rather sad for their plight."

"You and Cousin Wei Lai are alike," Lustrous-Gem retorted. "You both claim to be impressed by the constancy and singlemindedness of these women, but in fact, you are simply allowing yourselves to be titillated by something quite cheap and disgusting. I feel nothing but revulsion for people who fall head over heels in love at first sight, and declare their love to be true. If they were not even previously acquainted, from where does this affection spring? This so-called 'head over heels in love' is nothing more than infatuation and physical lust. Suppose one day you fell madly in love with an alluring female of stunning beauty. Then suppose that the next day she suddenly contracted a horrible disease, and her whole body was covered with pox, scabies, and ringworm, so thin her bones stuck out, her face the colour of clay, with an unpleasant odour. Strange indeed if you still felt yourself to be in love with her! But what if the same two people had been lovers for many years, and she had suffered such a tragedy when you were husband and wife? Would you feel disgust toward her then? Certainly not. Everyone takes pleasure in physical beauty. But unless two people are constantly in each other's company, going everywhere together, true love cannot grow. Unless they love and respect each other, and are able to forgive each other's faults, no bond will develop between them, and they will not have the sort of love that endures undiminished until death.

"But the Miao sisters, it seems, desire a man they have never before met as lifelong companion, and do not hesitate to resort to coercion to achieve their aims. What difference is there between that and the way you men so often force your lewd attentions on a woman? The novelty of it is that the Miao women are more forthright than a shy city girl. It's perfectly obvious to me that you are stirred to pity them because of their beauty.

"If we can think of a way to bring them to their senses without harming them, naturally that would be the best course. But what is all this talk of being so cautious about the results of our actions? If it were a pair of Miao men who were threatening violence to a woman, it would be strange indeed if you did not slay them outright!"

"No wonder I had to court you for so many years before you would consent to marry me!" Ding Shao laughed. "Now at last I understand your guiding principle!"

Lustrous-Gem's eyebrows rose, and her star-like eyes flashed dangerously. "Do you have more to say?"

Ding Shao's tone became more serious. "Since we do not intend open confrontation with the Miao, we must act in secret and with great caution. It may turn out that the best strategy will be to catch them by surprise by sending our guests off sometime tomorrow. In the meantime, I suggest you get as much rest as possible with us."

Zhao and his companions offered their thanks.

The following afternoon, Soaring Cloud and Wei Lai appeared, bringing along the two beasts. They announced that Lad-of-Heaven had already been sent on his way.

"In a short while a fog will rise," said Soaring Cloud. "We will escort you away under its cover. My mother is unfortunately occupied, so Elder Brothers Zhao and Wang need not worry about bidding her farewell. She looks forward to seeing you again the next time we meet."

Not a word was said about the Miao sisters. The affair evidently had been taken care of, so Zhao and his companions asked no questions. Ding Shao and his wife had prepared a farewell feast for them, which the company consumed with relish.

Not long afterwards, a dense fog appeared over the mountain and began to pour into the valley from all sides. Emerald and Snowy were waiting patiently outside, their bodies already expanded in preparation for flight.

"We insisted that Emerald remain here with us so that we could send you off," said Wei Lai. "The creature was naturally quite obstinate because of his loyalty to his young master. If the boy had not been given such a rare and marvellous opportunity, Emerald would never have agreed."

"Younger Cousin!" laughed Lustrous-Gem. "It is already getting dark. If you truly mean to avoid any conflict with the Miao sisters, you had best be off immediately, or your plan will fail, marvellous animals or not!"

"That's not quite the reason for what we are doing," said Soaring Cloud. "The Miao sisters are only exerting such coercion because they are hopelessly infatuated, not because they intend any harm. Certainly they have not been involved in the evil committed by Old Man Miao and his descendants in recent years.

"The Miao are always open and direct, so when the sisters departed they twice questioned us about our own intentions. Their suspicions had been aroused by Snowy and Emerald, whom they realized were capable of destroying any of their mutant beasts, and wondered if we intended to attack them. Also, I had reported failure in my mission as matchmaker. In answer I concocted a story about Lad-of-Heaven, whom they had seen, telling them that he was the adopted son of Shang Wu, Master of the Isle of Earth and Wood. I said that a friend had brought him to the mainland to visit an acquaintance, and had encountered and befriended the three of you along the way. I told them that one of you had been injured by the elixir venoms of a magical beast, and that my younger cousin and I had recognized the symptoms. Since we had effective medicines at home, we invited you here for treatment. We had kept Emerald here only to bear you home when you were recovered, and that you would shortly be leaving. I also said that Brother Lai and I would see you along a portion of your journey for your protection. This story seems to have allayed their suspicions, and will forestall trouble should you encounter them on the road."

Lustrous-Gem spoke. "Just yesterday I berated your Cousin Ding here for being partial toward the Miao sisters. Why is it that even you have now grown hesitant?"

Soaring Cloud whispered a few words into her ear. Lustrous-Gem appeared to disapprove, and shook her head several times.

"The mountain fog is now thick," said Ding Shao. "The time has come to convey you to the Peak of the Great Roc."

Zhao Lin and his companions thanked their hosts, and bade them farewell.

This time the three of them were to ride together on Emerald, with Soaring Cloud and Wei Lai accompanying them on Snowy. As they made ready to depart, Soaring Cloud explained the route to them.

"We will traverse the region of Meng Hua and the Southern Gorge, and from there take to the upper airs. Beyond the Dragon's Way there will be no more fog. We can take you as far as the Ridge of the Maiden Immortal in the Grief-at-Toil range before we must turn back. Not far past that is the Peak of the Great Roc. The crags and rocks below it are steep and dangerous, but we are permitted to proceed no further in that direction, so it is there that we must part. There is a mountain trail there overlooking the Yuan River, which offers the sole route to your Willow Lake. It is high and dangerous, but is only used by a few Miao medicine peddlers. Perhaps you three have been along that route before."

Zhao Lin thought for a moment. "I have never gone to Great Roc Peak, but we used to travel along the Ridge of the Maiden Immortal quite frequently. From there it is only twenty miles or so through the mountains to the river stockade where we relay goods to the valley."

"Excellent!" said Wei Lai. "We will drop you off at the Peak of the Great Roc and bid you farewell. You must exercise caution, however. The route along the river may be an easy one, but unforeseen obstacles and difficulties may pose serious risk. The pills presented to you by the Old One are potent against all manner of afflictions, and may be ingested if need arises. You may hear unusual sounds along your way; if so you may safely ignore them and continue on.

"Sixth Brother said yesterday that he is very fond of Elder Brothers Zhao and Wang. He has given you each an ancient jade talisman, and Elder Brother Zhu a powerful paper charm. With these you need not fear malign influences or poisons of a more ordinary sort. Remember, you may continue peacefully on your way no matter what strange sounds and threatening disturbances you may hear around you.

"Sixth Elder Brother has a large collection of protective talismans, given to him by his masters and elders over many lifetimes of training and cultivation. These particular specimens were delivered to him only yesterday by Cousin Ruan from the home of one of his friends. Sixth Brother himself does not prize them, and hands them out almost casually to his friends, though only as tokens of affection and regard."

The three men thanked their hosts gratefully.

Lustrous-Gem laughed. "You're the one who invariably benefits the most when Sixth Elder Brother distributes his magic treasures," she said to Wei Lai. "No wonder you flatter him to his face and praise him behind his back! But enough talk! Don't start off too late!"

Wei Lai laughed merrily. "It's only natural that Sixth Elder Brother should treat me better. He did give me another pair of magic treasures, and I'll show them to you when we return. We can't leave, though, until I have explained the use of the charm and pendants. We have been joking so much that I haven't had a chance to instruct you in their use. If you chase us away now, Elder Sister Gem, and they don't learn how to use them properly, then Sixth Brother's generosity will have been in vain."

He turned to Zhu. "Elder Brother Zhu, I must tell you frankly that I had reservations about you, but Sixth Elder Brother has taken great pains to persuade me otherwise; let there be no further rancour between us! Sixth Elder Brother only had two of the jade pendants. Since Elder brothers Zhao and Wang will be traversing the mountains to seek their teacher, they will have great need of them in times to come. You are a family man, in danger only through this current crisis. This paper charm has been carefully copied from primordial Immortal writings in the celestial realm of Supreme Clarity. Carry it on your person at all times, but use it only in case of great need. Once burned, its magic will last only two or three days, but is of much greater potency than that of the jade pendants. It is thus perfectly suited to your present need. Do not be tempted to trade these treasures back and forth once you have returned home to your mountain. Sixth Brother has provided for each according to your needs, and the nature of his gifts reflects this."

He then proceeded to reveal the method of activating each periapt, and they made ready to depart.

THIS TIME THE TWO BEASTS BORE THEM TO A FAR GREATER HEIGHT than previously. At first the sky was clear, the full moon bathing the ridges and gullies around them with a bluish light almost as bright as day. But then they crossed the ridge bordering the valley, and as they stared at the dark chasm and precipitous cliffs of Square-Bamboo Gorge where they had nearly been killed two days before, they plunged abruptly into the oncoming wall of dense fog. They found themselves in an opaque mass of darkness, relieved only by the glow flickering like lightning from the eyes of the two flying beasts. A fierce wind swept against their faces with such force that they could hardly breathe, and a constant roar thundered against their ears.

After a time the two animals rumbled quietly to one another, and the light from their eyes was abruptly veiled. Their speed increased still further. They plunged on through the inky blackness for a span of two hours, the three men enduring the constant stifling pressure of the chill and clammy air. Then at last they dipped suddenly downward, and the fog began to thin. The stars and moon gradually came into view, shining indistinctly through the mists ahead. Then they burst forth from a great mountain of cloud into the full splendour of the night sky.

They looked about them. Mountains, rivers, and forests spread out with crystal clarity far below; an immense jade vault of midnight blue stretched above. Behind them the great bank of dense fog pushed rapidly along against the wind; ahead all was clear. At that great height they seemed to be moving only very slowly. They recognized certain features of the terrain beneath their feet: River Outlook Station and the Ridge of Realm's Divide, two landmarks they had frequently passed before.

They descended and began to reduce their speed. They swept past the Peak of the Maiden Immortal at the level of its summit, but did not stop there. Soaring Cloud and Wei Lai now stood up on the back of the Linked Culmen and looked about with an air of tension. After a few moments, a weird peak came into view ahead. Astonishingly tall and steep, it towered far up into the moonlight out of a long ridge in the Grief-at-Toil Mountains. Its feet were carpeted in the great expanse of the tranquil forest surrounding it; the summit jutted out forward, and on either side two flat wide projections extended far over empty space. From a distance it looked like a gigantic strangely-formed bird, perched on a height, its wings outstretched to launch itself into the wind. Despite its massiveness, it looked almost alive. They guessed that this must be Great Roc Peak, the place where Soaring Cloud had said they would part.

Wei Lai in front of them uttered a sharp cry, and the two beasts descended toward the wide ridge below the peak. In the twinkling of an eye they had reached the ground, and at a word from Soaring Cloud they dismounted. Wei Lai addressed them.

"We have taken you as far as we are permitted," he said. "And in any case your excellent village at Willow Lake has long been removed from the world, and your laws bar entry to outsiders. Please forgive us for not taking you further. From here you have nearly thirty miles to go through deserted mountains and barbarian wastes, and obtaining food may prove somewhat inconvenient. We have prepared some coarse provisions for your journey, and would be honoured if you would accept them."

Three linen bags, each roughly two feet long, dropped to the ground beneath the Linked Culmen's belly where its strange mutant claw grew. Wei Lai lifted them up and passed them to Zhao and his companions, who accepted them with thanks.

"Everyone has a will and desires of his or her own," Soaring Cloud said to them. "Those who are not directly involved in an affair cannot force a resolution, and we are hampered because neither you nor the Dragon Miao sisters are willing to compromise. It is quite possible that you will find them waiting for you. Do not be afraid to speak plainly with them and explain your position. Somehow or other it will be resolved, though it would be best if both sides show a measure of flexibility. Dangerous animals and pests infest these mountains; exercise caution on the road ahead! I am truly sorry that we cannot conduct you any further. We will say good-bye for now, but will meet again before long."

Even as she spoke, Zhao and his companions thought they heard a sneering laugh from high up on the peak, putting their senses immediately on the alert. Each of them sensed that someone was spying on them from some hidden place. Soaring Cloud and Wei Lai continued to smile, seemingly unperturbed, though they exchanged glances. As the three men puzzled over what this portended, Wei Lai urged Soaring Cloud to hurry.

"Come, Elder Sister, our task is completed." He gave Zhao a meaningful look that Zhao was unable to interpret. As their hosts mounted the Culmen, Zhao and the others expressed their gratitude one last time. Wei Lai and Soaring Cloud saluted them in farewell, and ordered the beasts to depart. The three men stood forlornly in the moonlight as the animals rose into the sky and flew swiftly out of view.

CHAPTER 11

Savage Beasts

THE LIGHT AROUND THEM ABRUPTLY DARKENED. MAN-TIGER CRIED out in dismay; Zhao and Wang sprang quickly to either side and whirled about in fighting stance. A sudden harsh cry thundered in their ears, and a vast shadow with two glowing points of blue light swooped low over them. As it disappeared over the topmost branches of the nearby trees, they saw that it was an enormous mutant bird.

Zhao Lin knew that the Miao sisters were somewhere nearby, demonstrating their power in an attempt to intimidate them. He whispered a quick warning to Zhu and Wang to remain calm, and ignore any animals, snakes, or monsters unless they were actually attacked.

As they whispered together, there was a flicker of movement among the large trees ahead, and five huge tigers appeared. They were large as water buffaloes, with eyes gleaming malevolently beneath wide white foreheads. They padded slowly toward them, their long tails extended stiffly upward. The three men were little impressed; they had spent much time in the mountain wilds and captured or wounded many attacking tigers, though none as large and ferocious as these.

But then a massive rustling began all around them, and they turned to look. A tremendous host of tigers, panthers, bears, and savage beasts of every description had appeared on both sides and behind them. There were hundreds of them, crouched in stiff and threatening postures, glowing eyes all fixed hungrily on Zhao and his companions. There were far too many of them to fight off; they could neither advance nor retreat. Zhao, now thoroughly alarmed, thought desperately of a way to escape the trap.

The animals, seeing their quarry turning to look at them, gave voice to a terrible chorus of roars and growls. The sound echoed deafeningly off the cliffs all around, and a sudden wind blew up a great cloud of dust, partially obscuring the moon. It occurred to Zhao that a mob of such savage beasts, already stirred to a frenzy, might not obey the commands of their mistresses. Any provocation would be extremely dangerous.

The men stood still, not daring to move. But soon Zhao Lin noticed that the animals were not moving toward them. They growled without cease, but none was prepared to attack. The animals' purpose was clearly to intimidate them. By not moving the men only betrayed their own fear, so Zhao began to lead the way forward, ordering Zhu and Wang to keep a sharp lookout in all directions. The five tigers ahead were the largest and fiercest of the lot, but also the fewest in number. Anticipating a desperate battle if the tigers attempted to block their way, they called up reservoirs of strength and circulated energy through their bodies, all the time maintaining an appearance of easy calm.

The five tigers, however, padded slowly to either side before the men had reached the trees. There was a flurry of footsteps as the entire massive pack moved along with them, hemming them in on three sides. They kept in perfect pace with the men, the nearest of them no more than twenty feet away. This went on for some time, as the three wondered what the Miao women had in mind.

A sudden strange bellow and hiss erupted just off to the right, and they stopped dead in their tracks. A foul wind enveloped them, assailing their nostrils with the reek of carrion. Unable to retreat because of the dangerous predators stalking them from behind, the men leaped to the left, and turned to see what it was. In the trees above them coiled three black-scaled mutant pythons. They were enormous, the smallest of them over a foot in diameter and thirty feet long. The largest was easily fifty feet in length, so heavy that the tree in which it hung was bent almost double. The snakes had lunged as the men walked past. Their lust to feed was plain; huge blood-coloured mouths opened and closed, and forked tongues flickered in and out like crimson lightning. As the men stared, the serpent heads retreated back into the trees with incredible speed and agility. Their eyes glittered malevolently from the shadows as they kept their gazes fixed on the men, satisfied that their prey could not escape.

A great rustling and slithering began, and the trees all around shook. Leaves and broken branches fell like rain. The trees, rocks, and ground ahead were suddenly covered with pythons—smaller than the first three but still very large—along with enormous scorpions, centipedes, and other poisonous creatures. The least of these was over a foot in length. A bite or sting from any of them would bring a quick and inevitable death. Many spewed clouds of black vapour from their mouths, and the men soon found themselves surrounded by a noxious green mist.

They scanned the terrain around them. Circumstances did not seem to favour a bold advance as they had made a few moments before, particularly with the three mammoth pythons waiting to pounce as soon as they came within range.

The only possible avenue of escape seemed to be through the forest to their left, the direction in which the five tigers had now withdrawn. It did not seem to be far off their course. As long as the venomous creatures did not give chase, they could avoid them, and take the detour through the woods.

What the men did not realize was that the pythons had retreated into the trees because they were terrified of the jade pendants and the charm they bore. Had they but continued to press on as resolutely as before, the entire venomous swarm would have given way before them. The Miao sorceresses would then have concluded that they were being aided by powerful forces, and abandoned all thought of seizing them. Much trouble would thus have been avoided, even if the sisters' blind infatuation might have spurred them to resume their efforts at some

137

later date. But now the women were willing to risk their lives rather than let this opportunity pass.

Zhao and his companions went through the forest for a while, every now and then turning to look at the great pack of beasts that continued to stalk them. The snakes and other venomous creatures had stayed where they were. Since the three had managed to escape two traps with little difficulty, their confidence swelled. They chattered lightly as they walked along in a deliberate display of bravado. Unfortunately for them this complete lack of timidity only impressed their hidden adversaries all the more with their strength and courage. Their every word and move was under careful scrutiny.

They continued on for a while, laughing and talking to keep up their spirits. But before long they saw that the way ahead was growing steeper and more difficult. The five tigers had vanished; the disturbance behind them had abated. They looked around and discovered that the entire pack of beasts was gone.

Soon they came to a place three hundred feet from the cliff below the left wing of the Great Roc. To the left the way was blocked by a broad dark gully that had not previously been visible. On the other three sides a smooth slope rose, wide and only lightly forested. The trees were tall, but their slender trunks, with no branches or leaves below the height of twenty feet, afforded excellent visibility. Nowhere could the men see any sign of the animals, and they began to wonder why the great horde had been withdrawn. They could not fathom what their adversaries intended.

Zhu Man-Tiger laughed. "Well, from the look of things the Miao women have decided to let us pass. To tell you the truth, as far as beauty goes, those two were genuinely magnificent. If they would consent to be concubines, and the village Council of Elders granted permission, I wouldn't mind having them even now."

Zhao Lin glared at him, furious at his loose tongue. Danger lurked on all sides, and if anything the present quiet was more foreboding than ever. Man-Tiger had already caused a great deal of trouble, and had still not learned caution. Zhu closed his mouth, chagrined at his own imprudence.

Then a young woman began a song of sweetness and love somewhere on the road ahead. The voice was gentle and lovely, so hauntingly seductive that it moved the hearer to feelings of pity and affection. Zhao, mindful of the deadly creatures the Miao women controlled, whispered to Zhu and Wang to be on their guard, ready to activate the periapts given them by Sixth Brother Li Hong. He took the lead, warning them to act only if he gave the signal, and above all not to move hastily.

They continued for no great distance, and the voice of the singer grew ever nearer. There was no sign of anyone on hand to help them out of trouble, and Zhao grew steadily more apprehensive.

Then, high above them, they heard the sound of pipes playing on the mountain. It began clear and piercing, like phoenixes singing in harmony. It seemed to be issuing from the top of the right wing of the Great Roc, though they could see no sign that anyone was there. The Miao ballad was closer and more urgent, however, so they had little inclination to pay much heed to anything else. They looked around briefly, and then continued on as before, another twenty paces or so.

The ground was steadily rising. Ahead of them the song suddenly ceased. They came to a smooth clearing two or three acres in size. To the left the gully ended in a sheer drop overlooking the Yuan River eight thousand feet below. In front and to the right grew groves of huge pines and firs, their trunks three or more spans in circumference. The immaculate white of the moonlight cast tranquil shadows on the ground below, and the trees sighed gently in the breeze. The pipes on the crags above increased in clarity and volume, and after a time were answered by others, combining in deafening harmony.

Zhao Lin realized that the pipes were no mortal instruments of bamboo, and began to hope that help was near. Then, just outside the grove to the right of the clearing, he caught sight of a large rock shaped like a sleeping tiger, perhaps thirty feet in height. On top were Moon-Maid and Cunning-Maid, one sitting, one reclining. They gestured toward the three men and talked softly between themselves. One appeared angry, and was struggling to get her temper under control.

Zhao Lin had not paid the women much heed when he had first encountered them, and Wang Jin was seeing them for the first time. Both men now observed that they were shapely and voluptuous, glowing with health, though their beauty was of a style very different from Soaring Cloud and the other women they had seen on the Mountain of Verdant Spots. Their faces seemed moulded from jade, as beautiful as rare flowers, and their bodies were light and supple. Above the waist they wore only cloud-like blouses woven of feathers, decorated with innumerable bits of gold and jade, which barely concealed the shape of their well-proportioned breasts. Below they were dressed in short skirts of tiger skin which did not quite reach to their knees. Their arms, legs, and feet were bare, white skin shining like snow or jade in the moonlight.

The white apes and other beasts were not in evidence. Zhao guessed that the women intended to treat them with courtesy at first, holding their forces in reserve if coercion became necessary.

Under the circumstances, calling out a greeting to the women seemed inappropriate. Since they were not blocking the way ahead, the men pretended not to have seen them and continued forward. As they passed near the rock, however, they heard two sharp feminine cries, and the women jumped thirty feet from the top of the rock and descended like a pair of rainbow clouds, dropping lightly to the ground to cut off their path.

The younger, Cunning-Maid, smiled prettily at Zhao. "Do you not love me? What is it about me that displeases you? Tell me!"

At the same time Moon-Maid spoke coquettishly to Zhu Man-Tiger. "You're no better than that fellow Zhao! It was you who approached and proposed to me. Why do you evade me now? I know you Chinese men have no consciences, but you insult the brothers and sisters of the Dragon clan at your peril! Know that we sisters have fallen in love with you and your companion. We feared that you would think that we meant to coerce you, so we have sent even our Ape-children away. We will show you our true love and integrity, so that you will love us and desire to wed us.

"We differ from those other Miao women whom you Chinese people hold in such contempt. We do not follow the tawdry custom of snatching men in the wilds. I love you, and my sister loves your companion, and we will love no other. We have no objections if you wish to return home and explain the situation to your families before coming away with us to be wed. But if you have ideas of refusing us, that we will not allow. You in particular have no choice but to treat me fairly. Of course if you are really strong, you have an option: you may issue a challenge to do battle with us, and set a time to come to our Jade-Dragon Mountain. There, if you can defeat us, we will die gladly at your hands, should it come to that, and no man or beast of ours will ever trouble you again. Speak! What is your answer?"

Of the three Zhao Lin was the most familiar with the Miao temperament and psychology. He signalled to the others to stand close beside him and listen in silence as Moon-Maid spoke. He hoped to be able to use something she said to steer the conversation onto another track, and perhaps give them a chance to extricate themselves by cunning argument. The possibility of setting a date to challenge them on their mountain presented just such an opportunity, and he began to think hard.

When Moon-Maid had finished speaking, Zhao smiled politely. "Love between a man and woman comes about when both parties desire it. I must tell you that when I saw you set your animals on my friend with intent to injure him, I felt no love for you, but only dislike. My Second Brother Zhu here has a beloved wife and child already, and has no intention of abandoning them. He behaved as he did only because his wits were impaired, and in any case he spoke only of taking you as concubines. If your love for him is true, and you are willing to humble yourself in his household in a subordinate status, there is no reason why you could not go back with us. Otherwise, we cannot consent to your request. If you intend coercion, it does not matter how powerful your sorcery is, or how many animals you send against us. We three are unafraid of death, and if we lack the strength to resist you, we will stand unmoving and allow ourselves to be eaten alive ."

Cunning-Maid, scrutinizing Zhao Lin's powerful arms, hawk-like shoulders, handsome features and relaxed, open manner, felt that he was even more heroic than he had seemed before. Her passion for him flamed up, wild and irresistible. She listened to his unyielding tone with mounting alarm.

"Dear Chinese brother," she said anxiously. "I know that you are not married, and I am surely not ugly. Can it be that you feel no affection for me at all?"

Zhao Lin assumed a cool and haughty smile. "Of course you are not ugly," he answered. "You are extremely beautiful. But I have long since determined not to marry. It has nothing to do with beauty or ugliness. Love is completely out of the question."

Both women cried out in alarm. "You Chinese people always speak falsely!" said Cunning-Maid. "Who ever heard of not marrying at all? Agree to marry us, and as long as you are true to us, you can beat us, curse us, or do anything you want to us, and we will not resist. Perhaps it bothers you that we keep so many beasts. If so we will give them up."

The sisters were obviously sincere, and their passion ran deep. They were prepared to sacrifice almost anything without reservation.

Meanwhile, Moon-Maid, seeing Zhu Man-Tiger standing silent to one side, and mindful of the fact that he had once propositioned her, felt that there was still hope. She could not restrain herself from reaching out to tug urgently at his arm.

"Come, dear lover," she said. "Let's you and I go elsewhere to talk."

Zhu Man-Tiger tried to resist, but Moon-Maid's soft white hand, at first soft and gentle as a strand of cotton, tightened around his arm like a band of steel. He could not oppose her tremendous strength without fighting his way loose, which he dared not do.

"Isn't it the same if we talk right here?" he mumbled lamely as he was pulled along.

"I know you are afraid of Elder Brother Zhao, and don't dare talk to me," she said, turning to him with a pretty smile. "We won't go far, just over there. Don't be afraid! As long as the two of you accept us, we will agree to anything, and even if you don't, we won't harm you."

As she spoke her other hand stole around and circled his waist, and she sidled up to him. Her lovely face moved up close, and her white jade-like shoulder pressed against his. Grasping his hand in hers, she led him away. As she had promised she took him no further than the great rock she and her sister had been resting on. They mounted to the top and sat down side by side.

Zhao Lin realized he could do nothing to prevent this without risking open conflict. He signalled to Wang Jin to stand fast, and spoke out in a loud voice.

"You sisters are both beautiful and passionate, and can easily find Chinese men better than we are. I speak the truth to you: one of us is married, and the other is determined never to wed. We made this clear to Elder Sister Cloud and Elder Brother Lai when they acted as go-betweens on your behalf. Coercion is useless. If all else fails, I will follow your suggestion and swear to meet you on your mountain next year on this day."

As he spoke, Cunning-Maid's magnificent eyes remained fixed on his face, and tears began to flow down her cheeks. Her beautiful countenance fell in dejection.

"Why are you so cruel?" she cried out in anguish. She jumped toward him and embraced him tightly. Zhao had feared she might resort to this Miao custom of seizing a man and holding on to him at all costs, enduring any indignity he might offer her, and was prepared for it. He knew that he must not fight her in any way, and, in any case, felt sorry for her hopeless infatuation. He did not try to break free, but stood straight and unmoving while Cunning-Maid kissed him several times in succession. Seeing that he was not responding to her, she turned her cherry-red lips to the side and bit at his shoulder. Zhao, thinking that she was trying to hurt him, circulated his inner energies to his shoulder and tensed it to avoid injury. But Cunning-Maid only nipped him lightly, and turned away with a rueful smile.

"Do you take us for common Miao wenches, willing to settle for anyone who wants us? You are the best, and I will have only the best. If I cannot wed you, I will die before your eyes. No matter how cruel and heartless you are, your heart will soften. Perhaps I can win a drop of water from your eyes. It won't bring me back to life, but at least it will make my death worthwhile."

As she spoke great tears welled forth, but she forced them back. So melancholy was her expression that even Zhao was moved. As he prepared to speak words of comfort and encouragement, Cunning-Maid suddenly knelt before him and embraced his legs.

"Dear lover," she said mournfully. "You are so heartless! I am trying to speak directly and reasonably, but you won't respond. I can't interfere in what my older sister does, but for my part I will allow you and your friend to return in peace. My sister may not have heard what you said about challenging us on our mountain. This you must not do, no matter what happens!"

Wang Jin, standing quietly to one side, grew embarrassed at the sight of the girl's clinging and begging, and turned away. Cunning-Maid saw that he was no longer watching, and rose quickly to her feet.

"You have no small understanding of Miao custom," she said, smiling through her tears. "You will know what this signifies, and never be willing to wed another!"

So saying, she pulled off her blouse, and stood bare to the waist. Her snow-white skin and perfect jade breasts stood fully revealed in the moonlight, giving off a faint feminine warmth and fragrance. A Miao women of Cunning-Maid's status would reveal herself in such a way only to the man she was sworn to wed, this being the Miao way of swearing that she would never take another husband or lover. No other man was ever allowed to see or touch her breasts, and she would willingly fight to the death to protect herself if anyone tried to violate this rule.

"No!" Zhao blurted clumsily, trying to force a smile. "Beauty such as yours is rare indeed, such that a man might never hope to attain. But you

142

are struck by a passing infatuation, nothing more. You must understand that I wish to study the Dao, and will soon retire from the world of men. I cannot be adopted into your family in marriage. Please stop this at once!"

"Do you feel compassion for me then?" she asked softly.

Zhao Lin, fearing that he would become more deeply entangled, assumed an expression of rectitude and severity.

"When Heaven produces something beautiful, like a rare herb or famous flower, who does not feel love and compassion for it? But I have no intention of plucking it. That is why I must refuse the honour of your attentions."

"Then at least you will retract what you said about a challenge on our mountain, won't you?"

"Once a man says something, there is no way he can go back on it."

Cunning-Maid donned her blouse once more. "If you can feel compassion for me, that is enough," she said with determination. "You and your companion had best leave now."

"There is one more of our number here," said Zhao.

"I fear my sister will not let him go," sighed Cunning-Maid. "That Second Brother Zhu of yours will follow your wishes when you are together, but his heart and temperament are not like yours. If he agrees to her request, there is nothing you can do to stop her from taking him away. If he refuses, then the two of you are in danger. If I were to fight to the death on your behalf, I might save your life, but this Third Brother of yours—such a fine man—will likely not survive."

Zhao Lin was favourably impressed by the girl's innocence and integrity. Moon-Maid, though, was dangerous and unpredictable. She was still in the flower of youth, her romantic desires at a peak. His sworn brother Zhu was vain and lustful, and might prove too weak to resist her clinging charms. If he allowed himself to be confused and seduced, his intelligent and beautiful wife, their beloved son still nursing at her breast, and his own family would be divided and scattered by the Miao woman. The whole thing had come about because he, Zhao, had led them on an expedition to visit a friend. How could he ever face Zhu's family? He hardened his heart and raised his voice to answer Cunning-Maid.

"My Second Brother Zhu is not without feeling, but he has an aged mother, a beautiful wife, and a young son. His family is peaceful and happy. If your fine sister is willing to humble herself as a concubine on our barren mountain, I foresee little difficulty. If she is not, he would never be so befuddled as to agree. We cannot permit our sworn brother to remain here. At the very least we must ask your excellent sister to permit him to return home and wait patiently until we pay our visit to your mountain this day next year. We can discuss the matter further at that time."

Cunning-Maid listened alertly to his words. His expression and tone were harsh, and he was facing her as he spoke, but his eyes were fixed on Moon-Maid. Cunning-Maid grew ever more anxious, and when he said next year she rushed at him and tried to cover his mouth, but was too late.

"No!" she cried desperately, raising her hand to point at him. But before she could say anything more, they heard a feminine shout: "Agreed!" A breeze fanned his face, and a shadow flickered in front of him as Moon-Maid leaped from the rock and dropped beside him, holding Zhu Man-Tiger like a baby in her arms. She put Man-Tiger down, and stabbed her finger viciously at Zhao.

"My lover loves me, and he is willing. I knew all along the only reason he wouldn't say so was because you forced him not to, so I took him away from you to let him speak his mind. He was still afraid of you, and hadn't yet agreed, but I knew that he was beginning to waver. Then you started to shout, and scared him so much he shook his head, and refused to say another word! I know all about you Chinese people! You listen to advice from anyone, even a fuzzy-headed baby, as if he were a wise elder! If you advise him to wed me, I will thank you handsomely. If you keep on deliberately getting in my way, I'm going to duel with you right here and now!"

Zhao saw the savage gleam in her beautiful eyes, and knew that she was on the verge of violence. As he made ready to answer, Zhu Man-Tiger interrupted. Zhu was filled with shame at being carried about helplessly like a baby. He had indeed been stirred by Moon-Maid's tender caresses and gentle pleadings, but knew perfectly well that what she wanted could never be achieved without stripping him of his dignity, and he had wavered. When he heard her threats, he began to fear for the safety of his best friend. His youthful temper raged, and with a violent effort he wrenched himself free of her grip.

"Don't you dare touch him! He has nothing to do with this!" he shouted angrily, pointing his finger at her. "You are pretty, and I like you, but I have a wife and family, and I know you cannot break your laws and marry away from home! All I did just now was try to persuade you with kind words instead of giving you a harsh rejection. Why are you threatening my Elder Brother? I started this whole business, and I will bear the brunt of it! If you wish to kill me, I am ready!"

Cunning-Maid, seeing her sister's explosive anger, had turned white with alarm. She rushed up to Zhao and hushed him to silence, and turned to Moon-Maid with a placating smile.

"They speak the truth," she said. "I love Squire Zhao more than my life, but we cannot succeed in a day. As heartless as they may seem, they are not made of iron. The more resolute a man is, the finer he is. It is plain that neither of them is as unmoved as he pretends. If we press them now, we can only fail. Better to take a leisurely course; sooner or later we will get what we want. If Squire Zhu really loves you, then after he returns to his mountain he will not be able to forget you, especially if we go to seek them out. I say we allow them to return home."

Moon-Maid listened to her sister's argument without losing her temper, though she glared furiously at Zhao and Wang, a dangerous fire dancing in her eyes.

"He already intends to come to our mountain and fight to the death," said Moon-Maid angrily. "Why yield to him now?"

"I know I never had any hope," said Cunning-Maid dejectedly. "But I love him so. I can't bear it if you anger him, much less harm him. Now at least there is still a year's time. Who knows? Perhaps I can change his mind."

Moon-Maid laughed contemptuously. "I don't intend to wait a year. I lack your patience. He is the one who said he would come to our mountain, not Squire Zhu. You are too simple and honest. Leave this affair to me! I guarantee success!"

As she spoke, Wang Jin noticed savage beasts slipping in and out of view in the woods to the left. Red, green, and blue glowing eyes flickered in the shadows. Moon-Maid roared like an enraged tigress, her voice and expression disfigured by savage ferocity. Disaster was imminent. But then Cunning-Maid raised her voice in protest.

"Sister, we agreed to go about this without resorting to force. I don't care about anyone else, but Squire Zhao is mine, and I cannot stand to see him harmed or coerced! This fine Chinese fellow Wang, his close friend, has nothing to do with the business at all. You must allow me to convey the two of them home on the Green Simurgh."

Meanwhile Zhao was thinking hard. The help they had been promised had not arrived, but the jade pendants Li Hong had given them were supposed to ward off the attacks of serpents, animals, and other evils. Moon-Maid's rage and malice could not be soothed. Cunning-Maid was much more reasonable, but still determined to cling to him at any cost. Zhao could never allow an outsider to take them home, thus betraying the secret location of Willow Lake. Nor could he abandon Zhu Man-Tiger. He had little to lose at this juncture; why not test Moon-Maid's resolve? He drew himself up and interrupted Cunning-Maid, who was still arguing with her sister.

"Do not mistake our courtesy for fear of you!" he said to Moon-Maid. "It's only because Elder Sister Cloud and Elder Brother Lai are mutual friends that we have been unwilling to enter into unseemly conflict. We have dealt reasonably with you as long as we can. Your sister is in a similar position, but she at least behaves in a civilized manner. Look at yourself! How could any man of backbone yield to your rage and threats of violence! Even if you were able to carry us off to be married, we would never be able to give you the love you desire. Is that truly what you wish? Your capricious arrogance stems from the masses of savage beasts, birds, and poisonous vermin under your command. We will not leave one of our companions behind under any circumstances. If you agree to allow us to return without further trouble, you have my word that we will go to your mountain to settle all accounts before this day next year. When that time comes, if you are still resolved to coerce us under threat of violence, we will pit our individual strength and powers against each other to see who is superior and who must yield. If you are victorious you may murder us in any manner you wish, but otherwise you must release us, and stop using your sorcery against us. If this is agreed, then you must cease harassing us with your strange creatures and let us go in peace. Let me remind you that we have been accepted by an Immortal as his disciples, and have mastered some of his teachings. How do you know that we do not have the ability to resist you?"

Moon-Maid glared malevolently at Zhao with mounting fury. Cunning-Maid, knowing that Moon-Maid was capable of great violence, quickly interrupted, not giving her sister a chance to reply.

"Sister, if he wants to issue a challenge to duel, that is acceptable to me. You will go against Squire Zhu, and I against Squire Zhao. We will divide into separate pairs, and each will take care of herself." She then turned around to face Zhao Lin and continued on despondently. "The best thing would be for you to kill me by your own hand. Only then will my wish be fulfilled."

Zhao Lin could not help but be moved by this melancholy protest at his treatment of her. He would not take her as a wife, but could never bear to fight with her. He knew that if a Miao woman were desperate, and could not have the man she wanted, she would seek to die at the hands of her beloved. This was something he could not contemplate, and began to regret speaking too quickly. But Moon-Maid interrupted before he could reply.

"I know that Squire Zhu wishes to maintain his dignity," she said, a crafty smile on her face. "But he loves me all the same, and would never be willing to raise a hand against me. I am even less willing to defeat him if it will damage his self-respect. Your lover, and he alone, is responsible for the present impasse. I could chew him up and swallow him down, every bit of him! Unfortunately you cherish and protect him, for which I suppose you cannot be blamed. But I had an understanding with Squire Zhu before we came here, and I did not anticipate your Squire Zhao's spiteful interference. I doubt that you two could bring yourselves to fight any more than my lover and I could.

"I want Squire Zhu at once, and I mean to have him. If your lover allows Squire Zhu to remain here, our troubles are behind us. Order the Green Simurgh and the Piebald Vulture to convey them both back to our mountain! Wang here we will release to take word back to their families. That is my advice. Otherwise, let us see if his immortal magic is powerful enough to escape my Ninefold Dragon Circle of the Hundred Beasts! He is the only one of the three who has made any promise to challenge us on our mountain. If he now nods to me in agreement, and yields to me in my request for Squire Zhu, no one need ever know of this promise. For the sake of the sisterly love between us, I will spare him from my wrath. If he does not yield, I will exact certain revenge in one year's time, however you try to protect him. One word from him

146

now will decide whether I treat him with kindly affection or as a bitter enemy!"

When Cunning-Maid heard this, her face went white. She rushed over and grasped her sister tightly.

"Brother Zhao is a man of China," she said, her voice trembling. "He doesn't understand the law of our mountain. I don't know from what Miao tribe he picked up these ridiculously exaggerated notions of challenge and duel, but he's obviously just using them to make himself seem strong and heroic. Is there no love or honour left between us, Sister?"

Moon-Maid smiled contemptuously. "I love Squire Zhu as much as you do your Zhao. There was no difficulty until Zhao started yelling and interfering. You wonder that I hate him so?"

Zhao Lin had been stalling for time in the hope that help would eventually arrive. But as the two women continued to argue with no result, he grew annoyed, and decided to wait no longer. He evaded Cunning-Maid and stepped forward to confront Moon-Maid.

"These attempts at intimidation must cease!" he thundered. "I understand perfectly well what going to your mountain means, and am quite familiar with Old Man Dragon's power and influence. I do not fear to confront your Dragon people, as you will see when the time comes. Your hysteria and threats of violence are of little consequence. Summon your serpents and animals, and introduce us, so that we may be on our way!"

He had long since signalled to Zhu and Wang, who stood at the ready. When Zhao had spoken, they moved beside him and began shouting at her as well. Seeing Zhu Man-Tiger's enraged expression, so different from his gentle manner when they had been sitting shoulder to shoulder a few moments earlier, she erupted in fury. She spoke first to Man-Tiger.

"I never expected such cruelty and deceit!" she said, pointing at him with a bitter smile. Then she turned to Zhao Lin and fixed him with a baleful glare. "You have done me a serious wrong this night! This day next year, you will learn how dangerous I am!"

She threw back her head and howled at the sky. Strange and desolate echoes awoke around them. The strange pipe music begin again on the summit of the cliff. The unearthly sound, clear and penetrating, seemed to descend from high in the sky, striking the woods and the huge canyon far below. The first time this mysterious sound appeared, Zhao and his companions had assumed it was a signal indicating that the help Soaring Cloud had promised was not far away. The Miao women on top of the rock had looked about as if puzzled by the music. Then it fell silent, and no one appeared, but the men had still hoped that rescue was near. But now it seemed that the music had resumed in answer to Moon-Maid's cry, and they concluded that the players were in league with the sisters. The men positioned themselves back to back in triangular formation, prepared to fight for their lives, and made ready to activate their jade pendants and magic charm.

147

As Zhao and the others prepared themselves, the Miao woman uttered another furious howl, even more mournful and savage than the first. As the echoes faded, a wind rose about them. Sand and dust blew in their faces, and the surrounding woods thundered like an ocean surf. A fearful clamour approached. Animals roared, serpents hissed, and scores of unidentifiable creatures contributed their own weird howls and whistles to the deafening cacophony. The tranquil clearing, surrounded by crags and tall trees in the beautiful moonlit night, a perfect setting for lovers to court one another in intimate conversation, had in an instant been transformed into the battlefield of the Asura,* a hell in the world of men. A grim darkness eclipsed the moon's brilliance; a dusty mist filled the air. The forest shook to the tread of innumerable animal feet as dark shapes moved through the murk. First they saw only a vast constellation of glowing eyes, high and low, flashing red and blue from the concealment of the trees, but soon it became apparent that each pair of malevolent lamp-like eyes was attached to a large black form. The entire pack converged slowly upon them, surging like the tide.

Zhao and Wang, experienced and courageous, knew themselves to be in no immediate danger. They saw that the nearest of the malevolent eyes were over a hundred feet away, and approaching slowly. Moon-Maid's intention was clearly to intimidate by cutting off all escape; she wished to capture, not harm them. Zhao and Wang were both prepared to watch the situation develop before making any move of their own, and waited with hands on the jade pendants hanging within their garments.

Zhu Man-Tiger nudged them urgently from behind with his elbows. They turned to look, and saw the three huge apes standing only twenty feet away, their blood-red mouths slightly open to reveal rows of sharp fangs. Each of them was half again as tall as a man, steely eyes glinting; huge taloned hands, each the size of winnowing baskets, were reaching to seize them.

On another side were nine mammoth pythons, some coiled on the ground with foot-thick necks erected like pillars, others dangling from trees, stretched sinuously toward the three men. Red tongues flickered in and out like glowing flames. Surrounding these serpents was a vast horde of gigantic centipedes, scorpions, giant worms, and other poisonous vermin, which scuttled and slithered across the ground.

The three men kept a wary eye on this evil brood, saw that none of them had begun to spit venom, and if anything seemed more hesitant and less ferocious than before. The pipes on the cliff continued to play a slow tune, its languorous echoes drifting far over their heads.

The wind gradually quieted, and the sharp brilliance of the moon reasserted itself. The creatures about them came into clear view. There

* [In Indian mythology (known in China after the introduction of Buddhism) the Asura were the demons who battled against the god Indra.]

148

were more than twice as many as before. Besides tigers, panthers, elephants, bears, and apes, there were now also dozens of weird mutant creatures seldom encountered in the world, all fierce and savage, most displaying rows of needle-sharp fangs. Each of these was at least ten to twenty feet in length. The vanguard of the host had advanced to a distance of twenty or thirty feet, where they crouched in threatening postures. The men saw little chance of finding an opening through the ranks surrounding them.

The Miao women had returned to the top of the rock. It was hard to believe they would unleash this savage tide of claws and teeth against them, but Zhao worried that in a long tense stalemate with wild and savage creatures of this sort, the women might not be able to prevent an accident from occurring.

Zhu Man-Tiger in particular, already humiliated once, was now directly face to face with the three savage apes. He knew their malevolence and steel strength, and his terror mounted as three pairs of malicious fist-sized eyes fixed on him. He thought of activating the magical charm he bore, but hesitated, deterred by the recollection that it could only be used once. It would be a shame to waste it, and if it were not powerful enough to ward off the encircling animals, it might only enrage them. Better to let Zhao and Wang try their jade pendants.

The apes sensed his fear, and delighted in it. They took great pleasure in bullying human beings, and now bared their teeth and sliced their claws through the air in a menacing display. Zhu Man-Tiger, his hand on the charm, was now on the verge of panic. He whispered to Zhao and Wang to beware of the apes, and suggested that they activate their magic talismans simultaneously to take advantage of their combined power. But then Moon-Maid, watching from high up on the rock, grew anxious for her beloved and gave two sharp whistles. The apes backed away and stretched their blood-red lips into grotesque parodies of smiles, attempting to please their mistresses with a display of friendliness toward Zhu.

Everything might then have been all right, for the time being at least. But then Wang Jin intervened out of concern for Zhu. He perceived, as Zhu had not, that the Miao women were planning no worse than a stubborn deadlock, and intended them no bodily harm. He knew that Zhu was terrified of the white apes, so Wang touched Zhao with his elbow, signalling that the three of them should rotate their formation so that Wang himself faced the monstrous apes. The men were unaware that the creatures were under orders to remain motionless as long as their quarry did not move. If the three men did make any move, however, the animals were to rush in toward them, roaring in as menacing a manner as possible. As the men rotated their formation, it aroused a tremendous chorus of roars, growls, eerie howls and hoots. Their breath blew up a gust of wind, driving sand and dust into the air. The serpents and vermin stayed where they were, but the beasts rushed in from all sides, stopping barely twenty feet away. The three men had no idea it was all a bluff, and with savage creatures in such close proximity they panicked.

Of the three apes, the yellow one was the most cunning and mischievous. He was itching for trouble, and was frustrated at having been prevented from baiting Zhu Man-Tiger. He knew full well that Wang Jin was the only man not cherished by either of his mistresses, and felt free to taunt him. Impatient to vent his pique, he bounded forward and reached to seize him. He had no intention of doing Wang any real injury, but Zhao and Wang, seeing the speed of his forward rush, and mindful that the creature was powerful enough to rend a strong man limb from limb, feared that he was out of control. They hastily drew forth the magic pendants, and extended their left hands in the power-gesture demonstrated by Wei Lai. Two brilliant pillars of white light erupted about them, each ten feet in diameter. The light swept up and then almost immediately curled downward like a fountain to enclose the three men in an effulgent envelope of power. Its outer surface crackled with hair-thin threads of lightning, scattering like a fall of shining rain. This did not extend to any great distance, but the wild beasts which had ventured too close appeared to have suffered some injury.

The yellow ape, who had been on the verge of snatching Wang Jin out of the group and having some sport with him, was the closest to the wall of blinding energy, and the most badly hurt. He shrieked in agony and backed away as fast as he could. So urgent was his flight that he neglected to watch where he was going, and backed full-tilt into a large cypress a hundred feet away. The trunk snapped, the ape howled; he began leaping madly about, setting up a mournful wailing.

Seeing these developments, the front ranks of the encirclement beat a hasty retreat. Great confusion ensued as those coming up from the rear continued to press forward, ignorant of what was going on ahead. The yellow ape continued to wail and jump about, and the white apes, seeing their offspring so severely hurt by human beings, bellowed in outrage. All of the animals were in fear of the apes, who were stronger and more terrible than any of them, and a stampede ensued. Great clouds of dust were flung into the air; the moon and stars faded from sight. The thunder of pounding feet and the hideous chorus of howls and roars shook the mountains. The effect was more fearsome than any of the deliberate menacing that had preceded it.

The Miao women seemed greatly perturbed. They had not dreamed that Zhao and his companions were capable of such a feat. Moon-Maid gave a long sharp whistle, and drew forth a small folding trident concealed in the back of her garment. She shook it to extend it to its full length of three feet, and with her other hand produced a small golden bell from a leopard-skin sack at her waist. She tossed her head suddenly, and her long thick hair loosed and tumbled about her shoulders. She moved the bell back and forth in her left hand, and gestured violently with the trident in her right. Three flares of brilliant blood-red flame sprang from the head of the trident and burned in the air above her. The snakes and poisonous vermin, who had not participated in the encirclement, and had begun to retreat when the white effulgence had appeared, responded to the scarlet flame with a frenzy of hisses and shrieks. The other beasts calmed, and turned obediently to face Zhao and his companions. They approached once more to a distance of twenty feet, and resumed their menacing formation. Nonetheless they now seemed subdued and unenthusiastic, their roars sporadic and forced. None of them dared approach the strange ball of blinding white brilliance.

The three men were delighted at the power of the talismans. Zhao decided to try a further bluff. Wei Lai had warned them that since they did not yet have magic powers of their own, they should not attempt to travel while the shield was activated, but remain where they were until help arrived. The protected area inside the glowing bubble was more than ten feet in diameter, which gave them some freedom of movement. There was no longer any need to stand back to back. Zhao instructed the others to fetch out the provisions prepared for them by Ding Shao and his wife, and they sat down to eat with an air of easy nonchalance, talking and laughing all the while.

CHAPTER 12

The Music of Power

THE MIAO WOMEN DID NOT REACT IMMEDIATELY WHEN THEY SAW the glowing shield of force. They were deterred in part by the music of the pipes on the cliff. At the moment it was playing a clear and pleasant tune, and showed no signs of the threat they had originally anticipated, but the sisters were perturbed, and wary of provoking trouble with the unknown bystanders.

Moon-Maid was further agitated at the sight of the three men laughing and eating in such a free and easy manner. She pressed Cunning-Maid to summon the great marvellous birds she had trained, but Cunning-Maid was reluctant. Despite her stubborn and fiery temperament, Cunning-Maid was wiser than her sister, and knew that any attempt at violent coercion would only arouse the disgust of the man she was determined to win. He did not love her, but at the same time did not seem to feel the dislike toward her that he clearly harboured for Moon-Maid. She was determined to overcome his stubborn resistance with true love and yielding tenderness. She could not bear to see him harmed or disturbed in any way. She disapproved of Moon-Maid's tactics, and no matter how her sister cajoled and threatened, she refused to help. Frightened, humiliated, and outraged, Moon-Maid prepared to attack the three men on her own.

After a short time the men finished their meal and rose to their feet. Zhao Lin, safe in the protective glow, raised his hands and gestured at the two women.

"Moon-Maid!" he barked. "Look carefully! We bear Dharma-treasures transmitted to us by the Immortals! We are immune to evil sorcery and demonic arts! We have lingered here and not opposed you more vigorously only because you are friends of Sister Cloud and Brothers Wei and Ding. Also, most of these creatures you have raised are rare and valuable, and we wished to examine them. Did you really think you could hinder us? If you have any idea of what you are doing, recall your forces at once! Marriage between us is out of the question, but there is no reason we cannot be friends. If you do not agree to this, then we must wait to settle the affair next year when we challenge your mountain. If you will not listen to this friendly advice, we shall depart under cover of our protective treasure-glow. You can do nothing to stop us. Should you continue in these outrageous attempts to coerce us, we shall have no choice but to retaliate. You yourselves may not be affected, but we cannot guarantee the lives of your animals. IIs this really what you want?"

Despite his bold words, Zhao Lin felt little confidence. He addressed his speech exclusively to Moon-Maid, because she was the one acting against them. He hoped that Cunning-Maid would persist in her refusal to help, and that Moon-Maid, thus isolated, would be more likely to back down without loss of face.

Unfortunately for Zhao, his plan had unintended consequences. Cunning-Maid observed with satisfaction that he had been careful to say nothing to hurt her, and concluded that his attitude toward her had changed. Overjoyed, she was even more determined not to aid her sister, no matter what the cost.

When love is one-sided, the lover in most cases is prone to jealousy. Moon-Maid was no exception. When the magic shield sprang into life around the three men, she studied it carefully, and discovered that Zhu Man-Tiger also bore a charm, but had not activated it. Zhu had been facing in her direction before the men began to eat, which she interpreted as a covert signal to her. She grew ever more suspicious of Zhao. Why had he spoken only to her, and addressed none of his challenging remarks to Cunning-Maid? She knew he was not married. Could it be that he and her sister had come to a silent understanding, and were conspiring against her? Fury burned in her heart, and she began to harbour suspicion and resentment even against Cunning-Maid, with whom she had shared years of perils and difficulties.

"My hatred of you is as deep as the sea!" she raged at Zhao. "Your words mean nothing! I trained all of these animals and venom-bearing creatures myself, and without my command they will die rather than retreat. If you want to leave, fine! You need only kill me, or else break the Ninefold Dragon Formation of beasts around you, but to do this you must subdue them all! Otherwise, we will run you down even if you fly to Heaven! Bring forth your silly powers and Dharma-treasures, and do what you will with them! While my sister's heart yet beats, I have no desire to harm you, and am willing to let you and the Chinese man Wang leave. Not only will I let you go free, but the hatred and enmity between us will be completely expunged. I will even forget your promise to visit our mountain. All you need do is let me have my lover! But if you are determined to take him away, and persist in your provocations, our dispute can only be settled through conflict! It is not I who is breaking my word, or callously disregarding our sisterly bond. I have exhorted you many times, and given you many chances. I am going to give you one last chance!"

Zhao Lin listened in dismay. He had attempted a bluff and failed. The two women were obviously determined to hold on to them at all costs. Even if they could break through the encirclement, the sisters would trail them relentlessly. If the secret location of Willow Lake were revealed, it could spell the beginning of endless trouble. Zhao knew full well that he had no genuine power to overcome the sisters and break the deadlock.

As Zhao pondered, a voice rang out, seemingly quiet and yet clearly audible, from the top of the cliff.

"We have been sitting here minding our own business, playing the pipes and enjoying the moon," it complained. "Then along came this nasty brood of animals, squawking and yammering, filling the air with dust and noxious vapours. We weary of this. On one side of the conflict are the men: they are unwilling to join the women in matrimony among the Miao, and are unwilling to accept their kind affection despite all arguments. On the other side are the two Miao girls. One at least is honest and upright; her love has led her into error, but her conduct has not been particularly offensive. But the other grasps and clings in a disgraceful manner, and I tire of her histrionics. A fine deadlock, indeed! They ride the tiger, both unable to dismount. Pride precludes all compromise. A clear pleasant night like this is a rarity. I am of a mind to ask them to take their noisy argument elsewhere, and cease disturbing our quiet evening pastimes. Or perhaps we should save ourselves trouble and look for a quieter spot. What say you, Cousin?"

The music of the pipes broke off, and another voice answered.

"No, that wouldn't be right," it said. "Why should we defer to others when we are in the right? Tonight the moonlight is best in this spot, and the view is unusually clear and fine. We would have a hard time finding another spot as enjoyable as this. We were here first, after all, and we certainly have precedence over a pack of animals! People might even get the idea that we were afraid of them. If word of that ever got out, imagine the jokes at our expense! Mountains are open to all, not the exclusive preserve of anyone. We have no stake in the dispute, and must not intervene on either side. Since it is only the clamour of the animals that is bothering us, why not play a stronger tune on our pipes, and compete to see whose noise is the greater? Whoever loses the contest must agree to be silent."

During the time the mysterious voices were talking, Moon-Maid had gestured several times with her steel trident, and the scarlet flame hovering in the air above her head blazed up more brightly. The beasts, vermin, and serpents threatened with redoubled ferocity, roaring and howling. The din was terrific, shaking the mountains and thundering among the peaks, but, oddly, failed to drown out the conversation on the cliff. Every word the voices said was clearly audible.

The music of the pipes deepened and changed in pitch. It pierced the rocks and thrust into the clouds, echoed from the mountains and jolted the sky. The wooded slope began to shake. The animals roared for a time in an attempt at defiance, but many of them were already cowering in fear. Their efforts became more sporadic, each beast unable to do more than raise its head occasionally to growl, and the din lessened considerably. The serpents, scorpions, and other vermin were particularly terrified, every one as quiet as cicadas in winter, necks drawn in and heads lowered. Zhao looked around for the apes, but all three had disappeared.

The piping grew ever stranger and more terrible. Sometimes it resembled gargantuan thunderclaps shaking the sky above a raging surf; at other times it sounded more like a bloody duel between divine dragons, their long shrieks and bellows echoing through the void. The tempo quickened; a multiplicity of notes and sounds unfolded in an unfathomably complex harmony, a vast sky-wide orchestra of celestial gongs and drums beating in unison.

Even Zhao and his companions, safe within their glowing shield, felt their minds and souls shudder and flutter within them, and came close to fading into unconsciousness. Outside the glowing bubble a great wind rose, and racing clouds obscured the sky. Sand and leaves fell like rain. The beasts cowered in terror, heads down, tails tucked securely between their legs. All trace of fight was gone, and they huddled in an attitude of submission.

Zhao saw that the two women were also shuddering, mouths tightly closed, expressions at once mournful and indignant. Their courage and very souls wavered and weakened; they seemed to be losing control of their bodies, and began to twitch and shake in time to the music. Zhao recalled Wei Lai's warnings to disregard strange sounds along the way, and to use their pendants to escape all harm. Without their shield they might have found the terrible piping more than they could bear. The pipe players on the cliff must be their long-awaited saviours. The voices indeed seemed to be those of Hong Jade-Sheen and Ruan the Pellucid, the two beloved disciples of the Old One in Green. It was not unlikely that Sixth Brother Li Hong was along for the excitement as well. As Zhao viewed the devastation around him in wonder and amazement, the music broke off, and one of the voices rang out in indignant tones from the cliff top.

"You dare send your creatures to disturb us?" it barked. "We have been sitting here playing our pipes, not interfering with you or your doings in any way, and yet you order three nasty apes to come and do us harm! This action is spiteful, and cannot be tolerated! But we shall forbear for the time being, because you act from love and ignorance in your zeal to win husbands, rather than from malice. We shall do no more than make an example of this large and brazen beast. If you do not take this first hint, even Old Codger Miao will suffer the consequences of your folly!"

A white-clad figure seemed to appear briefly on the top of the cliff; the two white apes howled in agony somewhere in the darkness above. A large human figure flew down from the cliff top toward the Miao women. It came at tremendous speed, and Zhao and his companions assumed that one of the strangers on the cliff was swooping to attack the girls outright. But then a hideous thud shook the ground, and a cloud of dust leaped up in front of the rock. A crumpled corpse lay on the ground, not a man at all, but the yellow ape that had been threatening Zhu and Wang. Moon-Maid, angered that the strangers on the cliff had ruined their plans, had probably sent the beast to go up and deal with them. The strangers had seized it, killed it, and flung its body down.

155

Zhao and his companions were awestruck. The yellow ape was a fearsome creature like a giant mandrill, only half a foot shorter than its white parents. Its body was hard as iron, impervious to injury from knives and axes; its strength was almost limitless. And yet the men on the cliff had killed it in the time it took to raise a hand. The two older apes, which had accompanied it on its mission, had been injured and subdued, but not killed outright. The strength and power it would have taken to accomplish this was beyond imagining. The top of the left wing of the Peak of the Great Roc was several hundred feet above and behind where the Miao women were standing. The beast had been flung from a point far to the right. Even a crossbow bolt could not have been loosed from this distance with such accuracy. And yet the huge and clumsy body of the ape, several hundred pounds of dead weight, had been snatched up as if it were light as a feather, and hurled down like a lightning bolt to land right before the two sisters. It could only be the two flying warriors Hong and Ruan. Had they not been warned in advance to ignore any strange happenings around them, Zhao and Wang might have rushed forward eagerly to greet them and express their gratitude.

The Miao women seemed to realize at once that they had been sorely bested. Moon-Maid's tone grew a shade milder, but she addressed them boldly.

"As soon as we heard your pipes we suspected you intended evil," she said. "We twice ordered our apes to ascend and observe your movements, but they were unable to find your hiding place. We two sisters have never sought trouble with others, and on this night came to meet with someone. We certainly have no objections to your doing whatever you want. But, just as we expected, you were determined to harass us, and blew your sorcerous pipes to scare our animal hosts away. Now you have killed our Yellow Boy. Who are you? Why have you set yourselves against us? Show yourselves, and answer! Only thus can we find out who is the stronger, and who will live and who will die!"

A laugh rang out from the cliff top. "Ignorant Miao children! We came to sit and enjoy the moon. We had no more to do with you than the waters of a river have to do with a well. If you desire husbands badly enough to want to kidnap them, it is no concern of ours. But it was wrong of you to summon that animal rabble and cause such a rucus! Their disturbance raised a noisome wind, and the moon and stars lost their brilliance. You spoiled our pleasant evening frolic. We thought of running you off, but that would have put us to the trouble of coming out and threatening you. So we decided to follow your own example and play an unpleasant tune on our pipes; to contest with you and see who could make the nastiest noise.

"This mountain top is not the territory of your clan. You have the gall to challenge us? How shameless can you be? Considering what you tried to do to us, we have shown great forbearance. You must have lost the power of sight if you think we are hiding; we are here in plain sight on the cliff top. If you can't even see us, what makes you think you are worthy of meeting us in combat? If you know what's good for you, you will take that pack of brutes and depart, lest you bring shame and dishonour on your family and Old Man Miao. If you do not yet recognize that it is time to retreat, be warned! We never harm anyone without good cause, so you may not lose your lives. But do not think for a minute that a single one of your beasts will escape alive! The world would be better off without these noxious creatures in any case. Do not wait until it is too late to regret your mistake!"

The other voice broke in. "It is not strange that ignorant Miao girls of this type would be savage and barbaric. They're certainly not worth troubling about. Though I grant you if their dispositions showed a little more yielding tenderness, the gentlemen might be less inclined to reject their suit. The sisters seem not to have enjoyed the dragon-and-tiger-quelling tune I played; perhaps the music was too stern and vital for their taste. Why not play a more soothing air? Maybe that will calm their nerves, and stop them from raging like a pair of tigresses!"

Zhao and his companions furtively scanned the cliff, but could see no sign of their rescuers. Cunning-Maid stood on the rock with an air of great determination. She listened attentively to the voices above, but her eyes were fixed all the while on Zhao. Moon-Maid, however, clenched her teeth in anger and impatience, her attitude one of great malice. Before the voices above had finished speaking, she began her attack. She pointed her finger, and the crimson flame floating in the air above flared and shot up toward the cliff. Her lips moved as she recited a spell, and she gestured with her trident. Blood-red flames erupted from it, and a rain of crimson sparks exploded outward, beautiful as a New Year's bouquet. Great masses of this fire swept with lightning rapidity toward the top of the cliff, one after another. Her adversaries on the cliff, however, continued to speak as if unaware of the attack. By this time nearly a hundred blasts of flame had struck the cliff top, collecting there in a great glowing mass, seething and threatening to burst. But then a strange and barely visible auroral cloud flickered briefly among the crimson flames, and the fire was abruptly extinguished, as if it had never been.

Moon-Maid quailed, and hastened to withdraw her flames. But before she could do anything else, Cunning-Maid, whose expression had grown unhappy and resentful, uttered a long strange cry, suggestive of a magical bird like a phoenix or simurgh, but far more passionate and tragic. The sound echoed powerfully through the forests and wilds, gradually dissipating among the mountains. Before it had faded completely the pipes began to play once again.

The women were obviously anticipating a tune far more terrible than the first. But as their anger and terror reached its peak, a clear and delicate music began, completely different from the other. It warbled pleasantly in the ears like the pretty notes of a songbird, evoking images of flowing brooks and blooming flowers. After a while the key changed, and the music became more vibrant and imposing, but not threatening

157

like the booming gongs and drums of the previous tune. It was clear and penetrating, harmonizing in a lovely chorus that filled the sky with austere and stately music. Listening to it Zhao and his companions felt a curious awe and respect. Its effect on the Miao women was far greater. They looked like a pair of vengeful assassins who have come face to face with their enemy and are about to strike, but have been overcome by the overbearing majesty of their intended victim, too timid and dispirited to move.

Zhao and his companions, who harboured no enmity for the musicians, felt very little of this. They found the music lovely and pleasant, completely different from the earth-shaking and heaven-startling power of the previous tune. They wondered why the resentful and furious agitation of the women had so suddenly calmed.

But then a sudden furious squall blew up, bending the trees around with a great howl. In the sky, from both directions along the road they had been travelling, there appeared several huge shapes of different colours, some light, some dark. On each eyes glowed, stars of different sizes. They advanced with lightning speed, covering the sky and spreading shadows far out over the ground. In a twinkling they had arrived. Half the sky darkened, and the moon and stars disappeared from view.

The three men looked closely, and discovered that a flock of seven or eight mutant birds was wheeling overhead. One of them was of a size normal for a large bird, but the rest were gigantic. The wingspread of the largest was over forty feet. A strange long-tailed bird with green plumage was the one that had swooped over them after Soaring Cloud and Wei Lai had gone. Each of them had talons like iron; their steely eyes flashed like lightning. Their every move revealed a rapacious ferocity.

When the giant birds had approached to within seventy or eighty feet of the cliff, they hovered for a moment in midair. Blasts of wind from two or three slow beats of eight powerful pairs of wings tore several half-span pines and cypresses right out of the ground. A scattering of earth and rocks came out with the roots and was driven wildly about in a relentless hail-storm. The thunder of the beating wings and the crash of falling trees combined in a frightful earth-shattering din, so violent that the very mountains seemed ready to collapse. Had it not been for their glowing protective shield, the three men would have been blown off their feet or injured by flying rocks. Never had they seen creatures of such ferocious power and massive proportions.

The birds seemed to have come in response to Cunning-Maid's summons, but since their mistress had not yet told them what to do, they wheeled and awaited further instructions. The strangers on the cliff gave no sign that they were aware of the birds, though the music of the pipes gradually became finer, adding many melodious and mournful notes. Listening to it Zhao and his companions felt themselves overcome by indescribable grief and despondency. The tune conjured up images of a lonely wife awaiting a husband who would never return, heartbroken with grief as she watched in vain along an empty highway. After a while the music shifted again, now conveying the impression of languid daydreaming amid the bright warmth of spring, on beautiful days while plants and flowers grew and flourished. A curious feeling of weakness and lassitude made their limbs feel as soft as cotton strands. They felt a sense of helplessness, as though in the grip of a strange springtime languor that could not be fought off.

The three men sensed the power of the music, but remained largely unaffected by it. Their adversaries, however, both human and animal, were swiftly overcome. The Miao women, agitated as they were, did not have the strength to speak. Even the eight huge birds, at first so mighty and awesome, seemed to lose their savage power. Some of them continued to hover in the air, flapping weakly. Others had already folded their wings and dropped heavily to the ground near the base of the cliff. The large green mutant, accompanied by the one smaller bird and one other of the large ones, had not yet retreated.

As the three men stared in wonder, there came a single vast booming note. It echoed deafeningly through the mountains and valleys, so strong that it sent leaves flying through the air. The three mutant birds, like defeated fighting cocks struck a violent blow in the head, uttered tremulous cries of terror, and fled wildly in different directions, their wings flapping furiously. The small one flew fastest and furthest, and was the least visibly distressed. But before the two large ones had flown very far, their wings seemed to grow fatigued; they lacked the strength to carry themselves further. Losing control over their flight, they began to sag and drop downward. With great shrieks and squawks they struck and bounced against the ground several times in succession before they were finally able to struggle into the air again and escape. Huge clear swathes of crushed and broken trees, shattered by the iron-hard wings, marked those spots in the forest where they had struck the ground.

Zhao and his friends were well protected from the effects of the music, and felt little more than faint lassitude and fear. They never dreamed that the pipes could contain such terrible power. The strangers on the cliff had neither showed themselves nor engaged in direct conflict, but had driven the terrible mutant birds away in terror. This was magic of a very high order, and the three men were filled with awe and admiration.

The mutant birds had engaged their complete attention, and the men had not observed what was happening on the ground. When the birds retreated, Zhao and his companions discovered that the serpents and beasts had suffered even more. Some lay limply on the ground like dead things, others were stretched out in trees with barely a sign of life. All of them stared dully, eyes glassy, mouths closed, unable to utter a sound. They seemed completely paralysed. One of the Miao women was lying in a dead faint on the rock, and the other was half lying, half sitting, supporting herself with both arms in a feeble attempt to rise.

The music on the cliff top had changed once again. It became vast and ethereal, much as it had been at the beginning, only grander and more pleasing to the ear. Zhao Lin was the first to realize that their adversaries, both human and animal, had been utterly vanquished, and that the time had come for them to leave. He signalled to the others, and then addressed the two women on the rock.

"This is the effect of the pipes of the Immortals!" he shouted. "Your birds and animals have been vanquished! It is clear who is the victor, and who is the vanquished. We have yet other Dharma-treasures that we have not yet used. But since the conflict is now ended, and mindful of the fact that you were motivated by your desire for marriage rather than maliciousness, we are unwilling to retaliate.

"Heed my advice! There are many excellent Chinese men about; you should make other plans! You sent your beasts to harm us without good cause, and in addition disturbed Immortals making their music and enjoying the moonlit night. None of this embarrassment was necessary; you have brought it on yourselves. However, no one need know of it, and neither you nor we have been injured. Let us go our separate ways in peace! I have already said that I will visit your mountain, but if you continue to harass us in this preposterous manner, we shall have no choice but to cancel our visit."

Zhu and Wang chimed in to affirm their support for Zhao's words. The two women were now both struggling to rise, but without success, and showed no signs of having heard. Zhao judged that the sisters no longer had the strength to hinder their departure. He gave the word to depart, and they began to walk away. The glowing shield moved along with them. After they had gone a short distance, they turned to look. They were now out of sight of the rock, and the women did not seem to be following. The three of them bowed in gratitude in the direction of the cliff, and continued nonchalantly on their way, avoiding the serpents and vermin lying across their path. When they saw no more of the creatures, they deactivated their shield.

CHAPTER 13

A Last Embrace?

IT WAS THE HEIGHT OF SUMMER, AND THE NIGHT WAS SHORT. THE full moon hung high above the distant mountains in the west, but a faint glow already dimmed the stars to the east. Zhao was cautious enough to assume that the Miao sisters were not prepared to give them up. As soon as it was light, the pipe players on the cliff would depart. The women had suffered a crushing humiliation in full view of their intended lovers. They were helpless against the mysterious musicians, but judging by what Zhao knew of their temperaments and the customs of their people, the women would attempt to confront them once more. Failing that, they would probably try to trail them. If the men led them to Willow Lake, it would mean endless trouble for them in the future.

Fortunately, Willow Lake was located deep within a spur of the Grief-at-Toil range along the Coiling River. The entrance to the valley, and the station from which the transport of goods in and out was coordinated, were both directly on the river. The watery route to the valley was dark, well hidden, and circuitous, difficult to spot from the outside. Zhao hoped to elude pursuit and reach the entrance unobserved.

Once they passed beyond the Peak of the Great Roc, they soon found the road they had often travelled in the past. In order to throw the Miao women off the track, they decided not to follow this direct route, but instead plunged into the wild and trackless mountains. They left deliberate signs of their passage, discarding food and provision bags in several places. At every opportunity they climbed to high vantage points to scan for signs of pursuit. They went nearly eight miles out of their way in this fashion, clinging to precipitous cliffs and overhanging crags, climbing now upward and now downward, always taking the least obvious route.

At last it was now full daylight. They had seen nothing along the way except an occasional bird flying north or south across the sky. They climbed several more heights to survey the surrounding terrain, but still saw no trackers. They pressed on, crossing first a deep and luxurious wood, then rocky and precipitous crags, cliffs, and ridges. Nowhere there any sign of human presence, not even a woodcutter's trail.

They had been in constant danger since arriving at the Peak of the Great Roc the night before, and had now followed winding animal tracks through nearly sixteen miles of wild mountains with no opportunity for rest. As great as their martial skills were, fatigue was inevitable.

Zhu Man-Tiger in particular,, who had escaped death twice in as many days, felt dreadfully homesick, and wished fervently that he might be transported directly home. But he understood the necessity of preventing the enemy from finding Willow Lake, and forced himself to endure

161

his weariness and keep pace with his companions. Sweat poured down his back. He was utterly fatigued in both mind and body. His pride prevented him from complaining, but inside he was crying out in misery, clenching his teeth against the pain. Wang Jin finally noticed Zhu's condition, and called to Zhao Lin.

"Eldest Brother! We never expected the going would be so rough in this region. Perhaps we should rest here before proceeding."

Zhao still worried that the Miao women were on their trail. If the sisters had recovered in the early dawn, he estimated that they would catch up with them very soon. The terrain they now traversed was open and exposed, and he had not planned to stop until they crossed over the mountains and reached the river bank near the entrance to the secret tunnel, where there was a good deal more cover. If they could just gain the main road without being spotted, the Miao sisters would very likely be taken in by his strategy, and find it nearly impossible to track them down. Once safely through this one critical stage, they would have a full year to prepare for the next encounter.

His first reaction to Wang's plea was one of disapproval. But then he chanced to look around, and saw that Man-Tiger's face and neck were red and swollen, and that he was panting and sweating profusely. Even Wang Jin, whose physical condition and training were excellent, showed signs of strain. Zhao recalled then the Stone Milk elixir that he had ingested, and realized that his own strength and endurance must have been greatly enhanced.

He quickly scanned the terrain. The side of the ridge they were now following was open and exposed, but there were large trees and strange contorted rocks all around which would offer a certain degree of cover. Zhao chose a pair of huge ancient pines growing side by side. Beneath them was a patch of shade nearly a third of an acre in size. They concealed themselves below these trees to rest.

The barren mountains around them were empty and silent. There was no trace of any human presence. Weeds grew thickly about, still wet with the night's dew. The setting was thoroughly desolate and deserted.

"These mountains are full of weeds, plants, trees, and rocks," Wang Jin said with an uneasy laugh. "It offers excellent cover for birds and animals, but we have not seen a single living creature. Many traces seem to have been left by large and ferocious creatures. Where have they all gone? This is strange indeed."

Zhao reflected for a moment, and then answered. "Remember, we have been angling off and doubling back, so it is only natural that we feel as though we have travelled a long way. Actually, if you add it up, we have only come about eight miles. The pipe music was loud and potent, even when it sounded fine and delicate. I am quite sure that we are still within the area of its influence. All the birds and animals here must have been driven away."

Suddenly Zhu Man-Tiger pointed up into the sky. "Look! See that, flying toward us? Isn't it a large bird?"

Startled, Zhao and Wang looked upward. A bird was in the sky not far away. In the sunlight its yellow plumage flashed and shone like a fabric woven of gold thread. It was neither eagle nor crane. Its long feathered wings spread seven or eight feet as it soared rapidly with the wind. It was nothing like the mammoth birds they had seen the night before, but large and unusual birds of prey of this kind were seldom seen. It approached from the direction of the road to Willow Lake. When it was almost directly above them it wheeled suddenly to one side, and flew toward the upper reaches of the Coiling River.

When it did not return they decided that it was no more than a chance encounter, and gave it no further thought. They rested a while longer, and then took out their grain provisions and dried meats. After eating their fill, they found a mountain spring nearby and drank. Their strength had recovered to some degree, and they resolved to continue on once more.

After a time they drew near the road they usually travelled when they returned home. There was no trace of the Miao women, or of any living creature, save for one or two unusual birds flying past. In the barren mountains of the southern barbarian regions there had always been many strange, unidentifiable birds, most of which did not fly very high, so this was nothing to be wondered at. Beyond raising their heads briefly to watch them, and perhaps making a comment or two, the men paid little heed.

One last ridge remained between them and the river. To cross it they would have to travel along it to their right until they reached a break in the rock which afforded an easy way through. After that it would be only another ten miles or so to the water stockade through which goods were relayed to and from the secret valley. They moved to higher ground and carefully surveyed the surrounding terrain. From this altitude the visibility was excellent. It was not long past noon, and the sun hung high in a cloudless sky. They turned to look at the Peak of the Great Roc. It and the many layers of mountains between stood out clearly before them. They could trace every bit of the long winding route they had followed.

Zhao cursed himself for a fool. Because of his unfounded suspicions they had spent the better part of a day on a long, useless detour, and come no great distance. His two friends were exhausted. Had the Miao women been on their trail, it would have been an easy matter for them to send the animals under their command to track them down. The men had kept under cover as much as possible, but had been forced to travel part of the way in the open, and could have been spotted easily by anyone from a high vantage point like the one on which they now stood.

There was nothing for it but to continue. Before long they reached a wide open slope. It was not difficult to traverse, and the three men were swift of foot. Having just escaped from great difficulty, and with familiar mountains in view, they were doubly anxious to press on. Occupied with thoughts of home, they arrived at the break in the ridge almost before they realized it.

Beside them was an unbroken cliff; the Coiling River flowed along its base. In the past, they had often delighted in travelling along the top of this cliff, enjoying the sight of the river below. This time, however, they felt it prudent to take advantage of the cover provided by a twisting ravine running parallel to the river beneath the ridge. Someone on a prominence looking far out over the landscape would be unable to spot them there. They descended into the ravine, which turned off to the right along the base of the ridge.

They had gone barely a hundred feet when a parrot with multicolored plumage flew down from the treetops on the cliff above. It flapped over their heads and landed on a rock in the wall of the ravine not far ahead. It addressed them in a high-pitched squawk.

"Lover-brother Zhao, go no further! Aunt Cunning-Maid asks you please to wait, there is something she wants to tell you! She won't hurt you at all, oh no! Wherever you go Aunt Cunning-Maid knows. Why do you hide?"

The men were greatly startled and alarmed. They had some difficulty comprehending the parrot's speech, and it repeated the message. They were now close to the stockade, and dared go no further for fear of leading the enemy right to their home. They had no choice but to stop and wait. Zhao, realizing that the bird was intelligent, deliberately shouted at it.

"Hasn't your mistress given up yet? Fly back at once with this message! Marriage is based on mutual consent. There is no love between us brothers and you sisters. We made this quite clear to you last night. Why do you persist in following us?"

"I won't go tell her," the parrot shrieked. "I am afraid. Aunt Cunning-Maid will beat me. You can't get away either. Aunt Cunning-Maid will be here in a n instant."

All three of them felt that to wait there quietly was an admission of weakness. Zhao prepared to make further efforts to browbeat the parrot into leaving, but the bird squawked and began leaping up and down.

"Here comes Aunt Cunning-Maid on Old Goldie! My job is done!"

High up in the sky they heard the booming call of a very large bird. A bright golden star appeared in the sunlight, streaking toward them from the Peak of the Great Roc with preternatural speed. In the twinkling of an eye it had drawn close, and its form became clear. It was none other than the strange crane-like bird they had seen on the road that morning. A Miao woman was mounted on its back, and by the time they had recognized her as Cunning-Maid, the bird had already begun to descend toward them at an oblique angle, fast as a shooting star.

The bird was shaped very like a huge bat. Its wings were large and wide, and its body relatively small. It was covered with fine golden feathers, which reflected the sunlight as though wet or oily. On its forehead sprouted a single horn. Its eyes bulged strangely as though in anger. A curious beak, shaped something like a crane's, was slightly open, revealing rows of sharp teeth. Its body was short and thin, but from its underside there sprouted a pair of long thick legs with foot-long talons like steel hooks. When its wings were extended, they spread out over ten feet, but when it landed it tucked them neatly over its back, folded over three or four times. The entire effect was of a creature whose every part was poorly proportioned in relation to the whole. Compared with its graceful appearance in flight it seemed rather weird and ugly, though none the less frightening. They had not seen this particular specimen the night before. The men wondered where the two sisters had managed to collect such an enormous variety of creatures.

Cunning-Maid leaped lightly off the bird's back and approached Zhao Lin. She seemed worried and unhappy.

"I know you do not love me," she addressed him. "But I will not force myself on you like some ordinary Miao wench. You took a terrible risk provoking my sister. Whether or not your Second Brother Zhu rejects my sister of his own free will, it is wrong of you to interfere. She is convinced that you are opposing her out of sheer perversity, and is bitterly angry. She can be vindictive and violent, and I was afraid she might lose her temper and do you harm. So, before coming here I struck a bargain with her. We agreed to separate for a time, and each conduct our relations with you in the way we think best. We have sworn not to harm either one of you no matter what happens, and not to resort to violence or coercion. This oath between sisters cannot be broken.

"You haven't the least inkling of what you have done by committing yourself to visit our mountain. You seem to have the idea that you understand my people's ways from frequenting a few Miao market fairs. Why didn't you consult with Soaring Cloud and her friends before blurting out something of such mortal significance?

"If I may speak plainly, I have precious little respect for your Second Brother Zhu. For my part, I wouldn't tolerate the man at all except for the sake of you and my sister. He should never have flirted with my sister in the first place. If he were a proper man, he would stand straight and step forward to refuse her simply and directly. It was wrong of you to keep him from speaking for himself. He wouldn't give her a straight answer. He talked on and on without speaking plainly, and made no effort to resist her embraces. When you started shouting to her, she became convinced that he was actually willing. She thinks that all Chinese people are afraid of their elder brothers, and that you were deliberately taking advantage of your mastery over him to thwart her wishes.

"Last night, I had to go to great lengths to restrain her, and things might have gone badly if you had persisted in interfering. Your protective magic was given to you in secret just a few days ago, that much is obvious. Even those two weird men playing the pipes must have been persuaded to come and help you. My sister was fooled for a time, but I knew perfectly well what was happening. However would you have escaped without their aid?

"Your promise to come to our mountain was your greatest and most foolish mistake. The custom of the challenge is not known among many Miao tribes. Perhaps you learned of it from the Miao at Golden Flower Peak or Raven-Dragon Ridge, and assumed that our people resolved our conflicts through a duel, with the loser forced to obey the commands of the winner. Our people, however, name this custom 'Visiting the Mountain for a Trial by Fire'.Long ago our founding ancestor nearly met with death twice on account of this. Hence we all feel pain when it is mentioned, and it is shunned by all the Dragon Miao. The whole story is far too complex for me to explain now.

"I declare to you now that I am yours. Whether or not you accept me is up to you, but there is nothing you can do that will change my mind.

"This morning after you left, I felt no resentment against the pipe players. I was intoxicated by their music, and my whole body went limp, but I was not displeased. My sister, though, looked on the loss of her lover as a mortal insult, and blamed it all on you. She swore never to leave you in peace. After our mysterious adversaries left, she recovered, and resolved to return to our mountain to inform our people of this insult. She was determined to pursue her vendetta against your village during the coming year. It was only with great difficulty that I persuaded her not to do this. I told her that your master must be a mighty sorcerer, and if we acted too rashly, we would only bring shame on our parents and masters. A year would pass by soon enough, and she would have the opportunity to confront you honourably. I offered to go on ahead and speak with you. Only then did she finally agree not to carry word back to our mountain and bring forces to pursue against you, and to wait at the home of a friend until I reported the result of my discussion with you.

"I have a great many birds of considerable intelligence under my command. They can seek you out no matter how secret a hiding-place you might find. They communicate with others of their kind, and make inquiries of birds everywhere in their own language. After I took my sister to our friend's house, all I had to do was summon the Green Simurgh and instruct him accordingly. Before long he had communicated with others of his feathered folk, and learned that your people live beside a lake deep in the mountains not far ahead. They said your people had lived there for many years. They also told us how you had spent hours following a long and winding course through the wilds, which you must have done to throw us off your trail. You certainly can be infuriating!

"If you are willing to listen to my advice, stop trying to influence your sworn brother's decision, and let him speak for himself! If you do this, my sister will no longer be your enemy, and all will be forgiven. Otherwise, not only you but your entire village might not escape her retribution."

Before Zhao had a chance to reply, Zhu Man-Tiger interrupted. He was furious at Cunning-Maid's open contempt for him. Her words were full of barbs and jibes, and she seemed to be accusing him of putting his friends into danger. He was emboldened by the fact that the apes were not in evidence, and felt that the jade pendants of his companions would protect them if she resorted to violence. He laughed contemptuously at her.

"It seems that your sister is convinced that my Elder Brother Zhao is deliberately thwarting her. Well, let me tell you something. After seeing the unpleasant way she behaved last night, I wouldn't want her now even if she were willing to be my concubine. It will never come about, so how can she know whether or not anyone is interfering? Likewise, my brother won't accept you no matter what you do! Just what do you intend to do about that?"

The girl turned her clear sparkling eyes to give him a sidelong glance of chill contempt.

"If you were so firm and resolute, why didn't you come out and say so in the first place?" she answered him icily. "Decent people are suffering on your account! Don't think that I can be bullied because I did not act against you last night! It is quite true that your Elder Brother Zhao does not desire me, but at least he feels some pity and goodwill toward me. He is unwilling to reveal it in word or expression because he is afraid that I will cling to him. If he were to change his mind about retiring from the world and decide to take a wife, he would accept me at once. I can tell that his heart and word are one. He does not desire me, but he will desire another even less. If he were to accept me, then I would be happy beyond my wildest expectations, greatly fortunate to get such a perfect mate. But if he does not, my heart will still be at peace. I will miss him terribly and think of him always, but I won't hate him, and will never press him.

"As for you, my sister must be blind. She may actually get what she wants, though, so perhaps she is more practical than I. Marriage to a weak and wicked man like you would be shallow and meaningless. But because I love the man who has won my heart, I have bonds with all who are associated with him. I have hurried here at great risk to save him and the lives of all your people.

"Let me tell you something else. Don't think that you are safe from me because you are carrying some sort of magic charm. I don't know what devious trick you had in mind by not using yours along with the others last night, but the fact that you did *not* made my sister think that you still felt affection for her. I did not see what manner of object it was, but I can guess that the Old One in Green looked down on you, and would have given you one that was inferior to the others. You have no magical powers of your own. If I really wanted to destroy you, there would be plenty of weak points in your armour to attack. You are doing nothing more than basking in the reflected glory of my lover, and it is for his sake that I do not deal with you as you deserve. You are bold and shameless to speak to me in this way!"

Cunning-Maid clearly was ready to say a good deal more, but both Zhao and Wang could see that her expression was growing uglier by the minute. Zhu Man-Tiger was bursting with rage, barely able to restrain himself from attacking her, but not quite daring to do so. Zhao and Wang urged them to calm, but Cunning-Maid ignored them and continued to berate Zhu without mercy. Finally, fearing that Man-Tiger had been provoked to the point of violence, Zhao shouted at her to stop.

"Cunning-Maid!" he barked. "Be still! You say that you favour me, why do you not listen to me?"

Mindful of Cunning-Maid's powers, Zhao had been circumspect in his dealings with her up to that point, but when he heard her bitter denunciation of Zhu, his heart grew cold with fright. He was further distressed by the fact that she had discovered the secret location of the valley. In his mounting anxiety he failed to choose his words with care, and forgot that such a sharp and familiar tone should only be used with those with whom one is intimate. Only after it was too late did he realize this, and feared that she would misunderstand. And indeed her anger gave way instantly to joy, and she turned and moved close to him.

"I knew all along that you pitied and valued this unfortunate Miao girl," she said softly, smiling sweetly at him. "But do not fear. From now on I will never cling to you or trouble you again, and what is more, I will help you out of your current predicament, even if I die for it. This will be the token of my faith!"

She pursed her lips and gave a sharp whistle. As she berated Zhu Man-Tiger, she had given the bird a quick signal with her hand, and it had flapped into the air and begun wheeling above them, apparently keeping a lookout. When it heard the whistle, it dropped low. Its head darted beneath its wing for an instant, and it flung down a short arrow, which the Miao girl caught in her hand. She mumbled an oath over it, then broke it in half and flung the pieces on the ground. She turned to him.

"My lover, do you trust me now?"

Zhao chose his words with care. "I recognized from the first that you were superior to your sister. I am aware that your people treat the oath of the broken arrow very seriously indeed. Those of us among the Chinese people who value honour treat our friends with honesty and know one another's hearts. I already trusted you, and valued you; the ritual is superfluous, and I would have stopped you had I known what you intended."

Cunning-Maid smiled ruefully. "Hearing these words from you, I could go now to my grave without regret. Perhaps I am greedy, but I am still not satisfied. Just now I entreated you to tell me what is in your heart. If you are willing to say it, I will be happy for the rest of my life."

Zhao Lin did indeed find her graceful and beautiful as an Immortal maiden, her feminine charms superior even to those of Soaring Cloud.

168

But up to now he had been suspicious of her, and felt her words and actions to be overly direct. Young women, he had always thought, should be gentle and feminine, using subtle means to bind a man by a soft but unbreakable thread of love. Even if it were the woman who took the initiative, she ought to find a way of making her role seem a passive one. On the surface at least it would appear as though it were the man who had captured her and made her his plaything. In reality, he would have surrendered gladly, a mouse in her bag, free to move about and struggle as much as he liked, but never able to go so much as a single step beyond the bounds she set for him. Even a man who wooed a woman too aggressively, clinging and grasping at her for dear life, would eventually arouse only revulsion in the object of his love. This was, Zhao felt, even more the case with a woman. No matter how great her charms, such tactics would diminish her attractiveness, and arouse in the man only displeasure and contempt.

But Cunning-Maid had not offered violence the way her sister had, and had not persisted in clinging to him after her first attempt had failed. It was obvious that she thought herself very much in love with him, and wanted to take him away with her. But she was able to put aside her own selfish interests, and did everything she could to protect him regardless of the cost to herself, and even felt concern for those associated with him. Her direct and selfless manner was hitting home at his most vulnerable spot. Her tone was gentle and sweet, delightful to the ear, and her words reflected a lovely sadness that appealed directly to his own integrity and kind heart. No matter how stubborn he might be, at the very least he could not help but feel pity for her hopeless love and acknowledge her good intentions. He was an honest man with a strong sense of good. He heard her trembling plea, and saw the tears in her eyes. He felt no desire for her, but his heart softened. He could not restrain himself from blurting out words of comfort.

"You have read my heart correctly," he said. "My mind is made up to seek the Dao, and before long I intend to leave here and go elsewhere. That is truly the only reason why I do not desire to have a family."

"If so, then whether or not you marry me, you will never desire another woman," Cunning-Maid said happily.

"If even a beautiful and passionate woman such as you cannot move my heart, how could I ever desire another?" Zhao Lin answered readily. "But you must realize that the bond between me and my two friends is stronger than life itself. You ask me not to interfere in my Second Brother's affairs, but I cannot oblige you in this."

Cunning-Maid's face brightened when he first spoke, but then fell once more as he continued. Suddenly she reached out to seize his shoulders, and shook him sharply back and forth.

"Interfering will not be of any use at all," she said desperately. "It cannot help, and it could hurt. Please do as I say!"

Zhao Lin, facing her with his hands on his hips, made no effort to argue.

169

"I will not lie to you," he said simply. "I have said that I would go in challenge to your mountain, so I shall do just that. If your sister comes to seek trouble before the appointed time, how do you know that I do not have ways of defending myself?"

Cunning-Maid stood stupefied for a moment, her expression dark and uncertain, her beautiful eyes fixed on him. Suddenly she dropped to her knees and embraced his legs.

"You are truly my husband!" she cried out. "I saw right from the first that you were not one to go back on your word. It is just that the consequences are too terrible, so I thought that perhaps I could persuade you to change your mind to get you out of trouble. But since you are determined, I must help you to the bitter end. If everything turns out all right, well and good. If not, and I must give up this life to save you, it will not have been in vain. First I will take whatever measures I can to see that my sister does not try to harm you before the appointed time. After you have gone home, you must leave again in secret as soon as possible, and secure the help of powerful friends in your defense. Everyone in my clan has a good command of sorcery, so mere mastery of martial arts is quite useless. No matter how many ordinary warriors are arrayed against her, all my sister need do is send one white ape against them, and they will be torn to shreds. Only powerful allies like those two pipe players will be of help to you. When the time comes I will aid you without fail, either openly or in secret. With the compassion and aid of the gods of Heaven, I will not fear even if I am torn to pieces. All that I will seek is to maintain peace between you and our old Crag-Lord; if this can be done I will be satisfied.

"I have been away from home a long time, and must now return. If you feel any pity for me and my efforts for you, then will you not embrace me just once to show your kind regard?"

Zhao Lin, now more than ever aware of the danger he was to face, knew that he was fortunate to have an ally in the enemy camp. She would be able to keep many obstacles from his path in times to come. Already she had saved him much trouble. At the same time he was truly moved by her passionate love for him, and felt that it would be untoward of him to hurt her any more than necessary. He was also unwilling to give her the impression that he secretly felt her, a Miao woman, to be inferior to him, a Chinese man. He had made it clear that he was firmly resolved not to marry, so there could be no harm in embracing her. Under the circumstances, even if she had wanted to cling to him according to the typical Miao custom he would have been hard put to resist.

"Since you are good of heart, this I will do," he said.

He reached down to draw her up, and she stood willingly in response. She draped herself softly against him, her arms reaching around to embrace him. She asked him to hold her more tightly, and he obeyed. They held each other for a moment, her face against his. She was scantily dressed in the summer heat, exactly as she had been the previous night, covered by only a single layer of clothing. The deep

ravine was well shaded and almost cold. Zhao Lin, who had little experience of women, found that her skin was firm and deliciously smooth
and cool, like fine soft jade. Cunning-Maid, happy and content, worked
her charms to excellent effect. Her shining eyes, filled with limitless affection and ardour, were fixed on his face. She murmured 'Dear lover'
to him several times, vermilion lips and white teeth close to his own,
and a warm fragrance teased his nostrils. Zhao, in the arms of a woman
for the first time in his life, felt dizzy in spite of himself, though he tried
resolutely not to respond. A strange sensation stole over his body, and
he cried out to himself in dismay. He struggled to quiet the turmoil in his
mind, and his expression at last grew calmer. He tried to speak, but she
would not let him. She tightened her embrace, and kissed him three or
four times on the lips and cheeks. Then she suddenly let go and wiggled
free, smiling happily at him.

"You have given me my heart's desire," she proclaimed. "From this
day forward I am yours. Even if there is conflict because of it, my sister
and the others can no longer hold me responsible. Your village is located in an excellent spot, but it cannot be kept secret forever, even
though I can delay them from discovering it for a time. Did you not say
that you were going away to seek the Dao? It would be best if you leave
soon, before they find you. When you depart the valley, I will know of
it, and if you encounter trouble I will help. As long as you are not in the
village, she will not take her vendetta against your people there.
Whether your Second Brother accepts or refuses her, other people will
not be involved in any trouble. You have put your trust in me, but it is
hard to say the same for your Second Brother. He obviously hates me,
and will attempt to drive a wedge between me and my sister, but I do
not fear this. I must part from you now, lest my presence cause trouble
for you on your return."

The strange bird in the air above crooned deeply several times in
succession. Cunning-Maid looked uneasily upward, and gestured with
her hand. The huge bat-shaped mutant dropped like a stone to the
ground. Cunning-Maid pointed to the three men, and spoke to the bird.

"Ah-Ning, this is my man, and these are my man's good brothers. If
anything happens to them, you and your fellows must help them." Then
she looked askance at Zhu Man-Tiger and snorted at him in contempt,
and leaped lightly up onto the bird's back. The creature took off at once
into the air, and in a twinkling had flown high into the sky. But then it
wheeled about and swooped low over their heads. Cunning-Maid called
out to him once again.

"Please do take care of yourself, dear lover! You must do as I have
asked! Farewell!"

Zhao Lin, hearing the grief in her voice, and feeling great pity for her,
hastened to shout back in reply.

"Cunning-Maid, do not worry! I shall follow your advice!" His shout
was still echoing as the great bird once again mounted into the sky, dart-

171

ing in and out of the clouds, racing back the way it had come with the speed of a shooting star. An instant later it had completely disappeared.

"I never dreamed that a Miao woman would be so deeply in love," Wang Jin laughed, obviously embarrassed. "What we were told on the Mountain of Verdant Spots is true after all."

Zhao Lin shook his head and sighed. "From what I can see, this woman's passion will lead her to break the rules of her clan. The laws of the Miao people are strict, and are applied impartially to all, no matter how powerful their relatives might be. This woman's beauty, spirit, and virtue are all remarkable. 'The falling flower has desire, but the flowing water into which it falls feels nothing,' as the saying goes; if I do not love her, what can be done? Still, if she breaks her laws on account of me and is killed for it, it would be a terrible shame, poor girl."

Zhu Man-Tiger gave a malicious laugh. "What does it matter if one little Miao slut gets herself into trouble and is beaten to death for it?"

Zhao and Wang, seeing that Zhu was still incensed at the girl for her contemptuous treatment of him, and mindful of the fact that he had suffered a great deal throughout their journey, mentioned her no more. They looked about for the parrot, but it too had flown away; for the time being, at least, their movements were not being watched. In any case Cunning-Maid had promised to help them divert pursuit, and would prevent her sister from making trouble. They relaxed their vigil and continued boldly on, delaying any further plans until they had reached Willow Lake.

CHAPTER 14

Return to Willow Haven

THEY TRAVELLED ON FOR A TIME AT A LEISURELY PACE, AND SOON reached the receiving station on the river. There had been no unusual activity anywhere along the road. Zhao issued instructions to the man on duty in the stockade, and they rested there a short while. Then they made straight for the secret route through the cave. On the way they agreed that since it was nearly evening, and all of them were tired, they would do no more than report in after they arrived, and go directly to their homes. There was no point in causing an uproar, they reasoned, since nothing could be done at once in any case. The next morning they could give the Village Master and the Council of Elders a complete account of what had occurred, and let them deliberate on how best to deal with the situation.

Almost as soon as they arrived, their luck turned against them. Zhu Shi, the current Village Master, was Zhu Man-Tiger's uncle, and lived right next door to him. He saw at once from Man-Tiger's expression that something was wrong. When the others had gone, he pressed Man-Tiger for answers. Man-Tiger, who had been in an ill humour for many days, put up little resistance. He soon told the whole story, sticking mainly to the truth, except for a few embellishments at points where he had behaved foolishly.

Zhu Shi listened with mounting alarm. The safety of the entire village was threatened. He wanted to summon Zhao and Wang immediately, but Man-Tiger had begged him not to say that he had revealed anything in advance. Zhu Shi knew of their sworn brotherhood, and realized that there must be something wrong between them. He grew suspicious of Zhao and Wang, certain that his nephew was hiding something.

The next morning, as soon as it was light, Zhao and Wang came to see the Village Master. Man-Tiger had no opportunity to warn them of what he had already told his uncle. Zhu Shi soon found inconsistencies between Zhao's and Man-Tiger's version of events. Zhao carefully avoided any mention of magic, as well as anything that would embarrass Man-Tiger. He said that a misunderstanding had arisen because of a difference in languages, and that the women had set their animals on Zhu. Afterwards, one of them had taken a liking to Man-Tiger, and attempted to force him into being adopted into their clan in marriage. The other sister, Cunning-Maid, was hopelessly in love with Zhao, and in a pitiable state. She had agreed to aid them in secret, and act as an ally in the enemy camp. Zhao said nothing about the magical powers of their hosts on the Mountain of Verdant Spots, knowing that the Old One and the others did not wish to be known to the outside world.

173

Zhu Shi was astute and of a suspicious nature. He was proud of his handsome and heroic nephew, and the bond between them had always been close. Confronted with two contradictory accounts, it was only natural that he tended to believe Man-Tiger. Man-Tiger had said that Cunning-Maid was the more vicious of the two sisters. During their journey home, he asserted, she had hunted them down on the back of a strange bird, intending to do them harm.

After so many years of peaceful isolation, this was the first time the village had ever faced such a crisis. Zhu Shi, now thoroughly alarmed, began to question them in detail. Only Zhao's and Wang's excellent standing in the community prevented him from dealing with them more harshly. Wang Jin responded to the interrogation with his usual modesty and patience, but Zhao Lin soon grew irritated at Zhu Shi's insistent questioning. But since Zhu Shi was his senior, Zhao was in no position to defy him openly, so he kept his anger in check. Zhao and the Village Master now faced each other, polite on the surface but at odds underneath, each doing his best to suppress his mounting annoyance.

Meanwhile, community leaders and members of the Council of Elders began to arrive singly or in small groups. The Village Master had sent out messages the night before inviting them to a meeting after he had heard Zhu Man-Tiger's story. Zhao Lin himself had intended to meet with the elders to deliberate on how the crisis should be dealt with, but when they appeared without warning, he realized that the Village Master did not trust him, and intended to charge the three with a serious offense. The only thing Zhu Shi had not done was to take the irrevocable step of convening a public trial at the village temple. As he realized this, Zhao gave a contemptuous laugh, and refused to answer further questions until all of the elders had arrived.

The deliberations began, and Zhao repeated his story. Fortunately, the present members of the Council of Elders were for the most part steady and experienced, and knew of Zhao's unfailing honesty.

Zhao and Wang had long since agreed that they would not speak of the supernatural events which had befallen them, or reveal that they themselves were soon to go to the South-End Mountains to seek their appointed master. They respected the wishes of the Old One in Green, Chen Graceful-Equity, and all of their disciples, who did not want their existence known to outsiders. Accordingly, Zhao told the assembly that the man they had gone to visit was a high-minded and noble recluse. Zhu Man-Tiger, though envious of the two for their good fortune, had previously agreed to stand by this story. The jade pendants and the powerful charm, they claimed, were the gifts of a mysterious stranger on the road, and their only virtue was that of repelling the attacks of serpents and other evils. They displayed these objects to the assembly. The charm was written in red on yellow linen, covered with strange seal characters and incomprehensible talismanic diagrams. The two pendants were not particularly unusual, except that the design and workmanship was obviously of great antiquity, and the jade of unusually fine quality; they too were engraved with unrecognizable talismanic seal characters.

Zhu Man-Tiger, seeing the fear and worry of the assembled elders, wanted to demonstrate to them the awesome power of the pendants, but, seeing Zhao Lin's resentment at the proceedings, he held his tongue. The assembled elders inspected the objects with passing interest, and laid them aside.

After some deliberation, the two oldest and wisest of those present, both Village Masters of distinction in times gone by, put forward the view that no great harm had been done, and that the three men were guilty of no more than youthful inexperience. Were not the Miao people known as great tamers of beasts and serpents, and were there not many sword swallowers, fire eaters, and conjurors among them? Over a thousand years had passed since the first military campaigns had been waged by the Chinese against the Miao, during which the barbarians had been utterly defeated. Their magic, if it existed, had availed them little. The Miao sisters could not be as powerful as Zhao and his companions had supposed; otherwise how could the women have been so easily mesmerized by the pipe players' music? All the villagers need do to prepare for the crisis was look to their defences. If the Miao found the valley, it would be a simple matter to lure them into an ambush and kill them all. The two wise men's words carried conviction, and everyone's fears gradually calmed.

Zhu Shi was also persuaded. Perhaps he had lent too much credence to his nephew's frantic tale the night before, and entertained unnecessary suspicions. However, his anger at Zhao Lin's intransigence had not abated. He felt that Zhao, the leader of the expedition, during the course of a journey made for private purposes, had run the risk of revealing the secret of the valley's location, thus violating the strictest prohibition in their laws. When the enmity of the Miao women was aroused, why had he not found a way to lead them to some distant place? Zhao had been entirely too negligent, and Zhu proposed a public trial to determine the appropriate punishment.

Fortunately, the elders all thought very highly of Zhao Lin, and of his sworn brothers. Here were three fine young men, who would no doubt some day serve as capable Village Masters. They were guilty of error, perhaps, but punishing them now would only tarnish their future prestige. The elders conveyed to Zhu Shi by their expressions that he should withdraw his proposition, and some even opened their mouths to interrupt him as he spoke. Despite his authority, the Village Master had little choice but to swallow his anger and resentment, and drop the accusations.

As Zhao Lin grew ever more exasperated at the elders' inability to grasp the seriousness of the threat against the village, he recalled Cunning-Maid's advice to leave as soon as possible, since the rest of the village would be out of danger once he was gone. With this in mind, he addressed the assembly.

"It is true that none of us was injured," he said. "And none of the animals or serpents actually approached us. But after such a frightening experience we felt that we could not but make a full report to you upon our return. I respectfully urge that we maintain vigilance lest we be caught unawares. My Second Brother Man-Tiger has an amulet of great power, but it should not be used lightly. My humble recommendation is that he and Sister-in-Law should for the time being move to the Canyon of White Duckweed near the entrance to the cave. There they will be well hidden, but may still come and go with little inconvenience. Brother Jin and I will withdraw to a hidden spot in or around the forest. The Miao women's intention is purely to seek a mate. Old Man Miao forbids them from having any conflict with Chinese people unless they are provoked. If they should find their way to our front gate, and see that the three of us are not here, they will doubtless depart. If a conflict does occur, we three brothers will be guarding the two most vulnerable points of entry into the valley, and can ensure that you have plenty of time to prepare against them."

Wang Jin addressed the assembly as well, delivering an artful statement carefully worded so as to cool tempers all around.

Zhu Shi was astute and intelligent, and certainly not evil or treacherous, despite being somewhat vain and suspicious. Only a few years older than Zhao, he often felt that he was not held in as high regard as Zhao by the community at large, which caused him considerable indignation. Now soothed by Wang's conciliatory words, he considered the facts more carefully. It was not in character for Zhao, Man-Tiger and Wang to stir up such trouble purely out of lust for a pair of Miao women. There was no dearth of comely maidens in the wholesome climate of the valley, and more than one person had offered to find them suitable matches. A good many girls confident enough of their own charms had taken the initiative in approaching Zhao and Wang. This was not unusual in the valley, where men and women mingled on a daily basis without the sort of social conventions and embarrassment found on the outside. But Zhao and Wang had steadfastly avoided all advances. They had not mingled much with women, determined instead to dedicate themselves wholeheartedly to their training. Because of this they were jocularly known as the "Iron Idiots." Zhu Shi found it unlikely that either would have attempted to seduce the Miao women and aroused in them such fiery ardour. If the two sisters were all as dangerous as they said, how had the men been able to escape them so easily?

Zhu's temper cooled, and his words and manner became friendly once more. He smiled and laughed easily, and gave his support to Zhao and Wang's proposals. The meeting was adjourned.

As Zhao and Wang left the meeting, Zhu Man-Tiger did not accompany them out. Zhao guessed that Zhu and his young wife had much to say to one another after their prolonged separation. He wanted to visit them, but Wang advised against it. Unlike Zhao, he had perceived that Man-Tiger had told his uncle everything, despite their agreement of the evening before.

"We have already decided we must leave as soon as possible," Wang said. "It is necessary to act with great secrecy and caution. Our situation is quite different from usual, when no one leaves the valley except at need, and the matter has been deliberated in public. The fewer people know about our departure the better. They do not understand the true danger of the situation, and it seems that the Village Master is intent on bringing serious accusations against us. If he or the Elders find out we are planning to leave they will certainly forbid it.

"We could tell our Second Brother of our plans and trust him not to reveal our secret deliberately, but he might let it slip in casual conversation with his wife, or with his uncle. The way I see it, the best thing would be to depart at once, and leave him a letter explaining that the two of us are going to journey to the South-End Mountains to present ourselves to our new master there. We must begin as soon as possible to enlist strong allies with unusual powers to help us when we fulfil our oath to challenge Jade Dragon Mountain. We must urge our Second Brother to do as you suggested, and take Second Sister-in-Law to hide in the Canyon of White Duckweed. At the same time ask his uncle to tell the villagers that if they ever discover that any Miao people, men or women, have slipped into the valley, they must pretend as though they had not noticed. No matter what happens they must not move to seize or attack them. If strange beasts or serpents appear, these too should be ignored as long as they threaten no harm. If the Miao people come openly to ask after us, the villagers can make any reply that seems best, as long as they treat them with courtesy. They might tell them that no such person lives in the village, or perhaps something to the effect that we have accompanied two mysterious warrior Immortals back to their mountain, flying away on the magic glow of their enchanted swords, announcing before leaving that we were going into retreat on Yellow Mountain to cultivate the Dao. We must arrange it so that our letter to Second Brother does not come into his hands until after we are gone. Tomorrow we can say that we are going into the woods for a look around, and entrust the letter to a third person. Then we can set out directly through the forest.

"Two years ago, when I had nothing to do, I made two exploratory trips into the forest. I found a path through it, well hidden, almost impossible to see. My thinking at the time was that the cave was our only means of egress from the valley, and if by some mischance another landslide like the one that struck many years ago cut the tunnel off, we might find ourselves in considerable difficulty. Another way out would serve very well in such an emergency. But it was no easy task. Ever since our ancestors came through the forest at such terrible risk to themselves, no one has dared to go into its depths. I was afraid that if I proposed such an exploration, people would say I was meddlesome, so when the opportunity arose I went out on my own.

"Do you remember early last year when you couldn't find me, and went rushing to the woods to search, only to bump into me just as I was coming out? You never asked me much about it, so I said nothing. I made two trips into the forest. The only unpleasant thing about it was that there were too many poisonous snakes and insects. The second time I went, I killed a large venomous serpent, and nearly lost my own life, but in the end found the way through. This time we have our jade pendants to ward off evil. The normal route through the upper reaches of the Coiling River would expose us to the eyes and ears of the Miao sorceresses. The roads we must traverse in the neighbourhood of the Peak of the Great Roc would be even more hazardous if Moon-Maid is still somewhere nearby.

"When I won through to the far side of the forest I discovered that the terrain was unfamiliar, so I climbed to a high place to look around. The paths through the mountains there looked difficult, and there were toxic miasmas in different spots, but we will have no trouble with that.

"Our ancestors left secret records of the route they took from Hunan Province. The inscription on the stele at the village temple also tells us something of the terrain and the direction of their travel. We can find their route to Hunan, and there link up with the main road to the North. What do you think?"

Wang Jin was quite right in saying that they would not be granted permission to leave the valley. Even in normal times the village relied on Zhu's and Wang's talents; with this new threat from the Miao sisters the elders would be even more inclined to keep the two of them in the valley to aid in defense. Zhao began to feel that Wang Jin's argument was sensible, and agreed to his plan.

All through the day Zhao expected Zhu Man-Tiger to come and spend part of the day with them, as he had invariably done in the past, or consult with them about their plans. But, as Wang Jin had anticipated, he never appeared. Zhao Lin began to wonder what it was that Man-Tiger had told his uncle that he was now too ashamed to show his face. Or perhaps he was still disgruntled because Zhao Lin had not given Cunning-Maid the rebuff Zhu felt she deserved. But Zhao felt no anger toward him; they were after all close friends, and he only thought that Zhu was being a little silly and ridiculous. If Zhu did not want to see them, he did not go to look for Zhu.

The next morning Zhao Lin drafted a letter to Man-Tiger, and he and Wang Jin stopped by the Village Master's house to pay their respects. Then they returned home, and each prepared a small pouch of gold dust, a good selection of weapons, and a few changes of clothing packed in a bag. Then they started out toward the forest. If anyone asked, they intended to explain that they were going to look around in the forest to keep an eye on the many serpents and animals lurking there.

When they reached the forest edge, they went first to speak with the people stationed nearby. There were ten or so households in that area, and it was an easy matter for them to secure grain provisions and dried meat for the journey. They gave the letter for Zhu to a man there, asking him to take it back to the village in three days' time. Zhao explained that they were going into the woods to scout around, and perhaps do a little hunting. They expected to be in the forest for several days. They asked for two hammocks and some of the repeating flares and the noise-making signal rockets people lost in the woods used to summon help. No one showed much curiosity. They all took it for granted that Zhao and Wang were skilled explorers and fighters, and knew that Wang Jin in particular had on more than one occasion gone into the forest alone for seven or eight days at a stretch; they had never heard of his encountering any significant danger.

The forest was extremely dense, spreading over thirty miles of darkness, within which the light of day never penetrated in all but a few spots. Beneath the densely intertwined tangle of branches thick trunks grew in solid ranks, jostling and crowding one another, leaving little space for a man to get through. To make things worse, poisonous serpents infested the path, and flying insects descended in a constant rain. A bite from a snake was more than most men could bear, and the insects, which swarmed in numbers too great to be fanned aside, could be dangerous as well. Mosquitoes, flies, and ants grew three or more times larger than normal, and most were highly venomous. Individual insect bites would itch maddeningly and swell up into painful lumps, and as they increased in number, the poison would accumulate to the point where the victim would lose consciousness. Thousands of insects would then converge on the body, and in little time could reduce a man to a skeleton. As a result, it was the usual practice among the villagers to organize hunting or herb collecting expeditions during the middle of winter when many of the insects were dormant. They were adept at protecting themselves, and went equipped from head to foot. Except perhaps for huge venomous serpents, they feared little, but it was still an arduous business. No one had ever dared go deep into the woods during the summertime.

Zhao and Wang plunged boldly into the forest, trusting to the power of their jade talismans. Through the first section of woods no serpent or insect approached them, since it was an area where the villagers often came to cut wood, and there were still a good many spots where the light of the sun penetrated. But when they had followed the usual trail beyond familiar territory, and the passage grew ever more arduous and difficult, they began to encounter obstacles, and had to start making frequent detours or cut their way through as best they could. The last traces of daylight faded; they had reached the area where it was perpetually dark. Insects swarmed in great numbers. Finally they fetched out the jade pendants and activated them in the prescribed fashion, and once again two columns of shimmering light erupted and encased them in a bright shield. The darkness for a hundred feet or more around them was lit up as bright as day, and all serpents and insects stayed far away.

Oddly, peaches grew in the darkness, and, though green in colour, had ripened in the summer heat. They plucked the sweet and juicy fruit at will off the larger trees to relieve their thirst, and preserved the water in their bottles.

"We are making excellent progress," Wang Jin observed, much pleased. "We can see where we are going without having to light a lantern. Last time it took me five days, but if we keep on like this, we should be able to get through in two."

Both men were agile and strong, and save for quick stops to eat, took no rest during the day. In the black murk of the forest they had no idea whether it was night or day. When they estimated that it was evening, and happened upon a comparatively clear space, they strung their hammocks from the trees. Still within their glowing shield, they slept in comfort and safety.

When they awoke, they ate from their provisions, and Wang Jin led the way forward. The occasional spots where hints of daylight penetrated grew even rarer. They calculated the passage of time by their own hunger, and eventually settled for a second period of sleep.

When they got up, Wang Jin looked carefully around at the forest, found marks he had left the year before, and realized that they were almost through to the other side. He and Zhao estimated that the time was now the afternoon of the third day of their journey. But when they got to the edge of the woods and looked around, there was only a faint hint of daylight in the east. They had settled down to sleep too soon both times, and must have risen only a little after midnight of the second day. Surprisingly, they had managed to traverse more than thirty miles of ancient, nearly impenetrable forest in just two days and two nights.

They rejoiced and congratulated each other. They still had a long journey past countless mountains and rivers, but never would it be as arduous as this forest. They made preparations to travel swiftly toward the North, taking only provisions and water bottles, their weapons, clothing, and a single rope hammock. Everything else they hid within the forest. When their equipment was in order, the sky was already light.

Ahead of them was an unfamiliar terrain of ravines, swamps, and meadows, all overflowing with mists and unwholesome miasmas. Zhao was certain that the many fierce animals and birds under the control of the Miao sorceresses would be seeking them everywhere. Cunning-Maid of course did not intend them any harm, but she was excessively infatuated, and he felt it best to avoid her notice.

The miasmas were at their most poisonous during the dawn hours. Their jade pendants offered protection, but they had deactivated the glowing shield at the forest's edge, fearing it would attract unwanted attention. They had no alternative but to find a way over the hills and ridges where the poisonous vapours did not reach. There were many difficult climbs, but they were able to use their Light-Body techniques to good effect. They had also swallowed some of the potent elixir pills given to them by the Green-Clad Old One, and found their strength greatly enhanced. Although they had been hurrying along since midnight, they felt no fatigue.

Neither Zhao nor Wang had ever been beyond the borders of Yunnan Province. Two years previously they had gone as far as the border of Guizhou, but no further. They had studied their ancestors' account of the difficult and dangerous flight from Hunan through Guizhou to Yunnan, but did not realize that there was a direct route, and that the wooden platform-road built into the cliffs of the Thorn Mountains would have taken them straight to the South-End Mountains. Instead, they planned to go through Guizhou, from where they would turn eastward into Hunan. Once there, they wished to visit the scenic spots at the Mountain of the Goddess and Lake Dongting. Since youth they had read about this enchanted spot in the *Record of Yueyang Tower* by the scholar Fan Xiwen, and had always longed to see it. From there they would go to Wuchang and climb the Tower of the Yellow Crane, and see the sacred spot where an ancient Immortal had ascended to Heaven astride a crane. There they could make inquiries as to the best route northward to Shaanxi Province.

They had not at first fully taken into account the fact that their ancestors, as refugees fleeing the Mongols, had kept as far from civilization as possible. They had gone deep into the mountains and steaming jungles, following little-known, roundabout routes. Their records had little to say about the official postal highways. Zhao feared that they would lose time on detours through the unfamiliar wastes, burdened with provisions in the summer heat. Except for the first stage of their journey just beyond the forest, they decided not to follow the mountain route described by their ancestors, but take the official highways instead.

On the third day after leaving the forest they encountered two settlements of semi-civilized Miao. Zhao and Wang, both fluent in the Miao tongue, were well received. These Miao told them of a short cut through the mountains used by medicine peddlers. They took this path, though were careful not to tell the Miao where they were headed, and along the way they concealed themselves whenever other travellers, all of whom were Miao, came within sight. But the path was a good one; they gained the government postal highway without incident in a few days' time.

IV

On Central Mount the clouds begin to disperse;
the Goad and the Staff together
scale the Gorge of the Golden Lock;
before the leaves of Lake Dongting have fallen,
misty waves swamp the Magnolia Boat.

CHAPTER 15

The Mountain of the Goddess

DURING THE FIRST PART OF THEIR JOURNEY, ZHAO LIN AND WANG JIN proceeded with great caution, fearing that the Miao women might find them gone from Willow Lake and send spies to seek them out. They took great pains to conceal themselves whenever they spotted birds or animals which seemed at all out of the ordinary. Only when they had journeyed almost to the borders of Guizhou Province without incident did they relax their vigil.

Zhao Lin loved fine scenery, and, having encountered the Old One in Green, was aware that many unusual and mysterious people might be concealed deep within the mountains on high enchanted peaks. Their primary goal at present was to seek out their appointed master, but there were a number of places notable for magnificent scenery along the way, and Zhao intended to take advantage of the opportunity to visit them.

Zhao had long heard that Mount Qianling in Guizhou was exceptionally beautiful, and very much wanted to see it. Wang Jin, though he shared Zhao Lin's enthusiasm for mountain scenery, reflected on the fact that the border area between Yunnan and Guizhou was home to many Miao tribes, most of whom no doubt had frequent contact with their kindred further south. Cunning-Maid might learn of their whereabouts, and, though she did not intend them harm, her presence might prove troublesome. Wang urged Zhao to abandon the idea of visiting the mountain.

"At this stage it is important that we distance ourselves from the Miao people as quickly as possible," he argued. "Once we have found the people we seek, we can visit Mount Qianling on the way back."

Zhao Lin saw the truth of this at once, and agreed.

"Actually," Wang Jin continued, with a smile, "Cunning-Maid is a fine young woman. She has character, a good temperament, and remarkable abilities. The path we have chosen does not demand celibacy. Our own future master is married, and Elder Brother Ding Shao as well. All of them are mystic swordsmen far advanced on the path to immortality; obviously there is no prohibition on married couples cultivating immortality together. You are unmarried. If Cunning-Maid is willing to break with tradition and leave her people to go away with you, and our master and mistress give their permission, then what need is there to reject her so harshly?"

"Cease your jests, Third Brother!" laughed Zhao. "Small wonder Second Brother suspects me of taking a fancy to her! Of course I pity her, but my heart is truly fixed on the Dao. Our master and Cousin Ding are married, as you say, but they have no young children. That day at

Cousin Ding's house when you and Brother Wei Lai went outside to have a look around, our Second Brother Man-Tiger, with his characteristic lack of tact, observed that our Cousin Soaring Cloud was still very young, and asked why our master and mistress would encumber themselves with children after having achieved mastery of the Dao? Our Sister-Cousin Ding saw my efforts to shut him up, and laughed and said it didn't matter. She seemed to imply that our Sister-Cousin Cloud was an abandoned infant who ended up in the care of our mistress, which is how she has managed to achieve her present spiritual level. She mentioned also that her karmic burden in the world of dust was not yet expunged. We have very little understanding of our master and his people. All I know is that if I had a wife and children, they would be an impediment to my spiritual progress.

"I am not jesting," Wang replied. "I am quite serious. It is precisely her forbearance which poses a problem. She is both strong-willed and passionate. She loves you more than life itself, and will risk anything to save you. We are already seriously at odds with Moon-Maid, and when we go to their mountain next year we will surely make mortal enemies of the rest of their clan. How could Cunning-Maid's position be anything other than precarious? Whatever happens, she faces certain death with her own people, unless of course we are victorious and take her away with us. He has many sons and grandsons, most of them formidable. Enchanted traps and dangerous spells are bound to be woven thickly about the mountain. Cunning-Maid will aid us to the full extent of her ability, in violation of the prohibitions of her tribe. They cannot allow this to go unpunished; even Moon-Maid's hand will be turned against her.

"We have always prided ourselves on our chivalry and sense of justice. Surely you do not mean to suggest that we will stand idly by while this lovely, wise, and unhappy girl, our benefactress, is put to cruel torture and a horrible death? Could you endure this? Particularly when her love is so one-sided, and she so earnest and straightforward?

"She will do anything you ask of her. All she desires is to be near you. If you are afraid that marriage will interfere with your progress, perhaps she will be content to be your companion for the rest of her days, a wife in name only, with no desire to consummate her love. She will accept any terms. It is said that a third person is always impartial in such affairs, but when she came after us on the way home to say good-bye to you, even my heart went out to her. Don't tell me she didn't have a greater effect on you! It was obvious that you could not bear to leave her completely disappointed. Now she will risk even more for you, and make greater efforts to win your love.

"What happens if she is the one who saves us from danger, and risks losing her life as a result? I ask you, dear brother, what will you do then?"

"We will think of something when that time comes," Zhao answered. But as he spoke he reflected that if things really did come to such a pass, he would find himself in a difficult position indeed.

Wang Jin argued with him no more, but because of his urgings they did not go to Mount Qianling.

They did not know it, but at that very moment Cunning-Maid was indeed trying to find Zhao Lin. She intended to take him to meet a man of great power who might have given him important assistance. First she had taken the risk of hurrying directly to Willow Lake. There she was deceived and captured by Zhu Man-Tiger, and suffered a dreadful beating at the hands of the villagers. She endured the blows from sticks and canes with no attempt to retaliate, confident that Zhao's resistance to her suit would be further weakened when he learned of the event. Finally her great bird, the Green Simurgh, came to find her and bore her away.

She had at least discovered that Zhao and Wang were long gone. She concocted a story to explain her injuries to her sister, and sent her golden bird out to search for the two men. Assuming that the secret water route through the cave was the only exit from the secret valley, she was unaware of the direction of their travel. Finally, frustrated by their complete disappearance, she decided that they had been on the road for longer than she had thought, and ordered four of her swiftest birds to spread out in all directions to a distance of three hundred and fifty miles, each to make a careful survey of an allotted area and return to report. But the two men travelled quickly, and took pains to conceal themselves. The faithful birds soared about in diligent search, and on two occasions one of them wheeled right over the men. But the first time Zhao and Wang had chosen a concealed spot to rest, and on the second they were eating inside a house, and were not discovered. A day or two more, and they had passed beyond the birds' search areas.

When they crossed into western Hunan Province, they encountered an old and experienced wanderer, and learned for the first time of the quicker route through to the North from Sichuan Province. But now that they had already reached Hunan, they would have had to turn aside and follow minor roads up the Yangtze River to the west, and traverse the Three Gorges in eastern Sichuan. Having come this far, it would be best to proceed according to their original plan.

They went first to Baling, which lay along their route, to see the sights at the Mountain of the Goddess and Lake Dongting. There they planned to stop and take stock of the best route of travel onward, whether it would be quicker to go by land or by water.

Though educated and experienced, the two of them had lived all of their lives in a tiny and remote corner of the frontier, far from civilisation. As a secluded mountain haven in dark times Willow Lake was ideal, but the inhabitants were limited in vision and experience. Zhao and Wang had only travelled to Dali and a few other cities within the borders of Yunnan Province; even nearby there were many places they had never seen. On their numerous journeys out of the valley, they had become familiar with inaccessible mountains and raging waters, lands cloaked in drifting miasmas and the smoke of barbarian fires, but, busy with their missions, they had no leisure to seek out and enjoy areas of scenic beauty. All they could spare was a look as they went past, a hurried mouthful stolen from a sumptuous banquet table. The customs of the frontier region were restricted and provincial, the population sparse and widely scattered. Most of the people they met were Miao or other barbarians, strange in customs and speech, and they derived little pleasure from consorting with them.

All men take great interest in the novel and strange, and Zhao and Wang were no exception. When they reached the famed spots at the three tributaries of the Xiang River and the Seven Marshes in Hunan Province, it seemed to them that the mountains became sharper and the waters brighter, the people plumper and objects more substantial. Everything seemed to them utterly unlike the provinces of Yunnan and Guizhou. The famous Yueyang Tower, however, which they had long desired to see for themselves, was a disappointment: nothing but a small structure in the midst of the city, whose only remarkable feature was its excellent view of Lake Dongting. Zhao and Wang found it compared poorly to some of the towers built against the mountains overlooking their own Willow Lake.

Lake Dongting was at the heart of a land of abundance. As a major centre for traffic on both land and water, it was a place where merchants congregated in large numbers. A dense haze of smoke lay over the thickly populated area on its shores. Many-storied wine and tea houses lay everywhere, crowded with wealthy young rogues and crafty brokers, wreathed in the steam rising from endless tables of meat and heated wine. These establishments overlooked streets filled with the teeming thousands of ordinary folk, great rivers of pedestrians coming and going in all directions. The various sounds of the city merged into an undifferentiated roar which Zhao and Wang found overwhelming. They felt little desire to linger. If the area had been this noisy a few centuries before, they reasoned, then Lü Dongbin, the Immortal of Purest Sun-Energy, surely would never have been inclined to come here in search of fine wine and refined merriment.*

The lake itself, however, was magnificent. Far over the hazy stretch of waves and ripples a multitude of sails came and went, standing out sharply against the distant looming presence of the Mountain of the Goddess. On the far side of the lake twelve layers of mountain ridges, dark as charcoal, towered over a cloak of mist, seeming to float over miles of sapphire waves. Looking on it from afar the two men found it different from anything in their experience; their minds and souls grew calm within them.

---

* [Lü Dongbin was one of the famed Eight Immortals, said to have lived at the end of the Tang Dynasty.]

The two conferred for a while. The traces of the Immortal of Sun-Energy were so long cold that there was no point in looking for them. Better to go directly on to the mountain. Boat travel was convenient in those parts, and arrangements easily made on the spur of the moment. They elected to go by water, even though it was slower, so that they could rest from the travails of their journey.

Zhao and Wang had arrived in the city early in the day, and it was now barely noon. They went to an upstairs inn to eat their fill, and then descended into the streets and markets to sell gold dust and purchase clothing suitable for autumn weather. They then found their way to the shore, and soon hired a boat to take them to the city of Hanyang or the dry river channel on the far side of the lake, just below the Mountain of the Goddess.

The boatmen were father and son, and seemed simple and honest. The son, invariably cheerful and eager to please, was called Zhang the Fourth, and was just twenty years of age. Since childhood he had lived on the water, dressed in a boatman's coir raincoat and hat, and was a superb fisherman. He and his father had only recently constructed a fine new boat, and they did a brisk business transporting passengers and freight through the waterways of Sichuan, Hunan, Hubei, and Jiangxi Provinces. They also loved the mountains, and were familiar with most of the rivers and peaks along the routes they travelled. When they learned that their new passengers intended to visit famous sites along the route, they grew excited, and volunteered their services as guides. Zhao and Wang were delighted, and soon found themselves growing fond of the boatmen. Zhao ordered them to proceed directly to the Mountain of the Goddess, and plied them with questions about the famous sites around them. They spent the first hours of their journey in eager conversation, relieving the loneliness they might otherwise have felt.

"I have heard many stories of how the Immortal Lü three times drank himself into a stupor at Yueyang Tower," said Zhao. "I have also heard that the area of the three tributaries of the River Xiang and the Seven Marshes is one where mysterious people are said to wander or live in seclusion. Do such people really exist?"

Zhang the Fourth laughed. "You honoured guests come from far away, and know little of what goes on here. I have frequented the mountains since I was small, but never have I seen Immortals flying about on bits of mist and cloud. Everyone knows the story of the Immortal Lü's three drunken bouts in Yueyang Tower, but all we do is tell the story. If there really are Immortals, they certainly pay no attention to common folk like us.

"But strangely enough, something odd happened recently right on the Mountain of the Goddess. I can tell the story if you wish to hear it. It's only been a few days, so it is possible that the man has not yet left. I must warn you that much of it is just hearsay; I have not witnessed anything with my own eyes. You honoured guests are more educated and

187

knowledgeable than we, and will surely be in a position to evaluate the truth of the rumours during your visit. When we reach the Mountain of the Goddess, I can take you to see this man, if you wish."

Zhao and Wang asked what the strange event had been.

"THERE ARE MANY BUDDHIST AND DAOIST ESTABLISHMENTS ON THE Mountain of the Goddess," said Zhang the Fourth. "Long ago, there were only Daoist priests there. They were wealthy, and owned much land and property. But since the change of dynasty, government officials have believed only in the Dharma of the Buddha. The Daoists have been hounded and harassed, and gradually declined. Of the dozens of great Daoist abbeys on the mountain, most have fallen into the hands of foreign Buddhist monks.

"Only the Abbey of the Pure Void and the Bamboo-Immortal Abbey have continued to prosper as before. These two establishments are actually one. Their former abbot had at one time wandered the deserts of Mongolia, and befriended a number of royal princes there. By coincidence the Mongol prince leading the invasion of Hunan Province ninety years ago was one of these, a trusted friend of the abbot for many years. When the armies arrived, the prince went to pay his respects, and their friendship continued. It is said that the prince presented an iron plaque to the abbey, a token which has so far protected it from harm.

"In recent years barbarian monks have coveted the abbey property and the offerings it receives, and have come in strength to seize control of it. Some of these monks won the support of officials in their cause, and more than once everyone thought that the two establishments were done for. But somehow, without fighting or struggle, these monks, no matter how violent and ruthless, have always suffered ignominious defeat. The Daoist priests are quiet and unassuming, and you can't tell just by looking at them that they have any powers to speak of. But whenever an attack was launched, they went on about their daily business coolly and calmly as if nothing was amiss, and the attackers would eventually give up and leave. Everyone assumed that it was the royal authority of the iron plaque that kept them at bay. Someone actually inquired of the present abbot, whose name is Wang Pure-Wind, but he denied having any unusual powers. All they did, he said, was reason calmly with their adversaries, and then send them on their way. Nobody believes this, of course. They all reckon that this iron plaque is a mighty Treasure of Power, and that the priests are simply unwilling to acknowledge its existence to outsiders. But there is another side to the story.

"Formerly, there was a priest in tattered clothing living in the abbey. He never recited scriptures with the others, and in fact never involved himself in any of the abbey's affairs. What was worse, he loved wine more than his own life, and spent all his waking hours hopelessly drunk. Sometimes he would wander off and disappear for a year or two, but always returned to take up residence in the abbey once more. The ab-

188

bot was deeply fond of him, and the rest of the priests for the most part treated him kindly. They never tried to restrict his behaviour, and would even buy whole jars of excellent wine for his enjoyment. People living on the mountain say that he has no name or surname, and just call him the Drunken Daoist. He lived years and years in the abbey temple, always behaving in the same manner, never aging. He frequently emerged from the temple to buy wine, sometimes wandering as far away as the city of Yuezhou, where he cavorted drunkenly in the streets and markets.

"One night in the temple, as the priests were holding some ritual or other, the Drunken Daoist staggered back from a huge drinking bout, and behaved disgracefully in the main hall before a group of distinguished patrons and donors. He waved his arms and capered wildly about, howling abuse all the while. The abbot, saddened and embarrassed, spoke empty words of apology to the patrons, but did nothing to stop him. Two disciples in charge of the ceremony were standing by, and when they saw that the drunken priest was arousing the anger of the temple patrons, they grew fearful of the consequences, and hastened over to whisper words of caution. The Drunken Daoist paid no heed to them at first, but then flew into a rage. 'Ignorant, sinful bastards!' he shrieked. 'So you find me disgraceful, then! I grow weary of this place!' Then he staggered out. If he had not, the assembled company of distinguished patrons might have cursed or even beaten him.

"Oddly enough, as he stormed out, the abbot leaped to his feet in agitation and went after him. 'Master-Uncle, please wait!' he cried. 'Your humble disciple has something to say to you!'

"The assembled company finally realized why the abbot had treated this drunkard with such kindness over the years. The Drunken Daoist was the brother of his own master!

"The abbot rushed out as fast as his legs would carry him. No one had ever seen him run so quickly. It was night, but because of the warm weather and the religious festival then in progress, there were many boats moored at the Mountain of the Goddess, and directly in front of the abbey temple there were stalls selling midnight snacks. Many witnesses later said that the Drunken Daoist and the abbot Pure-Wind had emerged one after the other, and gone into the woods beside the temple. Then the moon ducked briefly behind a cloud, and when it reappeared the Drunken Daoist had vanished. Soon the abbot returned, dispirited and panting heavily. The patrons and other visitors asked him what had happened. If the Drunken Daoist was so anxious to leave, why not just let him go, even if he was the brother of the abbot's master? Anyone capable of raising such an uproar once would be sure to do so again.

"The abbot explained: 'I left my family for a life of asceticism as a small child, and it was this master-uncle who cared for me. He saved me more than once from serious illness, virtually resurrecting me from the dead. He is a respected elder to me, and a benefactor to whom I owe my life. I can never repay this debt. He was overly fond of wine, and gradually sank into drunkenness. He could never abide courtesy and social constraints. He spends most of his time on the opposite side of the mountain, drunk from dawn to dusk, except for occasional wanderings below the mountain. He ordered me never to reveal his status or address him as 'Master-Uncle', which is why no one ever knew who he was. Now he has lost his temper and left me, and I have failed to stop him. I feel deeply anxious .'

"The abbot was curiously dejected as he told his tale. He had always been well liked by all who knew him, and enjoyed the respect and friendship of the temple patrons. At the time they marvelled at the deep love and reverence he bore his benefactor, and the overwhelming grief he felt at the man's departure, but gave the matter no further thought. The Drunken Daoist was never seen again.

"Then, at the beginning of this month, two evil wandering Daoists visited the abbey. As soon as they entered the gate they began a campaign of violent intimidation. Strangely, the abbot seemed to fear them. For decades fierce and powerful enemies had failed to seize the abbey, but now it fell under the sway of these two dark priests. It is said that the abbot fell seriously ill from frustration and anger, and has withdrawn to the Bamboo-Immortal Abbey on the far side of the mountain to recuperate. The temple patrons were greatly outraged, and went to consult with the abbot, eager to redress the wrong. But they returned thoroughly dispirited, and would not mention the affair again.

"A few days ago I ran into a man on the street who hawks fish and vegetables outside the Abbey of the Pure Void. He said the two strange priests were dark and corrupt Daoists, great masters of demonic sorcery. They had engaged the abbot in a contest of power. Though himself a formidable magician, the abbot could not stand against them, and was badly wounded. He had no choice but to withdraw. The abbot was heard to say to his followers that if the Drunken Daoist had been present none of this would have happened. The fish seller had been asked by the abbot's disciples to cross the lake and keep an eye out for the Drunken Daoist in his old haunts, the wine shops of Yuezhou.

"Only then did we realize that the Drunken Daoist was mightier than even these demonic priests.

"The dark priests treated the abbot and disciples with great brutality, but seem to intend no evil to outsiders. They quietly took over as masters of the abbey, and have since attracted quite a number of new disciples. Power attracts favour, and some of the temple patrons, impressed by the magic and miraculous powers of the evil priests, have gone over to them as well.

"The Bamboo-Immortal Abbey across the mountain would have been the next to fall, except for a peculiar circumstance. In their first arrogant challenge to the abbot, the evil priests boasted that they were able to defeat him and anyone he cared to enlist in his support. When he was defeated, the abbot reminded his adversaries of their claim, and

190

demanded that they give him the opportunity to test this boast. With so many witnesses present, the dark priests were forced to agree to let the abbot remain unmolested at the Bamboo-Immortal Abbey for a period of three months, during which time he would be free to find capable allies for an attempt to win the abbey back. Come the end of the three months, the dark priests would be free to drive the abbot and his disciples out.

"The mountain inhabitants and fishermen were particularly angered by what had happened to the abbot. The abbot is a kindly man, and has always given aid to humble folk. Those seeking help were never turned away, and all of these people remain grateful and loyal. The dark priests at first showed no signs of animosity toward outsiders, but after they had become entrenched, great throngs of strange men and women in Daoist clothing, along with vile and ugly barbarian monks, began to frequent the abbey on a regular basis. They did not abide by the rules of purity and chastity, and there were many strange goings-on. The local people began to fear that as time went on this unpleasantness would affect those living nearby. When word got around that the Drunken Daoist could save the abbot, they began to make efforts to find him every time they left the mountain.

"The dark priests soon got wind of this. They made inquiries, and obtained a description of the Drunken Daoist. They seemed to realize at once that he posed a danger to them. They forbade the abbot and his disciples to leave the mountain. They announced that the whole business was an internal matter of the Daoist Church, and of no concern to outsiders. Anyone who attempted to interfere on behalf of the abbot risked retribution, they warned, and might be crippled or even killed. They wished to make this quite clear in advance, they said. They were not to be blamed for any unpleasantness. This of course made everyone hate the dark priests even more, but they had no choice but to conceal their anger, out of fear of provoking them.

"When the abbot was first defeated, he had sent two of his most capable disciples in secret to seek for help. A month passed quickly by without news. The abbot's health, exacerbated by anger and unhealed wounds, grew steadily worse. His disciples were anxious, but could think of nothing they could do to help. Finally they decided to send another messenger in secret over the lake to see what might be accomplished.

"Only moments after I heard this tale from the fish seller, a man came to hire passage on our boat to the Mountain of the Goddess. The lake was full of pleasure boats of every size and description, but he was uninterested in them. He wanted our boat, primarily a fast river craft for long-distance trips to outside ports. We assumed he knew nothing about boats, and my father tried to tell him that a pleasure boat would be better suited to his purposes. The man was dressed in rough and simple clothing, but was obviously a scholar and gentleman of some refinement. He gave his surname as Jian. He explained that he wished to make this trip to the Mountain of the Goddess to observe the powers of the evil priests, and discover why they felt free to abuse others in such a high-handed fashion. I immediately put our boat at his disposal.

"I reckoned that this impoverished scholar would have little cash, but he proved generous. He gave us five taels of silver in advance, half for the boat fee, and half towards wine and food for his enjoyment on board. He told us that he had business to attend to, and that he wished to set out at noon the following day.

"I urged him to reconsider. The Festival of Ghosts in the middle of the seventh month was only two days past, and the moon that night promised to be excellent. He could come late in the day and sleep on board, or sip wine and enjoy the moon in the cool of the night. My father and I could then row along at a leisurely pace, getting him to the Mountain of the Goddess early the next morning, rested and ready to see the sights. If we set out at noon, we could not reach the mountain before dark. But he would not listen, and seemed to have the notion that sailing with the wind was the same as rowing against it. He insisted that a favourable wind would get us there long before dusk. Setting out earlier would not be of any use either, he said, since the Ghost Festival celebrations had already come to a close, and there was nothing to see. We had given him fair warning that we would be unable to make it there before dark; if we failed it would be no fault of ours. So we accepted his instructions.

"The next day at noon he appeared right on schedule. He had no luggage except for two ancient books and a small leather bag, a foot or so long and two fingers in width, tied at his waist. It was the hottest time of the day, and the lake was as still as glass. There were no pleasure boats out, and only a few scattered commercial boats. The planks on the boat were so hot that they seemed to be on fire, but our passenger sat down at the window where the sun's rays beat right down on him, and began to read his books, every now and then pausing to gaze out over the water. He seemed not to feel any discomfort. He didn't even take off his long gown. From time to time he would hum or sing to himself.

"When we pushed off, we ran head-on into a burning wind that seemed to blast from the mouth of an oven. My dad began grumbling quietly to me that I should never have agreed to leave at noon. But a cool breeze sprang up from behind the boat, just as, out of the corner of my eye, I saw our passenger extend his hands forward in a peculiar gesture. As time went by the wind strengthened. It was most peculiar. The sun still blazed in the sky, but we felt cool and comfortable. Naturally we were delighted at not having to row, and went forward to hoist the sail. I went to the cabin to prepare some wine, and served it to our passenger. Master Jian was most considerate, and urged us to join him. We refused, of course, but he insisted, suggesting that we take turns eating while the other steered the boat. We found his generosity hard to refuse, and finally agreed.

"At one point when I was aft steering, I saw a pair of boats coming head-on toward us, their sails also stretched out before the wind. The passengers on these boats were stripped to the waist and covered with sweat, and vigorously fanning themselves. But on our boat it was perfectly cool, with not the slightest hint of heat. Also, it was quite impossible that boats could be sailing in exactly opposite directions. I wanted to ask our passenger what was up, but my father cautioned me to silence. He has been around for a long time, and knows of many strange happenings on the lake and the tributaries of the Xiang River.

"I kept my eyes open and observed our guest. The only odd thing about him was his eyes, which were a brilliant yellow gold, so bright that they were frightening. Otherwise he was quite ordinary, though refined and elegant. He made some casual inquiries as to the trails and roads on the Mountain of the Goddess, and wanted to know what had been happening around the Abbey of the Pure Void over the last month. His speech was sophisticated, and betrayed an excellent education. It did not seem to me that he was a man of strange powers. I convinced myself that the wind was one of those inexplicable phenomena that manifest themselves on the lake from time to time. I made no mention of it, fearing that if I did, the spell might be broken, and whatever deity had caused it would withdraw its favour.

"When the boat was about halfway there, our guest turned to the window, and his lips moved for a moment. Then he ordered us to steer the boat toward the Bay of Peaches.

"The boat was at that time racing right along, and we had very nearly reached the Mountain of the Goddess. If we changed course we would no longer be running before the wind, and would have to fight a strong current. But we were scarcely in a position to argue with him, and obeyed without comment. Strangely enough, though, as we started off on our new course, we found ourselves being blown along faster than ever. It was obvious that the wind had been summoned to speed our progress! We marvelled greatly at this.

"When the boat reached the bay, our passenger went on shore and entered the peach groves. He walked around there for a time, and then came back to the boat, and we continued on toward the Mountain of the Goddess.

"The wind continued to drive us directly toward our destination with remarkable speed. While we were on the boat we were not aware of how quickly we were really travelling, but when we reached the mooring at Old Fisherman's Bluff on the far side of the mountain and looked up at the sun, we found to our surprise that it was only the beginning of the Hour of the Sheep.* We had gone all the way from our starting point to the Bluff, including a two-mile detour to the Bay of Peaches, in less than an hour's time. People who had seen us that day later remarked that they had felt it a bit strange that we were coming at them head on

* [2–4 PM.]

193

against the wind with full sails, but had no idea we were going so quickly. A strange state of affairs, wouldn't you say?

"We thought to accompany him on the pretext of acting as guides, but he refused. He didn't require the boat any longer, he said, and preferred to roam idly about on his own. He had many acquaintances in the monasteries and abbeys on the Mountain of the Goddess, but at this time he wished to keep his arrival a secret. He asked us not to stay too long, or mention him to anyone else. Then he gave us thirty taels of silver, saying that it was for my wedding.

"My father had been wanting to get me a wife, and had calculated that the cost of all the ceremonies and various frills would come to exactly thirty taels! Just the evening before, when we had been unoccupied with any task, we had been discussing the possibility of borrowing the sum. I was afraid he would get himself into debt, and pleaded with him to give up the idea. How could this stranger ever have found out? We did our best to refuse, but he insisted. We were about to bow down to the ground in thanks, but he had already turned and left us.

"I shouldn't really be telling you this, but rumours about this man have spread everywhere. Apparently he has provoked the dark priests into a great fury over the last two days. Things have happened that are even stranger than what I have already related. You two honoured guests bear a certain resemblance to Master Jian, except that he is if anything even more refined. I wouldn't have mentioned it, but you inquired as to whether there were any unusual men or Immortal warriors on Goddess Mountain. I'm sure he has not yet left the Abbey of the Pure Void, so if you honoured guests go there, you might be able to meet him."

"If this man is opposing the evil priests," Zhao asked, "Why would he stay in the abbey itself? Isn't he afraid that they will try to kill him with their black arts?"

"I don't know the details," said Zhang the Fourth. "All I have heard is that on the day after he arrived he went looking for the evil priests. They were away, and their disciples answered the gates. He was polite to them, but somehow or other provoked them into a fury. First they tried to intimidate him, confident of the terror their dark masters had inspired, but he overwhelmed them with casual ease. He then departed, leaving a message for the evil priests to seek him on the far side of the mountain.

"When the two evil Daoists returned and learned of what had happened, they went off that very evening in a rage to find him. They encountered him in a grove on the far side of the mountain, and held a duel of sorcery with him. Some people saw wild flickers of lightning, but we don't know exactly what happened.

"The next day the gentleman moved right into the abbey, taking up residence in the small tower next to the Cupola of the Demon Guardians. Every day he goes off to roam the far side of the mountain. He goes in and out by himself, and continues to look as calm and well-mannered as ever. There is no sign from him that anything is out of the ordinary, and no one has seen him in any further confrontation with the evil priests or their disciples. Everyone is puzzled. If he is their enemy, considering how ruthless and violent the evil priests have shown themselves to be, it hardly seems likely that they would prepare a room and issue a polite invitation to stay with them. If they have become friends, then it makes no sense that the evil disciples curse him so spitefully behind his back. If he is still residing in the abbey, you will have no difficulty finding him there. But remember that the evil priests are not the sort of people one should provoke. If you go to the abbey to look for them, I'm sure that they will suspect that you are confederates of his, and will likely seek to do you harm.

"I'd like very much to see Master Jian again too, but I am not sure what advice to give you. It would be best if you seek him on the far side of the mountain, where you can be more certain of meeting. If I am not with you when you see him, could you give him a message from us? Say that my father and I are grateful for his kind help, and that I am to be married next month.

"Remember: the dark priests have violent tempers. Just a few days ago a couple of people went to see the abbot, and on the way back allowed their tongues to wag. The evil priests overheard, and very nearly hounded them to their deaths. My father is old, and we rely on the waters about here for our livelihood. He fears that the evil priests might direct their anger at me and work some grim mischief. Otherwise I would gladly go with you to see him."

ZHAO AND WANG WERE ANXIOUS TO FIND A MAN OF POWER exactly like this Master Jian to help them. Zhang the Fourth had not known much about him, but it was obvious that he was a tremendously powerful adept and magician. Accepting Zhang the Fourth's advice, they instructed him to proceed directly to Old Fisherman's Bluff on the far side of the mountain.

Zhang the Fourth leaped to obey Zhao and Wang's instructions. The dark priests did not engage in indiscriminate violence, but disaster was certain for anyone who disregarded their warnings, and he had not dared to make any effort to find Master Jian. Now he had an excuse to go to the far side of the mountain and discover what was really happening, and if all was safe, perhaps he would be able to visit him. Old Fisherman's Bluff was quiet and remote, inhabited only by two or three fishing households. The dark priests would have no reason to go there, and perhaps they could meet with the stranger without the knowledge of their foes.

CHAPTER 16

The Devil Monk

THEY HAD SET OUT FROM THE CITY RELATIVELY LATE IN THE DAY, and by the time they circled around to the far side of the mountain, it was near evening. Zhang the Fourth led them first to the house of an honest old fisherman, where they made inquiries about the whereabouts of Master Jian. When Zhang mentioned that Master Jian was staying in the Abbey of the Pure Void, the old man's expression changed. He said that he knew nothing, and looked frightened. As Zhang turned to leave, Wang Jin spoke up in a casual tone.

"It is getting late, so he must already have gone back to the abbey. Why not go straight there, and pretend to be sightseers? We can handle the situation as it develops, and if we manage to find him, all the better. If he is not there, then we can converse with the Daoist priests and find out what manner of men they are. After that we can stroll back to the boat in the moonlight, and return here in the morning. What do you think, Elder Brother?"

These words had the desired effect. Before Zhao Lin could answer, the fisherman turned to Zhang the Fourth and addressed him in a loud voice.

"We seldom have live fish, because we normally catch them with trained water birds. But today you are fortunate! A customer ordered live carp, and we still have a few on hand. They are small, but if our guests would care to purchase them and enjoy them with wine while viewing the lake, you are most welcome to step within and see if they are suitable for your needs."

The old man obviously had something on his mind, so they accompanied Zhang the Fourth into the house. Inside, the fishermen addressed them in an anxious whisper.

"It is plain that you honoured gentlemen are honest and kind, but you are outsiders. What is wrong with roaming about the lake on your own? If you are not Master Jian's friends, why risk meddling in his affairs?"

They asked him to explain.

"Except for several of the Daoists at the Bamboo-Immortal Abbey, one or two people living on the front side of the mountain, and myself, no one knows the truth," the old fisherman replied. "I didn't want to say anything at first, but I can see that you are all young, and have no conception of the danger. It would be a shame if you threw your lives away for nothing, so I will tell you what is happening with Master Jian.

"The dark priests occupying the abbey are cruel, venomous, and mighty in sorcery. But they are helpless against Master Jian. They have sent for aid, but it has not yet arrived. Every day they sit, anxious and

196

dejected, while their disciples roam the mountain, victimizing the innocent on the slightest pretext.

"The evil disciples' eyes are sharp and ears keen. Yesterday three men came across the lake in search of Master Jian, but were unable to find him. When they gave up and embarked on the return journey, the evil acolytes worked sorcery on them, and overturned their boat. Fortunately Master Jian arrived to rescue them, or they would probably have drowned. The most humorous thing of all was that the three visitors never recognized the man who saved them from being murdered. They had come because of his reputation for remarkable powers, but when he actually appeared, they did not pause to consider how strange it was that a single man had managed to save them from drowning and get them safely back to shore through a strong wind and heavy waves. They never noticed that he was not wet, even though he had gone into the water to save them. Master Jian pretended that he was only a weak and refined scholar, and gave several impoverished bystanders credit for helping with the rescue. He suggested that the three visitors part with a small sum by way of a reward. The visitors grew annoyed and berated him for being an interfering busybody. He took leave of them with a polite smile, finding them rather too pompous for his liking. Then one of the bystanders, unwilling to accept money when he had done nothing to earn it, informed them that the scholarly man who had just left was the very Master Jian they had been seeking. The three visitors became rather huffy, and sniffed that the man himself did not match his reputation. They accused him of being in collusion with the bystanders in an elaborate swindle to extract money from travellers! Can you imagine the gall of these fools?

"In any case, the evil priests loathe Master Jian with a passion. They know that he will not fight except in defense. They have mounted a vigil to prevent the Daoist masters at the Bamboo-Immortal Abbey from summoning other powerful allies. Each day their evil followers spy about the mountain, and we often see them here. For you to have landed here on a deserted shore not far from the Bamboo-Immortal Abbey is suspicious enough, but then you asked after Master Jian himself without a thought as to who might be listening! If they find out you will be attacked, and either injured or killed outright. Why involve yourselves in trouble of this sort? If something unpleasant happens, only Master Jian can help you.

"The two Daoist masters in the Bamboo-Immortal Abbey learned of Master Jian's remarkable powers, and have been coming out of the abbey to seek him. Three days ago in the afternoon they were caught by some of the evil disciples. They might have been killed, except that Master Jian happened by and frightened the evil disciples away. The Daoist masters persuaded him to accompany them to the Bamboo-Immortal Abbey. I have heard that Master Jian has befriended the old abbot of the Abbey of the Pure Void, and they meet each day. Since

197

then, the roving evil disciples have not dared to enter the bamboo grove which surrounds the abbey.

"The rear gate of the Bamboo-Immortal Abbey is right on the lake shore nearby, but if you go by that route you risk great danger, even if you do not encounter the evil disciples. If you really want to see Master Jian, my advice is that you do some casual sightseeing for the rest of the day, and when it gets dark return to your boat to enjoy the coolness of the evening. Early tomorrow morning a lesser priest will come to buy fish for the old abbot in his illness. I will ask him to carry a message about you to Master Jian. If he is willing to see you, he will come to you of his own accord. If he is not, you would not have been able to find him in any case. You can only cause trouble for yourselves by trying to find him."

Zhao and Wang were greatly encouraged. The presence of this mysterious man presented a rare and wonderful opportunity. By the look of things, Master Jian was mightier than the dark priests, and would soon move against them. Once the enemy was ousted, Master Jian would probably depart. If so, Zhao and Wang had to seek him out at once, lest they miss him. The evil priests might be deadly, but Zhao and Wang had their jade amulets for defense.

Zhao smiled and answered the old fisherman.

"We chanced to hear someone talking about him, and our curiosity was aroused. We thought we would come in person to find out what had really happened. We have no particular reason for wanting to see him. But if you are willing to ask the lesser priest to take him a short message, we would be grateful."

He purchased a pair of live fish for a few silver coins, and instructed Zhang the Fourth to take them back to the boat. When they had taken their leave of the fisherman, Zhao glanced around, and, seeing that no one was near, asked Zhang the location of Bamboo-Immortal Abbey, and where on the lake shore its back gate might be found.

Zhao and Wang agreed they should continue their efforts to find Master Jian themselves. Returning to the boat with Zhang the Fourth, they ate a hasty cold meal. Then they left Zhang and went ashore.

Rather than risk going straight to the abbey, they wandered over to the general vicinity in a casual and aimless fashion, trying to give the impression that they had discovered the establishment by accident and gone over for a closer look. Surreptitiously, however, they were keeping a careful watch.

The abbey was on a prominence halfway up a nearby hill. One side overlooked the lake, with stone steps leading down to the shore. Approaching it by water would almost certainly have aroused the suspicions of the dark priests and their cohorts. On the other side of the abbey, facing the mountain, lay an extensive grove of giant bamboos. A bare earthen slope opposite the grove afforded an excellent view of the lake, which gave Zhao and Wang a pretext for ascending it.

Halfway up this slope, they turned to face the lake, and beheld a scene more perfect than any painting. The evening sun hung low in the west; the smoke of cooking fires rose from temples, monasteries and homes scattered across the slopes. Far out over the lake stretched a limitless expanse of mist and waves, through which the sails of pleasure boats moved lazily back and forth. Lit by the setting sun, the vast surface of the lake threw back the sunlight in a glittering blaze of golden scales. The songs of herdboys and the evening cries from the fishing boats drifted up the slopes. A breeze off the lake dispelled the last traces of heat. The thousand or so inhabitants of the mountain, peasants and fisherfolk, were returning to their homes, their straw and coir hats moving in and out of view through the groves and meadows.

As they stood on the dirt slope marvelling at the view, they were startled by a voice speaking softly from the concealment of several large pines only a few paces to the side.

"Elder Cousin," it said. "Why not go back?"

Zhao and Wang, who had been proceeding all the while with great caution, instantly froze. They listened as another voice answered.

"This is all Eldest Cousin's fault!" the second voice complained. "It was his idea to come up here every day and pretend to be gathering pine needles! We've been keeping watch here for days, and haven't seen a thing, suffering for nothing through the heat of the day. We can't very well go back yet, though. I say we go down to the lake for a swim!"

Zhao and Wang guessed that the two were disciples of the dark priests sent to spy on the abbey. Zhao and Wang had kept mostly to the concealment of rocks and trees, and seemed to have come right up beside the acolytes' hiding place without being discovered. Afraid that their sudden presence would now be discovered and arouse suspicion, Zhao Lin deliberately bumped into Wang Jin and stamped his feet noisily on the ground. He laughed out loud.

"We've not come very far," he complained. "It seems a waste of effort to me. This whole side of the mountain is deserted, just like the boatman said. I don't see a single temple. Let's rest our feet here for a while, and then go back to the boat to enjoy the breeze."

As he spoke he turned away from the pine grove, and they pretended as though they had only just come up the slope. The voices in the grove instantly fell silent. Wang, aware of Zhao's intentions, replied.

"I am in better condition than you are," he said. "But the first twenty feet of climbing were more than enough for me. I say we have suffered quite enough of this the last few days."

No sooner had he spoken than two village lads, perhaps fifteen or sixteen years of age, sauntered out from the pines. They carried bamboo baskets full of pine needles. They wore short peasant's garments and went barefoot, but they were strong and muscular, and something about their appearance suggested malice and a capacity for casual violence. They glanced nonchalantly over at Zhao and Wang, and strode down the slope toward the side of the mountain. They turned and looked back twice, talking and gesticulating between themselves. It was perfectly obvious that they were a pair of evil disciples in disguise.

Zhao and Wang pretended to take no note of their presence. They talked and laughed together, pointing at the mist-shrouded peak. They cast covert glances at the prominence opposite them, but saw only a calm and secluded grove of thousands of tall slender bamboos, halcyon branches sighing in the wind. They decided that Bamboo-Immortal Abbey must be concealed within its depths.

Glancing back, they saw that the two lads were a considerable distance away. The earthen hill on which they stood was deserted and silent, as was the bamboo grove below. There seemed little chance of their being discovered by the evil disciples, so they walked down toward the grove opposite.

The bamboos grew tall and dense over the prominence on which the abbey stood. There was a path, but the two men, anxious to penetrate directly to the abbey, used their Light-Body breathing techniques to scale the steep slope through the bamboos. Oddly, they found themselves unable to progress at any speed. The bamboo grew ever more densely, obstructing their way at many points. From deep within the grove they heard someone chanting scriptures. They recognized the words of 'Autumn Waters' from the venerable *Southern Floriate Scripture.*

Zhao and Wang reflected on how the Daoist abbot maintained such calm while surrounded by spies and cut off from outside visitors; obviously he was no ordinary man. They attempted to move in the direction of the voice, but the more they walked, the further it seemed to recede from them. The grove, which had been in shade, grew dark as night. It had been daylight when they entered the grove, and they had been in it for only a few moments. What was happening to them?

The chanting ceased, and a glimmer of light appeared to their left. They moved in that direction, and the sky above them brightened once more. Through gaps in the grove they could see the sun floating over the surface of the water, beginning to set, but not yet gone. The evening sky was clear and bright; there had been no change in the weather. They looked back and tried to make out their course through the grove. All of their climbing and walking had somehow brought them back to where they started. They found this strange, but in their eagerness to find the abbey they assumed that it was because they had lost their way in the murk of the grove. They plunged in once again, seeking a path.

Wang Jin grew aware that the grove should not have seemed so dark, even allowing for the fact that their eyes might have had trouble adjusting to the gloom. He stopped and spoke.

---

* [The *Southern Floriate Scripture* was the name for the ancient philosophical text *Zhuangzi* (or *Chuang-tzu*) adopted as a sacred text by religious Daoist adepts. It has been translated into English by H. A. Giles, Burton Watson, and most recently by A. C. Graham.]

"Elder Brother, did you feel that it was unusually dark just now, as if the sky had changed?"

Zhao Lin had been asking himself the same question, and began to feel somewhat alarmed. But at that moment a young Daoist stepped out of the bamboos ahead and hastened forward to intercept them.

"You must pardon our lack of courtesy," he said. "The abbot of our Bamboo-Immortal Abbey is sequestered within, recovering from illness. We have little space to spare. For that reason we are at present unable to entertain visitors. There are poisonous snakes and insects in the grove whose bites are difficult to treat. Perhaps you honoured gentlemen would prefer to remove your august presences to another establishment where you can enjoy yourselves in a manner better suited to your tastes."

The young Daoist was refined in appearance and manner, though somewhat nervous and hurried. His priest's robes were plain and simple, but his speech was far removed from the common vernacular. They recalled how the sound of chanting had just stopped, and so smiled and addressed him.

"Was that you by any chance reciting the *Southern Floriate Scripture* ?" they asked.

The Daoist, seeing that the two evidently intended to remain and ask questions, grew even more anxious.

"That was a friend of my master's, who has just now departed, heading back to the front of the mountain. Please do not be annoyed with this impoverished priest for being ill-mannered, exalted guests, but please turn back!"

"We are not sightseers," replied Zhao Lin. "We have come to pay our respects to your excellent master. Perhaps we could trouble you to take a message to him."

"You must not remain here," the priest said, growing more agitated than ever. "If you do not go now, no good will come to either you or ourselves. Our master is ill and resting in quiet. He cannot even see his dearest friends, much less guests whom he has never met. My rudeness is for your own good. You must listen to me!"

Zhao and Wang realized that there must be a reason for the suspicion in the priest's manner, but they were anxious to find the mysterious man Jian. Having come this far and finally made contact with one of the abbey's members, they could not bring themselves to leave without trying to learn more.They addressed the priest once more.

"If your excellent master is unwilling to receive visitors, we will certainly not press him. But please tell us one thing. Is Master Jian in the abbey? Would it be possible for you to take us to see him? Or perhaps you could reveal to us his present whereabouts, so that we may go to seek him ourselves, and so leave here at once."

As Zhao Lin spoke the priest glanced this way and that with a worried expression.

"Who? Master Jian? I am aware of no such person. Our master and his disciples have seen no one outside the abbey for many days, so how could we know of such a person? I am telling you this for your own good. Why won't you listen?"

As he spoke the priest lifted his arms, as if wishing to push them physically out of the grove but hesitating to do so. Zhao and Wang, both modest and retiring in nature, could not bring themselves to press him further. They had no choice but to withdraw. As they did so the priest's manner grew calmer. He accompanied them out of the grove and onto the main road, where he smiled and addressed them once more.

"You exalted guests are men of understanding and magnanimity. I can see that you are good and kindly. The one you seek is in fact present on the Mountain of the Goddess, and I am sure you will eventually find him. But the hour grows late, and it would not be convenient to pay him a visit at this moment. I have heard talk of barbarian monks and evil men who have of late been frequenting the temples and abbeys on the front of the mountain. It would be most unwise to go there tonight. It would be best if you return where you came from, and go tomorrow morning to the area around Little Green-Coil on the lake out back. There it is just possible that you might meet him. It is dangerous to remain anywhere in this vicinity; evil men often come to oppose us, and may seek to do you harm. If it is so fated, perhaps we shall meet again!"

Without waiting for a reply, the priest hurriedly retreated into the grove.

Zhao and Wang were disappointed. Zhao Lin even began to think that they might as well go directly around the mountain to the Abbey of the Pure Void to look for him. But Wang Jin, considering carefully what the priest had said, and recalling how the grove had become so dark all of a sudden, realized that something mysterious was afoot.

"I am sure that there was more to the Daoist's parting words than was evident on the surface," he said to Zhao. "He was particularly insistent about warning us not to remain here. I suspect the two opposing sides are planning to make some move tonight. The priest claimed at first not to know any mysterious stranger, and yet later told us to go to Little Green-Coil tomorrow morning to look. He was obviously giving us a rather clear hint on how we might find him. If we cannot go to the front of the mountain, why not do as he says? We can go back to the boat and wander about the lake, and then wait at Little Green-Coil tomorrow morning."

Zhao Lin saw the sense of this, but his curiosity got the better of him. He determined to try the grove one last time. But the result was the same; the giant bamboos grew so thickly that they could not walk more than two or three steps in any direction before they found their path completely blocked. Once again it became as dark as night. They gave up and retreated; once again the grove viewed from without seemed normal. In the light from the setting sun the halcyon green trunks and fresh foliage within its depths were clearly visible throughout. It was obvious that a defense on the order of a magical Eight-Rank Diagram maze had been activated. They became even more convinced that something was going to take place that evening.

Zhao Lin turned to Wang Jin. Why not seek out an elevated spot from which they could watch whatever transpired? They were uninvolved in the conflict, and a threat to neither side; in any case they had their amulets for protection. Ding Shao had warned them that students of the Dao could not afford to be fainthearted; Zhao felt this was an opportunity they should not miss. They could observe for themselves which side was really good and which was evil, and watch to see if Master Jian took part before going to seek him out the next day.

If the evil priests were defeated in the encounter, they would naturally have little leisure to pay Zhao and Wang any heed. In the unlikely event that they were victorious, they would be greatly delighted, and surely disinclined to make trouble for people uninvolved with the enemy.

Wang Jin felt that this would be hazardous, but he had always tended to follow Zhao Lin's lead, and agreed to his plan. The crest of the hill on which the abbey stood seemed the ideal spot, but as the Daoist priest had warned them not to remain, Wang Jin argued for greater caution. The dirt hill opposite was fairly high, and directly faced the bamboo grove, affording an excellent view of it.

Their minds made up, they went down the hill to enjoy the sights, planning to return later that night to see if anything unusual was afoot.

By this time the Crow of the Sun had vanished in the west, and the Toad in the Moon was ascending.* The Mountain of the Goddess stood high over the vast still lake, sky and water both equally clear, each seemingly contained in the other. The moon was unusually bright. Intermittent breezes had dispelled the last traces of heat. Intent on enjoying the mountain and lake in the clear moonlit night, Zhao and Wang lost track of time. Before long they found it was already late in the Hour of the Pig or early in the Hour of the Rat.† They had strayed far from the bamboo grove, and decided that it was time to return.

"We have seen nothing strange anywhere about," said Zhao. "Have we misread the situation?"

"It is still early in the Hour of the Rat," Wang replied thoughtfully. "Don't forget that it was late at night that we were trapped at Great Roc Peak. Sorcerers avoid the eyes and ears of common folk, and there are many people out on the lake enjoying the cool night air. It may be that the time has not yet arrived. Why not go back to the dirt slope and keep watch?"

Zhao Lin recalled the two evil disciples in the pine trees on the dirt hill. The enemy was adept at magic, and might not need to penetrate the grove to fight at close quarters, especially if they were wary of traps and

_____

* [In Chinese mythology a three-legged crow inhabited the sun, and a toad the moon.]
† [9 –11 PM and 11 PM to 1 AM respectively.]

defences prepared for them within. What if the dark Daoists were also lying in wait on the same dirt hill? If Zhao and Wang blundered in, the evil priests would naturally assume that they were agents of the abbot. Zhao and Wang stopped, and conferred in hushed whispers. In the end they concluded that the top of the prominence on which the abbey stood would be safer from the enemy, but still afford a good view of what transpired below.

At first Zhao Lin wanted to play the part of sightseers once again and scout around the area in front of the dirt slope. From there they could ascend the hill on which the abbey stood, and walk close by the edge of the bamboo grove to see if anything unusual was going on inside. Wang Jin disagreed.

"It's getting late," he said. "If they plan to start at midnight, both sides must already have drawn their swords and strung their bows, and are right now waiting to attack. If we go barging into the middle of the battleground, it might prove awkward. I think it would be best to go straight to the hilltop, and stay well out of harm's way."

Perhaps it was their destiny that saved them that night. They stayed well away from the dirt slope and bamboo grove, and, at Wang Jin's insistence, they held their concealed amulets at the ready, prepared to activate them at an instant's notice. Then they crept quietly toward the hill above the abbey.

The dirt hill opposite soon came into view, and they thought they saw brief yellow and green flashes among the pines, but these almost immediately ceased. After the experience gained on their trip to the Mountain of Verdant Spots, they recognized the lights as being akin to the flash of a Flying Sword or some other sorcery. Their own movements must already have been observed. Zhao nudged Wang with his elbow. Since they had already been discovered, they should pretend to be completely at ease, and avoid anything that might be interpreted as furtive behaviour. They walked along in a casual manner, laughing and talking, pretending to be sightseers climbing the hill to look at the moon. When they reached the lake side of the hill on which the abbey stood, and were out of sight of the dirt slope, they stretched out their legs and hurried to the top. It was not very high, and it took them barely a moment to reach it.

Large rocks and trees on the flat top of the hill offered concealment, giving the two men an excellent opportunity to observe what went on below without risk of their own presence being discovered. The hill was clear and isolated. Save for the mountain path which led down to the Bamboo-Immortal Abbey, no other road led up to it. They had missed this spot before because the young Daoist had warned them off the hill, and because the dirt slope across from the grove had first caught their attention as the most obvious vantage. Delighted by this unexpected luck, they found a good hiding place behind a rock and peered downward.

They were disappointed to find that the abbey and the entire bamboo grove were hidden by a dense cloud of mist. They looked over at the dirt slope across the way. There, in a level space roughly thirty feet in diameter amid a sparse grove of ten or so pines, stood two Daoist priests with swords strapped to their backs. They were attended by a pair of young acolytes. At that moment they were talking, gesturing in the general direction of the abbey. There was no further sign of the yellow or green light. A large octagonal shape had been marked in the dirt beside them, but it did not seem that they had yet made any move. The two priests seemed almost identical in age, dress, and appearance; it was impossible to tell which was the senior. Their manner and bearing reflected an extreme arrogance, and Zhao and Wang heard curses and jeering laughter.

The abbey below was silent, with no trace of movement or activity. Any passer-by would have found nothing unusual about the scene, and probably assumed that the four Daoists across the way had merely gathered to converse while enjoying the cool night air.

It was now the middle of the Hour of the Rat.[*] The moon was so bright that only a few of the brightest stars were visible. Every now and then a lone cloud would glide swiftly over the midnight blue void. Further down the mountain there was little sign of activity, except for a few dim lamps and the occasional sound of bells or chimes from the abbeys and monasteries around them. The sightseers and people out for the cool night air had gone to bed; the pleasure boats were moored by the lake shore, lamps extinguished. The cool shimmering beauty of the mountain and lake lay in complete tranquillity.

Zhao and Wang watched for some time without noticing anything strange. Then they caught sight of a small cloud over the far side of the mountain. The other clouds drifting by in the moonlight were white, but this one was dim and grey. It was small, perhaps only a few feet in diameter, and looked rather tenuous as it hung in the clear night sky, so they paid little attention to it. They glanced about in all directions, and then found a spot amid the jumble of rocks where they could hunch down and speak to each other, every now and then looking out at the hill opposite.

For a time nothing happened. The four Daoists across the way stopped their jeers and taunts, and each reclined against the base of one of the pines and spoke quietly to one another. Their voices were nearly inaudible. They seemed even more at ease than before.

Zhao and Wang were themselves just observing that in two more hours it would be light, and wondering why nothing had happened, when the sky abruptly darkened above them. They looked up to discover that in the space of a few moments the small grey cloud they had noticed on the far side of the mountain had expanded to obscure the moon. A sudden wild wind arose, like the change before a violent squall.

[*] [Around midnight.]

It had not been the sort of weather which produces sudden storms, however, and the cloud had appeared first over the front side of the mountain. The dark Daoists were evidently up to some mischief. Zhao and Wang scrambled to their feet and peeked out at the slope opposite. The original four Daoists were still there, but two other men had joined them, a Daoist priest and a Buddhist monk.

The Daoist was tall, lean, and imposing. He held a yak-tail wand in one hand; the handle of a sword and a banner strapped to his back protruded diagonally from behind his shoulders. He was garbed in a magnificent robe of shimmering feathers and wore a hat decorated with stars and constellations.

The Buddhist was shorter and more massively built. He was dressed in the orange robes of a foreign monk, which left his feet and right shoulder bare. He bore a monk's dagger and a bottle gourd. A sack containing something unrecognizable was slung over his shoulder. His swarthy face projected an aura of hellish malevolence.

The cloud filled the sky. The whole area was plunged into darkness, except for the clearing in the pines, which was now brightly illuminated by a sultry green light.

When the newcomers joined the others, they appeared to consult with them for a moment. The Daoists seemed unaffected by what they learned, but the monk was visibly enraged. He strode to the centre of the clearing, and then turned to face the Bamboo-Immortal Abbey. He drew forth his monk's dagger and made several passes over the ground, chanting a Sanskrit spell. He made a sudden movement with both arms, and an enormous octagonal platform, a fearsome altar of demonic magic, rose from the pattern inscribed in the dirt. It was roughly two feet in height, ringed with red and yellow fire. Uncountable phantom shapes danced indistinctly within the flames, all more or less human in form, though much larger and taller, like celestial gods and evil demons bearing ghostly standards in their hands. At the centre of the altar rose a brilliant pillar of flame seven or eight feet in diameter. The top of this flared green and was formed into the shape of a lotus roughly five feet across. The monk leaped up onto this huge blossom with incredible agility, and seated himself, his legs crossed. He ceased his Sanskrit chant, and stabbed outward with his knife. A stream of blazing scarlet fireballs the size of wine-cups erupted from the blade and shot toward the abbey.

For some time the abbey had been completely hidden within a mass of impenetrable white cloud, which had now expanded to about two acres in size, covering a whole section of the lower half of the hill. The monk's fireballs struck with extraordinary velocity, but were repelled by an unseen barrier before they reached the cloud. They bounced upward and downward, striking again and again at the cloud above and below, but were unable to break their way in. The barbarian monk gesticulated several times with his knife; the fireballs shot forth with even greater speed and violence.

Zhao and Wang watched in wonder as the scene grew ever stranger and more unearthly. The white cloud over the ground had been almost invisible when the grey cloud filled the sky above, but when struck by the monk's demonic flames, it stood out clearly once again, its surface lit with a bright orange glow. The monk used his sorcery to spur the swarm of fireballs to still greater agitation. They now numbered in the hundreds, leaping and darting like fiery bullets, striking the cloud again and again at every point. Soon the cloud began to glow alternately orange and white, strange phantom images flickering over its surface in beautiful, constantly changing patterns.

The situation remained deadlocked. The fireballs were unable to penetrate, the glowing cloud was stable and unmoved. Finally the monk, failing to provoke any response from the other side, rose and began to leap up and down in frustration. His eyes blazed in fury, and his mouth gaped wide to emit a brief inch-wide shaft of dull red light, exactly the colour of blood. Fast as an arrow, it shot into the swarm of dancing fireballs. As it touched them, the fireballs each expanded to nearly a hundred times their original size. They struck against each other, breaking open and melding into a ponderous mountain of flames which pressed relentlessly down on the cloud. The hills shook with a booming roar like an unending succession of thunderclaps. The defending cloud now glowed a steady cherry red, but did not weaken.

The monk's fury knew no bounds. Once more his mouth opened to spew forth a steady beam of light with even greater force, a dull red rainbow linking him and the flaming cloud. The fire grew immeasurably stronger. The cloud began to ripple upward, seemingly unable to withstand the attack. An expression of pleasure spread across the face of the monk.

Zhao and Wang watched with growing amazement. They knew that the abbey lay directly beneath the cloud. The abbot within was defending himself without counterattacking, and appeared to be getting the worst of it. The flames were so intense that if the cloud barrier gave way even for an instant, the abbey and the whole grove around it would be instantly incinerated. As the two men watched, anxious for those within, a spot on top of the cloud where the flames beat most powerfully suddenly sagged and fell inward like a whirlpool. The huge fiery spheres and the red beam penetrated this gap at once, and the storm of surrounding flame rushed after them in a raging tide.

Zhao and Wang were certain that the abbey was done for, but then, in the twinkling of an eye, they heard an enraged roar, and the rainbow-shaped dull red beam snapped in two. One half withdrew into the monk's mouth. They could not see exactly what happened to the rest, but they seemed to glimpse a shaft of light ten feet or so in length following the tide of flames into the whirlpool, from which it never reemerged. The fires thinned, and then vanished like a stone into the ocean. The cloud around the whirlpool surged up and darkened suddenly, and was whole once again. Beneath the cloud the sound of a voice chanting became audible, the same 'Autumn Waters' of the *Southern Floriate Scripture* Zhao and Wang had heard at dusk.

The monk on the hill opposite had suffered a serious setback. Sweat poured down his face. He drew himself up and hurled three flying tridents at the cloud, each shimmering with a dim emerald radiance. As fast as he was, the opposition was faster. By the time the tridents reached the cloud the whirlpool had vanished, and they were unable to penetrate the barrier. The monk clenched his teeth and shouted curses, but was now somewhat dispirited.

As the monk's attack began, the five Daoist masters and disciples standing by had been eager and full of high spirits. They encouraged the monk with curses and taunts.

"You dog priests!" they roared. "If you surrender the abbey, and submit, we will allow you and your master to flee with your lives. If you have a man of ability supporting you, let him stand forth for a duel! If you do not recognize your danger, and persist in a silly display of vision-blocking techniques, you will annoy this Buddhist master and your own rightful patriarch, and be burnt to cinders!"

They rejoiced still further as the blood-red beam spewed forth by the monk caused the cloud to waver. Little did they know that this was a ruse designed to draw the monk off balance and destroy the Vital Breaths he had long cultivated.

"Ignorant dog priests!" they howled in triumph. "If you want to stick your nose into the affairs of others, why are you so terrified when things get nasty, hiding your heads in a hole? It is too late for you now! Your dog lives are forfeit even if you do admit your faults and surrender!"

They fell silent when the flames vanished without trace into the cloud.

The blood-red beam spewed forth by the monk was a direct projection of his vital breaths. He had battered against the cloud with the flames for quite some time without effect, and decided to risk some of the spirit substance of his own being. In doing so, he overextended himself, and a good portion of his vital energies were absorbed by the enemy. These primal breaths were a condensed elixir of his own spirit, and their loss was of mortal significance. Even minor damage to them could only be healed after days of bitter training.

Fortunately for the monk, his sorcery was powerful and his reflexes quick. As his red flames began to sink into the cloudy whirlpool, he sensed a massive force drawing with irresistible might from beneath the cloud. Greatly startled, he firmed his stance and attempted to withdraw the red beam of his vital energy. But it was held firmly at the far end, and would not move. Realizing that he was in serious trouble, he broke the beam in two at once, even though he had to sacrifice a part of himself to do so. Had he tried to recover it all, it might have meant his death. A capable sorcerer could have struck at him while he was struggling to withdraw his energy, and absorbed it himself to augment his own power. Such an enemy might also have released the stream of power and allowed the monk to reabsorb it, but concealed Treasures of Power within it. These would have been almost impossible to detect, and so sucked directly into the monk's belly. From there the enemy could have detonated them, blasting him into tiny fragments from within.

The monk had no choice but to endure the intense pain, gritting his teeth as he sucked back at his energy for a brief instant, paused, and then deliberately severed it. This sacrifice removed him from immediate danger, and gave him a moment to find a way to avenge the shame of defeat. His life was preserved, but his vital breaths were seriously diminished.

It was increasingly evident which side was the stronger. The monk began to realize that all of his sorcery and Treasures of Power were insufficient against his foes. But if he simply fled with his disciples, the public humiliation would be intolerable. He would have to force himself to speak bold words, and find some ploy to maintain his dignity, even though he was now dispirited to the point where such a sham would be difficult.

Zhao and Wang, viewing from the sidelines, had an excellent view of the proceedings. They were out of range of the flames, though Wang Jin in particular was cautious enough to keep an eye on their route of escape. They grew more apprehensive when the barbarian went mad with rage, seemingly undeterred by his setback. The great demonic fires had been quenched, but the dim spectral flames continued to play around the magic altar, phantom gods and demons dancing in and out of visibility in their depths. The three tridents the monk had launched, glowing with a ghastly green radiance, continued to dart and strike at the cloud. The monk's hellish visage, distorted by evil rage, was plainly visible above the flaming green lotus. The entire scene had taken on an aura of grim spectral horror far more frightening than the pyrotechnics of a few moments before.

A voice still chanted the *Southern Floriate Scripture*. Zhao and Wang were convinced it was Master Jian. Since his spiritual powers were obviously very great, Zhao and Wang wondered why he had not drawn the glittering tridents into the cloud as well, and come forth to exterminate the hellish menace once and for all. What was the purpose of sitting there quietly and reading a book?

After the barbarian monk had unleashed his tridents, he raised his bared right arm in a magic *mudra*, controlling the flight of the tridents in midair and sending them again and again to the attack. His other hand gripped the bottle-gourd at his waist. His eyes glared malevolently forward. He seemed to be fully aware that his flying tridents could not penetrate the cloud, and evidently intended it as a feint as he watched for an opportunity to strike with something more deadly. The sound of the voice reading the scripture grew ever louder and more resonant. Glancing up at the sky, Zhao and Wang noted that there was barely an hour left before daylight.

The barbarian monk's sorcery was now complete. He reached back and struck the bottle-gourd with his fist. Blood-red flames leaped up ten feet or more, and then curled down to envelop his body. From a distance he looked exactly like a man of glowing blood, his true body completely concealed. The evil Daoist priests and their disciples stepped back in obvious alarm, drawing the swords and demonic banners they wore on their backs, and extending their hands toward the monk in magic *mudras* to ward off danger.

As Zhao and Wang wondered what sort of devilry he was up to now, the voice chanting in the grove fell silent. Simultaneously there was a flicker at the head of the figure of blood-fire, and out flew a homunculus of brilliant red, barely a foot tall, holding a monk's dagger in one hand and a golden ring in the other. It looked exactly like the barbarian monk in miniature. It flew at blinding speed, and in a twinkling stopped to hover above the cloud over the abbey.

The three flying tridents came instantly to meet it, and circled its head. The hovering homunculus pointed with its knife, and a small dim sphere of blood-red light shot down into the cloud.

The foot-high homunculus was in fact the barbarian monk's own vital spirit, which had separated itself from his body. The spectral sphere it wielded was not very bright, and looked less menacing than the massive flames which had scorched the hill previously. Zhao and Wang assumed that the white cloud guarding the abbey was far too potent to be affected, but they were wrong. The blood-like light dropped down onto the top of the cloud, where it bobbed softly up and down for a moment, and then penetrated into the interior of the cloud. There was no sign of the whirlpool effect which had earlier swallowed the flames. There was a deep, very faint detonation far within the cloud, and a hole appeared. The homunculus plunged downward with great delight.

Seeing this, the evil priests and their disciples began to rejoice, and gave vent to threats and encouragement. Then a great deal happened very quickly. Just as the homunculus penetrated the cloud, and the evil Daoists were starting to rejoice and curse, a loud guffaw rang out from the blood-fire on the altar which concealed the monk's body.

"Ignorant, vile degenerate!" a booming voice chortled. "Evil to the core! You have walked into a trap!"

The red homunculus reemerged from the cloud. Its tiny body seemed to have been almost completely drained of the glow of blood which had suffused it. It looked frightened and thoroughly beaten. Quick as an arrow, it darted back toward the monk's body. But a prodigious thunderclap split the sky, and a golden bolt of lightning burst from the form of blood-fire on the altar, scattering it in all directions like driving raindrops. Then a Daoist, a red bottle-gourd strapped to his waist, materialized in the air above.

The evil Daoists had long since taken to their heels, knowing as soon as they heard the booming voice that the duel was lost. The red homunculus had nearly gained the altar, but when the thunderbolt destroyed the monk's body, it flew madly back the way it had come.

Zhao Lin guessed the priest who now hovered in mid-air over the ruined altar must be the Drunken Daoist their boatman had described. Unable to suppress his excitement, he called out to Wang.

"Look!" he shouted. "The Drunken Immortal!"

The red homunculus, the barbarian monk's vital spirit, had plunged into a carefully-prepared ambush. The Drunken Daoist had unleashed the mysterious Divine Thunder of the Grand Monad, a terrible golden thunderbolt from the ultimate Pole of the cosmos, which spanned the sky as it descended to shatter the barbarian monk's material body. His vital spirit was still alive, but seriously injured, and now had no body to return to. The homunculus was nervous and fearful of every threat. The monk's formidable Treasures of Power had been destroyed with his body, leaving him with nothing more than the tattered remnants of his blood-energy. He dared not approach the altar. As he fled madly back along the way he had come, he was too terrified by the suddenness of the golden thunderbolt to consider the best route of escape. When he passed over the abbey, he suddenly recalled the powerful enemy beneath him, and he veered off to the left in a panic, planning to cross the top of the hill and get safely away. In so doing, he flew straight toward the spot where Zhao and Wang were hiding.

The barbarian monk was at that moment consumed with fury and resentment. His cruel and violent nature, long exacerbated by his obsession with dark sorcery, needed an outlet. Anyone in his path at that juncture would have incurred his wrath, and Zhao Lin had been indiscreet enough to reveal sympathy for the Drunken Daoist. The monk saw that they were ordinary Chinese men, weak and defenceless. His ire blazed up, and an evil thought struck him. He sent down the remnants of his blood-fire to strike at them, intending to pluck the living souls from their bodies as he passed.

Zhao Lin must have been fated to meet with this disaster. Up to this point he and Wang had been on their guard, ready to release the magic glow of their jade amulets if it appeared things were going ill for the abbey. But when the enemy was defeated by the unexpected intervention of the Drunken Daoist, the two men were greatly relieved, and relaxed their vigil, assuming that the power of the enemy had collapsed. Also, the homunculus had seemed to be flying toward the abbey, and his sudden change of course directly toward them caught them completely unprepared.

The homunculus came at tremendous speed; by the time they could react it was too late. Zhao Lin caught a glimpse of a tiny blood-red figure pressing down directly above his head. His nostrils filled with the scent of blood, and he dimly sensed a strange silvery light burst into life around him. He fell unconscious to the ground as he groped for the amulet at his breast.

Fortunately, Wang Jin was standing further to the rear. He had been clutching the amulet inside his shirt all the while, ready to activate it. When Zhao Lin pointed out the Drunken Daoist, Wang's eyes remained fixed on the slope below. He saw the demonic homunculus cut suddenly off to one side and dart straight up toward them. His heart leaped. He drew forth the jade amulet and activated it in the proper manner, pressing the magic symbol on its surface and lifting it upward. The blazing shield rose up to surround them, but a fraction too late; the homunculus had already felled Zhao Lin with its spectral blood poison.

The shield from the amulet caught the homunculus completely by surprise. The monk had not expected that two ordinary men would command rare periapts of such power. He and Wang Jin had moved almost simultaneously. The blazing shield swept up and struck the homunculus, the last remnants of the monk's vital spirit. Only one of its intended victims fell, and was not dead, but only unconscious. The glowing shield destroyed most of the blood-fire which protected him. The homunculus rose unsteadily into the air and attempted to fly away, but before it had gone more than twenty feet, a blinding shaft of white light lanced out of the bamboo grove and encased the monk's vital spirit in a glowing envelope. The envelope contracted, and Wang heard a muffled shriek of agony. The homunculus burst into a multitude of smoke streamers, which dissipated almost instantly in the wind. A few wisps of blood-fire still drifted aimlessly in the air above; a bolt of golden lightning blazed from the slope opposite and destroyed them with a deafening thunderclap.

CHAPTER 17

Dispersal of Spectral Poisons

THE STRANGE DARK CLOUD OVERHEAD HAD BEEN DISPELLED BY THE first thunderbolt; the white cloud was now withdrawn as well. The moon shone brightly once more, revealing one corner of a temple wall in the bamboo grove below. The abbey they had tried so hard to find was now revealed. The stars in the east were beginning to dim as the glow of dawn approached. The lake, calm and flat, was a boundless mirror of midnight blue. The utter tranquillity of the scene made it seem as if all that Wang Jin witnessed had never happened. Every last trace of the spectral emanations had disappeared.

Wang was overcome by a wave of despondency. With the battle over, the two men should have had the opportunity to meet genuine Immortals, but then, in the twinkling of an eye, tragedy had struck. Wang's closest friend was stricken by a grim spectral poison, and lay near death. In a twinkling the Drunken Immortal had withdrawn, deserting them in a strange land. There was no friend to whom he could turn. In desperation, he bent and lifted Zhao Lin up, and began calling for help.

"O Drunken Immortal, take pity on the guiltless! Please help us quickly!"

There was no response. His heart felt as though it had been pierced by a knife. It seemed there was nothing he could do for his friend. But then someone emerged from the bamboo grove on the slope beneath them and ran to the top of the hill. Wang's mood grew easier as he recognized the young priest they had met in the evening.

"Come quickly, Daoist Master!" Wang cried urgently.

The priest hurried up to him, and instructed Wang to withdraw his shining shield.

"You very nearly got yourselves into serious trouble!" the Daoist scolded in an injured tone. "It is fortunate that your friend is in no great danger. If the Drunken Master-Uncle had not come back in time, and Master-Uncle Jian had not lured the enemy into a trap, the demon monk would have slipped out of the net. Had he escaped, our master might never have lived in peace again. The whole region might have been devastated, reduced to wasteland and noisome swamps. Tens of thousands of lives were hanging in the balance. How on earth could you have expected the Masters to allow themselves to be distracted by your requests to see them at such a critical time? There were enemy spies lurking about, and if the Masters agreed to see you, our secret plans might have been betrayed.

"When you two first appeared Master Jian was in the midst of weaving his defensive spells. I urged you over and over again to go elsewhere, but you refused to listen!

"Our Drunken Master-Uncle is no longer here. He has gone to the Abbey of the Pure Void to force the evil Daoists to send their disciples away and restore the abbey to our master with a public apology. Then he plans to escort the dark priests away to another place. Your excellent friend is fortunate not to have been killed outright. He may not recover from effects of the psychic poison of the blood-fire at once, but he will assuredly be revived with no great difficulty, and has accrued considerable merit for helping destroy the primal spirit of that horrible monk.

"I should warn you that Master Jian is somewhat eccentric. When you see him you must say as little as possible, and follow all his instructions. If there is anything on your mind, he will know what it is before you speak. If he is able to help you, he will certainly do so, but if not, you must not press him. But let us get your friend back to the abbey."

As the man spoke, Wang Jin knelt to the ground to express his gratitude, and thanked him for his advice. He asked the priest his name.

The priest saluted politely in return, and drew Wang back to his feet.

"My name is Shen the Lute," he said. "I felt that there was an affinity between us from the moment we first met. I sense that before long you two gentlemen will become members of our Daoist order, and gain spiritual advancement even greater than what you have now achieved. There is no need for such courtesy between us. Come, let's get back to the temple."

Wang Jin thanked him again. He followed the priest down the hill into the grove, carrying Zhao Lin in his arms.

The buildings of the Bamboo-Immortal Abbey were tucked neatly against the hill. None was more than two stories high, and the complex covered only a small area. It was completely surrounded by the bamboo grove, and set about with beautiful rocks and flowers. The site was delightfully pure and secluded. The rear buildings on the slope loomed high over the lake, its towers and cupolas in excellent repair. None of this had been visible prior to the great battle with the monk, when the entire establishment had been sealed off from the outside by powerful spells.

Wang Jin learned that the mysterious man Jian was named Ice-Purity. It was he who had been up in the tower defending against the attacks of the enemy, chanting the *Southern Floriate Scripture* as a ruse while he worked his powerful arts. His plan had been to enrage the monk and try to provoke him into sending his vital spirit to the attack. Once the monk's vital spirit had been lured out, Master Jian would attempt to destroy it, and smash the magic altar. But Master Jian's strategy contained an element of extreme risk. The spectral fire of blood essences in which the demon monk had cloaked himself was replete with psychic poisons foul and deadly beyond imagining. If these had scattered in midair, the white cloud would have been seriously weakened, and un-

214

able to repel a determined attack. The abbot and his disciples in the temple might have been seriously injured.

Then the Drunken Daoist had returned to the mountain, and arrived at the scene just before the plan was put into effect. As the monk prepared to unleash his vital spirit, the Drunken Daoist cloaked himself in invisibility and flew up onto the altar to secrete himself within the spectral flames protecting the monk's material body.

Thus the demon monk was ambushed, suffered serious injury, and was stripped of his Treasures of Power. When his vital spirit was finally destroyed, the Drunken Daoist had gone in pursuit of the evil Daoist priests, leaving only the Immortal Jian in the tower.

Soon Wang and Shen the Lute reached the tower at the rear of the abbey. As they came to a halt, Wang Jin prepared to wait until Shen had ascended to announce their presence. But a voice high up in the tower called down to them, instructing Shen to conduct the visitors immediately upstairs. Wang Jin, polite and respectful as always, put Zhao Lin down, made a formal bow toward the upper part of the tower, then lifted Zhao again and followed Shen up the stairway to the top, where they entered a small chamber.

A middle-aged man sitting on a cloud-bed awaited them within. He had thin and refined features, and was dressed in the garb of an impoverished scholar. His unusual appearance and golden yellow eyes matched exactly Zhang the Fourth's description. Hastily Wang laid Zhao on a bed to one side, and went forward, prepared to announce his name and kneel to beseech him for aid. But the man spoke first.

"It is fortunate that you and your companion are tough and hardy," said Jian Ice-Purity. "The fiery blood essences are deadly. Under normal circumstances it takes up to a year to recover from the effect of these poisons even if an alchemical elixir is administered. But it would appear that this man, poisoned though he is, is not as badly hurt as I had anticipated. A strange business indeed! You bear protective Treasures of Power, your physiognomies show signs of latent immortality, and yet you are not initiated as men of the Dao. Is it possible that your companion has ingested some sort of unusual drug or elixir in the past?"

Wang Jin told him how Zhao Lin had unintentionally ingested a measure of the Stalactite Milk on the Mountain of Verdant Spots, and also that they had received a gift of alchemical elixir from the Old One in Green.

"Ah!" said Jian Ice-Purity. "All is now clear. So you are to be the disciples of Zhu the Fifth! This simplifies matters considerably. Here are three cinnabar pills which you must administer to your companion at once. In a short while I shall apply a simple technique to flush the spectral emanations from his body. He will revive speedily enough, but even so it would normally be a hundred days before he recovers completely. But I am informed that you have come a thousand miles through the mountains from your distant home on business of considerable urgency. My Drunken Master-Uncle has recently obtained a potent drug that will not only restore your companion to perfect health at once, but also considerably enhance his original mental and physical powers. At present, though, the Drunken Master is otherwise occupied, and the medicine is not here. It will be necessary for you to make your way to Southern Mount with my calling card to seek Grandmother Gold, surnamed Luo, in the Grotto of the White Sparrow."

Wang Jin knelt in gratitude.

"Come now!" said Jian Ice-Purity. "Excess courtesy brings me no pleasure! Sit, and I shall tell you the story of what has transpired.

"Recently my roamings happened to bring me to the area of Lake Dongting. There I learned that my Disciple-Nephew Wang, the abbot, had been humiliated by wicked Daoist priests. I came across the lake at once to offer my assistance. It seemed at first a simple matter to drive these sorcerous priests away. But while investigating the matter I discovered the hand of the devil-monk Hawuni in the affair. With him and the dark priests in league, their demon sorcery was very great. They were working great mischief, and had harmed many innocent people. I resolved to lure the monk here and dispose of this hellish menace once and for all. It was not until today that this dangerous undertaking was brought to a successful conclusion. Tomorrow I must go to the Eastern Sea to visit an old friend, and regret that I will be unable to stay on longer. But come! Let us revive your companion."

So saying, he instructed Wang to lift Zhao and seat him upright on the cloud-bed. By this time Zhao's face was as yellow as gold paper, and his limbs limp as cotton. He was not breathing. Except for a hint of warmth on his chest, and an occasional heartbeat, his appearance was more frightful than that of one newly dead.

Wang Jin, blinking back tears, whispered into his ear. "Courage, Elder Brother! A Master Immortal has kindly saved us, and you will soon be brought back to life."

As he spoke, he lifted Zhao Lin in his arms, and seated him gently on the bed with his legs crossed. Jian Ice-Purity sat down opposite him while Wang Jin supported him from the rear. The older man's eyes closed, and he circulated mysterious energies within his body for a few moments. Then his eyes opened wide, and his lips parted slightly. Out of his mouth came a narrow stream of white vapour, no wider than a chopstick. The vapour stream shot into Zhao Lin's left nostril. Zhao's body began to shudder. The vapour exited his left nostril and went into his right ear, and then in and out of his seven orifices in succession, before finally shooting back into Jian Ice-Purity's mouth.

An evil vapour, dark red like blood, issued from Zhao's mouth, nose, eyes, and ears, and floated one or two inches from his face. Jian Ice-Purity reached out and made a snatching motion with his right hand. The evil smoke gathered into a single cloud, and rose upward with his hand. Then he closed his left hand over the cloud, and it disappeared. Zhao Lin opened his eyes, and his colour gradually improved. His heart was beating wildly, however, and his whole body was still limp as cotton. He was unable to speak or move.

Jian Ice-Purity ordered him to lie back, close his eyes, and rest quietly. Then he took out a red pill and put it into his mouth, and gave him half a cup of pure water. Wang Jin spoke once more in Zhao's ear.

"Rest peacefully, Elder Brother. I will tell the Immortal Master Jian about our problem with the Miao."

Wang got off the bed, and prepared to bow down in supplication. But Shen the Lute, still standing to one side, stepped up and stopped him.

"Master Jian has little fondness for excess courtesy," he said. "If you have something to say, do not hesitate to speak plainly. When Master-Uncle comes forth to roam in the world of mortal men, he often aids those in peril and distress. You two in particular should have nothing to fear. Since you are future disciples of Fifth Uncle Zhu, this venerable gentleman will assuredly not stand idly by if you are in trouble. You have knelt down twice now, which rather annoys Master Jian. You are fortunate that you are an honest man, and have made a good impression on him. Master-Uncle has seen many a man who, in his words, comes to embrace the feet of the Buddha only in time of need. Such a one can knock his head a thousand times against the ground, but will accomplish no more than making an ugly spectacle of himself. Speak!"

Wang Jin agreed, and then respectfully turned to tell his story. But before he could begin, Jian Ice-Purity laughed and gestured at Shen the Lute.

"What fine excuses you make for me! Your own part in the affair should not be overlooked! If you had made certain that they went back to their boat, and told them what was really afoot, this evil would not have happened."

"But there were enemies everywhere," Shen the Lute protested. "Also, they said that they had come because they had heard of your reputation, not because they knew you personally. I had no idea who they really were. With demonic acolytes spying from outside the grove, how could I have revealed our secrets for all to hear? I know now that they are not really outsiders. We only hope that you can extend your aid and protection to your younger disciples to the fullest possible extent, and be so magnanimous as to go to the Miao crag on Jade Dragon Mountain to help them in their moment of peril."

"A simple enough thing to say!" said Jian Ice-Purity. "You should know how deadly Old Man Miao can be, especially with his entire family and all his supporters. Even my Disciple-Brother, the Old One in Green, who has been cultivating himself for seven lifetimes, who in three centuries is to take over as the exalted Patriarch of the Omei school, and who is a good deal more powerful than I, would not intervene directly against them. Even he did no more than send two beloved disciples of many years' standing to fend off the Miao daughters in secret. Do you think this sort of incident is going to be a pleasant one?"

217

Then he turned to Wang Jin. "There is no need for you to tell us your story. One of my Daoist brethren has already informed me of what has happened to you. There have been developments since you left home of which you are probably unaware.

"After the two of you departed Willow Lake, the Miao child Cunning-Maid, pining desperately for your companion Zhao Lin, found a pretext to go to your valley, hoping to see him again and inform him of secret events which had transpired within her clan. But her presence was detected by your companion Zhu Man-Tiger, who was able to snare her by trickery and had her cruelly beaten by your people. She could have doomed the entire valley to destruction with a single gesture of her hand, but she forbore, and accepted the pain and indignity, desiring to move Zhao Lin's heart."

Wang (and Zhao, who was conscious enough to hear what went on about him) listened in astonishment as Master Jian told them all that had happened.

WHEN CUNNING-MAID FIRST APPEARED, SHE WAS ON FOOT, AND behaved with meekness and courtesy. The Village Elders, following Zhao Lin's advice, treated her with kindness and hospitality. They invited her to a banquet, and during the course of it she began to reveal the story of how she and her sister had met Zhao and his companions. Zhu Man-Tiger, driven by his hatred of her and fear that his own part in the affair would become known, schemed to destroy her. He made accusations against her, which the Village Master believed. Acting against the wishes of the Elders, the Master gave the order that she be seized and beaten.

The Green Simurgh which had borne Cunning-Maid to the valley eventually returned to look for her. It soon found her, broke her bonds, and bore her away. The great bird was enraged at the indignity suffered by its mistress, and desired revenge. With one long cry it summoned its companions, her entire flock of extraordinary birds. Cunning-Maid stopped them from doing anything, but two of the deadliest and most ferocious, particularly loyal to their mistress, were reluctant to obey at once. Cunning-Maid had to work a powerful spell of prohibition before she finally induced them to depart. They made no direct attack, but the great wind from their wings as they swooped low uprooted trees and damaged a few homes. Had Cunning-Maid been an instant slower to control them, many people would have been killed or injured. As she left, she addressed the townsfolk from the back of the great bird.

"Were it not for my Prince Zhao, none of you would be alive now!"

She went on to recount to the Elders all that Zhu Man-Tiger had done. Only then did they realize that he had been the one behind the trouble right from the start. Through his efforts to silence Cunning-Maid, he had nearly caused the destruction of the village. The Elders had no choice but to convene the villagers and pass sentence. They removed the Village Master from office for his part in the affair, and recalled his predecessor from retirement to take up his duties.

Zhu Man-Tiger, however, learned of the assembly one day in advance, and avoided the judgement of the community by taking flight. He left a letter saying that he was going out of the mountains to seek Zhao and Wang (though he did not reveal where Zhao and Wang actually were), and slipped away. The news of his escape was greeted with considerable relief. The Elders felt that this action on his part removed a painful burden. If he succeeded at his quest and returned, he would redeem much of his guilt, and the unpleasant task of passing sentence upon him might no longer be necessary.

But when he left, his heart was full of anger and resentment, exacerbated by his knowledge that Zhao and Wang were destined for immortality, and he was not. Before the Miao girl had left the valley, she had cursed him shamefully before all, and the villagers had believed her. He felt there was nowhere he could turn. Even if the affair blew over and he was able to return home, the memory of his public humiliation would be unbearable. The more he thought the angrier he became. He resolved to seek a master, so that he might ultimately have the power to exact his revenge on Cunning-Maid. He thought that in spite of his shame on the Mountain of Verdant Spots, he had been on rather good terms with Ding Shao and his wife. If Ding would not consent to be his master, then at least Man-Tiger could implore him to offer advice on how best to proceed. In either case, he felt there was some hope for him.

Cunning-Maid had said that Zhao Lin's promise to visit their mountain was already known to all her people, and that it was more difficult than before for the two Miao sisters to get permission to go abroad. Nonetheless Man-Tiger was still fearful at the prospect of meeting up with them. If he encountered Moon-Maid, it would be easy enough to explain things to her, but he was terrified at the prospect of being found by Cunning-Maid.

When he escaped, he stole an exit pass from his uncle's house. After leaving the river stockade, he went straight to a Miao market and purchased what he needed to disguise himself as a peasant. Then he struck out for Dali at best speed.

Ever since the debacle at the Peak of the Great Roc, Master Jian explained, Moon-Maid had suspected that some of the Immortal warriors at the Mountain of Verdant Spots had intervened to help the three men escape. Old Man Miao feared the Old One in Green, so Moon-Maid dared not risk a confrontation with them over this. Certain that Man-Tiger and his companions had no magic powers of their own, she anticipated that they would seek help at the Mountain of Verdant Spots before making good their pledge to visit Jade-Dragon Mountain. She sent her evil apes, snakes, and tigers to keep all the major approaches to the mountain under surveillance.

Meanwhile, the astute Cunning-Maid observed that her sister was growing suspicious of her. The two of them might long since have quarrelled and become estranged, except that Cunning-Maid had been able to concoct a plausible story to explain her absence, and could point to the wounds she had received at Willow Lake as evidence that she had suffered a misadventure. She greatly feared Man-Tiger's deviousness. If the opportunity presented itself, he and Moon-Maid would join in an instant. Man-Tiger hated Cunning-Maid with a passion, and would certainly waste no time turning Moon-Maid against her. He might even force Moon-Maid to take revenge on Cunning-Maid as a condition for marriage. And if his position in the village became untenable, he would doubtless slip out of the valley, and be caught by her sister's evil apes and other creatures as soon as he emerged.

Moon-Maid was prevented by the laws of Jade Dragon Mountain from attacking Zhao Lin at Willow Lake prior to the time appointed for his challenge. But there was no regulation against seizing or killing him at a location away from their respective homes. If she found Zhao and Wang in the wild, she was perfectly capable of provoking an incident with her snakes and animals, and using this as an excuse to attack the men. Cunning-Maid needed to prepare for this eventuality as soon as possible.

Cunning-Maid ordered her simurgh, crane, and other extraordinary birds to maintain a constant search from the air. Her birds flew faster than Moon-Maid's animals could run, and they found Man-Tiger in less than two days. At this point a signal from her would have sufficed to snuff him out, achieving a sweet revenge, and preventing much trouble later on. But her love for Zhao Lin was too strong, and she was afraid of causing him grief. The idea tempted her, but she decided not to strike. At the same time, though, to prevent Man-Tiger from turning Moon-Maid against her, she approached her sister.

"The man you love seems to have left Willow Lake," she said. "He hates me bitterly. If you marry him, he will surely seek to destroy the sisterly love which exists between us. If you swear not to listen to his slander, I will help you win him. But remember, he is in disguise, and difficult to recognize. The Green Simurgh was flying high at the time, and I cannot be sure that it saw clearly. If it does not work out as we expected, I cannot be blamed."

She demanded that Moon-Maid swear the Miao oath of the broken arrow before she would reveal her plan.

Moon-Maid, utterly convinced that Man-Tiger loved her, was overjoyed by this news. Man-Tiger would not escape her if he went near the Peak of the Great Roc and the Mountain of Verdant Spots, but she worried that he might set out in another direction. Her snakes and beasts had been lying in wait for many days without news. Success would be certain, if Cunning-Maid were willing to help with her gigantic birds. She did not pause to reflect on Cunning-Maid's motives, and agreed to her sister's proposal at once.

220

Cunning-Maid entrusted command to the Green Simurgh. When this bird departed, she gave it secret orders. If Man-Tiger had not been recognized by the snakes and beasts, then the bird was to ignore him. If he was in danger of capture, the bird was to move in and seize him ahead of the others, and bring him back to the mountain. She ordered the parrot and the golden crane to go along to render whatever assistance they were able.

When they arrived at the Peak of the Great Roc, the birds saw that Man-Tiger had already been cornered by Moon-Maid's pythons, and that the evil apes were hurrying to seize him. The giant crane, in a flurry of desperation, swooped down to snatch him up.

Man-Tiger had realized that there was something strange about the huge pythons which confronted him, and heard the answering cries of the apes and tigers as they approached from further away. He guessed that all of these creatures had been sent by Moon-Maid, and was not unduly worried, though he prepare d his paper talisman just in case. When he saw the simurgh and the crane swooping down on him, he immediately recognized Cunning-Maid's ferocious birds, and assumed that they intended to murder him. He activated his talisman at once. The charm emitted a sheet of blinding white light which almost caught the giant crane by surprise as it reached for him. Fortunately, the bird had cultivated the techniques of Internal Alchemy for many years. Before the deadly white blaze reached it, the bird turned down and exhaled jets of green vapour to ward off the white fire, and was able to snatch Man-Tiger up and fly away.

But the crane soon found that it could not long withstand the deadly power of the charm, and before long its strength began to flag. The parrot and simurgh had been following close behind the crane's tail, and now dipped beneath it to catch Man-Tiger in case he should fall. So potent was the charm, however, that Man-Tiger's entire body was enveloped in the blazing light. If he did fall, there was no way the simurgh could grasp him. The parrot ordered the two larger birds to drop close to the ground, and flew close to address Man-Tiger in human speech. It told him that their intentions were good. They had come on the orders of Moon-Maid and her sister, and would take him back to the Miao mountain to meet with her.

"The crane's claws are sharp as razors," the parrot announced. "If it had wanted to hurt you, it could have killed you when it first swooped down. If you don't turn off your magic glow, you might fall ten thousand feet and be smashed to bits! What a shame to die for nothing! Be a nice man, and come back with us quietly! If hanging by its claws makes you uncomfortable, you may ride on its back."

As the parrot spoke, the crane was already reaching the point where it could bear up no longer, but Man-Tiger was unaware of this. He also did not know that the power of the glow would protect him from injury regardless of how far he fell. He grew fearful for his life, and was at the same time encouraged that the birds had been sent by Moon-Maid. He withdrew the talisman's glow.

The crane searched desperately for a place to land, in such severe pain that it could no longer hold up. It was only by forcing itself to endure that it was able to alight without letting Man-Tiger fall. It was so exhausted that it would be quite impossible for it to take off again with Man-Tiger on its back. Man-Tiger, however, did not notice this. The parrot squawked urgently at him.

"The Green Simurgh is more comfortable to ride! It flies smoothly and at great speed! If you don't hurry and climb on its back, it will grab you in its claws again!"

Man-Tiger's capture of Cunning-Maid at Willow Lake had been accomplished mainly through the threat of his talisman. When he saw how the crane was capable of warding off the glow with jets of green vapour from its beak, he assumed that its potency was diminished because it had been used once before. The Green Simurgh looked a good deal more imposing and dangerous than the crane, and he dared not disobey the parrot's instructions.

Once at Jade Dragon Mountain, spurred by a combination of fear and lust, Man-Tiger agreed to all of Moon-Maid's demands. Moon-Maid made formal announcement to Old Man Miao, and they were married. Before long Man-Tiger had grown hopelessly infatuated with Moon-Maid's voluptuous charms, and lost all thought of home. The only flaw in his joy was his hatred of Cunning-Maid. He did everything he could to trap and subvert her. Moon-Maid kept her oath to her sister for the time being, and spoke soothing words to allay her fears. But Cunning-Maid feared that she would eventually fall victim to his wiles.

In desperation Cunning-Maid made a trip to the Mountain of Verdant Spots on the pretext of collecting water from the enchanted springs. Once there, she sought out the wife of Master Zhu Blue-Lotus, the Immortal woman Chen Graceful-Equity, and knelt before her in tearful supplication. Graceful-Equity, aware of all that had befallen the unfortunate girl, gave her comfort and advice on what to do.

"THE POSITION OF WILLOW LAKE IS SECURE FOR THE TIME BEING," continued Jian Ice-Purity. "Old Man Miao honours his agreements, and will not molest the villagers in any way until the year is up. Zhu Man-Tiger's native goodness is not completely gone. He resents the villagers, but they are after all his own people, and he still has fond memories of them. For the time being at least, nothing unpleasant will happen there.

"The people at the Mountain of Verdant Spots are another matter. Man-Tiger has already told of the secret aid you received from its inhabitants. He has not yet mentioned the Old One in Green, and has instructed Moon-Maid not to spread the story around, but sooner or later Old Man Miao will get wind of it, and direct his attention there. The Old Man has dangerous allies. Should any of them intervene to oppose you—as they might if the people at the Mountain of Verdant Spots are known to be involved—you will come under attack, and if defeated, will probably be killed. The lives and property of the entire Willow Lake community will then be in peril."

Master Jian explained that even with the help of capable allies, Zhao's and Wang's ordinary martial skills would be helpless against the sorcery of the Miao. But because Zhao was the principal in the encounter, Miao etiquette demanded that he appear in person.

The Old One in Green had long foreseen this eventuality. He had observed that Zhao and Wang were good and pure in nature, and their facial features showed physiognomies indicating latent immortality. This was the reason why the Old One had gone to some trouble to insure that they became the disciples of the Terrestrial Immortal Zhu Blue-Lotus, who was now cultivating himself in seclusion on the South-End Mountains in the North. Zhao and Wang would have no hope in a duel with the Miao sorcerers unless they had first mastered something of the magic sword-arts of the Immortals.

Jian Ice-Purity told them that Zhu Blue-Lotus was from an excellent family from the township of Minx-Woman Springs in the province of Anhui. This family was, in fact, descended from the great Confucian Master of the Song Dynasty, Zhu Xi. Blue-Lotus grew up amid wealth and opulence. His wife, Chen Graceful-Equity, was a lady of jade bones and ice-like skin, highly accomplished in both the literary and martial arts, incomparably wise, graceful, and lovely. But the joys of mortal existence soon palled, and when they reached middle age without children, and began to reflect on the fact that their twilight years were soon approaching, they grew sad and troubled. It was then that certain karmic roots came to fruition, and they encountered the Old One in Green and his wife.

As soon as the two couples met they felt a remarkable intimacy, and established close ties. The Old One had only just been reunited with his children from former lives, whom he had drawn with him through the difficult karmic mode of rebirth. His full awareness and powers had been suppressed before his present birth by his own master, the great Perfected Immortal of the Long Eyebrows. The Perfected Immortal had done this to ease the pain of returning to mortal life, but had left other memories of their former incarnations intact. While living as ordinary mortals the entire family, parents and children, felt a strong yearning for the Dao, and their dedication remained firm. The marks of immortality were visible in their features, but aside from this their native powers had not been restored. The spell of suppression was to be broken when their seventh and youngest daughter Li Zheng had been born. The Perfected Master had also hidden the family's many Treasures of Power and their Flying Swords, and at that time had not yet returned them.

The Old One and his wife received the aid of other intimate friends from their previous lifetime, in particular the Terrestrial Immortals Yi Zhou and his wife of the Southern Sea. Before their rebirth they had arranged to be reunited with these two. Yi Zhou bestowed upon them a strong spell-breaking mantra, as well as several types of very powerful magic, including the Arcana of the Primordial Numerological Flux.

The Old One's piety and sincerity had given him the power to perceive and measure the karmic burden remaining to be expunged. Recently he had discovered that although seven or eight tenths of his family's karmic burden had yet to be worked off, they would in their next lifetime encounter a spiritual nexus, a rare opportunity to break free of the cycle of rebirth. The Old One would then be able to inherit the great Daoist tradition led by the Perfected Immortal of the Long Eyebrows, and revitalize the great Omei sect, opening up the riches of that great mountain and its mystic school once again.

Still, the road ahead of them was far from easy. They would undergo two great crises, cataclysms of earth-shattering power, whose aftershocks would reverberate through all time and space. Success or failure would be decided in the blink of an eye. At times of great danger they would have to be prepared to wrench themselves away from major karmic catastrophe by main force; the slightest slip could destroy all of the merit they had accumulated over many lifetimes. They laid their plans with care, calculating their chances in these two fateful encounters with mingled apprehension and joy.

When the Old One and his wife befriended Zhu Blue-Lotus and Chen Graceful-Equity, they made them aware of the possibility of immortality, and began guiding them along the same path they themselves had followed, thinking that the two couples might cultivate themselves together, and leave another wondrous tale in the archives of the Immortal worlds.

But Zhu and Chen felt that to cultivate the same arduous path as the Old One and his family might prove too perilous for them. An easier path existed, that of the Terrestrial Immortals who remain on earth. These lesser beings were still subject to severe karmic nodes every few centuries, but these could be avoided, and Terrestrial Immortals could look forward to enjoying a carefree and delightful existence on earth. Chen Graceful-Equity approached Madame Li, the Old One's wife, to explain their decision, and to entreat them to impart some of their esoteric teachings.

The Old One, who himself had only just advanced to the point where there existed some hope of success, was sympathetic.

"At present all I can do is transmit to you the most basic breathing exercises," he told them. "When my own powers have been recovered later in this lifetime, and I have once again seen my master and fellow disciples from my past lives, I will make certain that you are introduced to them. My prognostications have shown that you are not fated to be my disciples."

From that time on, the two families were constantly together, each undergoing spiritual training in their own manner. Before long, the Old One met his master and fellow disciples once again, and full awareness was restored to him. He entrusted Zhu and his wife into the care of an advanced Terrestrial Immortal, under whom they finally mastered the Dao.

Afterwards Zhu Blue-Lotus and his wife continued to dwell in secret at their hidden retreat on the far side of the Mountain of Verdant Spots, where they performed the techniques transmitted to them by their master. The great karmic node of the Daoists, which occurred every four hundred and ninety years, as well as the final limit of approximately thirteen hundred years to which Terrestrial Immortals were subject, was still a long way off, but Zhu was a prudent man, and knew that it is always best to make plans for danger while one enjoys safety. He began to seek for ways to surmount these obstacles, and in recent years had gained possession of an arcane Daoist book which detailed techniques efficacious in warding off the karmic nodes.

This Daoist book was rare and precious, one of the esoteric scriptures of the sect of Supreme Clarity. Members of all sects would seek to win possession of it if they learned of its existence. Even worse, the application of the techniques set forth in the book involved a great uprush of spiritual forces, a sudden release of malignant vapours and concentrated light in the direction of the Milky Way. The alchemical elixirs produced in accordance with the recipes in the book were also redolent with a penetrating and highly distinctive fragrance. Anyone making use of the book thus risked being discovered and losing it to the machinations of treacherous spectral forces. The practices could only be performed in solitude; no second person could stand guard nearby.

The solution was provided by Tao Si, another Terrestrial Immortal and one of Zhu's closest friends, who dwelt in a cave deep within the roots of Yellow-Ear Crag on the South-End Mountains. Zhu used the Art of the Rock-Shattering Shout to excavate three new stone chambers far below the rear grotto of Tao Si's dwelling, and took up residence there to perform the practices and smelt the elixirs according to the instructions in the book.

Tao's grotto was concealed deep within the belly of the mountain. The new stone chambers were fully two thousand feet further down, and the passage down to them was protected by three layers of guardian spells. The blazing flames and strange fragrances created by the Supreme Clarity practices could be concealed with little trouble. Even if evil powers were able to discover his location, the formidable Tao Si remained on guard above to ward them off, ensuring that no one could interrupt him at a crucial juncture and ruin his practices.

Jian Ice-Purity assured Wang that because of his friendship with the Old One, Master Zhu would certainly receive the two of them.

"However, if you go directly there, you might not be able to see him at once. He will be sequestered for another three months with a difficult set of practices. But then again, if the Old One instructed you to seek him out, there must be a good reason for it."

JIAN ICE-PURITY HAD HEARD THESE DETAILS FROM A THIRD PARTY during his travels. The night before he had noticed that Zhao and Wang were glimmering with a magic glow, but had not yet realized who they were. Now that the evil on the Mountain of the Goddess had been rooted out, he was free to take an interest in their affairs. He had seen to it that Zhao Lin would receive the marvellous drug recently acquired by the Drunken Daoist, which would enable him to recover in short order, and bring him a good deal of additional benefit besides. In addition, Master Jian intended to introduce Zhao and Wang to other Immortals dwelling not far away. Luo Violet-Mist, styled Grandmother Gold, and the two men of Central Mount, Zhu Mai the Short Man and the Chaser-of-Clouds Bai Guiyi, had recently come to Southern Mount to construct a separate residence which they planned to make their permanent home at some future date. These three Immortals were on Southern Mount at that very moment. They commanded powerful magic, and were known to be fond of extending a hand to those less advanced than themselves. Each had been close friends of the Old One in Green and his wife over two or three lifetimes, and would surely do something to help Zhao and Wang. Master Jian urged the two men to make the most of their opportunity.

Wang Jin took great comfort from all of this. Zhao Lin was also conscious enough to have heard most of what had been said. He tried to climb out of bed to express his gratitude, but Jian Ice-Purity stopped him.

"No need for that," he said. "What you must do now is sleep here all day and overnight, and then set out tomorrow morning in your boat."

Wang Jin asked for directions on how to find the grotto they sought. He feared that the boat would be too slow, and that they might reach their destination too late to catch the Immortals they were to meet.

"Do not worry!" said Jian Ice-Purity. "The Drunken Daoist will not be leaving quite as soon as that. As for White Sparrow Grotto, once you reach Southern Mount, you should proceed to the far side of Fire-God Summit, then to the Gorge of the Golden Lock. A large ridge bars access from an area of many monasteries and temples only eighteen miles away. From the bottom of the Gorge of the Golden Lock, you should scale the next ridge, go around two turns, and you will find the entrance to the grotto. It will be difficult going, but with your good command of the Light-Body breathing techniques, you should encounter little difficulty.

"My Dao-Companion Luo, Grandmother Gold, is kind and affable, and you will find her easy to approach. When she finds out why you have come, she will take you to see the others. My Dao-Companions Zhu and Bai enjoy playing chess beneath an old pine outside the grotto, and others of their kind often come to watch their contests. Recently they have seldom strayed from the area, which will make it all the more likely that you will find them. They are eccentric, however, and you must be circumspect in your speech; they are acquainted with the Red-

Haired Patriarch, who is Old Man Miao's mightiest friend. When you see them, do not say you intend to destroy Old Man Miao and his sons, but say that you promised to go to their mountain because honour demanded it, and that your only intention is to survive the encounter without harm to yourselves. If you explain matters in this way Zhu and Bai should agree to lend a hand.

"Once you have obtained the Drunken Daoist's elixir, you must depart at once for the South-End Mountains, regardless of whether you have been able to see all three of the Immortals on Southern Mount, and go straight to Yellow-Ear Crag. If your excellent master Zhu is sequestered and you are unable to see him at once, you may enlist the aid of your Master-Uncle Tao Si to get a message to him. This man Tao Si is alert and canny. He is not fond of involving himself in the affairs of others, but for the sake of the Old One and your own master he will not send you away. As long as your master is willing to keep you there, you will not be wasting your time or delaying important tasks.

"I regret that our meeting has been so hasty, and that I have not been able to devote more attention to this matter. But I foresee that you will get through without mishap. If it were up to me to oversee this affair, and I did not have any commitments in the realms beyond the Seas,* I would do more to help you. It is a shame that the Old One and your master Zhu will also be occupied when the time for your encounter comes, and cannot intervene in person. You will have to arrange things as best you can next summer, though it is possible that I will be able to lend you a hand.

"The most important thing for you at present is that you be united with your master as soon as possible. You will be able to meet both the Drunken Daoist and the abbot at a later date; there is no pressing need for you to pay courtesy calls on them now, and they are in any case occupied with the repossession of the Abbey of the Pure Void. The breathing techniques they practice are different from those that you will be learning. Zhao Lin needs a period of quiet rest while the drug I have given him does its work. Tomorrow morning you should set out as early as possible.

"I regret very much that I must leave you now."

He stood and lifted one arm. A blinding sheet of light flashed briefly, and he was gone. Wang Jin bowed in farewell to the space where he had stood. He looked around the rest of the room, and found that Shen the Lute had also departed; only a single Daoist lad remained. The boy explained that because of the urgency of repossessing the other abbey, only two of his older fellow-disciples had been left behind to see to their needs. Shen the Lute, his eighth Disciple-Brother, had a favour he wished to ask of Master-Uncle Jian, and had gone ahead to Old Fisherman's Bluff to wait for him there. But he had left a message for Zhao and Wang. He regretted having to leave them so suddenly, he said,

* [The lands beyond the Four Seas were inhabited only by the Immortals.]

227

but the favour he required of Master Jian could not be performed by anyone else, and it was rather awkward for him to make his request in the presence of others. If it should happen that he could not return that night, and was not in time to see them off the next morning, he begged them not to take offense. At the time of their appointment with Old Man Miao on Jade Dragon Mountain, he promised, he would think of a way to join them there. His own powers were limited, and would probably not be of much use, but at least they would have the opportunity to meet again. Right from the first he had felt that they were like old friends. The Daoist lad delivering the message was his young Disciple-Brother, whose name was Secure-in-Tranquillity.

Secure-in-Tranquillity appeared to be fourteen or fifteen years old. Wang Jin, engaging him in conversation, found him alert and agile, and suspected that he had a thorough grounding in the martial arts. They soon found themselves liking one another.

Before long, a young Daoist serving lad appeared with a fresh and clean vegetarian meal of wild vegetables and bamboo shoots. Zhao Lin was sound asleep, so Wang set aside a portion of the food in case he awoke. When he and Secure-in-Tranquillity had finished, the serving boy came to clear the table.

Secure-in-Tranquillity urged Wang Jin to get some sleep after his long and difficult night, and promised to tend to Zhao Lin's needs if he awoke. He noticed how Wang Jin's eyes turned constantly toward Zhao Lin's face as they had been talking, and how he reached out every now and then to feel Zhao's forehead, chest, and hands. Secure-in-Tranquillity could not restrain himself from uttering a sigh.

"How close these two fellow disciples are!" he said under his breath. "This is the way disciples of the same master should be! I wonder if this Elder Disciple-Brother Zhao is this good to him?"

Wang Jin heard him, and it was in his mind to tell him that the bond between them in fact had nothing to do with their being fellow disciples. But Wang was tired, and his back was to Secure-in-Tranquillity. When the lad said nothing further, he was overcome by a great languor, and a moment later was asleep and dreaming.

After a time he awoke, and looked about him. The sun was low in the west. He and Zhao Lin, still asleep on the opposite side of the bed, were alone in the room. Wang Jin slid over toward Zhao Lin and examined him carefully. He was delighted to find that his complexion was normal, and his body warm. No trace of the spectral illness remained. For a moment Wang wondered if he should feed him, but he recalled that the Village Elders at Willow Lake, whose medical knowledge was considerable, had always said that sick patients would recover more quickly on an empty stomach. Food was ready and waiting if Zhao should require it. Wang Jin let him sleep.

He got off the bed. A pot of fine tea was waiting on the table, still hot. Evidently Secure-in-Tranquillity had only just left them. Wang felt somewhat guilty about putting the boy to so much trouble. He heard

228

footsteps on the stairs below, and two people entered the room, Secure-in-Tranquillity in the lead. Following behind him was their boatman, Zhang the Fourth. Wang Jin broke out into a broad grin when he saw him.

"However did you find us?" he asked.

"Last night, after you two honoured guests failed to return, we saw a thick fog rise up about Bamboo-Immortal Abbey, and before dawn we heard two loud thunderclaps. Later Master Jian appeared with a young priest. He told us that the demonic Daoists had been driven out, and that Abbot Wang was restored in the Abbey of the Pure Void. Our passenger Zhao, he said, had caught a chill during the night, and was resting in the abbey.

"He said you two guests would depart for Southern Mount tomorrow morning, and should not be disturbed until evening. He assured us that a favourable wind would speed us to Southern Mount in a single day. I know that both he and the Drunken Daoist are Immortals, and that the wind we will get will be as fast as the one which drove us across the lake with Master Jian the first time. He gave my father a pill, saying that it would prolong his life by ten years, and make him stronger and more agile. I was delighted, as you can imagine.

"During the day I hurried over to the front side of the mountain to see what was happening. The evil Daoists made a public speech to the crowd, admitting that they had seized the abbey out of sheer spite. Now the two oldest of their number were formally restoring the Abbey of the Pure Void to their excellent Dao-Companion Wang, and would depart that very day with their disciples. They bade the abbot a courteous farewell, and the abbot personally came out with all of his disciples to see them off as they boarded their small boat. As they left, I was standing quite close, and overheard the chief evil priest say to the abbot, 'I never dreamed that you would treat me with such great kindness, Elder Dao-Brother!' It seems as if all the ill-feeling between the two sides has been expunged.

"I never saw any trace of the Drunken Daoist. The abbot told me to return here, and not spread any wild stories. I reckoned that you two honourable guests would be rising soon, so I hurried back as quickly as I could. This young Daoist gentleman came down to ask me what I wanted, and said that you two guests had not yet awakened. A moment later we heard the sound of footsteps moving around upstairs, and came up to see if you had risen. Food, rice, wine, and fuel have already been laid in on the boat; we can leave any time you honoured guests give the word."

Wang Jin told him that they would leave the next morning, and instructed him to wait on board the boat. Zhang the Fourth bade them farewell and left.

Soon dinner was brought up to them. Zhao Lin had awakened by this time, and told them what had happened. When he had been struck by the spectral emanation, he said, his whole body had seemed to swell and grow numb, and he felt an unbearable itching and soreness. His veins and arteries felt as though they were distending and spewing forth their contents, causing a dreadful piercing pain. But when he had ingested the potent drug and received treatment from the Immortal Master Jian, he felt a burst of warm vapour suffuse his body, easing the terrible discomfort wherever it touched, and soon he fell into a sweet sleep. After awakening, except for a certain weakness in his limbs, he felt normal, his speech and movements unimpaired. Wang Jin told him all that had happened, and introduced him to Secure-in-Tranquillity.

Secure-in-Tranquillity questioned them eagerly about Willow Lake and how they had incurred the enmity of the Miao sorceress. The time passed swiftly; it was midnight before they realized it. Zhao and Wang were well rested and unwilling to sleep, so they sat in tranquil meditation in the fashion they had seen on the Mountain of Verdant Spots. Secure-in-Tranquillity, unwilling to leave them, sat on the bed on the other side of the room to meditate.

The short summer night passed quickly. Wang Jin rose first. Seeing that it was still dark, he did not rouse Zhao Lin, wanting him to rest as long as possible. He went quietly over to the other bed. Secure-in-Tranquillity was deep in a trance, performing some sort of breathing practice. Every now and then two jets of white vapour darted out of his nostrils to a distance of a foot or so, and then were drawn back. Ding Shao and Wei Lai had spoken of this practice, and told them that he and Zhao would have to pass this stage when they took up the practice of the Flying Sword arts. From the look of things, Secure-in-Tranquillity was already quite advanced. Wang Jin realized that the abbot Wang Pure-Wind and his disciples were no ordinary men. He wondered why someone of such attainment as the abbot, who counted so many remarkable Warrior-Immortals among his 'Master-Uncles', had not gone into the remote mountains to cultivate himself, preferring rather to remain for decades at the Mountain of the Goddess, an area close to a great city and frequented by large numbers of travellers from all directions.

Zhao Lin awoke, and the two talked for a while. By this time it was daybreak, and they bade Secure-in-Tranquillity farewell. The lad, now out of his meditative trance, insisted on seeing them to their boat. Zhao Lin, thanks to his native strength and a good night's rest, felt no discomfort, but was weaker than before. When they reached the boat they conversed with the lad a while longer. Finally when Secure-in-Tranquillity saw that it was broad daylight, and that he was delaying their departure, he knew he could keep them no longer. Reluctantly he grasped their hands and bade them farewell, and returned to the abbey. Zhao and Wang instructed the boatmen to set out for Southern Mount.

Southern Mount, or Mount Heng, in ancient times was called the Sacred Peak of the South. It was famed for the imposing beauty of its Seventy-Two Crests. The highest of these was the Summit of the Fire God. This prominence seemed to reach halfway to the sky, and was swathed in roiling clouds and mists which seldom cleared. The entire mountain was nearly a hundred miles in circumference, located east of the Xiang River. Popular legend had it that Immortals came and went from time to time, leaving traces of their presence. It was eleven miles (or nine miles, according to some) from the county capital of the same name.

Zhao and Wang had long yearned to visit this mountain. Now they were overjoyed to learn that there really were Immortals there, Immortals that they themselves were soon to visit.

As soon as they pushed off, a brisk tailwind arose, and they moved along at an extraordinary clip. As predicted, they arrived at Southern Mount the following day. When they disembarked, each of them bowed off into empty space in gratitude to Jian Ice-Purity.

They paid the boatmen and saw them off. It was already the Hour of the Horse,* so they sought out a place of lodging in a town near the mountain, where they bathed and took a vegetarian meal. Then, having inquired as to the best route onto the mountain, they set out on foot. They climbed all the way up to the base of the Summit of the Fire God, where they encountered a pair of woodcutters. When they asked them the way to Gorge of the Golden Lock, the woodcutters pointed to a ridge far beyond the peak.

"It is easy enough to find. Go around the mountain peak, and you will reach Golden-Lock Gorge. But whatever takes you to such a dangerous place? The area is blocked off by snow and fog all year around. Also, a strange monster with eyes of shining indigo frequently appears and disappears within the fog. We have never heard of anyone being harmed, but it is frightening to behold. In the gorge itself there are only old vines and a few common medicinal herbs. No one ever bothers to go there. If you feel a desire to wander about on the mountain, we suggest Violet Canopy Peak. The mountains and waters there are lovely."

"We seek a particular medicinal herb," Zhao Lin replied. "It is urgently required to cure an illness. Only this particular variety will do. Snakes, beasts, and monsters are of little concern to us. We only beg that you point out the way to us, Elder Brothers!"

The woodcutters, approving of their pleasant and affable tone, obliged by describing the route to them in greater detail.

* [11 AM–1 PM.]

V

Through reincarnations, the twin braids are preserved;
a jade staff spans the sky as a thousand-foot rainbow;
seeking for help, the stalwarts encounter two old men;
past a thousand peaks of stone,
they call on the Perfected Immortal.

CHAPTER 18

Ambush of the Annealed Spirits

ZHAO AND WANG SET OFF TO FIND THE ROUTE DESCRIBED BY THE woodcutters. They went three or four miles over several ridges, and found the place they sought. Below them yawned a vast gorge, whose opposite side was a ponderous and lofty mountain ridge. In every direction wild hemp exploded from the ground; thorny brambles grew in profusion. The path they had been travelling grew difficult and precarious. A desolate wind moaned through the wastes; there was no sign of human presence.

The path downward grew ever more steep and dangerous. Normally, with their experience travelling through the wild tracks of Miao-controlled mountains, they would not have found the going particularly difficult, but Zhao Lin, recovering from his ordeal, was fast weakening. The weather was hot and the sun was high. Wang Jin had to assist him through the steeper and more arduous spots. It was only after a considerable effort that they reached the bottom of the gorge.

Looking up at the mountain on the other side of the gorge, they found themselves confronted by a sheer wall of rock, with no apparent path for the climber. Worse, the upper half was completely obscured by dense white clouds. The Immortals were close by, but there seemed no way to reach them. In desperation, they knelt, and Zhao began a quiet supplication.

"Your humble disciples, following the orders of the Old One in Green on the Mountain of Verdant Spots, are proceeding to the South-End Mountains to take up our apprenticeship under the Immortal Master Zhu Blue-Lotus. Unexpectedly, I was struck down by the spectral sorcery of the Barbarian Monk on the Mountain of the Goddess. We were fortunate enough to receive the aid of the Immortal Master Jian Ice-Purity, who ordered your humble disciples to proceed without delay to the Gorge of the Golden Lock and visit Grandmother Gold and the Drunken Immortal Master. We humbly entreat the two exalted Masters not to abandon these two foolish mortals, and open the clouds to grace us with a sign."

He spent nearly half an hour at this without response. There seemed little choice but to make a desperate attempt to scale the cliff with Wang Jin in the lead, and himself tethered to Wang with a rope, following as best he could. Their jade amulets would afford protection when the time came to penetrate the ominous band of cloud above.

There was a faint rustle from the brush to one side. Thinking that some sort of beast or snake was trying to approach them unawares, they turned quickly to look. A young woman in Daoist garb, perhaps seventeen or eighteen years old, was approaching along the base of the peak further up the gorge to their right.

She was innocent and beautiful, her features refined and spiritual. Her Daoist garment was white as snow, a strange misty gauze that was neither silk nor cotton, unsullied by any trace of dust. Such a person would be a rare sight in the midst of civilisation, not to mention a deep valley on a remote and desolate mountain. Surely she was the Immortal woman Luo Violet-Mist, the Grandmother Gold described to them by Master Jian.

They turned hastily and bowed politely.

"We humbly beg leave to speak to you, Immortal maiden!" Zhao Lin said. "Are you by any chance Grandmother Gold, the Immortal Master Luo?"

The girl smiled. "I am Nineteenth Sister Xiao. The Grandmother Gold you speak of is my eldest Disciple-Sister. I have only just left her in White Sparrow Grotto. I caught sight of you two kneeling here in prayer. It appears that you are unaware that this spot is right behind her grotto. What business brings you here?"

The two men, delighted to find that she was a disciple of the same master as Grandmother Gold, bowed down once more, briefly recounted what had happened to them, and stated their reason for coming. They told her that they were unable to scale the cloud-shrouded mountain.

Nineteenth Sister Xiao smiled and told them to rise.

"It always gives me pleasure to aid people whose hearts are good," she said. "The Old One in Green was kind enough to assist me once in the past, and it still disturbs me that I have been unable to repay the debt. Unfortunately, the Drunken Daoist has departed. My eldest Disciple-Sister has been busy the past few days with an important matter, and in the normal course of events would not have time to see you. Your physiognomies show an excellent command of the martial arts,* but the mountain path to the grotto is arduous for mortals. Most dangerous of all is the Divine Roarer which guards the grotto entrance. Unless it has instructions to the contrary, it never allows anyone past the halfway point on the mountain. You cannot force your way past this beast, even though you bear rare Treasures of Power.

"But I will help you, and ensure that you meet my Eldest Disciple-Sister. I will also arrange it so that when the time comes for your appointment on Jade-Dragon Mountain next year, she will be present to increase the strength of your forces. I shall lend you a green jade staff. It was given to me by my honoured former Mistress, the Seven-Fingered Dragon Mother Who Leans on the Void. The divine beast who guards the grotto will recognize this treasure, and not hinder you. The staff is a

---

* [It is believed that adepts in the martial arts undergo certain changes in physiognomy. It is thought, for example, that the bone and muscle around the temples becomes more pronounced, causing the eyebrows to slant upwards.]

234

special token of trust between me and my eldest Disciple-Sister. She knows that I never lend it to anyone without dire need, and will be certain to treat you with great favour.

"I will clear a way for you through the clouds and mists on the upper half of the mountain. The grotto is on the other side, and a hidden ravine affords passage up the cliff. Not far away at the foot of the mountain you will find a stalagmite growing out of the ground; this marks the way. If you reach a dangerous area, strike the staff against the ground. A glowing shield will protect you and convey you safely past the obstruction."

She reached into a pouch of blue brocade at her waist, and drew out a three-inch object resembling a jade hair clasp. She shook it once in the wind. There was a green flash, and the object transformed into a long staff of pure emerald-green jade, the top fashioned into the head of a dove. She handed it to Zhao Lin. The two men, delighted by this unexpected stroke of good fortune, received it with a grateful bow.

"How should we return this treasure?" Zhao Lin asked. "Should we give it directly back to you, or should we leave it in Grandmother Gold's keeping?"

"Neither," answered Nineteenth Sister Xiao. "I am on my way back to the Temple of the Sky-Woman on Mount Min in Sichuan. I will remain there until I have undergone one full Cycle of sixty years, because I cannot bear to part with the material husk of my former mistress. This treasure is directly linked to my soul, and cannot be lost or stolen. When you see Grandmother Gold, explain that I directed you to her, and show her the staff. When you have done this, lift it up and call out my name, 'Nineteenth Younger Sister Xiao!' three times. The staff will leave your hand and fly back to me. But now you had best be going."

A shaft of white light lanced up into the layer of clouds above, and the girl was gone. The two of them bowed and set off, staff in hand.

It seemed at first that the gorge came to a dead end ahead of them, but as they went on they discovered that it doubled almost completely back and became a rift which sliced directly up the mountain. The reason for the name 'Golden-Lock Gorge' became apparent; its shape in fact resembled that of an old-fashioned Chinese lock, a groove turning one way and another, with the passage to the grotto far up at the top.

The ominous mass of clouds and mists obscuring the upper half of the mountain had lifted, and the ridge with its ravines and gorges now stood mostly revealed, reflecting violet and green like the rainbow shimmer of a bubble. A belt of white cloud still clung to the mountain's waist, which made it seem all the more beautiful and imposing, inspiring in Zhao and Wang longing for the Immortals who dwell beyond the sky. This cloud belt curled and undulated, floating free of the rock in certain spots, looking as though it might any moment drift away on the wind. Fearing that the clouds would soon close in around the mountain once more, Zhao and Wang made ready to scale the mountain as quickly as possible.

In case of accident, they followed Zhao Lin's earlier plan of tethering themselves together with his Pliant Claw rope. Zhao held the green jade staff, and Wang took the lead. They proceeded up the hidden ravine, clinging to vines and creepers, using their Light-Body techniques to best advantage as they scaled the steeper spots. Trees and vines provided ample handholds, making the climb easier than it had seemed from below. The magic staff gave them added confidence.

Zhao Lin did nothing with the staff during the first stage of the climb. Before long they approached the belt of white cloud at the halfway point. The slope ahead grew less steep, and looked easily passable, though fewer trees and plants grew in the chill mountain air which prevailed at this higher altitude.

A huge, oddly formed rock loomed suddenly in front of them, its surface thickly covered with moss and lichens. They had already encountered several steeply-sloped rocks of this sort, and found them difficult to traverse. Wang Jin went first, climbing cautiously across it to the other side, and then found a spot where he could stand firm and wait for Zhao Lin.

Zhao Lin was by this time severely exhausted, but was relieved to see that once this last obstacle was surmounted, the road ahead was smooth and easy. He was determined not to show any sign of weakness, despite the complaints of his bones and muscles. He told Wang Jin to dangle the rope off to one side, and started across the surface of the rock. Mosses and lichens, constantly moistened by the vapour of the clouds, had grown thick and lush, and were as slippery as oil. Zhao Lin lacked the strength to perform his Breath-Lifting techniques, and after just two steps, his weary feet slipped out from under him, and he slid helplessly downward.

Wang Jin, unaware of the extent of Zhao's distress, was caught somewhat by surprise. In desperation, he bent his knees and planted his feet, holding tightly to the rope to break Zhao's fall. But at that instant Zhao, falling over to the side, instinctively reached out with the staff in a futile effort to keep himself from tumbling over. As the staff struck the rock, a burst of green light enclosed him. It righted him and supported his weight as he strode easily up the face of the rock, looking somewhat surprised.

At once alarmed and delighted, Wang Jin asked him what had happened.

"My foot slipped, and I thought it was the end. I completely forgot what Xiao Nineteenth-Sister told us."

They started up the gentle slope above the rock as they spoke, and the magic glow vanished. A strange roar thundered above their heads. They realized it must be the cave guardian trying to frighten them off, which meant they must now be within a hundred feet of White-Sparrow Grotto.

They advanced shoulder to shoulder, both grasping the staff, prepared for anything. Another roar, more savage and thunderous than the

236

first, sounded in front of them. A powerful mountain wind shrieked around them. The clouds raced overhead and the trees and plants lashed wildly; a frightful din echoed from the mountains all about. Zhao Lin recalled the Immortal maiden's warning that the creature was deadly, and began to fear that it might come upon them too suddenly to see the staff. He waved the staff in his hand, and called out.

"O divine creature, calm your fury! We come on the orders of Xiao Nineteenth-Sister to seek the master of the cavern, Grandmother Gold. We bear a token, this green jade staff. Please grant us passage!"

A golden monster nearly twenty feet long, with glowing indigo eyes the size of rice bowls, swooped down on them. The green fire from the staff welled up once more and encased the two men in a protective shield. The huge golden form darted off to one side to avoid the glow, and landed on their left. They heard the sound of heavy breathing, and turned to look at the beast.

A frightful monster stood facing them on the path. It vaguely resembled a lion or tiger, but was neither. Its body was twenty feet long and ten feet high, with a large head and stout body. Protruding red lips rimmed a huge blood-coloured mouth the size of a basin. A golden mane twitched and waved around the head; a short flat tail stood erect over its rump. The creature was a bright golden yellow, contrasting sharply with the dull grey stone on which it stood. A pair of bulging hemispherical eyes, large as rice bowls and glinting with indigo sparks, regarded the men with some surprise.

The green glow from the staff vanished, and they realized that they were free to continue. They bowed respectfully to the creature, and Zhao Lin repeated his speech one more time. The creature, taking no notice, turned its mammoth squat head to the side and bellowed several times at the mountain top, apparently announcing their presence.

Zhao and Wang advanced, but before they had gone a few steps, the beast bounded forward and blocked their way. Zhao Lin lifted the staff once more and began to repeat his speech. A sheet of green light descended from the sky and coalesced into the form of a young girl, perhaps thirteen or fourteen years old, her hair done up in the fashion of a maidservant. She began speaking before they could address her.

"My name is Vortex-of-Tranquillity. My mistress has ordered me to receive you two honoured and most excellent guests. You may mount this Divine Roarer who guards the grotto, and ride him the rest of the way. Please, you may climb directly on his back!"

The Divine Roarer crouched low to let them clamber up. The two men begged the creature's pardon for putting it to trouble, put away the Pliant Claw rope, and mounted. Vortex-of-Tranquillity gave a shout, "Go!" A green blaze of light came up before them, and men and beast flew up to the top of the mountain, all within the girl's shield of green light.

237

They flew over the belt of cloud around the mountain in the twinkling of an eye, and landed on a stone ledge above it. The two men dismounted.

They found themselves amid a scene of entrancing beauty. The ledge was three acres in size, covered with a profusion of rare flowers and exotic herbs. Seven or eight stone spires, like stalagmites, were scattered about, stabbing twenty or thirty feet up into the clouds. They turned away from the ledge to look, and discovered the entire splendour of Southern Mount and its environs spread out before their eyes. The Yangtze and Xiang rivers curled this way and that, giant silk sashes surrounded by lakes and lesser tributaries in a complex pattern of interwoven silver and white jade. A vast expanse of flat fields and lush wilderness dazzled their eyes with verdant splendour. The high mountain air was like crystal; clouds and mists boiled just below their feet. Looking out over the rest of the mountain they saw that the various summits, Fire-God, Violet Canopy, Brocade Screen, and Jade Maiden, along with the road they had just climbed, were once again almost completely hidden, leaving only a handful of scattered islands floating in a sea of cloud.

Vortex-of-Tranquillity and the guardian Divine Roarer conducted them to the cliff outside the entrance to White Sparrow Grotto. The girl explained that her mistress Luo Violet-Mist was at that moment engaged in a difficult feat of magic, congealing and strengthening the spirits of two of her disciples, and would in a short while emerge to escort these disciples back to the mortal world. Vortex-of-Tranquillity asked them to wait outside the entrance to the cave, and went in.

Zhao and Wang waited a considerable time, but Vortex-of-Tranquillity did not reappear. They began to wonder if the Immortals were subjecting them to a test. They endured their hunger, which was now considerable, and settled down to wait in an attitude of humility. But then Vortex-of-Tranquillity emerged once again. She smiled at them in friendly fashion.

"My mistress is still in the rear cavern working her arts," she said. "She had no idea that you would arrive so quickly. Not long ago my Master-Aunt Xiao, on her way back home, sent word to my Mistress to let you through the cloudy girdle around the middle of the mountain. Only my Mistress and myself are here, and we had no choice but to make you wait outside the grotto. I imagine that by this time you must be thirsty and famished after travelling since morning. Our task in the cave is almost complete; forgive me if I must make you wait a little while longer. Afterwards we shall entertain you properly."

The two of them assented, and expressed their gratitude.

"In a few moments the living vital spirits of my two older Disciple-Sisters will emerge from the cave," Vortex-of-Tranquillity continued. "My Mistress has to remain within a while longer to contain the forces of the magic. I am young and weak, and will be completely alone out here.

238

If something unexpected happens before my Mistress comes out, perhaps I could call on you Elder Brothers for assistance."

Zhao and Wang, chivalrous and accustomed to rendering aid to others, agreed without giving the matter much thought. But when the girl had vanished into the cave, it occurred to them that she was the disciple of an Immortal, and in possession of remarkable powers; if even she were in difficulty, what could they do to help?

After a short while, they heard an urgent cry behind them.

"Elder Disciple-Brothers, quickly! Stand to either side of the entrance! Work a protective spell for me! My Disciple-Sisters are coming out!"

The two took up positions beside the cave mouth. A sphere of icy green light floated from the opening, enclosing the figures of two young women barely a foot in height. Vortex-of-Tranquillity followed closely behind, holding a short sword of gold in one hand, and extending the other at the sphere in a *mudra* of power.

When she reached the ledge outside the cave, she stopped. The two young women in the glow appeared to be in considerable discomfort. They lunged frantically in every direction, but were firmly imprisoned, unable to escape.

"Disciple-Sisters!" Vortex-of-Tranquillity called. "You should be wise enough to know what is happening! You have already withstood the agony of annealing your spirits for many days! What difference is a few more minutes going to make? Our Mistress must dismantle the magic altar before she can take you back. With enemies as dangerous as yours, do you think you can leave without our Mistress on guard?"

The two tiny women calmed somewhat, but soon began to crane their necks this way and that, their lips moving urgently without sound. They seemed more agitated than ever.

"You fear the enemy will strike before our Mistress comes out, is that it?" said Vortex-of-Tranquillity. "I am too young and weak to help if the enemy comes now while you are in the open, and these two excellent Elder Disciple Brothers have no magic of their own, only borrowed Treasures of Power that are no match for real evil sorcery. Don't worry! Our Mistress has made thorough preparations. There are spells of prohibition above and below and all over the mountain. If there is any sign of trouble, we will know of it at once. The guardian Divine Roarer's eyes are sharp! If you are really in danger, we'll take shelter in the cave."

Zhao and Wang caught sight of a dull yellow light and several jets of greyish vapour flickering in and out of view to either side. Vortex-of-Tranquillity, her attention focused on the two tiny women, seemed not to have noticed. After watching the battle on the Mountain of the Goddess, the two men had gained some experience. They wanted to alert Vortex-of-Tranquillity, but desisted while she comforted the tiny women in the sphere. The grey vapour, though, seemed particularly suspicious. They signalled to each other with a quick glance, prepared for trouble.

There was a sharp cry, suddenly cut off, and the sky darkened. The ledge outside the cave was abruptly cloaked in a dim spectral mist. Two men in Daoist clothing materialized in the air, one short, one tall. Their malevolence was unmistakable. The short one swooped down on Vortex-of-Tranquillity, and a beam of dim greyish light lanced at her from his hand. The other, tall and lean, held a brown hemp banner roughly a foot across, covered with strange sorcerous designs, flickering with a ghostly fire. From it shot seven beams of a sickly and evil green light, which struck directly at the glowing envelope around the two tiny women.

Mindful of Vortex-of-Tranquillity's request for assistance, Zhao and Wang had been holding their amulets and Nineteenth Sister's green jade staff at the ready. They drew forth the amulets and activated them, performing the appropriate *mudra* with their hands. Two columns of light burst forth, encasing their bodies in a protective shield. Without any prompting, the jade staff transformed into a rainbow arc of halcyon light and extended far into the air.

The sorcerers closed in; Zhao and Wang prepared to leap forward within their magic shields and render whatever assistance they could.

Vortex-of-Tranquillity cried out in shrill defiance.

"Idiot sorcerers! You have jumped right into the net! Try and escape now!"

There was a sudden boom. The sky above them turned golden, and the mountainside was bathed in brilliant light. The Divine Roarer began to bellow. The dense spectral mist dissolved, like clumps of snow attacked by a blazing fire.

The short and fat sorcerer had been in the lead, attacking Vortex-of-Tranquillity with his beam of grey light. As the golden blaze erupted, Vortex-of-Tranquillity raised her shining sword and fended off the sorcerer's attack. The sorcerer retrieved his beam of light and attempted to flee back the way he had come, but found his way blocked by the halcyon rainbow transformed from the jade staff. Cringing in fear, he tried to avoid it. As he was thus occupied, a circle of bright silver lightning sprang up around the perimeter of the ledge. The golden fire above pressed down, joining with it to form an impenetrable dome of force, trapping friend and foe alike.

Both sorcerers, desperate for their lives, flung themselves wildly against the glowing barrier at various points, seeking to break through. Vortex-of-Tranquillity, paying no further attention to the two tiny women, took off after the enemy, wielding her Flying Sword with deadly effect.

Zhao Lin watched, uncertain of what to do. He did not know how to control the green staff once it had been activated. He had also learned the value of caution after his bitter experience on the Mountain of the Goddess, and feared that the sorcerers might turn on him and inflict another dose of spectral poison. It was evident that the lean Daoist with the magic banner was trapped, and in no position to continue his attack against the tiny women. The fat one was wounded and doing his best to escape. The outcome of the encounter seemed in little doubt; Zhao saw no need to involve himself.

Vortex-of-Tranquillity flew in determined pursuit of the sorcerers. The fat one transformed himself into a gleaming grey cloud, and circled the ledge in a frantic effort to escape, avoiding only the grotto entrance. The halcyon arc still hovered motionless overhead. On impulse Zhao called out in an effort to control it.

"Nineteenth Immortal Master Xiao, hear me! Swiftly manifest your spiritual communication with the staff! Order it to slay these two demonic attackers!"

No sooner had the words left his mouth than the halcyon beam expanded to span the entire ledge. With lightning-like rapidity it scythed overhead just as the glowing grey cloud flew toward it. They struck head on, and the beam folded, its two halves sweeping around to crush the cloud like a nutcracker. There was an agonized scream; blood and fragments of flesh splattered in all directions. The cloud dissipated, and the ruined corpse of the short Daoist dropped to the stone of the ledge.

The lean Daoist was considerably more powerful than his companion, and his reactions were quicker. He had been wielding his sorcerous banner to seize the two tiny female figures, transformations of the living souls of Grandmother Gold's disciples. But as the green demonic blaze flew forth from the banner his spell was broken by the golden fire above. The evil Daoist observed that the golden light had emerged from the cavern mouth, and knew that he had been tricked. He might have escaped if he had fled at once, but the magic banner dropped from his hand, and he was unwilling to abandon it. It took him only an instant to retrieve, but his enemy moved with preternatural speed.

As the evil sorcerer's hand closed over the banner, and he made ready to flee through the air at speed, a tiny needle of golden light, barely three inches long, flew out of nowhere. There was a tiny crack of thunder, and his banner exploded into fragments. He tried to escape, but got no more than ten feet before his left arm went numb, struck by another of the tiny needles. As he cried out to himself in dismay, his arm, completely severed, dropped to the ground. In desperation, he clenched his teeth, and used his inner control to staunch the flow of blood. He moved once again to escape, abandoning all thought of striking back.

He felt a burning sensation in his left leg, as though something had seized him about the thigh, cutting right to the bone, and he was dragged relentlessly downward. He looked down, and saw the Divine Roarer. Following the instructions of its mistress, it had lain quietly in wait while the evil Daoists broke through the protective spells and mounted their attack. Now it had slipped soundlessly from its hiding place and leaped over to seize the luckless priest's leg in its huge bloodred maw and bring him down.

The evil Daoist knew that the beast was imbued with a rare and deadly venom. If its bite broke the skin, death was inevitable. If he could not break free at once, his real enemy would emerge, and both his body and his living soul would be lost. In desperation, he invoked a spell of Body Division, and both legs detached themselves from the hips and dropped away. A protective demon fire sprang up to enclose him, and he attempted once again to flee.

But in the time it took for this to happen, the halcyon beam swept toward him, and the golden roof above pressed relentlessly down. The ground shook with a second great thunderclap, and the air about the ledge filled with lances of golden fire. The evil Daoist did not even have time to scream. His body was perforated in a thousand places and torn instantly to shreds. Nothing was left but a few smears of blood, a few bits of flesh, and an unpleasant burning smell.

CHAPTER 19

The Drunken Daoist

THE HALCYON BEAM CONTINUED TO ROVE BACK AND FORTH ABOVE
the ledge, and Zhao Lin wondered if he should make an attempt to retrieve it. But then a rich golden light blazed from the cave entrance. An
old Daoist lady with white hair, a bright red face, and a kindly expression flew through the air out of the cave. She smiled and nodded to
Zhao and Wang in friendly fashion as she passed, and moved to the
shining green sphere. As she came near, it vanished, and the two tiny
figures escaped. Without slowing her forward motion, the old lady
reached out to grasp the tiny women and tucked them securely into her
sleeve. Then she shot like an arrow into the clouds and disappeared.
The glowing dome over the ledge vanished as she left.

Zhao and Wang knew that this personage could only be
Grandmother Gold, the mistress of the cave. They dropped respectfully to their knees as the glowing dome of force vanished. The halcyon
arc that had been the green jade staff suddenly shrank, and turned into a
tiny sliver of light two or three inches long. With one quick flicker it
flew off into the southwest and disappeared. As the two men knelt in
some bewilderment, Vortex-of-Tranquillity addressed them.

"My Mistress has left, and Master-Aunt Xiao has recovered her staff. I
have work to do here. Please, do get up!"

Zhao and Wang climbed to their feet, and went to the edge of the
ledge. It was now late in the day. Half of the great fiery orb of the
evening sun had sunk out of sight. Ten thousand red rays painted the
meadows and forests below a golden orange. The evening wind moaned
over the deserted mountain. The belt of white fog was once again securely in place around the middle of the peak. Scattered pink clouds
drifted free through the sky or rested against the rocks. These lustrous
hues and pigments, set against layer after layer of peaks fading into the
misty distance, left Zhao and Wang entranced with wonder.

As they stood marvelling at the vista below their feet, Vortex-of-
Tranquillity worked diligently to clear the bloodstains and fragments of
flesh from the stone. Her task complete, she came over to address
them once again.

"I have been so busy all day that I forgot to prepare any food or
drink," she said. "You two excellent Elder Disciple-Brothers must be
famished!"

The two of them, in their astonishment at what had just taken place,
had forgotten their hunger and thirst.

"We are quite all right," said Zhao Lin. "Though if you have a mountain
spring here, perhaps we could have a small amount of water."

Vortex-of-Tranquillity led them into the cave, chattering all the while.

243

"Our Mistress has not eaten solid food for many years, but her disciples have not yet reached this level, and we still maintain cooking fires. My two Elder Disciple-Sisters, who bear a heavy karmic burden and must undergo rebirth, were particularly fond of fine food and clothing, and not well suited to asceticism. They decided to concentrate their training exclusively on the practice of virtuous and chivalrous deeds. Our Mistress loves them for their thoughtfulness, integrity, and sweet natures. She is so fond of them that she permitted them to practice the Dao in the outside world without supervision, using the Treasures of Power and Flying Swords she had given them to perform chivalrous deeds and accumulate a store of merit. Not only did they continue to eat mortal food, but, on fine days of spring flowers or beautiful nights under the autumn moon, they were accustomed to inviting a handful of their Daoist Disciple-Sisters up to the mountain to indulge in feasts. The two of them would take turns minding the kitchen, taking pains to perfect their culinary skills.

"They paid a price for this, though. Their powers were not great enough when they met with Dissolution, and their vital spirits were unsteady, which is why they had to undergo the agony of soul-annealing before being reborn. They left behind a considerable store of food in the cave.

"You and I follow the same school of teachings; you are like members of our family. If you require anything, do not hesitate to speak plainly. There is no need to be polite."

The two of them thanked her.

The cave they had entered was long and deep, divided into three levels. They descended to the third and innermost level, a hemispherical chamber twenty feet in diameter. The furnishings were clean and simple. Next to the wall was a round stone bed, on which was spread a thick quilt woven of feathers. In the left wall was a small door, five feet in height, which led to two more chambers. These two inner chambers, surprisingly, were opulent. Upon questioning, they learned that this set of rooms belonged to Vortex-of-Tranquillity. The girl's two fellow disciples, who were extremely fond of her, had provided the furnishings and decoration. Vortex-of-Tranquillity told them that in a few more years these fellow disciples would complete the transition through their karmic node and be reborn, and would eventually return to their Mistress and resume spiritual cultivation.

She invited them to be seated. She formed a *mudra* with her hand in the direction of the wall. There was a faint rumble, and a small hidden door opened in the stone. Zhao and Wang looked in, and discovered a kitchen, very ordinary in all respects, though somewhat cleaner than usual. Vortex-of-Tranquillity went in and busied herself for a while. Soon she emerged with platters of bamboo shoots and roasted pine nuts, and three sets of bowls, cups, and chopsticks, which she arranged on small tables of green jade beside their seats. She filled the cups with spring water and invited them to drink, and returned to the kitchen.

The water cups were jade of the highest quality. They were small, no larger than a fist, and exquisitely crafted in an ancient style. Zhao and Wang lifted the cups and tasted, and found the water delicious, incomparably cool and sweet. They drained their cups with a single swallow. Their thirst vanished in an instant, and their spirits surged. They tasted the bamboo shoots and pine nuts, and found them rich and delicious, like nothing they had eaten before. Knowing that the Immortals did not pay much attention to formality, they helped themselves to more of the water, pouring it from a bottle gourd, and toasted each other. After a while Vortex-of-Tranquillity returned with a profusion of food, eight different dishes in all, half vegetarian, half with meat, the latter mostly made from pickled or cured meats. There was a pudding made from golden pine nuts and sweet fragrant rice. Everything was delicious and savory. Vortex-of-Tranquillity sat with them, and served them attentively.

As they ate, she asked them why they had come, and what had happened to them. They told her everything.

"I would like to meet this hapless Miao girl, who is so desperately in love," she said with a smile. "I don't know whether you Elder Brothers would be willing to permit this."

Given the girl's extraordinary command of the Flying Sword and magical arts, Zhao and Wang would be fortunate indeed if they could persuade her to go with them on their appointment at Jade Dragon Mountain, especially if she came in the company of her mistress.

"It is we who are in the position of supplicating you, our Elder Disciple-Sister, for aid," Zhao said. "Anything you are willing to do is more than we would ever dare ask. There is no question of us being unwilling to permit you to meet the Miao woman!"

"I am only fourteen years old," Vortex-of-Tranquillity laughed. "When I was very small my father died, and I accompanied my widowed mother back to her own family. There I was caught in a tornado and blown high into the air. I would have fallen to earth and been killed, but my Mistress rescued me. She divined my karmic background, and accepted me as her disciple. I began my training when I was three, and have been at it for eleven years. My Mistress and Elder Disciple-Sisters have always loved and cared for me. My powers are not good for much, but I can already merge myself with my Flying Sword. I have borrowed two of the Treasures of Power left by my Disciple-Sisters after their dissolution. I think I can handle the minor sorcery possessed by Old Man Miao and his daughter.

"Unfortunately, two of my Mistress' three disciples have been lost. My two Elder Disciple-Sisters cannot return to continue their studies until another sixty years have passed. It is still too early for me to descend from the mountain and begin accumulating merit through good deeds, and my Mistress may not give me permission to go. But remember, even though my Mistress—the chief of the Three Women of Min Mountain—is noted for her ruthless suppression of evil over the years, she is in fact very much like her close friend Qie Yin, the Saintly Maiden from the Pool of Phantom Waves, easily moved to acts of kindness. She is particularly fond of furthering those less advanced than herself. As long as she sees that you are good, she will agree to anything you ask. She has only seen you once, but it looks to me as though she already thinks highly of you. I don't think you need make any sort of direct plea to her. When you meet, just briefly mention how dangerous Old Man Miao is, and ask if she would be willing to let you take me along to lend a hand. I will take care of the rest."

Zhao and Wang readily agreed. They felt it would be rather impudent of them to make direct requests of Grandmother Gold at their first meeting. If Vortex-of-Tranquillity was willing to persuade her mistress, Zhao and Wang would be spared the indignity of a desperate plea for help.

Zhao and Wang soon ate their fill, and Vortex-of-Tranquillity cleared away the remains of the meal. She brought out more cups of spring water to toast her guests. As the two of them accepted their cups with thanks, they heard the distant howl of the Divine Roarer out by the grotto entrance.

Vortex-of-Tranquillity jumped up in delight. "My Mistress is back!"

She ran from the room. The two men felt it would be somewhat awkward of them to go running after her, so they remained where they were. After a short while, Vortex-of-Tranquillity returned to summon them.

"Elder Disciple-Brothers, you are in luck! My two Master-Uncles Zhu and Bai, and my Drunken Uncle, have all come with my Mistress! This will save you the trouble of making a trip to find them, not knowing whether they are at home or not. Hurry, come to the front of the cave!"

Rejoicing, Zhao and Wang followed her out.

They went to a stone chamber to the side of the outermost level of the cave. This room was the place where Grandmother Gold and her disciples normally received guests. The furnishings and appointments were exquisite. A bed made of jade stood at the head of the room, on which were seated two old men. Both were short and thin. One had a round face, with sparse yellow whiskers sprouting from his chin and jaws. His clothes were shabby, and he looked considerably travel-stained. The other was thin of face. Short tufts grew on his chin, through which his skin was clearly visible. His eyes squinted into mere slits. His linen shirt was shabby, but clean. Neither of them looked particularly impressive, except that their eyes gleamed with an uncanny light.

Seated below them on a jade footstool was a Daoist priest with an enormous red bottle-gourd strapped to his back. This was the Drunken Daoist they had seen at the Mountain of the Goddess. Grandmother Gold was seated on a stool opposite.

Overawed, Zhao and Wang dared not look at these august personages, and prostrated themselves on the floor, prepared to make a formal statement of their reasons for coming.

"Come, get up at once, and tell us why you have come!" laughed Grandmother Gold. "The old gentlemen Bai and Zhu have an aversion to excess courtesy. The more casual you are in their presence the better."

Vortex-of-Tranquillity, standing to one side, also signalled them to rise. Zhao and Wang peeked furtively at the old men, and saw that they indeed seemed somewhat displeased. Zhao climbed back to his feet at once, but Wang, of a modest and respectful nature, hesitated for an instant.

"Grandmother Gold, you know I can't stand people bowing and scraping for no good reason, cutting themselves down to half their usual height! This fellow Wang is thoroughly spineless. I don't care to involve myself in his affairs. Forgive me if I leave now."

"Shorty Zhu, one moment!" the other old man shouted, but there was a muted flash of golden light, and the first old man was gone.

Zhao and Wang were greatly alarmed. Vortex-of-Tranquillity rushed over to Wang Jin.

"Quickly, get up!" she said. "If you are not careful, this honourable Short Master-Uncle Bai will leave too, and your problems will be more difficult to solve."

Wang Jin hurriedly rose.

"You're being decidedly impudent, Little Vortex!" laughed Grandmother Gold. "Why did you add the word 'short' when speaking Master-Uncle Bai's name?"

The old man's squinting eyes opened wide, and he laughed. "Why do you think? It's because you've spoiled her, you fat old lady! We all know the sad tale of how you accepted the three disciples as a favour to another, and worked hard on their behalf, only to have two of them murdered by evil sorcerers, leaving only this little imp here. It's small wonder that you dote on her and let her do what she pleases. It will be a miracle if you can keep her alive until she is a hundred, at the rate you're going!"

Grandmother Gold smiled, but did not answer.

"Your humble disciple would never dare such a discourtesy," said Vortex-of-Tranquillity, smiling boldly. "Nor has my Mistress been at all slack toward me. Ever since I was small, being raised by my beloved Mistress, Master-Uncle's mansion has been barely a stone's throw away. I have always gone to you for help and advice, and you have treated me with kindness and understanding. I know very well that you two Short Master-Uncles value candour and straightforwardness. We can engage in playful banter without fear of giving offense. You have been indulgent with disciples and other juniors.

"Ever since the Southern Song era, the 'Two Short Men of Central Mount' have been famed far and wide for terrorizing evil and demonic powers. Your reputation is inextricably linked with this title 'Short'. Some people have felt that 'Short' is undignified, and call you the 'Two Old Men.' But you two Master-Uncles have disported yourselves with great humour in the world of men, helping the good and rooting out evil as you laugh and scold your way along. The word 'Old Man' is meaningless for beings as ageless as yourselves, and I have been told that you Master-Uncles are not particularly pleased by it. By calling you 'Short', I was acting in accord with your own express wishes.

"At the same time, I addressed you in this manner because this fine Elder Disciple-Brother Wang is unacquainted with you, and has no understanding of your character and temperament. Master-Uncle Zhu has for some reason made his excuses and flown away. If Master-Uncle Bai does the same, the lives and property of thousands of people at Willow Lake will be in jeopardy. Old Man Miao on Jade Dragon Mountain has been growing ever more arrogant and wilful, and if not checked, may call in all his supporters. If so, this incident will have extensive and complex repercussions.

"It was out of concern over this business that I in my ignorance laid myself open for your rebuke and used this straightforward manner of address to keep my Master-Uncle from leaving. I wished to give Elder Disciple-Brothers Zhao and Wang a chance to tell what has happened to them. You have always treated me with great kindness, and I used the title 'Short' to please you. If you find me wild and unrestrained, it is only because you two Master-Uncles yourselves have been lax toward me. My Mistress is not to blame. Your humble disciple only begs that these two men be allowed to finish what they have to say before you leave. I will willingly accept punishment of any severity, if only it will dispel Master-Uncle's wrath."

"You brash little imp!" the old man scolded. "You have been a good deal more crafty than your Disciple-Sisters, feigning innocence all these years! You stick close to your Mistress to devote yourself to hard training, and stay out of trouble, purely because you have been afraid that some evil person would harm you. But this time, goodness knows why, you want to go to extra trouble for another's sake. Very well, if you want to meddle, then we will see to it that your training will cease to be so carefree and easy! This will be your punishment: next year, at time of the Double-Fifth festival, you must make a trip to Jade Dragon Mountain, if you dare!"

This of course was exactly what Vortex-of-Tranquillity wanted, though she was careful not to reveal her delight.

"Your humble disciple is truly unlucky," she said, keeping a straight face. "But with my two short Master-Uncles leading the way, I would dare to go anywhere, no matter how dangerous. However, I do not know if my Mistress will give her consent. I dare not make such a decision on my own authority."

"If you accept your punishment and go, of course we will be there," the short old man grumbled.

The Drunken Daoist roared with laughter. "This girl-child has a quick wit and a ready tongue. She is itching to go to Jade Dragon Mountain, to involve herself in the excitement and test the powers she has built up over the years. You've ordered her to do exactly what she wants. She knows of the rare treasures you received from Master-Uncle Linked Mountain in the Sea of Fire at Man-Child Mountain, including the Dragon Sparrow Ring and the Sword of Golden Scales. She knows perfectly well she can borrow them from you to protect herself from mishap. And here you sit, patting your breast in satisfaction, apparently unaware that one of your advanced years has fallen victim to this girl-child's wiles."

The old man opened his eyes wide. "Stop your babbling, you drunken sot! This is exactly how I want it. Do you think that this business will be settled as easily as all that?"

"All right, all right! Do it your own way," laughed the Drunken Daoist.

Grandmother Gold smiled as the others talked, saying nothing.

Zhao and Wang, seeing that the banter had stopped for the moment, and that Vortex-of-Tranquillity had gone back to stand at her mistress' side, made ready to speak once more.

"I know your story," laughed the Drunken Daoist. "You need say nothing. I have here the drug which Zhao Lin requires, and have already enhanced its potency by mixing in a measure of alchemical elixir. A day after you ingest it, your original health will be restored, your breathing will be strengthened, and your body will become lighter. It will be of advantage to you in your future training. Wang Jin I perceive to be sincere, loyal, and prudent. Your bone structure and physiognomy are excellent. To you I will give three pills of cinnabar elixir which have the power of restoring someone even in death. These you must keep against a time when you must face a great crisis.

"It so happens that I have business in the Shaanxi Plain to the north. You two may fetch your packs, and I will transport you to the South-End Mountains on my way. We shall be there at dawn. This will save you a great deal of unpleasant travelling."

So saying, he produced three cinnabar pills from his pouch and handed them to Wang Jin. Then he reached down to the jade table by his side and picked up a cup of medicine, already mixed, and gave it to Vortex-of-Tranquillity, instructing her to conduct Zhao Lin to the rear of the cave and administer it with two cups of spring water. When this was done, she was to bring him back.

Overjoyed at their good fortune, Zhao and Wang bowed in gratitude. They had secured Vortex-of-Tranquillity's promise that she would go to Jade Dragon Mountain, and felt that it would have been awkward of them to make any further requests, and so they said nothing to Grandmother Gold. When they left the room, Zhao Lin spoke to Vortex-of-Tranquillity.

"Elder Sister Vortex, Master-Uncle Bai has already spoken on your behalf. Before we leave, is there anything else you would like us to do?"

Vortex-of-Tranquillity smiled. "I have not yet got my Mistress' explicit permission to go next Double Fifth, but one way or another I will be there. If I can leave early enough, perhaps I will make a trip to your Willow Lake first. Also, I feel great pity for the Miao girl Cunning-Maid.

She has suffered greatly because of her desperate love and miserable luck. At this moment you two Elder Brothers have no powers to speak of, but when you return from the South-End Mountains, Master-Uncles Zhu and Bai will beyond a doubt transmit further esoteric teachings to you, and you should be considerably advanced. There may also be other powerful people aiding you. The Old One in Green could reduce Old Man Miao and his entire clan to ashes were he so minded, but he is unlikely to intervene in such worldly conflicts. But his disciples, Elder Brothers Hong and Ruan, are bound to be furious if Old Man Miao intimidates others. They will intervene, either openly or in secret. You two Elder Disciple-Brothers are acquainted with them, and your respective masters are as intimate as if they were from the same family. If, when the time comes, one of them arrives to resolve the situation, things will go well for you. If not, you must do everything you can to preserve this girl Cunning-Maid. Do not let her be killed! I tell you this partly out of commiseration for the poor girl, and partly for your own sake, Brother Zhao. 'True integrity always achieves its goal, and neither metal nor stone can stand in its way.' This woman is only in love. She has never committed any faults or worked evil. If you cannot come to an accommodation of some sort with her, and she comes to grief, you will in the future find yourself ensnared in evil karmic bonds, and it will be difficult to work free of them. One of my two Elder Disciple-Sisters was harmed in this way, and after three lifetimes we still do not know whether she is free of it. The situation was virtually the same as yours, except that the sexes were reversed. You, Elder Brother Zhao, have just encountered an opportunity for immortality, and are determined to pursue it. You cannot afford to be careless with this matter!"

Zhao and Wang listened respectfully to her words. They would have liked to speak with her at greater length, but feared that the Drunken Daoist would grow impatient if they kept him waiting. In the innermost chamber of the cave, Vortex-of-Tranquillity fetched clear spring water, and handed Zhao Lin the jade cup.

The medicine looked like milk, with a faint pink glow. As he drank he found it sweet, cool, and smooth. His mind and spirit immediately felt wonderfully clear and refreshed. He drank two cupfuls of spring water and retrieved his pack.

When they returned to the front part of the cave, they found that the Cloud-Chasing Gentleman Bai Guiyi and the Drunken Daoist were gone. Only Grandmother Gold was still seated there. Thinking that the Drunken Daoist had left without them, their hearts filled with dismay.

Grandmother Gold laughed. "Do not fear! My Drunken Dao-Companion has gone to see Dao-Brother Bai back to his cave. He will return in a moment.

"You have already been informed that you may not be able to meet your master immediately. Also, you still require solid food. When you are staying in Master Tao's front cave, you will have to go out daily to forage in the wilds. The cave is in the rear part of the South-End range, a remote and dangerous region. Even with your jade amulets you will be at risk from unexpected accidents. You have come a long distance to see me, and I have done nothing to help you. I will, however, give each of you a Flying Trident. They have no great power, but are effective against evil influences, and will fend off fierce animals and poisonous vermin."

Amazed and delighted, they accepted the gifts. Grandmother Gold instructed them in the proper method of use and the necessary spells. Always quick to learn, the two of them soon mastered the knowledge. At this moment, the Drunken Daoist returned.

"Will you look at them!" laughed Grandmother Gold. "They are so happy their spirits are bursting through the roof! I have a premonition that when they reach the South-End Mountains, they will obtain something unlooked for, an auspicious encounter above and beyond meeting their master. For this reason I have given them two Flying Tridents. We shall see what their destiny brings!"

"My Golden Dao-Companion is solicitous and enthusiastic in her aid for novices," replied the Drunken Daoist. "I believe your premonition is right. I sense that the 'Oblique Jade Hooks' may be involved in this business. Except for my Seventh Disciple-Brother, the Old One in Green, who talked about them once before in his previous incarnation, no one has mentioned them for many years. Had you not brought up the 'auspicious encounter' these two are destined for, I might never have recalled that we are within six months of the time when it was foretold that these extraordinary treasures would reappear in the mortal world. Why would the Old One in Green entrust these two into the care of Zhu Blue-Lotus so far north in the South-End Mountains, when he could just as well have asked Brother Zhu's wife, Chen Graceful-Equity, to begin their training close to home on the Mountain of Verdant Spots? They won't even be able to meet Brother Zhu while he is sequestered with his dangerous practices. What would have been the point of sending them on such a long and difficult journey if there were not a hidden reason ? I suspect that these two are meant to be involved somehow in the reemergence of these mighty treasures!"

Grandmother Gold smiled and nodded.

The Drunken Daoist stood. Together with Zhao and Wang he bade Grandmother Gold and her disciple farewell. Vortex-of-Tranquillity accompanied them out of the cave.

The Drunken Daoist instructed Zhao and Wang to close their eyes. He made a quick gesture with his hand, and they flew immediately into the air in a flash of light, headed in the direction of the South-End Mountains.

CHAPTER 20

To the Seat of the Master

THE SOUTH-END MOUNTAINS ARE CALLED BY SOME THE MOUNTAINS of Thorn. This cluster of mountains extends nearly three hundred miles cutting directly across the south of the Shaanxi Plain. Their peaks and ridges stand out with stark beauty, concealing the secluded glens and mountain valleys which have afforded refuge to high-minded recluses since the distant dynasties of Han and Tang.

Their destination, Yellow-Ear Crag, was in a remote valley on the far side of the mountains, a hundred and twenty miles from South Mountain, the main peak, which lay not far from the ancient imperial capital of Chang'an. The area around Yellow-Ear Crag was wild and dangerous. There was nothing but a wild jumble of chaotic peaks, cut through by scores of intersecting gorges and chasms. Except during the winter, when the leaves were gone, dense vegetation blanketed the landscape, affording cover for savage beasts and serpents. The terrain immediately in front of the crag was particularly treacherous. Jagged ridges stabbed high into the sky, enclosing yawning chasms which ran for thousands of feet. There was not so much as a single woodcutter's trail within a radius of twenty or thirty miles, and in some places the area was so impenetrable that even a monkey or gibbon might have difficulty finding a way through. Such was the secret and well-guarded site for which they were now headed.

When they first left the ground, Zhao and Wang felt an irresistible floating force carrying them swiftly into the air. When they reached a certain height, they began to accelerate forward. Their progress was as steady as a boat. They felt no wind, in contrast to their airborne journeys on the backs of the beasts at the Mountain of Verdant Spots, when the winds of the upper airs beat on their faces with such violence that breathing became difficult.

After they had flown for a while, the Drunken Daoist spoke.

"Your bones are remarkably well developed. I feel no strain carrying you along. We are now twenty thousand feet above the ground, and the sky is clear. I am deflecting the astral fluxes of the upper airs, so there is no reason why you cannot open your eyes."

Zhao and Wang opened their eyes. There was no longer any trace of the glow which had accompanied their departure. They were enveloped in a dull, white cloud, which parted to enclose them on either side. They were travelling along close behind the Drunken Daoist in the light of day. Only when they looked above and below did they realize the extraordinary speed at which they were moving.

It had not been light for long. The sun, a deep and brilliant orange, had only just risen, a great many-rayed wheel, framed in a curtain of pink auroral clouds spanning the eastern sky in a great arc. Above their heads stars were still visible, larger and brighter than those they were accustomed to seeing. The great cerulean void, pure and clean as washed crystal, stretched for thousands of miles around them. The massive earth spread in endless mountains and hollows beneath their feet. Flying here and there in the air were layers of cloud as white as snow. Sometimes these clouds would come soaring straight toward them, fast as a sword whistling through the air, but far slower than they themselves were travelling. In a twinkling they would shatter these clouds with tremendous force, the vapours scattering into countless bits of mist, showers of white blossoms scattered by the powerful forces of the Daoist's magic sword.

The rays of the sun, shining upwards from the horizon, illuminated streamers of mist like lengths of gauze fabric, twisting and rolling in the winds as they went past. In the short time it took Zhao and Wang to turn and look, the view was already fading far into the distance behind them. The powerful wind of the upper airs roared, but not a breath of it touched them. The whole vista about them was extraordinary beyond anything in their experience. Time passed swiftly; the sun ascended the sky. Far ahead of them, barely visible in a huge depression filled with murky clouds, a long mountainous scar cut across their path. The clouds they passed loomed higher and higher. Everything took on a different cast from the regions they traversed before: the clouds were whiter, the sky bluer, the mountains a richer green, the waters a deeper indigo. The Drunken Daoist addressed them.

"Yellow-Ear Crag is behind those mountains in front of us. We are almost there."

They plunged into murky clouds and dim fogs, and the speed of their flight diminished considerably. In a moment they cleared the mountain range and began descending toward its far side. The air felt rich and moist. They were surrounded by a general grey blur in which nothing could be distinguished. A sudden crash of thunder boomed from the mountains around them, and the sound of wind and rain began; they realized that they were in the midst of a thunderstorm. In a twinkling they flew through the shower, and alighted near a cleft in an enormous precipice.

"This is the Ravine of Green Vines," said the Drunken Daoist. "Follow it toward the east until it comes to an end, climb the slope, and turn to the left. There you will find the entrance to my Dao-Companion Tao's cave. When you see him, tell him that I have business in the Shaanxi Plain, and regret that I have no time to visit him."

Realizing that he was about to leave them, the two of them bowed and thanked him profusely. The Drunken Daoist did not wait for them to finish, however, and shot into the sky once more, heading toward the north.

The rain gradually subsided, though the thunder continued to rumble. The interior of the ravine was dim and dank; the smell of decaying vegetation was overpowering. Following the Drunken Daoist's instructions, they went along toward the east. Soon they reached the end, and began to climb a slope out of the ravine. There was a sudden flash of lightning behind them, and the sky shook with a tremendous crash of thunder. They turned to look, and saw a great ball of electrical fire drop down from far above to strike the western end of the ravine.

They were in a cloud-shrouded depression. The air around them was thick with mists and vapours, and, preoccupied with negotiating the dangerous terrain, they could not be sure they had seen clearly. But it had seemed that a tiny black human figure had darted up into the air, illuminated by the steely flash of the sphere of lightning. Whatever it was, it flickered out of view in an instant; all was now dim and murky as before.

It seemed unlikely that any sorcerous evil would lurk so near the secret dwelling of an Immortal, so they paid the matter no further thought. They began to ascend the cliff to their left in search of the cave.

They soon found themselves in another valley, considerably broader than the Ravine of Green Vines. They followed this for nearly a mile, and discovered yet another secluded ravine leading off past the cliff ahead on the right. The sides of the ravine hollowed out gradually as it led inward from the mouth, and finally met at the top to form a deep and dark tunnel like a dim murky alley. The crag above it, which covered several acres, was the highest point in the immediate vicinity, commanding the approaches on all sides. When Zhao and Wang first caught sight of this crag, waterfalls gushed over its outer face and down into the valley which they now traversed. These streams, the overflow from the heavy thundershower, formed tumbling dragons of white jade, which divided the rock into many sections. With the passage of the storm these waterfalls were now gradually shrinking.

Zhao and Wang realized that this lofty eminence along the side of the valley must be Yellow-Ear Crag. In great haste they wiped the traces of water from their bodies, and changed into clean clothes and shoes, before continuing forward in search of the cave.

The crag was shaped like half a roll of bread, long and round. It was formed of stone like yellow jade, smooth, even, and shiny. There was no trace of vegetation on its surface. At first they thought the cavern opening would be in the dark narrow ravine ahead, but before they reached it, they came upon a hidden hollow in the crag. Two curving paths in the rock came into view, twisting upward toward the round entrance of a cavern. The entire hollow with its opening and twisting paths looked very like a human ear. The mouth of the cave was completely clean, free of any soil or dust. Inside were twisting and tortuous tunnels, which seemed to lead deep into the mountain.

They decided this must be the abode of the Immortal. As they made ready to ascend one of these paths to the entrance, they heard a strange sharp whistle, like nothing they had ever heard before, and a human figure flew of the cave and descended through the air toward them.

254

The two men dodged quickly to one side, and turned to face the stranger as he dropped to the ground. Before them stood a Daoist youth clad in yellow robes, sallow of face, with a leonine nose, heavy eyebrows, and tiger eyes. A javelin was strapped to his back. A strange beast had followed him out, a large fire-red creature with a lion-like head and a single horn, its body armoured with dense scales. This creature seemed to be about to attack, but changed its mind and crouched down once more. Zhao and Wang stepped forward to speak, but the youth had already begun questioning them.

"This cave belongs to my master, the Perfected Immortal Tao," he stated. "The two of you do not look like demonic sorcerers. This area is surrounded by the Valley of the Ninefold Sheep's Intestines, infested with poisonous snakes, and extremely difficult for ordinary men to negotiate. How did you get here?"

Hearing this, the two of them knew that they had arrived at their destination. Rejoicing, they saluted the youth.

"My name is Zhao Lin, and that of my companion is Wang Jin," Zhao said. "We have come to this mountain of the Immortals in accordance with the instructions of the Old One in Green, wishing to become disciples under the tutelage of the Perfected Immortal Zhu. We humbly beg our Elder Disciple-Brother to reveal to us your exalted name and surname, and to announce our presence to your master, for which we would be eternally grateful."

The Daoist youth hesitated a moment. "My name is Lu Xiao," he replied at last. "You two Elder Disciple-Brothers are here on the orders of the Old One in Green? Were you aware that my Master-Uncle Zhu is not free to see anyone at this time?"

"The Old One warned us that our master would be sequestered far below the cavern to perform practices set forth in tomes of celestial origin, and would be unable to come out to see us immediately. If there was anything we needed, we were instructed to seek the aid of Master-Uncle Tao to convey a message to him. When we set out, the Old One gave us a letter of introduction, which we have here. We have already been presented to our Mistress, the Lady Chen, and have been assured of receiving his kind acceptance. But our yearning for the Dao was too strong, and we have certain matters on which we need to seek his help, and so have no choice but to come with all haste to present ourselves before Master-Uncle Tao and reside temporarily in his Immortal abode, seeking his instruction and advice. We have also met with Grandmother Gold and her elders, the venerable Master-Uncles Zhu and Bai from Central Mount, and Master Uncle the Drunken Daoist, in the White Sparrow Grotto on Southern Mount. They informed us that after we arrived here we would be certain to secure Master-Uncle Tao's kind permission to lodge here. Our Drunken Master-Uncle was also kind enough to bring us here himself, and it was he who set us down in the ravine off to the south. This is how we were able to find our way here."

Lu Xiao did not reply, but a voice called out from far within the cavern.

"Young Xiao! Why don't you bring them in?"

Lu Xiao called out in answer, and then spoke to them.

"My master summons you in to see him... "

So ends the first volume of
THE SWORDMEN'S HAVEN AT WILLOW LAKE.

The publisher invites those readers
eager for more adventure
to write and subscribe
to the concluding volumes.